Praise for the reigning queen of romance,

DIANA PALMER

"Palmer's talent for character development and
ability to fuse heartwarming romance with nail-biting
suspense shine in *Outsider*."
—*Booklist*

"A gentle escape mixed with real-life menace for fans of
Palmer's more than 100 novels."
—*Publishers Weekly* on *Night Fever*

"The ever-popular and prolific Palmer
has penned another sure hit."
—*Booklist* on *Before Sunrise*

"Nobody does it better."
—Award-winning author Linda Howard

"Palmer knows how to make sparks fly…heartwarming."
—*Publishers Weekly* on *Renegade*

"Sensual and suspenseful…."
—*Booklist* on *Lawless*

"Diana Palmer is a mesmerizing story teller who captures the
essence of what a romance should be."
—*Affaire de Coeur*

"Nobody tops Diana Palmer when it comes to delivering
pure, undiluted romance. I love her stories."
—*New York Times* bestselling author Jayne Ann Krentz

DIANA PALMER

HARD TO HANDLE

HQN™

HQN™

ISBN 13: 978-0-373-77261-2
ISBN-10:   0-373-77261-0

HARD TO HANDLE

CONTENTS

HUNTER

1

The silver-haired man across the desk had both hands clasped together on its surface, and his blue eyes were narrow and determined.

Hunter wanted to argue. He'd protested assignments before, and Eugene Ritter had backed down. This time the old man wouldn't. Hunter sensed Ritter's determination before he even tried to get out of the job.

That didn't stop him, of course. Phillip Hunter was used to confrontation. As chief of internal security for Ritter Oil Corporation for the past ten years, he'd become quite accustomed to facing off against all manner of opponents, from would-be thieves to enemy agents who tried to get the jump on Ritter's strategic metal discoveries.

"The desert is no place for a woman," he told the old man. He sat back comfortably in the straight-backed chair, looking as formidable as his Apache ancestors. He was very dark, with jet-black hair conventionally cut, and eyes almost black in a lean, thin-lipped face. He was tall, too, and muscular. Even his perfectly fitted gray suit didn't hide the hard lines of a body kept fit by hours of exercise. Hunter was ex-Green Beret, ex-mercenary, and for a short time he'd even worked for the CIA. He was an expert with small arms and his karate training had earned him a black belt. He was thirty-seven, a loner by nature, unmarried and apt to stay that way. He had no inclination to accompany Eugene's sexy field geologist out to Arizona on a preliminary survey. Jennifer Marist was one of his few ongoing irritations. She seemed to stay in hot water, and he was always deputized to pull her irons out of the fire.

Her last exploration had put her in danger from enemy agents, resulting in a stakeout at her apartment a few months ago. Two men had been apprehended, but the third was still at large.

Hunter and Jennifer were old sparring partners. They'd been thrown together on assignments more often than Hunter liked. Like two rocks striking, they made sparks fly, and that could be dangerous. He didn't like white women, and Jennifer was unique. Her soft blond beauty, added to her sharp intellect, made him jittery. She was the only female who'd ever had that effect on him, and he didn't like it. The thought of spending a week in the desert alone with her had him fuming.

"Jennifer isn't just a woman, she's one of my top field geologists," Eugene replied. "This is a potentially rich strike, and I need the new capital it will bring in. Jennifer can't go alone."

"I could send one of my operatives with her," Hunter replied.

"Not good enough. Jennifer's already been in danger from this assignment once. I want the best—and that's you."

"We don't get along, haven't you noticed?" he said through his teeth.

"You don't have to get along with her. You just have to keep anyone from getting his hands on her maps or her survey results."

He pursed his lips. "The site's in Arizona, near the Apache reservation. You can go see your grandfather."

"I can do that without having to follow your misplaced ingenue around," he said coldly.

"Jennifer is a geologist," the older man reminded him. "Her looks have nothing to do with her profession. For God's sake, you get along with my other female employees, why not with Jennifer?"

That was a question Hunter didn't really want to answer. He couldn't very well tell Eugene that the woman appealed to his senses so potently that it was hard to function when she was around. He wasn't in the market for an affair, but he wanted Jennifer with a feverish passion. He'd managed to contain his desire for her very well over the years, but lately it was becoming unmanageable. The temptation of being out on the desert with her was too much. Something might happen, and what then? He had good reasons for his dislike of white women, and he had no desire whatsoever to create a child who, like himself, could barely adapt to life in a white world. White and Apache just didn't mix, even if he did frequently wake up sweating from his vivid dreams about Jennifer Marist.

"You can always threaten to quit," Eugene advised with a sharp grin.

"Would it work?" Hunter queried.

Eugene just shook his head.

"In that case," Hunter said, rising to his feet with the stealthy grace that was unique to him, "I won't bother. When do we leave?"

"First thing in the morning. You can pick up the tickets and motel voucher from my secretary. You'll need time to lay in some camping equipment, so the motel room will be necessary the first night. You and Jennifer will be pretending to be husband and wife when you switch flights in Phoenix to head down to Tucson.

That's going to throw any followers off the track, I hope, and give you both time to scout the area before they discover their mistake and double back. Better get in touch with our operatives in Arizona and advise them of the plan."

"I'll do that now."

"Try not to look so dismal, will you?" Eugene muttered darkly. "It's demoralizing!"

"Stop sending me out with Jennifer Marist."

"You're the only man in my corporation who could complain about that."

"I'm Apache," Hunter said with quiet pride. "She's white."

Eugene had been married twice and he wasn't stupid. He could read between the lines very well. "I understand how it is," he replied. "But this is business. You'll have to cope."

"Don't I always?" Hunter murmured. "Will you tell her, or do you want me to?"

"I'll enjoy it more than you would," Eugene chuckled. "She's going to go right through the ceiling. It may shock you to know that she finds you offensive and unpleasant. She'll fight as hard to get out of it as you just did."

That didn't surprise Hunter. He had a feeling Jennifer felt the same unwanted attraction he did and was fighting it just as hard. From day one, their relationship had been uneasy and antagonistic.

"It won't do her any more good than it did me," Hunter murmured. "But if she ends up roasting over a campfire, don't say I didn't warn you."

Eugene's blue eyes twinkled. "Okay. I won't."

Hunter left and walked along the corridor with an expression so cold and so fierce that one employee turned and went back the other way to avoid him. He had a fairly decent working relationship with some of Eugene's people, but most of them kept out of his way. The icy Mr. Hunter was well-known. He was the only bachelor who didn't have to fight off feminine advances. The women were too intimidated by him. All except for Jennifer, who fought him tooth and nail.

And now a week on the desert with her, he mused. He lit a cigarette as he walked and blew out a thick cloud of smoke. He'd just managed to give up cigarettes the week before. He was getting hooked again, and it was Eugene's fault. For two cents, he'd quit and go back and raise horses on the reservation. But that would bore him to death eventually. No, he'd just have to find some way to survive Jennifer. One day, he promised himself, he was going to walk out the door and leave Eugene with it.

2

ennifer Marist shared an office with several other geologists, a roomful of high-tech equipment, maps and charts and assorted furniture. On good days, she and the other geologists who worked for the Ritter Oil Corporation could maneuver around one another as they proceeded with their individual and collective projects. Unfortunately this wasn't a good day. Chaos reigned, and when the big boss himself, Eugene Ritter, asked Jenny to come into his office, it was a relief.

She took her time going down the long hall enjoying the glass windows that gave such a beautiful view of Tulsa, Oklahoma, and the lush vegetation that accented the walkway. Jenny was twenty-seven, but she looked much younger. Her long blond hair was soft and wavy, her deep blue eyes full of life and quiet pleasure. She wore a white knit sweater with simply designed gray slacks, but she still looked like a cover girl. It was the curse of her life, she thought, that men saw the face and not the personality and intelligence beneath it. Fortunately the men in her group were used to her by now, and none of them made sexist remarks or gave wolf whistles when she came into a room. They were all married except Jack, anyway, and Jack was fifty-six; just a bit old for Jenny's taste.

All told, though, Jenny had given up on the idea of marriage. It would have been lovely, but despite the modern world she lived in, the only two men she'd ever come close to marrying refused to share her with her globe-trotting career. They wanted a nice little woman who'd stay at home and cook and clean and raise kids. Jenny wouldn't have minded so much with the right man, but she'd spent years training as a geologist. She was highly paid and tops in her field. It seemed wasteful to sacrifice that for a dirty apron. But, then, perhaps she'd just never met the man she'd want to compromise for.

She glanced around as she entered the waiting room of Eugene's plush carpeted office, looking for Hunter. Thank God he was nowhere close by. She let out a tense sigh. Ridiculous to let a man get to her that way, especially a cold-blooded statue like Mr. Hunter. He was the company's troubleshooter and there had been a little trouble just lately. He and Jenny had partnered up for an evening to catch enemy agents who were after Jenny's top-secret maps of a potential new strike in strategic metals. It had been an evening to remember, and Jenny was doing her best to forget it all. Especially the part that contained him. They'd caught two men, but not the ringleader himself. Hunter had blamed her. He usually did, for anything that went wrong. Maybe he hated blondes.

She lifted her eyebrows at Betty, Eugene's secretary, who grinned and nodded.

"Go right in. He's waiting," she told Jenny.

"Is Hunter in there?" she asked, hesitating.

"Not yet."

That sounded ominous. Jenny tapped at the door and opened

it, peeking around to find Eugene precariously balanced in his swivel chair, looking thoughtful.

"Come in, come in. Have a chair. Close the door first." He smiled. "How's the world treating you?"

"Fair to middling," she replied, laughing as she sat down in the chair across the desk.

He leaned forward, his silver hair gleaming in the light from the window behind him, his pale blue eyes curious. "Getting lonely since Danetta married my son and moved out?"

"I do miss my cousin," Jenny replied, smiling. "She was a great roommate." She leaned forward. "But I don't miss the lounge lizard!"

He chuckled. "I guess she misses him. Danetta's iguana is living with us, now, and my youngest son Nicky and he are best friends already. Cabe has promised Danetta a nice stuffed one for a pet anytime she wants it."

Jenny smothered a grin. Her employer's older son Cabe was well-known for his aversion to anything with scales; especially iguanas named Norman. Jenny had gotten used to the big lizard, after a fashion, but it was a lot more comfortable living without him.

"I've got a proposition for you," Ritter said without further preamble. "There's a piece of land down in Arizona that I want you to run a field survey on. I'll send down your equipment and you can camp out for a few days until you can get me a preliminary map of the area and study the outcroppings."

She knew she was going white. "The Arizona desert?"

"That's right. Quiet place. Pretty country. Peace."

"Rattlesnakes! Men with guns in four-wheel drives! Indians!"

"Shhhhh! Hunter might hear you!" he said, putting his finger to his lips.

She glared at him. "I am not afraid of tall Apaches named Hunter. I meant the other ones, the ones who don't work for us."

"Listen, honey, the Apaches don't raid the settlements anymore, and it's been years since anybody was shot with an arrow."

She glared harder. "Send Hunter."

"Oh, I'm going to," he said. "I'm glad you agree that he's the man for the job. The two of you can keep each other company. He'll be your protection while you sound out this find for me."

"Me? Alone in the desert with Hunter for several days and nights?" She almost choked. "You can't do it! We'll kill each other!"

"Not right away," he said. "Besides, you're the best geologist I have and we can't afford to take chances, not with the goings-on of the past month. And our adversary is still loose somewhere. That's why I want you to camp in a different section each night, to throw him off the track. You'll go to the target area on the second night. I'll show you on the map where it is. You aren't to tell anyone."

"Not even Hunter?" she asked.

"You can try not to, but Hunter knows everything."

"He thinks he does," she agrees. "I'll bet he invented bread..."

"Cut it out. This is an assignment, you're an employee, I'm the boss. Quit or pack."

She threw up her hands. "What a choice. You pay me a duke's ransom for what I do already and then you threaten me with poverty. That's no choice."

He grinned at her. "Good. Hunter doesn't bite."

"Want to see the teeth marks?" she countered. "He snapped my head off the night we lost that other agent. He said it was my fault!"

"How could it have been?"

"I don't know, but that's what he said. Does it have to be Hunter? Why can't you send that nice Mallory boy with me? I like him."

"That's why I won't send him. Hunter isn't nice, but he'll keep you alive and protect my investment. There isn't a better man for this kind of work."

She had to agree, but she didn't like having to. "Can I have combat pay?"

"Listen or get out."

"Yes, sir." She sat with resignation written all over her. "What are we looking for? Oil? Molybdenum? Uranium?"

"Best place to look for oil right now is western Wyoming," he reminded her. "Best place to look for moly is Colorado or southern Arizona. And that's why I'm sending you to Arizona—molybdenum. And maybe gold."

She whistled softly. "What an expedition."

"Now you know why I want secrecy," he agreed. "Hunter and you will make a good team. You're both clams. No possibility of security leaks. Get your gear together and be ready to leave at six in the morning. I'll have Hunter pick you up at your apartment."

"I could get to the airport by myself," she volunteered quickly.

"Scared of him?" Ritter taunted, his pale eyes twinkling at her discomfort.

She lifted her chin and glared at him. "No. Of course not."

"Good. He'll look after you. Have fun."

Fun, she thought as she left the room, wasn't exactly her definition of several days in the desert with Hunter. In fact, she couldn't think of anything she was dreading more.

Back in the office she shared with her colleagues, two of her coworkers were waiting. "What is it?" they chorused. "Moly? Uranium? A new oil strike?"

"Well, we haven't found another Spindletop," she said with a grin, "so don't worry about losing out on all that fame. Maybe he just thinks I need a vacation." She blew on her fingernails and buffed them on her knit blouse. "After all," she said with a mock haughty glance at the two men, "he knows I do all the work around here."

One of her coworkers threw a rolled-up map at her and she retreated to her own drafting board, saved from having to give them a direct answer. They all knew the score, though, and wouldn't have pressed her. A lot of their work was confidential.

She'd just finished her meager lunch and was on her way back into the building when she encountered a cold, angry Hunter in the hallway that led to her own office.

The sight of him was enough to give her goose bumps. Hunter was over six feet tall, every inch of him pure muscle and power. He moved with singular grace and elegance, and it wasn't just his magnificent physique that drew women's eyes to him. He had an arrogance of carriage that was peculiarly his, a way of looking at people that made them feel smaller and less significant. Master of all he surveys, Jenny thought insignificantly, watching his black eyes cut toward her under his heavy dark eyebrows. His eyes were deep-set in that lean, dark face with its high cheekbones and straight nose and thin, cruel-looking mouth. It wouldn't be at all difficult to picture Hunter in full Apache war regalia, complete with long feathered bonnet. She got chills just thinking about having to face him over a gun, and thanked God that this was the twentieth century and they'd made peace with the Apache. Well, with most of them. This one looked and sometimes acted as if he'd never signed any peace treaties.

In her early days with the company, she'd made the unforgivable mistake of raising her hand and saying "how." She got nervous now just remembering the faux pas, remembering the feverish embarrassment she'd felt, the shame, at how he'd fended off the insult. She'd learned the hard way that it wasn't politic to ridicule him.

"Mr. Hunter," she said politely, inclining her head as she started past him.

He took a step sideways and blocked her path. "Was it Eugene's idea, or yours?"

"If you mean the desert survival mission, I can assure you that I don't find the prospect all that thrilling." She didn't back down an inch, but those cold dark eyes were making her feel giddy inside. "If I got to choose my own companion, I'd really prefer Norman the Iguana. He's better tempered than you are, he doesn't swear, and he's never insulted me."

Hunter didn't smile. That wasn't unusual; Jenny had never seen him smile. Maybe he couldn't, she thought, watching him. Maybe his face was covered in hard plastic and it would crack if he tried to raise the corners of his mouth. That set her off and she had to stifle a giggle.

"Something amuses you?" he asked.

The tone was enough, without the look that accompanied it. "Nothing at all, Mr. Hunter," she assured him. "I have to get back to work. If you don't mind...?"

"I mind having to set aside projects to play guardian angel to a misplaced cover girl," he said.

Her dark blue eyes gleamed with sudden anger. "I could give you back that insult in spades if I wanted to," she said coldly. "I have a master's degree in geology. My looks have nothing whatsoever to do with my intelligence or my professional capabilities."

He lifted a careless eyebrow. "Interesting that you chose a profession that caters to men."

There was no arguing with such a closed mind. "I won't defend myself to you. This assignment wasn't my doing, or my choice. If you can talk Eugene into sending someone else, go to it."

"He says you're the best he has."

"I'm flattered, but that isn't quite so. He can't turn anyone else loose right now."

"Too bad."

She pulled herself up to her full height. It still wasn't enough to bring the top of her head any higher than Hunter's square chin. "Thank you for your vote of confidence. What a pity you don't know quartz from diamond, or you could do the whole job yourself!"

He let his gaze slide down her body and back up again, but if he found any pleasure in looking at her, it didn't show in those rigid features. "I'll pick you up at six in the morning at your apartment. Don't keep me waiting, cover girl."

He moved and was gone before she recovered enough to tell him what she thought of him. She walked back to her own office with blazing eyes and a red face, thinking up dozens of snappy replies that never came to mind when she actually needed them.

She pulled her maps of southern Arizona and looked at the area Eugene had pinpointed for her field survey. The terrain was very familiar; mountains and desert. She had topographical maps, but she was going to need something far more detailed before Eugene and his board of directors decided on a site. And her work was only the first step. After she finished her preliminary survey, the rest of the team would have to decide on one small area for further study. That would involve sending a team of geologic technicians in to do seismic studies and more detailed investigation, including air studies and maybe even expensive computer time for the satellite Landsat maps.

But right now what mattered was the fieldwork. This particular area of southern Arizona bordered government land on one side and the Apache reservation on the other. The reservation was like a sovereign nation, with its own government and laws, and she couldn't prospect there without permission. What Eugene hoped to find was in a narrow strip between the two claimed territories. He had a good batting average, too. Old-timers said that Eugene could smell oil and gold, not to mention moly.

It was too short a day. She collected all her equipment to be taken to the airport and the charts and maps she expected to have to refer to. With that chore out of the way, she went home.

Jenny cooked herself a small piece of steak and ate it with a salad, brooding over her confrontation with Hunter and dreading the trip ahead. He didn't like her, that much was apparent. But it shouldn't have affected their working relationship as much as it did. There were other women in the organization, and he seemed to get along well enough with them.

"Maybe it's my perfume," she murmured out loud and laughed at the idea of it.

No, it had to be something in her personality that set him off, because he'd disliked her on sight the first time they met.

She remembered that day all too well. It had been her first day on the job with the Ritter Oil Corporation. With her geology degree under her belt—a master's degree—she'd landed a plum of a job with one of the country's biggest oil companies. That achievement had given her confidence.

She'd looked successful that day, in a white linen suit and powder-blue blouse, with her blond hair in a neat chignon, her long, elegant legs in sheer hose, her face with just the right amount of makeup. Her appearance had shocked and delighted her male colleagues on the exploration team. But her first sight of Hunter had shocked and delighted *her,* to her utter dismay.

Eugene Ritter had called Hunter into his office to meet Jenny. She hadn't known about his Apache heritage then; she hadn't known anything about him except his last name. He'd come through the door and Jenny, who was usually unperturbed by men, had melted inside like warm honey.

Hunter had been even less approachable in those days. His hair had been longer, and he'd worn it in a short pigtail at his nape. His suit had been a pale one that summery day, emphasizing his darkness. But it was his face that Jenny had stared at so helplessly. It was a dark face, very strong, with high cheekbones and jet-black hair and deep-set black eyes, a straight nose and a thin, cruel-looking mouth that hadn't smiled when they were introduced. In fact, his eyes had narrowed with sudden hostility. She could remember the searing cold of that gaze even now, and the contempt as it had traveled over her with authority and disdain. As if she were a harem girl on display, she thought angrily, not a scientist with a keen analytical mind and meticulous accuracy in her work. It occurred to her then that a geologist would be a perfect match for the stony Mr. Hunter. She'd said as much to Eugene and it had gotten back to Hunter. That comment plus the other unfortunate stunt had not endeared her to Hunter. He hadn't found it the least bit amusing. He'd said that she wouldn't appeal to him if she came sliced and buttered.

She sighed, pushing her last piece of steak around on her plate. Amazing that he could hate her when she found him so unbearably attractive. The trick fate had played on her, she thought wistfully. All her life, the men who wanted her had been mama's boys or dependent men who needed nurturing. All she'd wanted was a man who was strong enough to let her be herself, brains and all. Now she'd finally found one who was strong, but neither her brains nor her beauty interested him in the least.

She'd never had the courage to ask Hunter why he hated her so much. They'd only been alone together once in all the years they'd know each other, and that had been the night they'd staged a charade for the benefit of the agents who were after Jenny's survey maps.

They'd gone to a restaurant with Cabe Ritter and his then-secretary, Danetta Marist, Jenny's cousin. Jenny had deliberately worn a red, sexy dress to "live down to Hunter's opinion" of her. He'd barely spared her a glance, so she could have saved herself the trouble. Once they'd reached the apartment and the trap had been sprung, she'd seen Hunter in action for the first time. The speed with which he'd tackled the man prowling in her apartment was fascinating, like the ease with which he'd floored the heavier man and rendered him unconscious. He'd gone after a second man, but that one had knocked Jenny into the wall in his haste to escape. Hunter had actually stopped to see that she was all right. He'd tugged her gently to her feet, his eyes blazing as he checked her over and demanded assurance that she hadn't been hurt. Then he'd gone after that second man, with blood in his eye, but he'd lost his quarry by then. His security men had captured a third member of the gang outside. Hunter had blamed Jenny for the loss of the second, who was the ringleader. Odd how angry he'd been, she thought in retrospect. Maybe it was losing his quarry, something he rarely did.

She washed her few dishes before she had a quick shower and got into her gown. The sooner she slept, the sooner she'd be on her way to putting this forced trip behind her, she told herself.

She looked at herself in the mirror before she climbed wearily into bed. There were new lines in her face. She was twenty-seven. Her age was beginning to bother her, too. Many more years and her beauty would fade. Then she'd have nothing except her intellect to attract a husband, and that was a laugh. Most of the men she'd met would trade a brainy woman any day for a beautiful one, despite modern attitudes. Hunter probably liked the kind of woman who'd walk three steps behind her husband and chew rawhide to make them soft for his moccasins.

She tried to picture Hunter with a woman in his arms, and she blushed at the pictures that came to mind. He had the most magnificent physique she'd ever seen, all lean muscle and perfection. Thinking of him without the civilizing influence of clothes made her knees buckle.

With an angry sigh, she put out the light and got under the sheets. She had to stop tormenting herself with these thoughts. It was just that he stirred her as no other man ever had. He could make her weak-kneed and giddy just by walking into a room. The sight of him fed her heart. She looked at him and wanted him, in ways that were far removed from the purely physical. She remembered hearing once that he'd been hurt on the job, and her heart had stopped beating until she could get confirmation that he was alive and going to be all right. She looked for him, consciously and unconsciously, everywhere she went. It was getting to be almost a mania with her, and there was apparently no cure. Stupid, to be so hopelessly in love with a man who didn't even know she existed. At her age, and with her intellect, surely she should have known better. But all the same, her world began and ended with Hunter.

Eventually she slept, but it was very late when she drifted off, and she slept so soundly that she didn't even hear the alarm clock the next morning. But she heard the loud knocking on the door, and stumbled out of bed too drowsy to even reach for her robe.

Fortunately her gown was floor-length and cotton, thick enough to be decent to answer a door in, at least.

Hunter glowered at her when she opened the door. "The plane leaves in two hours. We have to be at the airport in one. Didn't I remind you that I'd be here at six?"

"Yes," she said on a sigh. She stared up at his dark face. "Don't you ever smile?" she asked softly.

He lifted a heavy, dark eyebrow. "When I can find something worth smiling at," he returned with faint sarcasm.

That puts me in my place, she thought. She turned. "I have to have my coffee or I can't function."

"I'll make the coffee. Get dressed," he said tersely, dragging his eyes away from the soft curves that gown outlined so sweetly.

"But..." She turned and saw the sudden flash of his dark eyes, and stopped arguing.

"I said get dressed," he repeated in a tone that made threats, especially when it was accompanied by his slow, bold scrutiny of her body.

She ran for it. He'd never looked at her in exactly that way before, and it wasn't flattering. It was simply the look of a man who knew how to enjoy a woman. Lust, for lack of a better description. She darted into her room and closed the door.

She refused to allow herself to think about that smoldering look he'd given her. She dressed in jeans and a pink knit top for travel, dressing for comfort rather than style, and she wore sneakers. She left her hair long and Hunter could complain if he liked, she told herself.

By the time she got to the small kitchen, Hunter was pouring fresh coffee into two mugs. He produced cinnamon toast, deliciously browned, and pushed the platter toward her as she sat down with him at the table.

"I didn't expect breakfast," she said hesitantly.

"You need feeding up," he replied without expression. "You're too thin. Get that in you."

"Thank you." She nibbled on toast and sipped coffee, trying not to stare. It was heart-breakingly cozy, to be like this with him. She tried to keep her eyes from darting over him, but she couldn't help it. He looked very nice in dark slacks and a white shirt with a navy blazer and striped tie. He wore his hair short and conventionally cut these days, and he was the picture of a successful businessman. Except for his darkness and the shape of his eyes and the very real threat of his dark skills. He was an intimidating man. Even now, it was hard going just to make routine conversation. Jenny didn't even try. She just sat, working on her second piece of toast.

Hunter felt that nervousness in her. He knew she felt intimidated by him, but it was a reaction he couldn't change. He was afraid to let her get close to him in any way. She was a complication he couldn't afford in his life.

"You talk more at work and around other people," he remarked when he'd finished the piece of toast he'd been eating and was working on his second cup of coffee.

"There's safety in numbers," she said without looking up.

He looked at her until she lifted her head and then he trapped her blue eyes with his black ones and refused to let her look away. The fiery intensity of the shared look made her body go taut with shocked pleasure, and her breath felt as if it had been suspended forever.

"Safety for whom?" he asked quietly. "For you?" His chin lifted, and he looked so arrogantly unapproachable that she wanted to back away. "What are you afraid of, Jennifer? Me?"

Yes, but she wasn't going to let him know it. She finished her coffee. "No," she said. "Of course not. I just meant that it's hard to make conversation with you."

He leaned back in his chair, his lean, dark hand so large that it completely circled the coffee mug. "Most people talk a lot and say nothing," he replied.

She nodded. Her lips tugged up. "A friend of mine once said that it was better to keep one's mouth closed and appear stupid than to open it and remove all doubt."

He didn't smile, but his eyes did, for one brief instant. He lifted the mug to his lips, watching Jenny over its rim. She was lovely, he thought with reluctant delight in her beauty. She seemed to glow in the early morning light, radiant and warm. He didn't like the feelings she kindled in him. He'd never known love. He didn't want to. In his line of work, it was too much of a luxury.

"We'd better get going," he said.

"Yes." She got up and began to tidy the kitchen, putting detergent into the water as it filled the sink.

He stood, watching her collect the dishes and wash them. He leaned against the wall, his arms crossed over his chest. His dark eyes narrowed as they sketched the soft lines of her body with slow appreciation.

He remembered the revealing red dress she'd worn the night they'd staked out her apartment, and his expression hardened. He hoped she wasn't going to make a habit of wearing anything revealing while they were alone together. Jennifer was his one weak spot. But fortunately, she didn't know that and he wasn't planning to tell her.

"I'll get your suitcases," he said abruptly. He shouldered away from the wall and went out.

She relaxed. She'd felt that scrutiny and it had made her

nervous. She wondered why he'd stared at her so intently. Probably he was thinking up ways to make her even more uncomfortable. He did dislike her intensely. For which she thanked God. His hostility would protect her from doing anything really stupid. Like throwing herself at him.

He had her bags by the front door when she was through. It was early fall, and chilly, so she put on a jacket on her way to the door. He opened the door for her, leaving her to lock up as he headed toward the elevator with the luggage. They didn't speak all the way to the car.

3

~~~

J enny was aware of Hunter's height as they walked to the car in the parking lot under her apartment building. He towered over her, and the way he moved was so smooth and elegant, he might have been gliding.

He put the luggage into the back of his sedan and opened the passenger door for her. He had excellent manners, she thought, and wondered if his mother had taught him the social graces or if he'd learned them in the service. So many questions she wanted to ask, but she knew he'd just ignore them, the way he ignored any questions he didn't want to answer.

He drove the way he did everything else, with confidence and poise. Near collisions, bottlenecks, slow traffic, nothing seemed to disturb him. He eased the car in and out of lanes with no trouble at all, and soon they were at the airport.

She noticed that he didn't request seats together. But the ticket agent apparently decided that they wanted them, to her secret delight, and put them in adjoining seats. That was when she realized how lovesick she was, hungry for just the accidental brush of his arm or leg. She had to get a grip on herself!

He sat completely at ease in his seat while she ground her teeth together and tried to remember all the statistics on how safe air travel really was.

"Now what's wrong?" he murmured, glancing darkly down at her as the flight attendants moved into place to demonstrate emergency procedures.

"Nothing," she said.

"Then why do you have a death-grip on the arms of your seat?" he asked politely.

"So that I won't get separated from it when we crash," she replied, closing her eyes tight.

He chuckled softly. "I never took you for a coward," he said. "Are you the same woman who helped me set up enemy agents only a few weeks ago?"

"That was different," she protested. She lifted her blue eyes to his dark ones and her gaze was trapped. Her breath sighed out, and she wondered which was really the more dangerous, the plane or Hunter.

He couldn't seem to drag his eyes from hers, and he found that irritating. At close quarters, she was beautiful. Dynamite. All soft curves and a sexy voice and a mouth that he wanted very much to kiss. But that way lay disaster. He couldn't afford to forget the danger of involvement. He had a life-style that he couldn't easily share with any woman, but most especially with a white woman. All the same, she smelled sweet and floral, and she looked so beautifully cool. He wanted to dishevel her.

He averted his face to watch the flight attendants go through the drill that preceded every flight, grateful for the interruption. He had to stop looking at Jennifer like that.

They were airborne before either of them spoke again.

"These people that you think are following us," she said softly, "is it the same group that broke into my apartment?"

"More than likely," he said. "You have to remember that strategic metals tend to fluctuate on the world market according to the old law of supply and demand. When a new use is found for a strategic metal, it becomes immediately more valuable."

"And an increase in one industry can cause it, too," she replied.

He nodded. She was quick. He liked her brain as much as her body, but he wasn't going to let her know that. "We didn't pick up the ringleader, you remember. He got away," he added with a cold glare at her.

She flushed. She didn't like being reminded of how helpless she'd felt. "I didn't ask you to stop to see about me," she defended.

He knew that. The memory of seeing her lying inert on the floor still haunted him. That was when he'd first realized he was vulnerable. Now he seemed to spend all his time trying to forget that night. The agents, his job to protect Jenny and the company, had all been momentarily forgotten when the agent knocked her down in his haste to get away. Hunter had been too shaken by Jennifer's prone position to run after the man. And that was what made him so angry. Not the fact that the agent had gotten away, but the fact that his concern for Jennifer had outweighed his dedication to his work. That was a first in his life.

"We're transferring to another flight in Phoenix, under different names," he said, lowering his voice. "With luck, the agents will pursue us on to California before they realize we're gone."

"How are we going to give them the slip? Are they on the plane?"

He smiled without looking at her. "Yes, they're about five rows behind us. We're going to get off supposedly to stretch our legs before the plane goes on to Tucson. We transfer to another airline, though, instead of coming back."

"What if they follow us?"

"I'd see them," he murmured dryly. "The rule of thumb in tracking someone is to never let your presence be discovered. Lose the subject first. This isn't the first time I've played cat and mouse with these people. I know them."

That said it all, she supposed, but she was glad she could leave all the details to him. Her job was field geology, not espionage. She glanced up at him, allowing herself a few precious seconds of adoration before she jerked her eyes back down and pretended to read a magazine.

She didn't fool Hunter. He'd felt that shy appraisal and it worried him more than the agents did. Being alone with Jennifer on the desert was asking for trouble. He was going to make sure that he was occupied tonight, and that they wouldn't set out until tomorrow. Maybe in that length of time, he could explain the situation to his body and keep it from doing something stupid.

It was a short trip, as flights went. They'd just finished breakfast when they were circling to land at the Tucson airport.

Hunter had everything arranged. Motel reservations, a rental car, the whole works. And it all worked to perfection until they got to the motel desk and the desk clerk handed them two keys, to rooms on different floors.

"No, that won't do," Hunter replied with a straight face, and without looking at Jennifer. "We're honeymooners," he said. "We want a double room."

"Oh! I'm sorry, sir. Congratulations," the clerk said with a pleasant smile.

Dreams came true, Jenny thought, picturing all sorts of delicious complications during that night together. The desk clerk handed him a key after he signed them in—as Mr. and Mrs. Camp. Nice of Hunter to tell her their married name, she thought with faint amusement. But it was typical of him to keep everything to himself.

He unlocked the door, waited for the bellboy to put their luggage and equipment in the room, and tipped the man.

They were alone. He closed the door and turned to her, his dark eyes assessing as he saw the faint unease on her face. "Don't start panicking," he said curtly. "I won't assault you. This is the best way to keep up the masquerade, that's all."

She colored. "I didn't say a word," she reminded him.

He wandered around the room with some strange electronic gadget in one hand and checked curtains and lamps. "No bugs," he said eventually. "But that doesn't mean much. I'm pretty sure we're being observed. Don't leave the room unless I'm with you, and don't mention anything about why we're here. Is that clear?"

"Why don't we just go out into the desert and camp?"

"We have to have camping gear," he explained with mocking patience. "It's too late to start buying it now. The morning's over. We'll start out later in the afternoon."

"All right." She put her suitcases on the side of the room that was nearest the bathroom, hesitating.

"Whichever bed you want is yours," he said without inflection. He was busy watching out the window. "I can sleep anywhere."

And probably had, she thought, remembering some of his assignments that she'd heard about. She put her attaché case with her maps on the bed, and her laptop computer on the side table, taking time to plug its adapter into the wall socket so that it could stay charged up. It only had a few hours' power between charges.

"Give me that case," he said suddenly. He took the case with the maps and opened it, hiding a newspaper he'd brought into the case and then putting it in a dresser drawer with one of his shirts over it. The maps he tucked into a pair of his jeans and left them in his suitcase.

Jenny lifted an amused eyebrow. He had a shrewd mind. She almost said so, but it might reveal too much about her feelings if she told him. She unpacked her suitcase instead and began to hang up her clothes. She left her underthings and her long cotton gown in the suitcase, too shy of Hunter to put them in a drawer in front of him.

The gown brought to mind a question that had only just occurred. Should she put it on tonight, or would it look like an invitation? And worse, did he sleep without clothes? Some men did. She'd watched him put his things away out of the corner of her eye, and she hadn't seen either a robe or anything that looked like pajamas. She groaned inwardly. Wouldn't that be a great question to ask a man like Hunter, and how would she put it? Isn't this a keen room, Mr. Hunter, and by the way, do you sleep stark naked, because if you do, is it all right if I spend the night in the bathtub?

She laughed under her breath. Wouldn't that take the starch out of his socks, she thought with humor. Imagine, a woman her age and with her looks being that ignorant about a man's body. Despite the women's magazines she'd seen from time to time, with their graphic studies of nude men, there was a big difference in a photograph and a real, live man.

"Is something bothering you?" he asked suddenly.

The question startled her into blurting out the truth. "Do you wear pajamas?" she asked, and her face went scarlet.

"Why?" he replied with a straight face. "Do you need to borrow them, or were you thinking of buying me a pair if I say no?"

She averted her face. "Sorry. I'm not used to sharing a room with a man, that's all."

No way could he believe that she'd never spent a night with a man. More than likely she was nervous of him. "We're supposed to be honeymooners," he said with faint sarcasm. "It would look rather odd to spend the night in separate rooms."

"Of course." She just wanted to drop the whole subject. "Could we get lunch? I'm starving."

"I want to check with my people first," he told her. "I've got a couple of operatives down here doing some investigative work on another project. I won't be long."

She'd thought he meant to phone, but he went out of the room.

Jenny sprawled on her bed, cursing her impulsive tongue. Now he'd think she was a simpleminded prude as well as a pain in the neck. Great going, Jenny, she told herself. What a super way to get off on the right foot, asking your reluctant roommate about his night wear. Fortunately he hadn't pursued the subject.

He was back an hour later. She'd put on her reading glasses, the ones she used for close work because she was hopelessly farsighted, and was plugging away on her laptop computer, going over detailed graphic topo maps of the area, sprawled across the bed with her back against the headboard and the computer on her lap. Not the best way to use the thing, and against the manufacturer's specs, but it was much more comfortable than trying to use the motel's table and chairs.

"I didn't know you wore glasses," he remarked, watching her.

"You didn't?" she asked with mock astonishment. "Why, Mr. Hunter, I was sure you'd know more about me than I know myself—don't you have a file on all the staff in your office?"

"Don't be sarcastic. It doesn't suit you." He stretched out on the other bed, powerful muscles rippling in his lean body, and she had to fight not to stare. He was beautifully made from head to toe, an old maid's dream.

She punched in more codes and concentrated on her maps.

"What kind of mineral are you and Eugene looking for?" he asked curiously.

She pursed her lips and glanced at him with gleeful malice. "Make a guess," she invited.

She realized her mistake immediately and could have bitten her lip through. He sat up and threw his long legs off the bed, moving to her side with threatening grace. He took the laptop out of her hands and put it on the table before he got her by the wrists and pulled her up against his body. The proximity made her knees go weak. He smelled of spicy cologne and soap, and his breath had a coffee scent, as if he'd been meeting his operatives in a café. His grip was strong and exciting, and she loved the feel of his body so close to hers. Perhaps, subconsciously, this was what she'd expected when she antagonized him…

"Little girls throw rocks at boys they like," he said at her forehead. "Is that what you're doing, figuratively speaking? Because if it is," he added, and his grip on her wrists tightened even as his voice grew deeper, slower, "I'm not in the market for a torrid interlude on the job, cover girl."

She could have gone through the floor with shame. The worst of it was that she didn't even have a comeback. He saw right through her. With his advantage in age and experience, that wasn't really surprising. She knew, too, from gossip that he disliked white women. Probably they saw him as a unique experience more than a man. She didn't feel that way, but she couldn't admit it.

"I'm not trying to get your attention. I'm tired and when I'm tired, I get silly," she said too quickly, talking to his shirt as she stiffened with fear of giving herself away. Odd, the jerky way he was breathing, and the fabric was moving as if his heartbeat was very heavy. Her body was melting, this close to his. "You don't have to warn me off. I know better than to make a play for you."

The remark diverted him. "Do you? Why?" he asked curtly.

"They say you hate women," she replied. "Especially," she added, forcing her blue eyes up to his narrowed dark ones, "white women."

He nodded slowly. His gaze held hers, and then drifted down to her soft bow of a mouth with its faint peach lipstick, and further, to the firm thrust of her breasts almost but not quite touching his shirtfront. He remembered another beautiful blond, the one who'd deserted him when he'd been five years old. Her Apache child had been an embarrassment in her social circles. By then, of course, her activist phase was over, and she had her sights on one of her own people. Some years back, he'd been taken in by a socialite himself. An Apache escort had been unique, for a little while, until he'd mentioned a permanent commitment. And she'd laughed. My God, marry a man who lived on a reservation? The memories bit into him like teeth.

He released Jennifer abruptly with a roughness that wasn't quite in character.

"I'm sorry," she said when she saw the expression in his dark eyes. She winced, as if she could actually feel his pain. "I didn't mean to bring back bad memories for you."

His expression was frightening at that moment. "What do you know about me?" he asked, his voice cutting.

She managed a wan smile and moved away from him. "I don't know anything, Mr. Hunter. Nobody does. Your life is a locked door and there's no key. But you looked…" She turned and glanced back at him, and her hands lifted and fell helplessly. "I don't know. Wounded." She averted her eyes. "I'd better get this put away."

Her perception floored him. She was a puzzle he'd never solved, and despite his security files, he knew very little about her own private life. There were no men at the office, he knew. She was discreet, if nothing else. In fact, he thought, studying her absently with narrowed eyes as she put away her computer, he'd never heard of her dating a man in all the years she'd been with the company. He'd never seen her flirt with a man, and even those she worked with treated her as just one of the boys. That fact had never occurred to him before. She kept her distance from men as a rule. Even out in the field, where working conditions were much more relaxed, Jennifer went without makeup, in floppy shirts and loose jeans, and she kept to herself after working hours. He'd once seen her cut a man dead who was trying to make a play for her. Her eyes had gone an icy blue, her face rigid with distaste, and even though she hadn't said much, her would-be suitor got the message in flying colors. Hunter wouldn't admit, even to himself, how that action had damned her in his eyes. Seeing her put in the knife had made him more determined than ever not to risk his emotions with her. There were too many hard memories of his one smoldering passion for a white woman, and its humiliating result. And, even longer ago than that, his mother's contempt for him, her desertion.

He turned away from Jennifer, busying himself with the surveillance equipment one of his cases contained. He redistributed the equipment in the case and closed it.

"Why do we have to have all that?" she queried suddenly.

He nodded toward her computer and equipment. "Why do you have to have all that?" he countered.

"It's part of my working gear," she said simply.

"You've answered your own question." He checked his watch. "Let's get something to eat. Then we'll have a look at camping supplies."

"The joy of expense accounts," she murmured as she got her purse and put away her reading glasses. "I wonder if Eugene will mind letting me have a jungle hammock? I slept in one when I was a kid. We camped next to two streams, and they were like a lullaby in the darkness."

"You can have a jungle hammock if you think you can find a place to hang it."

"All we need is two trees…."

He turned, his hands on his lean hips, his dark face enigmatic. "The desert is notorious for its lack of trees. Haven't you ever watched any Western movies?" he added, and came very close to a smile. "Remember the Indians chasing the soldiers in John Wayne movies, and the soldiers having to dive into dry washes or gulches for cover?"

She stared at him, fascinated. "Yes. I didn't think you'd watch that kind of movie…" She colored, embarrassed.

"Because the solders won?" he mused. "That's history. But the Apache fought them to a standstill several times. And Louis L'Amour did a story called *Hondo* that was made into a movie with John Wayne." He lifted an eyebrow. "It managed to show Apaches in a good light, for once."

"I read about Cochise when I was in school. And Mangas Coloradas and Victorio…"

"Different tribes of Apache," he said. "Cochise was Chiricahua. Mangas and Victorio were MimbreÑos."

"Which…are you?" she asked, sounding and feeling breathless. He'd never spoken to her like this before.

"Chiricahua," he said. His eyes searched her face. "Is your ancestry Nordic?" he asked.

"It's German," she said softly. "On my father's side, it's English." Her eyes wandered helplessly over his lean face.

Her intense scrutiny disturbed him in a new and unexpected way. Her eyes were enormous. Dark blue, soft, like those of some kitten. He didn't like the way they made him tingle. He turned away, scowling.

"We'd better go, Jennifer."

Her name on his lips thrilled her. She felt alive as never before when she was with him, even if it was in the line of duty.

She started toward the door, but he turned as she reached it, and she bumped into him. The contact was like fire shooting through her.

"Sorry!" She moved quickly away. "I didn't mean to...!"

He put a strong hand under her chin and lifted her face to his eyes. Her eyelids flinched and there was real fear in them at close range. "You really are afraid of me," he said with dawning comprehension.

She hadn't wanted him to know that. Of course she was afraid of him, but not for the reasons he was thinking. She moved back and lowered her eyes. "A little, maybe," she said uneasily.

"My God!" He jerked open the door. "Out."

She went through it, avoiding him as she left. She hadn't expected the confession to make him angry. She sighed heavily. It was going to be a hard trip, all the way, if this was any indication. He was coldly silent all the way to the motel restaurant, only taking her arm when they were around people, for appearance's sake.

They were halfway through their meal when he spoke again.

"It's been years since I've scalped anyone," he said suddenly, his angry eyes searching hers.

The fork fell from her fingers with a terrible clatter. She picked it up quickly, looking around nervously to see if anyone had noticed, but there was only an old couple nearby and they were too busy talking to notice Jennifer and her companion.

She should have remembered how sensitive he was about his heritage. She'd inadvertently let him believe that she was afraid of him because he was an Indian. What a scream it would be if she confessed that she was afraid of him because she was in love with him. He'd probably kill himself laughing.

"No, it's not that," she began. She stopped, helplessly searching for the right words. "It's not because you're..." She toyed with her fork. "The thing is, I'm not very comfortable around you," she said finally. She put down her fork. "You've never made any secret of the fact that you dislike me. You're actively hostile the minute I come into a room. It isn't exactly fear. It's nerves, and it has nothing to do with your heritage."

She had a point. He couldn't deny that he'd been hostile. Her beauty did that to him; it made him vulnerable and that irritated him. He knew he was too touchy about his ancestry, but he'd had it rough trying to live in a white world.

"I don't find it easy, living among your people," he said. He'd never admitted that to anyone before.

"I can imagine," she replied. Her eyes searched his. "You might consider that being a female geologist in an oil company isn't the easiest thing to do, either. I loved rocks."

His dark eyes conquered hers suddenly. The look was pure electricity. Desert lightning. She felt it all the way to her toes.

"I find you hard going, too, Miss Marist," he said after a minute. "But I imagine we'll survive. Eugene said we were to camp on the actual site the second night."

"Yes." Her voice sounded breathless, choked.

He found himself studying her hand on the table. Involuntarily his brushed over the back of it. He told himself it was for appearances. But touching her gave him pleasure, and she jumped. He scowled, feeling her long fingers go cold and tremble. His eyes lifted back to hers. "You're trembling."

She jerked her hand from under his, almost unbalancing her water glass in the process. "I have to finish my steak." She laughed nervously. "The stores will close soon."

"So they will."

The subterfuge didn't fool him, she knew. Not one bit. His chin lifted and there was something new in the set of his head. An arrogance. A kind of satisfied pride that kindled in his eyes.

He was curious now. A beautiful woman like Jennifer would be used to giving men the jitters, not the reverse. He let his gaze fall to her soft mouth as it opened to admit a small piece of steak, and he felt his body go rigid. Over the years, he'd only allowed himself the occasional fantasy about making love to her. As time passed, and he grew older, the fantasies had grown stronger. He could keep the disturbing thoughts at bay most of the time. But there was always the lonely night when he'd toss and turn and his blood would grow hot as he imagined her mouth opening for him, her hands on his back, her soft legs tangling with his in the darkness. Those nights were hell. And the next few, alone with her, were going to sorely test his strength of will. For her it would be a field expedition. For him, a survival course, complete with sweet obstacles and pitfalls.

He had to remember that this was an assignment, and enemy agents were following them. Strategic metals always drew trouble, not only from domestic corporations struggling to get their hands in first, but from foreign investors interested in the same idea. He had to keep his mind on his work, and not on Jennifer. But her proximity wasn't going to make that job any easier. He almost groaned aloud at the difficulties. There hadn't been a woman in a long time, and he was hungry. He wanted Jennifer and he was relatively sure that she was attracted to him. She was certainly nervous enough when he came close.

But, he thought, what if her fear of him was genuine and had nothing to do with attraction? Her explanation that it was because they were enemies didn't hold up. It was far too flimsy to explain the way she trembled when he touched her hand. Fear could cause that, he had to admit. And he had been unkind to her, often. He sighed heavily. Thinking about it wasn't going to make it any easier.

They went to a hardware store when they finished their meal, and Jennifer watched him go about the business of buying camping supplies with pure awe. He knew exactly what to get, from the Coleman stove to the other gear like sleeping bags and tent and cans of Sterno for emergencies. Jennifer had gone out into the field before, many times, but usually there was some kind of accommodation. She hadn't relished the idea of camping out by herself, although she loved it with companions. Hunter, though, was going to be more peril than pleasure as a tent mate. She had to get a grip on herself, she told her stubborn heart again. The prospect of a few nights alone with him was sending her mad.

He loaded the gear into the four-wheel drive vehicle he'd had waiting for them at the airport. It was a black one, and he drove it with such ease that she suspected he had one of his own at home. That brought to mind an interesting question. Where was home to him? She knew he had an apartment in Tulsa, but he spent his time off in Arizona. Near here? With a woman, perhaps? Her blood ran cold.

"We'll be ready to go in the morning," he told her when they were back in the motel room again, with their gear stowed in the locked vehicle outside. All except her computer and his surveillance equipment, of course. He wasn't risking that. "Do you want to shower first?"

She shifted uncomfortably. "If you don't mind."

"Go ahead. I'll watch the news."

She carried her things into the bathroom, firmly locking the door, despite what he might think about the sound. She took a quick shower and put on clean blue jeans and a clean white knit shirt. She felt refreshed and sunny when she came back out, her face bright and clean without makeup.

He was sprawled across a chair, his shoes off, a can of beer in his hand. He lifted an eyebrow. "Do you mind beer, or does the smell bother you?"

"No. My father likes his lager," she said as she dealt with her dirty clothes.

He finished his drink and stood, stripping off his shirt. "If you're finished, I'll have my shower. Then we'll think about something for dinner."

She was watching him as helplessly as a teenage girl staring at a movie star. He was beautiful. God, he was beautiful, she thought with pleasure so deep it rivaled pain. Muscles rippled in his dark torso from the low-slung belt on his jeans to the width of his shoulders as he stretched, and her eyes sketched him with shy adoration.

He was aware of her scrutiny, but he pretended not to notice. He got a change of clothes to carry into the bathroom with him and turned, faintly amused by the way she busied herself with her computer and pretended to ignore him.

Her helpless stare had piqued his curiosity. He deliberately paused just in front of her, giving her an unnecessarily good view of his broad, naked chest.

"Don't forget to keep the door locked," he advised quietly, watching the flicker of her lashes as she lifted her blue eyes to his. "And don't answer it if someone knocks."

"Yes, sir, is that all, sir?" she asked brightly.

He caught her chin with a lean hand and his thumb brushed roughly over her mouth, a slow, fierce intimacy that he watched with almost scientific intensity. She knew her eyes were wildly dilated as they looked into his, and she couldn't help the shocked gasp that broke from her sensitized lips or the shiver of pleasure that ran through her body.

His dark eyes didn't miss a thing. Her reaction, he decided, was definitely not fear. He couldn't decide if he was pleased about it or not. "Don't be provocative," he said softly, his voice an octave deeper, faintly threatening. "Get to work." He moved away before she could find anything to say that wouldn't be provocative.

She sat down at her computer, her fingers trembling on the keyboard.

He closed the bathroom door behind him. His action had been totally unexpected, and it made her even more nervous than she already was. If he was going to start doing that kind of thing, she'd be safer in the lion cage at the zoo.

She was uncertain of him and of herself. Being around him in such close quarters was going to be a test of her self-control. She only hoped that she wouldn't give herself away. She'd had some naive idea that because Hunter disliked women, he didn't sleep with them. But she was learning that he knew a lot more than she did, and the sultry look in his dark eyes really frightened her. If she didn't watch her step, she was going to wind up with more than she'd bargained for.

His motives were what bothered her most. He didn't like white women, especially her, so what had prompted that action? She didn't want to consider the most evident possibility—that he thought she was fair game, and he had seduction on his mind. She ground her teeth together. Well, he could hold his breath. She wasn't going to be any man's light amusement. Not even his.

4

〜〜〜〜〜〜

When Jenny heard the shower running, she got up from her computer and sat in the chair Hunter had occupied to watch television. The chair still smelled of him. She traced the armrests where his hands had been and sighed brokenly. Jenny felt like a fool. She had to stop this!

She got out of the chair and went to work on her contour maps, trying to pinpoint the best place to look, given the mineral structure of the area. She'd begged time on Landsat earlier for another project, using the expensive computer time to study the satellite maps of this region of southern Arizona. The terrain they were going to survey was between the Apache reservation on one side and government land on the other. A narrow strip of desert and a narrow strip of mountain made up the search area, although they were going to be camping in several different spots to throw any would-be thieves off the mark.

She was deep in concentration when Hunter came back out of the bathroom, wearing clean jeans and no shirt, again. She had to bite her lip to keep from staring at him. He was unspeakably handsome to her, the most attractive man she'd ever known, but she couldn't afford the luxury of letting him know that. Especially not after the way he'd touched her mouth...

"Found what you're looking for?" he asked, placing one big hand on the table beside her and resting the other on the back of her chair. He leaned down to better see what she was studying. His cheek brushed hers and he felt her jump. His own breath caught. He wanted her. He should never have agreed to come on this expedition, because being close to her was having one hell of a bad effect on his willpower and self-control. He'd thought of nothing except the vulnerable look in her eyes when he'd touched her mouth so intimately, the yielding, the fascination. He wanted to grind his mouth into her own and make her cry out her need for him.

She was feeling the same tension. She knew he sensed her reaction, but she kept her head. "You startled me," she said breathlessly.

He knew better. His lean, warm cheek was touching hers as he stared at the map on the computer's small screen. She looked sideways and saw the thick, short lashes over his dark eyes, the faint lines in his cream-smooth tan. "Hunter..." His name was a soft whisper that broke involuntarily from her throat.

His head turned, and his eyes looked deeply into hers from scant inches away. She could taste his breath on her mouth, smell the clean scent of his body, feel the impact of his bare arms, his chest. He intoxicated her with his nearness, and she saw the hot glitter of awareness in those black eyes. She could see the thick dark lashes above them lower as his gaze suddenly dropped with fierce intent to her parted lips.

She shivered. All her dreams hadn't prepared her for the impact of this. Like a string suspended from a height, waiting for the wind to move it, she hung at his lips without breathing. A fraction of an inch, and his mouth would be on hers...!

The knock at the door startled them both. Hunter stared at her and cursed himself for his own vulnerability. She was intoxicating him, damn her. He was a new experience for her, that was all. He had to get himself under control.

He jerked erect and moved to the door. "Yes?" he asked as he opened it.

"Mr. Camp?" a feminine voice said loudly enough that anyone listening could hear. "I'm Teresa Whitley." A tall brunette moved into Jennifer's line of vision. The woman was smiling up at Hunter. "You requested some information about tour spots?"

"Inside," he said, holding the door open. He actually smiled at the woman, and Jennifer wanted to scream.

"Miss Marist?" Teresa smiled warmly, extending a hand as Jennifer came forward. They shook hands. "Nice to meet you. I'm with the corporation—under Mr. Hunter, in fact, so I'd better call you Mrs. Camp outside this room."

"Good idea," Jennifer replied absently. She was still vibrating.

"I've got some more information for you about the area. It's all here, on disk." She frowned. "I'm still learning about computers, I'm afraid. You do use the 312 inch diskettes in your laptop?"

"I have a hard disk drive," Jennifer told her. "But I can use the diskettes, as well."

"Thank goodness!" She handed the diskette, in its plastic case, to Jennifer. "I'm afraid I don't know much about science." She sighed, and her dark brown eyes sought Hunter's flirtatiously. "I'm just a security officer, so I deal with people instead of machines."

And, oh, I'll just bet you do it well, Jennifer thought. She didn't say so. She murmured something about checking out the new data and went back to her computer.

"If you'd like, we can run by the office and I'll give you the results of that security check you had us run," she told Hunter. "We could have dinner afterward, if you haven't already eaten?"

Jennifer ground her teeth together. She knew now what Hunter had meant earlier when referring to his "other project." This was it, and it had brown eyes and a svelte figure. Jennifer wished she'd dressed to the hilt and put on her makeup. In full regalia, she could have given that exotic orchid a run for her money, but she'd thought dressing up might give Hunter wrong ideas about her.

"Fine," Hunter replied tersely. "Let me get my shirt on."

Finally, Jennifer thought. He hadn't bothered before, but perhaps he didn't want to drive Miss Security Blip out of her mind by flashing his gorgeous muscles.

Hunter glanced at Jennifer, watching the way she studiously ignored Teresa, not to mention him. He glared at her as he pulled a pale gray knit shirt out of his drawer and put it on. He ran a comb through his hair, with Teresa sighing audibly over him.

"You haven't met Teresa before, I gather, Jennifer?" he asked too casually.

"No," she replied, forcing a smile.

"She's Papago." He said it with bitter pleasure, knowing Jennifer would catch the hidden meaning. This woman was Indian.

"Tohono O'Odham," Teresa teased. "We changed our name from 'bean people' in Zuni to 'people of the desert' in Papago."

"Sorry," he said with a smile.

Jennifer hated that damned smile. She'd never seen it, but this woman was getting the full treatment. Of course, Teresa wasn't a blond scientist, she thought darkly. Well, he needn't think she was going to play third fiddle while he courted his secret agent here.

"I'd rather you stayed here...." he began as Jenny said, "I have a headache...."

He cocked an eyebrow and she cleared her throat.

"I'll order something from room service," she continued. "If I feel like eating later," she amended without looking at him. "I've spent too much time at the laptop. The screen bothers my eyes." God knew why she was trying to justify her nonexistent headache. He and his brunette wouldn't notice.

"I hope you feel better," Teresa said.

"Thanks."

"Shall we go?" Hunter asked as he pulled on his tan sports coat over his knit shirt. He turned at the door. "Keep the door locked. If you have room service, check credentials before you let anyone in here."

"Yes, sir," she said with resignation.

He let Teresa out and started to close the door. He looked back at Jennifer first, and the intensity of his stare made her lift her head. His eyes held hers for one long moment before they went to her mouth and back up again.

"Don't wait up," he said, but there was another, darker meaning in the casual remark.

"You can depend on me, sir," she saluted him.

He shook his head and went out the door.

She picked up one of her shoes and threw it furiously at the closed door. It connected a split second before he opened it again. The expression on his face was priceless, she thought.

"I forgot my car keys," he said, watching her narrowly as he went to the dresser to get them. On the way back, he reached down and picked up her shoe, cocking an eyebrow at it. "Target practice?"

She tried to look innocent. "Would I throw a shoe at you?"

He studied her for a long moment before he dropped the shoe on the floor. "I'll be back before midnight. You should be safe enough."

"Definitely safer than Miss Whitley," she said, and could have bitten her tongue clean through.

His head lifted. "That's true. Most men react to a deliberate invitation. Even me," he added, angry at his vulnerability and lashing out because of it.

Her face colored. "I did not—" she began.

"Invite me?" He let his eyes drop slowly to her mouth. "Yes, you did. But it won't work a second time. You're not my type, cover girl," he added with a mocking smile. "I like a woman with less experience than I have. Not more."

He went out without a backward glance, missing the fierce anger that burned in her cheeks. She hadn't invited him! She groaned. Yes, she had. She wanted him and it showed, but he thought it was because she was experienced and used to a full sexual life. What a laugh!

She went back to her computer. Anyway, he'd just warned her off, and maybe it was a good thing. He seemed to prefer Miss Whitley, and he could relate to her. She was from his world, and Jennifer was just a diversion that shouldn't have happened.

She glanced at her reflection in the mirror and sighed angrily. "You should have stayed home in Missouri and married a mountain man and had two point five children," she told herself. "Instead of joining an oil company and getting tangled up with Mr. Native American."

She refused to let herself think about that one weak moment she'd shared with Hunter. She ordered a fish dinner and coffee to be sent to the room, and she ate it in silence, hoping the fish would leave its scent and drive him crazy. She'd heard someone say that he hated fish. Good enough for him. She hoped his girlfriend gave him warts.

It was only ten o'clock when she put on her cotton gown—deciding to let Hunter think what he liked—climbed into bed and turned out the lights. She didn't mean to go to sleep, she was too fired up by the long day and longer evening. But she was tired and the day caught up with her. She closed her eyes and slept like a baby.

Hunter came in just after midnight, sick of Miss Whitley's too-obvious adoration, and found Jennifer sprawled on her bed in a gown that would have raised a statue's temperature.

The covers had been thrown off, and the gown was up around her thighs. She was lying on her back with one arm thrown over her head, and the bodice was half off, baring the exquisite pink curve of one firm breast. Her clothes hid most of her figure. She didn't seem to go in for revealing things, except for that one night when she'd sent him up the walls in a low-cut red dress that showed every man around just what he was missing.

She was no less lovely now in that white cotton gown with its delicate embroidery. With her long blond hair spread around her perfect oval of a face, her lips parted in sleep, her body totally relaxed, she made a picture that he was going to have hell forgetting.

He managed to turn away from her at last and stripped down to his shorts. He almost removed them, too, but her remark about pajamas came back to twist his lips into a smile. He turned back his covers and set one of the security devices, just in case. From what Teresa had found out for him, the agent had been misled by this "vacation trip" and had followed their flight on to California, not realizing that Hunter and Miss Marist had suddenly turned into Mr. and Mrs. Camp in Tucson. But it didn't pay to get careless.

He had to remember that, he thought, looking at Jennifer one last time before he turned out the light. It had been one close call tonight, when Teresa had interrupted them. Another few seconds, and he'd have taken Jenny's sweet mouth without one single thought for the consequences. She'd have let him. That memory haunted him until he fell asleep. For a woman who purported to hate him, she was remarkably responsive to his touch. He had to convince her that he wasn't interested, no matter what it took. Her responsiveness could have terrible consequences if he let himself take advantage of it.

The next morning, Hunter was awake and dressed and had breakfast waiting when Jennifer smelled the coffee and food and forced her eyes open.

She sat up, barely aware of her state of undress until she saw Hunter scowl and avert his eyes. She tugged down her gown, angry at having given him a show, and quickly got her clothes together to dress in the bathroom.

She fixed her hair and put on makeup this morning, and she was wearing a blouse for a change, one that buttoned up and emphasized the exquisite shape of her breasts and her narrow waist. It was red, to go with her white jeans, and as she looked at her reflection, she hoped Hunter had fits because of her outfit. Miss Whitley, indeed! This morning she was more than match for the security lady.

When she went back into the room, Hunter was dishing up eggs and bacon. "Coffee's in the pot, pour your own," he said curtly.

"Thanks." She took the plate from him, aware of her beauty and its effect, tingling when she saw his dark eyes glance over her body and away.

"We aren't going to a party," he informed her curtly.

Her eyebrows arched. "Jeans, a short-sleeved blouse and sneakers aren't exactly party gear," she pointed out.

He lifted his head, and his eyes made threats. "I'm not a eunuch. We're going out into the desert, where we'll be completely on our own for several days. Don't complicate things. You looked better yesterday."

"Did I? Compared to what?" she demanded coldly. "Or should I say to whom?"

He let out a heavy sigh and leaned back in his chair to study her. "Teresa is an operative. When she isn't trying to compete for attention, she's very good at her job. I'm not her lover, nor likely to be. Nor yours," he added with a cold stare.

She had to grit her teeth. "I wasn't inviting you to be my lover. I'm tired of knit blouses. It gets hot on the desert. This blouse is cooler. So are the white slacks—they tend to reflect heat."

"God deliver me from scientific lectures before breakfast," he said icily, his narrow dark eyes making her nervous. "The fact is, Miss Marist, you saw Teresa as competition and you wanted to show me that you could beat her hands down in a beauty contest. All right, you have. You win. Now put on something less seductive and eat your breakfast. I'd like to get started."

She shook with mingled fury and humiliation and indignation, her fists clenched at her sides. No man had ever enraged her so much, so easily. She could have laid a chair across his skull with pleasure. Except that he was right. She *had* been competing for his attention. She just hadn't wanted him to realize it.

She grabbed up the same white knit shirt she'd worn the day before and pulled it on over her blouse, tugging her shirt collar through the rounded neckline. She didn't say another word to him. She sat down at the table and ate her breakfast. She was getting used to not tasting what she ate when she was with him. One way or another, he always managed to kill her appetite.

He finished his bacon and eggs and leaned back to sip his coffee, his gaze level and speculative. "Pouting?" he taunted. He wanted her and he couldn't have her. It was making him irritable. "You should know better than to throw yourself at men."

Her dark blue eyes flashed fire. She put down her coffee cup. "I don't pout," she said coldly, getting to her feet. "And I don't need to throw myself at men! Especially you!"

He got up, too, towering over her, his eyes dark with mingled frustration and anger. It got worse when she tried to step back and her cheeks flushed.

"To hell with it," he murmured roughly. He caught her waist and jerked her against his lean, powerful body, holding her there while his mouth bent to hers.

He didn't look in the least loverlike. He looked furious. "Hunter, no...!" she whispered frantically, pushing at his chest.

His lips poised just above hers, his dark eyes holding hers, his breath on her face. "You're going to push until you find out, aren't you?" he asked roughly. "Well, for the book, Apaches don't kiss their women on the mouth. But I'm no novice with your race or your sex. So do let me satisfy your curiosity."

The tone was smooth and deep, pure honey. She watched his hard lips part and then they were on her mouth, fierce and rough but totally without feeling. His breath filled her mouth with its minty warmth, his mouth moved with expert demand. But his body showed no sign of arousal, and he might have been holding a statue for all the warmth he projected.

She'd wanted this. She'd waited forever to be close to him like this, to feel his arms closing around her, enfolding her, to feel his hard mouth on hers. She breathed him, anguished pleasure racking her body at the taste of him, so intimate on her mouth.

But he was feeling nothing, and she realized it quite suddenly, with bitter disappointment. Almost at once he lifted his head. She opened her eyes and saw nothing in his face. No desire, nor need, nor love. There was nothing there except a cold curiosity. She was hungry, but he wasn't. Not a hair out of place, she thought with faint hysteria, Mr. Cool.

He let her go with a smooth, abrupt movement of his hands, putting distance between them effortlessly. "If you know as much about men as I think you do," he said quietly, "that should tell you exactly what I feel." He smiled, but it was a mocking, cold smile. "Bells didn't ring. Horns didn't blow. The earth didn't move. You have a pretty mouth, but I wouldn't kill for it. So now that we've breached that hurdle, can we go to work?"

She swallowed her pride and hurt. "By all means," she said. "I'll get my gear."

It was dark and they were camped on the peak of a small hill, under a palo verde tree. No jungle hammock, just a tent with two sleeping bags inside it. The bags were positioned as far apart as Jennifer could get them. Equipment was set up to monitor any movement for miles around. The computer was busy. There was no conversation. Jenny hadn't said one single word to Hunter since they left the motel, and if she had her way, she never would again. She didn't care about him, she told herself. She couldn't love a man who could be that cruel.

He was aware of her hostility, but he preferred it to those melting glances she'd been giving him. He'd deliberately been ice-cold with her when he'd kissed her. It had been imperative to show her that he felt nothing. Now he'd convinced her, and he wasn't pleased with his handiwork.

Jenny had withdrawn from him, into her work. Now it was she who was ignoring him, and it disturbed him to feel the distance he'd created. Not that it wasn't desirable. He couldn't afford the luxury of involvement with Ritter's top field geologist. It would complicate his own job, especially when the affair ended. And it would end. He and Jennifer were as different as night and day. He wanted her. She wanted him. But desire would never be enough to keep them together. He was old enough to know that, and she should be.

She was so different like this. They'd never been alone together on assignment, there had always been other people around. He saw a Jennifer that he hadn't known existed. A shy, uncertain woman with a keen analytical mind who actually downplayed her extraordinary looks. Or she had, he amended, until Teresa had tried her hand at upstaging Jennifer. Jennifer had tried to compete, to draw his attention. He should be flattered, he supposed, but it had made him angry to be the object of a female tug-of-war.

"Do you want anything to eat?" he asked when the silence became too tense.

"I had a candy bar, thanks," she replied. She was putting away the computer, her attention elsewhere.

"I brought provisions. You can have anything you like, including a steak."

"I don't want anything."

"Starve yourself if you like," he said, turning his back to fix himself a steak on the Coleman stove. "Pride doesn't digest well."

"You'll never know," she said under her breath.

He glared at her. "Do you have to have every man you meet on your string?" he asked. "Does your ego demand blind adoration?"

She closed her eyes. The pain was unbearable. "Please stop," she said huskily. "I'm sorry. I won't do it again."

He felt a strange empathy with her at times. He seemed to sense her feelings, her emotions. He was doing it now. She was wounded, emotionally.

He got to his feet and knelt beside her, his dark eyes enigmatic. "Won't do what again?" he asked.

"I won't...how did you put it?...try to get your attention." She stared at the darkening ground. "I don't know why I tried."

He studied the shadows on the ground. Night was coming down around them. Crickets sounded in the grass. A coyote howled. The wind caught her hair and blew it toward his face, and he felt its softness against his cheek.

"How old are you?" he asked suddenly.

"Twenty-seven," she replied, her voice terse because she didn't like admitting her age.

He hadn't realized she was that old. He frowned, wondering why on earth a woman so lovely should be so alone. "You don't date," he persisted.

"Checked the file, did you?" She pushed back her hair and glanced up at him and away as she closed the laptop and put it aside. "No, I don't date. What's the use? I was almost engaged twice, until they realized that I had a brain and wanted to use it. I wasn't content to be a room decoration and a hostess to the exclusion of my career. I've gotten used to being alone. I rather like it."

"Except sometimes on dark nights, when you go hungry for a man's arms," he added with faint insolence.

She stared at him with equal insolence. "I suppose you're in a position to know that," she agreed, nodding. "I've been alone too long, I suppose. Even you started to look good to me!"

He didn't answer her. He had to admit that he'd deserved that. He shouldn't have taunted her, especially about something that she probably couldn't even help.

She got up and moved away from him, tense and unnerved by his continued scrutiny.

"Come and eat something," he said.

She shook her head. "I meant it. I'm not hungry." She laughed bitterly. "I haven't tasted food since Eugene forced us on this ridiculous assignment. The only thing I want is to get it over with and get away from you!"

His dark eyes caught hers. "Do you, Jennifer?" he asked softly, his voice deep and almost gentle in the stillness.

She felt that tone to the soles of her feet and she turned away from him. It wasn't fair that he could do this to her. "I'd better get my equipment put away."

He watched her go. She seemed to bring out the very worst in him. "There's no need to run," he said mockingly, glaring at her through the growing darkness. "I'm not going to touch you again. I don't want you. Couldn't you tell?"

"Yes." She almost choked on the word. She turned toward the tent. "Yes, I could tell."

Her voice disturbed him. It seemed to hurt her that he didn't find her desirable. He drew in a slow breath, wondering what to do. It had seemed the best idea at the time, to put her at ease about his intentions. But he'd done something to her emotions with that cold, angry kiss. It hadn't been anything like the kiss he'd wanted to give her, either. Nothing like it.

He cooked his steak and ate it, feeling vaguely disturbed that he couldn't make her share it. He put out the fire, set his surveillance equipment, and went into the tent.

She was already in her sleeping bag, zipped up tight in her clothes, her eyes closed. But she wasn't asleep. He could hear her ragged breathing and there were bright streaks on her cheeks in the faint light of the flashlight he used to get to his own sleeping bag.

He put out the light angrily and took off his boots, climbing in fully clothed. He lay back on the ground, his eyes on the top of the tent, his mind full of thoughts, mostly unpleasant.

Jenny was crying. He could hear her. But to go to her, to offer comfort, would be the biggest mistake of all. He might offer more than comfort. Not wanting her was a lie. He did. He always had. But she'd want something more than desire, he thought. And desire was all he had to give.

She wiped at her tears, trying not to sniff audibly. She never cried, but she'd set new records tonight. Why did he have the power to hurt her so badly? She pushed the damp hair out of her eyes and stared at the wall of the tent, thinking back to camping trips with her parents and her cousin Danetta when they were girls. How uncomplicated and sweet life had been then. No career, no worries, just long, lazy summer days and hope.

A coyote howled and she stiffened under the sleeping bag. Was it a coyote, or a wolf?

"It's a coyote," he said, giving it the Spanish pronunciation. "We call them songdogs. They loom large in our legends, in our history. We don't consider them as lowly as whites do."

"If you dislike white people so much, why do you work with us?" she asked angrily, her voice hoarse from the tears.

"It's a white world."

"Don't blame me. None of my ancestors ever served in the U.S. Cavalry out west. They were much too busy shooting Union soldiers."

"Was Missouri a southern state?"

"I'm not from Missouri originally. My parents moved there when I was seven. I was born in Alabama," she continued. "And that *is* a southern state."

"You don't have an accent."

"Neither do you."

He felt his lips tug into a smile. "Should I?"

"I wouldn't touch that with a pole, Mr. Hunter," she replied. "I've had enough of that big chip on your shoulder. I'm not aiming any more punches at it."

"Poles and chips and punches, at this hour of the night," he murmured gently.

"You don't have to talk to me, you know," she said wearily. "We can manage this assignment in sign language."

"Do you know any?" he asked in a dry tone as he crossed his arms over his head, stretching.

"A few phrases," she admitted, reluctant to confess it. "Eugene sent me up to Montana once and I had to parley with two Dakota Sioux. They spoke no English and I spoke no Sioux, so I learned to talk with my hands. It was very educational."

She was full of surprises. His head turned and he stared at her through the half darkness. "I could teach you to speak Apache."

She closed her eyes. "I don't want you to teach me anything, Mr. Hunter," she said huskily.

"Too bad," he replied, trying not to take offense. After all, he'd given her a hard time. "You could use a little tutoring. For an experienced women, you don't know much about kissing."

She couldn't believe what she was hearing. She sat up on the sleeping bag. "This from a man who already admitted that Apaches don't do it...!"

"That was back in the nineteenth century," he mused. He propped himself on one elbow and stared at her, his blood beginning to burn at the sight of her, so beautiful with her long hair around her shoulders. "How can you be twenty-seven and not know something so elementary as how to kiss a man properly?"

"You only did it to humiliate me...!"

"You didn't know that," he replied. He remembered her shy response, and it made him feel worse. Apparently the men in her life had been more interested in their own pleasure than hers, because no one had ever taught her about loveplay. He wanted to. His body went rigid as he realized how much he wanted to.

"I told you," she said, trying to salvage some of her pride. "I've been alone for a long time..."

"Have you? Why?" he asked.

She didn't want to go into why. He'd managed to cut her to the bone already with his cold manner, without the insult about the way she kissed. It hurt even more that he'd noticed, despite his lack of interest in her.

"Never mind," she said wearily. She lay back down and closed her eyes. "I just want to go to sleep. It's been a long day."

"So it has. We'll move camp tomorrow."

"Could we move it to Mars?" she asked. "It wouldn't make much difference, considering the lack of vegetation."

"You aren't seeing. The desert is alive and beautiful, if you know what to look for."

"You do, I suppose."

"I'm an Indian, remember?" he asked with rough insolence.

"How could I forget?" she muttered. "You never let anyone forget…"

"Go to sleep," he said shortly. He closed his own eyes, out of patience and totally out of humor. She was really getting to him. He turned his head on the sleeping bag and his eyes wandered slowly over the curve of her body under the quilted fabric. Damn Eugene, he thought furiously, closing his eyes against the sight of her. He'd never forgive him for this assignment.

Jennifer, meanwhile, was thinking much the same thing. He blew hot and cold, friendly one minute and hostile the next. She didn't know how to get along with him. He seemed to resent everything about her. Even the way she kissed, she thought bitterly. Well, hell would freeze over before she was going to kiss him again! She rolled over. Maybe in the morning, things would look better.

5

❧〜❧ 〜❧〜 ❧〜❧

B ut things didn't look better in the morning. Hunter was unapproachable. When he did glance her way, it was like an Arctic blast. Nothing she did was ever right, she thought ruefully.

She busied herself with getting her equipment together, trying not to let him know how hurt she was by his coldness. Worse, trying to forget the feel of him in intimacy, the hard expertness of his mouth on hers. Dreams had sustained her for so long. Now she had at least one bittersweet memory to tuck away. But like all memories and dreams, it wasn't enough.

They loaded the four-wheel drive and set off for the next site— the real one this time. It was back in a canyon, beside a stream under a nest of cottonwoods and oaks. Behind it was a mountain range, smooth boulders rising to jagged peaks high above and only a small rutted road through the dust to get to it.

"It's very deserted here," Jennifer murmured, thinking she wouldn't want to be here on her own. It was probably haunted....

"One of the old Apache camps," he said, looking around. "I feel at home." He glanced at her with faint menace. "But I can imagine that you don't. White captives were probably brought here."

She turned away. "If you don't mind sparing me your noble red man impersonation, I'd like to get my equipment."

He lifted an eyebrow. That was more like it. He'd grown weary of her attempts not to mention his ancestry or her embarrassment when she did.

"Apaches weren't the only tribe around here," he remarked as he lowered the tailgate and began removing equipment and sleeping gear. "Comanches roamed this far south, and Yaquis came up on raids from Mexico. There were bandidos, cavalry, cowboys and miners, gunfighters and lawmen who probably camped in this area." He glanced at her with a faint smile. "I hope that makes you less nervous."

Her eyebrows arched. "I'm not nervous... Oh!" She jumped when a yelp sounded somewhere nearby, and got behind Hunter, sheltering behind his broad shoulders.

He chuckled with pure delight, savoring that one surge of femininity from Miss Independence. "A coyote," he whispered. He glanced down at her as the yelps increased. "Fighting. Or mating," he added, his eyes burning into hers from scant inches.

She went scarlet, swallowed, and abruptly tore away from him with her heart beating her to death. It wasn't what he'd said, it was the way he'd said it, his black eyes full of knowledge, his voice like that of a lover.

"Could you set up the tent, so that I can get the portable generator hooked up to my laptop?" she said with shivering dignity.

He put down the sleeping bags and glanced at her. "What's wrong?"

"You're very blunt," she said stubbornly. "I wish you wouldn't go out of your way to make me uncomfortable."

His expression gave nothing away. He studied her curiously. "Did I embarrass you? Why? Mating is as natural as the rocks and trees around us. In fact," he added, his voice deepening, "some native tribes weren't that fanatical about purity in their young women. Adultery was the sin, not lovemaking."

She glanced at him angrily. "The Cheyenne were fanatical about maidenly purity, for your information," she told him curtly. "And the Apache were just as concerned with virtue…"

"Well, well," he murmured. "So you do read about Indian history?" A faint smile appeared on his dark face. "Do you find the subject interesting?"

Not for anything was she going to admit that she did because of him. She'd read extensively about the Apache, in fact, but she wasn't going to admit that, either.

Nevertheless, he suspected it. He pursed his lips. "Did you know that Apaches disliked children?"

"They did not," she said without thinking. "They even kept captive children when they raided, raising them as their own flesh and blood… Oops."

He laughed. His face changed, became even more handsome with the softness in his black eyes, the less austere lines of his face. "So they did," he murmured.

She turned away. "That wasn't kind."

"Why does it bother you to be curious?" he asked pleasantly. "I don't mind. Ask. I'll tell you anything you want to know about my people."

She put down her computer and her blue eyes searched his black ones. "I didn't want to offend you," she said. "You've always been reticent about your ancestry, especially with me. I know I got off on the wrong foot with you, right at the beginning," she added before he could speak. "You frightened me, and what I did, I did out of nervousness. I never meant to offend you."

"That was a wholesale apology," he murmured, watching her. "I'll add one of my own. You frightened me, too."

"Me?" She was astonished. "Why?"

His eyes darkened and he started to speak, but the sudden beat of helicopter blades diverted him. He looked up, glad that he'd parked the vehicle under the thick cover of the cottonwood trees.

He caught Jennifer's arm and propelled her close to the Jeep, at the same time reaching behind him, into his belt, for the .45 automatic he always carried.

The sight of the cold metal in his hand made her nauseous. Sometimes it was easy to forget exactly what he did for a living. But this brought it home with stark clarity. He knew how to use the gun, and probably had, many times. She knew he'd been shot a time or two, and she'd seen one of the scars against his tanned shoulder, when he'd taken a shower two nights earlier. She shivered, remembering how he earned his living, what risks he took doing it.

He felt her tremble and glared toward the departing sound of the helicopter. He'd never known her to be afraid. This had to be a first.

"It's all right," he said, feeling unusually protective toward her. "I won't let anyone hurt you."

She looked up at him, glad he'd misjudged the reason for her unsteadiness. "Thanks," she said huskily. She looked toward the canopy of leaves. "Was that them, do you think?"

"Very likely." He put the safety back on the automatic and reholstered it with practiced ease. "We'll make a smokeless fire, just in case."

She smiled at him. "I suppose woodcraft, or the desert equivalent, was part of your upbringing?"

He nodded. "One of my ancestors fought with Cochise," he said. "When I was a boy, I knew how to find water, which plants I could live on, how to find my way in the darkness. Did you know that an Apache can go without water for two days by sucking on pebbles?"

"Yes," she said simply. Her eyes lingered on his dark face. "I...read a lot," she explained.

He let his gaze fall to her soft mouth. He had to stop remembering how silky and warm it felt, like a rose petal kissed by the sun. She wasn't a woman he could have, ever. Not as long as they both worked for the corporation. It would be the kiss of death to become involved on the job. One of them would have to go, and that wouldn't be fair. Jennifer was good at her job, and she loved it. He loved his, as well. Better to avoid complications.

She frowned slightly. "What are you thinking?" she asked.

He smiled faintly. "That a hundred years or so ago, I could have carried you off on my pony and kept you in my wickiup," he murmured. "My other wives might have beaten or stoned you when I was out making war, of course."

"Other wives, the devil," she said firmly. "Polygamy or no polygamy, if I'd lived with you, there would have been one wife, and it would have been me."

He smiled at her ferocity. Amazing that she could look so cool and professional, but under the surface there was fire and independence and passion in her. He could imagine her with a rifle, holding off attackers and defending her home. Children playing around her skirts on lazy summer days. He frowned. His eyes fell to her flat stomach and for one insane moment, he let himself imagine...

"Why are you looking at me like that?" she asked softly.

His gaze came back up to hers, the expression in his eyes unreadable. "We'd better get things set up. I'll pitch the tent."

He became unapproachable again, withdrawing deep into himself. Jennifer was sorry, because just for a few minutes it had seemed that they were on the verge of becoming friendlier. But Hunter was Hunter again when he had the tent up and the portable battery backup working. He left her to her computer and charts, busying himself with securing the parameters of their small camp and setting up his distance surveillance equipment.

She put on a pair of hiking shorts and long socks with her thick-soled walking boots and a button-up khaki blouse. She had a hat, an Indiana Jones one, in fact, that she used to keep the sun from baking her head. One thing she'd learned long ago was that a hat in the desert was no luxury. One case of sunstroke had taught her that, and Hunter had given her hell when he'd found her lying on the ground far away in the Middle East, where they were working on assignment one time, searching for oil.

He glanced up when she came out in her working gear, nodding at the hat. "You remembered, I see," he remarked.

"You gave me hell," she recalled, smiling.

"You deserved it."

"Yes, I did. All the same, you got me to a medic in short order. You probably saved my life."

"I don't want hero-worship from you," he said flatly, staring back at her. "We'd better get going. Keep to the trees if you can. We know we're not alone. It's best not to take chances."

"The stream bed is where I want to be," she said coldly. "And it isn't hero-worship."

"No?" He gave her a mocking appraisal. "Then what is it?"

"Fascination," she said with a mocking smile of her own. "You're different."

He didn't betray so much as a flicker of an eyelash, but the words hit home. She'd accidentally betrayed what he'd suspected all along, that she coveted him because he was a new experience for her. Like another white woman, years before, who'd been entranced not by who he was so much as what he was.

"Different," she emphasized. "Hardheaded, cold-eyed, bad tempered, unpredictable and totally exasperating!"

None of which had anything to do with being Apache, he mused, relaxing a little. He smiled with reluctant amusement.

"I could go on," she added. "But I do have a job to do."

"I'm not the only one here with a bad temper," he replied as they started out. "And you have a hard head of your own."

"I wouldn't have a bad temper if you'd stop stripping around me," she blurted out.

His eyebrows arched. "When did I do that?"

"At the motel."

"Oh." He chuckled as he strode along beside her. "I wanted to see if it would affect you." He glanced down. "It did."

"Most men your age are as white as dead fish and flabby," she remarked, refusing to let him get to her. "I can't be the only woman who's ever found you fascinating without your shirt."

No, but she was the only one it mattered with, he admitted to himself. He found her equally disturbing, but it wasn't a good time to say so. His eyes were alert, watching for signs.

"Look!" she exclaimed, bending down at the creek where tracks were visible in the wet sand. "A cougar!"

He knelt down beside her. "So it is. How did you know?"

"Big print, no claw marks," she explained. "Dogs and wolves

can't draw their claws back in like a cat can, and they leave claw marks. Look at this. It's a buck deer—cloven hoofprint. A doe's is rounded."

He met her eyes with grudging admiration. "Tracking interests you, I gather?"

"It always has. My father hunts deer every fall. He taught me."

"Kill Bambi?" he exclaimed with mock horror.

It was the first real flash of amusement she'd seen in him. She laughed delightedly and impulsively pushed him. He fell heavily onto his side, laughing, too.

"You hellcat," he murmured, reaching out with a lightning movement to drag her down heavily against him. He rolled her in the damp sand, pinning her, his face hard, his eyes glittering with excitement as he loomed over her. His gaze went down to her breasts, where the buttons of her blouse had parted during the struggle, leaving her cleavage bare. His breath quickened as he looked at her, his expression changing from humor to intent male appreciation.

The feel of all that hard muscle so close made her tremble with pure need. She could smell the scent of his clothing, the cologne that clung to his skin. She looked up into his black eyes and knew in that moment that he was everything she'd ever want. She wanted him to bend down, to pin her body to the damp sand. She wanted his hard, warm mouth to crush into hers and kiss her senseless. She wanted him.

And the ferocity of her desire made her ache. "Kiss me," she whispered, unbearably hungry for him. She reached up and touched his lean, hard face with hands that trembled, loving the warm strength of him. "Hunter...!" She managed to lift herself enough to reach his hard mouth, and hers touched it with helpless need.

He froze at the contact, his breath catching as he felt her lips so soft and warm against his own. For one insane second he almost gave in to his own hunger. But she was off-limits. She had to be, because there was no future in it for either of them. He forced himself to go rigid, despite the fact that his damned heart was beating him to death as he struggled with desire.

His lean hands caught her wrists and he pushed her down, tearing her mouth from his as he loomed over her, looking cold and dangerous. "Stop it," he said curtly, forcing the words out.

She felt the rejection right through to her heart. He didn't want her, so why couldn't she stop offering herself? She hated having him know just how vulnerable she was. How could she have done something so stupid? She flushed beet red. Yes, she was vulnerable, but not Hunter. Mr. Native American was steel right through.

"Let me get up, please," she said, her voice trembling.

Pure bravado, and he knew it. He could have her, right here, and she'd give herself with total abandon. But he knew, too, that once would never be enough. He'd have her and then he'd die to have her again. The fever would never be satisfied.

He let go of her wrists and got to his feet, turning away to keep his vulnerability from her as he stared up at the mountains with apparent unconcern. God, that had been close! He wondered if he could ever forget the way he'd seen her, the sound of her soft voice begging for his kiss, the petal softness of her seeking lips on his mouth…!

Jenny shivered with reaction, barely able to breathe. She got up and her eyes went helplessly to his back. Well, he'd made his lack of interest clear enough. Maybe her body would eventually give up, she thought with hysterical humor. Despite her beauty, he simply did not want her. It was the most humiliating lesson of her life.

She looked away, gathering her savaged pride. "I'm supposed to be working," she said in a thready whisper.

"The sun's getting high," he said without looking at her. "Get your samples and then we'll find something to eat."

She felt totally drained. She picked up her hat with a shaken sigh and retrieved the backpack with her tools. She didn't even remember dropping it, she'd been so hungry for the touch of him.

His dark face gave nothing away as he glanced once at her and turned away. "Where do you want to look? And for what?" he asked curtly. "Gold? Is that why this operation is so secretive?"

She glanced up at him, twisting her contour map in her hands. "I know what you must be thinking," she said. She could still taste him on her mouth and it made her giddy. "Gold and Indians don't mix. White man's greed for it has cost the Native Americans most of their land."

"There was a flurry here a year or two ago when someone found a very small vein of gold," he said. "There were amateur prospectors everywhere, upsetting the habitat, invading private property, some of them even came on the reservation to dig without bothering to ask permission. The Bureau of Indian Affairs takes a very negative view of that kind of thing, and so does the tribal government."

"I don't doubt it. But gold isn't what I'm after right now. I'm looking for a quartz vein, actually."

"Quartz?" He glared at her. "Quartz is a worthless mineral."

"Perhaps, but it can lead to something that isn't. I'm looking for molybdenite ore."

He frowned. "What?"

"Molybdenum is a silver-white metallic chemical element, one of the more valuable alloying agents. It's used to strengthen steel, which makes it of strategic worth. Like oil, it's a rather boom-or-bust substance, because its value fluctuates according to demand. Back in 1982, weak market conditions led to the closure of most primary molybdenum mines. Now there's a new use for it, so it's back in demand again. The United States produces sixty-two percent of all the world's moly, and that's why we've got competition for new discoveries."

"So you're looking for molybdenum," he murmured, trying to follow the technical explanation.

"I'm looking for its source ore, molybdenite, a sulfide mineral. It looks very much like graphite, but its specific gravity and perfect cleavage differentiate it from that. It's found primarily in acid igneous rocks such as granite in contact metamorphic deposits, and in high-temperature quartz veins. That's why I'm looking for quartz veins." She smiled at his confusion. "Don't look so irritated, Mr. Hunter. I couldn't fieldstrip an Uzi or set up surveillance equipment, either. If what I'm doing is Greek to you, what you do is another language to me, too."

That eased his bruised pride a little. He turned away. "Then we'd better get going. This area looks promising, you said?"

"Yes. The lay of the land and the mineral outcroppings I've found so far look very promising here."

"Moly. You say it's used to strengthen steel," he said, watching her.

She nodded. "A very profitable mineral to mine, too. There's already a deposit of it here in southern Arizona, another one in Colorado."

"But if you found gold instead, you'd put a real feather in your cap, wouldn't you?" he persisted, his eyes narrow and watchful.

"Oh, for heaven's sake!" She threw up her hands, her blue eyes blazing with hurt and anger. "You just love to think the worst of me, don't you? If I find gold, I'll take out ads in all the national tabloids and give interviews and send millions of people out here to harass the locals…!"

Involuntarily he put his thumb over her lips, stilling the words. "All right," he said quietly. "My mistake," he said, and his eyes fell to her mouth. His thumb moved caressingly over it, and his body began to tense. Her lips trembled under his touch. She was so vulnerable, and he hated hurting her. He wanted her, too, but it was simply impossible.

She couldn't bear to give herself away again. She drew back from him, still wounded from his earlier harsh rejection. "I'll just take some samples here," she said in a subdued tone, and without looking at him. "And get a few instrument readings."

He didn't say another word. But he was more watchful than ever for the rest of the day. He couldn't seem to take his eyes off her, and the more he looked, the more he wanted her. He almost groaned out loud when she stretched and he could see the sweet curves of her breasts outlined against the thin fabric of her blouse. She wouldn't deny him, and knowing it made the desire even greater. He had to get a grip on himself!

He prowled around his surveillance equipment, trying to get his mind off Jennifer's gorgeous body. When he couldn't prowl anymore, after dark, he stretched out on his sleeping bag and read by the light of the Coleman lantern while Jennifer rummaged in her suitcase.

Jenny was fascinated when she saw his books, the text indecipherable to her, despite her cursory knowledge of Spanish and French and a few words of Sioux.

"It loses something in the translation," he remarked when he noticed her interest. "I prefer the original language. This is Greek," he added, smiling faintly at her blush when she'd told him that what she was doing must seem like Greek to him.

She recovered quickly, though. "How did you learn Greek?"

"Overseas. I was CIA, didn't anyone tell you?"

She nodded, her eyes openly curious. "About that. And that you were in the special forces, and briefly a mercenary. You've done a lot of dangerous things, haven't you?"

"A few," he said, refusing to elaborate on it.

She gave up and busied herself getting a clean T-shirt and bra out of her suitcase. "It's dark. Do you think it would be all right if I bathed off a little of this dust? Are we safe here?"

"If you've got skinny-dipping in mind, I wouldn't advise it," he began.

"No, just my face and arms," she replied.

"Go to it. It's relatively protected here, and I've got sharp ears."

"Okay." She wanted some verbal reassurance that he wouldn't look, but he'd been withdrawn since they came back to camp. Probably she left him so cold that he wouldn't buy a ticket to see her totally nude. She felt terribly demoralized. Ironic, that men usually went crazy to have her, and Hunter wouldn't have her with cream and sugar.

The light from the smokeless campfire gave her enough to see by. She pulled off her khaki blouse and, glancing behind at the half-closed tent flap, her bra. The cool water felt like heaven on her hot skin. She sponged herself off, thinking that Indian women must have bathed like this a century before, in this clean, cool glade with the sounds of crickets in the brush and the distant howl of coyotes or wolves and the faint swish of the trees when the wind blew.

Hunter tried to read his book, but the thought of Jennifer out there alone was too disturbing, especially after the chopper that had come so close. He didn't want to spy on her, but he justified his flash of conscience by telling himself that he'd been assigned to protect her.

He opened the tent flap and moved outside, silhouetted by the smokeless campfire that was still burning under a pot of brewing coffee. Its dark, rich aroma filled his nostrils as he moved closer to the stream under the dark shadows of the trees.

Jennifer had her blouse and her bra off. He could see her smooth, silky back in the firelight, see the white lines where she'd sunbathed and the sun hadn't been able to reach. Odd that she didn't sunbathe nude, with a body like that, he thought stiffly.

He couldn't help looking. She half turned, her arms uplifted as she dashed water on her breasts, and his breath caught in his throat. They were full. Very full and very firm, and tip-tilted. Her nipples were hard from the cold water, dusky against the white streaks that cut across where her bra would have been. His body tautened and he felt himself beginning to tense with desire. He'd dreamed of seeing her this way, but the reality was devastating.

Jennifer, unaware of his scrutiny, finished her half bath and stretched, her body sensuously arched because the air was just cool enough to be delicious on her bare skin, and there was faint light from the nearly full moon. She sighed, brushing her long blond hair away from her freshly scrubbed face. The action lifted her breasts and they were high and firm and softly glowing in the light from the campfire.

Hunter heard himself speaking, when he'd never meant to betray his presence. "In the old days, the penalty for an Apache warrior who spied on a woman at her bath was death. The risk seems worth it to me right now, Jennifer. I've never seen anything quite so beautiful."

His voice had startled her. She whirled from the big rock she was sitting on, her body poised for flight, so shocked by his eyes and nearness that she hadn't the presence of mind to cover her breasts.

He was looking at them, too, with blatant appreciation, without even trying to hide that he was studying her. "Your breasts are lovely," he said quietly, his voice a whisper of deep tenderness in the night. "Much fuller than I thought. Pink and mauve, like clouds on the horizon just at dawn when the sun touches them."

Poetry, she thought dizzily. He was wooing her with words and she wanted his eyes so badly that she couldn't even do the decent thing and pretend to hide herself. All day she'd felt him watching her. If only he felt as she did, shared the fiery attraction that made her too weak to deny him now. She stood, proud in her seminudity, letting him look, feeding on his eyes. If that wasn't desire in his face now, she thought, awed, then she couldn't recognize it at all. He wanted her! The knowledge took away her reserve, her inhibitions. She walked toward him, her heart in her eyes.

His jaw tensed. He watched her come toward him and he ground his teeth together in one last effort at sanity. Her lips were parted, her eyes soft and hungry, her breasts rising and falling jerkily with her unsteady breathing.

She stopped just in front of him, her cheeks faintly ruddy with embarrassment and excitement. She couldn't have imagined doing this, but it seemed the most natural thing in the world. She looked up at him, meeting his dark, fierce gaze, trembling a little, because he looked capable of anything at that moment. For all her loving bravado, she was innocent and he wasn't. The complications of her actions could be extreme.

His chin lifted as he watched her, his gaze a conqueror's, his face rigid. "You're asking for something you may not be able to handle," he said quietly. It was a warning.

She swallowed. "Would you...hurt me?" she whispered.

He nodded slowly. "Very probably," he said, letting his dark eyes fall to the perfect symmetry of her breasts. "I've gone a long time without a woman and I'm not particularly gentle even when I haven't. You don't have a lot of experience with men." His eyes shot back up, catching her surprise. "That surprises you? Didn't you know that sophistication is hard to fake?" He smiled gently. "You're blushing. You had to fight not to cover yourself when I looked at you. You're still fighting your primary instinct, which is to turn and run away before I give you what you think you want."

"What I think I want?" she asked in a shaky whisper.

He reached out and the backs of his fingers brushed very lightly over one taut nipple in a blatant, deliberate caress.

She gasped and jerked away, and his eyes reflected the smile on his firm lips.

"You see?" he asked softly. "You'd give yourself to me, with a little coaxing. But not in cold blood. You aren't used to this kind of intimacy with a man."

She did follow her instincts then, and folded her arms over her breasts, shivering as she lowered her eyes to his shirt.

"Twenty-seven. And so inhibited." He sighed heavily. "What happened, Jenny? Was the first time so traumatic that you didn't have the nerve to try again?"

"You don't have the right to ask me questions like that...."

He caught her by the shoulders. "You offered yourself to me," he said curtly. "That gives me the right. Was the first time difficult?"

She couldn't tell him that there hadn't been a first time. That was just too humiliating. "Difficult enough," she said unsteadily. "Please...I'm sorry. I'd like to go in, now."

It was what he'd guessed. She was probably afraid of being with a man intimately because some man had hurt her. It irritated him to think of someone hurting her. He wouldn't have. His hands stilled on her upper arms, feeling the silky warmth of them. He hesitated. He wanted her like hell, but his mind was in control— just barely.

With a rough sigh, he picked her up suddenly and carried her slowly back into the tent, his eyes holding hers. He laid her down gently on her sleeping bag and sat beside her, frowning at the way she crossed her arms over her breasts.

"Don't," he said softly, and moved her arms back to her sides. "Don't cover yourself. Let me look at you. God knows, that's all I can do now."

"You said you didn't want me...." she whispered.

He sighed heavily, his expression sterner than ever, his dark eyes intent on hers. "Yes, I said it. My God, don't you have instincts about men? Don't you know..." He stopped, suddenly aware of the unblinking fascination of her eyes on his face.

Her blond hair was spread around her flushed face in glorious disarray, her small waist and flat stomach faintly visible where her shorts were a little large in the waistline. But he didn't touch her, yet. Only his eyes did, very slowly, very thoroughly, and she trembled all over from just that.

"You're helpless when I look at you," he said quietly. "When I touch you. Is there anything you'd deny me?"

She shook her head slowly, beyond denial. Her body trembled. "But you don't want to make love to me, do you?" she whispered.

"I can't," he said evasively. It wouldn't do to let her know how badly he did want her. His hand went out and she shivered with anticipation, but it was her hair he touched and nothing else, smoothing it away from her face. "I'm not prepared."

"Prepared?" she echoed the word blankly.

He wrapped a strand of blond hair around his forefinger and tugged it gently. "I could make you pregnant," he said simply. "Making love is one thing. Making a baby is something else. It shouldn't happen because two people are careless."

"No," she agreed. She couldn't tell him that to her it wouldn't be careless, that she wanted him and she wanted his child. Loved him, deathlessly. She felt warm all over. Her body arched gently, inviting his eyes. "Oh, please, couldn't you...?" she whispered brokenly.

His breath came jerkily. His eyes slid down her, lingering on her taut nipples. "You ache for me, don't you?" he asked, and there was a kind of bitter compassion in the words.

"So...much," she whispered mindlessly. "More than you'll ever know!"

His jaw clenched. She was every man's dream, lying there like that. She was his dream, surely, and it took every ounce of will-power he possessed to hold back.

Despite the hurting tautness of his body, the fever in his blood, he controlled the urge. He bent and gently brushed his lips against hers in the soft stillness of the tent. "Go to sleep," he whispered.

"Hunter," she moaned, her body on fire. Her arms locked around his strong neck, trembling, her eyes frantic. "Please!"

He groaned. "Jenny, you don't understand...God!" His mouth opened and crushed down on hers suddenly, and he allowed himself the pleasure of one long, endless kiss. His lips twisted against hers, his chest levered down over her bare breasts. He could feel them through the thin fabric of his shirt, the nipples biting into his skin and he shivered with reaction. She smelled of flowers. Her arms held him, her fingers in his thick, dark hair, caressing him. His hands slid under her bare back and brought her even closer, his tongue starting to probe her lips. She stiffened, surprising him, because her ardor had been so headlong and eager.

He lifted his dark head, breathing unsteadily. "Don't you like deep kisses?" he asked huskily.

"I...I didn't," she said, her own voice shaking. "Not with anyone else." She moved her fingers down to his mouth and touched it hesitantly. "Could you...teach me how?" she breathed at his lips.

The words kindled something explosive in him. It glittered in his eyes. "Yes," he said roughly. "I can teach you."

She was as close to heaven as she'd ever dreamed of being. His mouth bit hers gently, lifting and probing, delicately coaxing. His breath became ragged, and so did hers. He heard her soft gasp as his tongue probed her lips softly, felt her fingers tangle, trembling, in his thick hair.

"Are you ready for me?" he whispered deeply, and felt her shiver. "Open your mouth, and I'll let you feel me...inside you."

She cried out. The sound of her voice, the eager parting of her lips sent him over some vague precipice. He groaned, too, as his tongue penetrated her roughly, deeply, in thrusts that lifted her against him and made her weep with reaction. He made a sound deep in his throat and for feverish seconds, he gave her the weight of his body, the unrestrained ardor of his devouring mouth. His hands slid over her bare, silky back, feeling the warm softness of it with blind pleasure, savored the trembling hunger of her mouth. But then he became slowly aware of her uncontrollable shivering, felt the tears in his mouth. Her very abandon was what brought him to his senses. God, what was he doing?

He dragged himself away and sat up, ripping her hands away from his head, her wrists turning white under the involuntary pressure of his lean, dark fingers.

"No!" he said fiercely.

She looked at him through a sensual daze, her eyes smoky with desire, her face expressionless with it. "Hunter," she whispered weakly.

His hands tightened. "I'm Apache," he said harshly. "You're white. My God, don't you understand? We belong to different worlds. This whole damned situation is impossible, Jennifer!"

She realized belatedly that he'd stopped. Her mouth throbbed from the drugging contact with his, and she only began to realize how close he'd come to losing control. So had she. He'd wanted her for those brief seconds, and she gloried in the way he was loving her until he came to his senses. She looked at him hungrily, loving him, awash in sweet pleasure.

"Do you hear me?" he asked, his voice a little less cutting. "Jenny?"

"Yes, I…hear you." She caught her breath, her eyes searching over his dark face. "I can't stop shaking," she whispered, surprised by the reactions of her body—new reactions, although he wouldn't realize that. She was a newcomer to raging, abandoned desire. "Oh…my!" she whispered, moaning a little with frustration.

"Shhh," he whispered. His voice sounded actually gentle. "I know. It hurts. But I can't take the risk." He brought her hands to his mouth before he put them down and gently pulled the sleeping bag over her taut breasts, covering her. She was crying. He bent and kissed away the tears, his lips tender on her wet face. "Breathe deeply, little one. It will pass."

He moved away and she watched him through her tears. "My things," she remembered. "I left them by the stream."

"I'll get them." He looked back at her. "I'm going to have a cup of coffee before I come to bed. Do us both a favor and try to be asleep when I come back," he added quietly. "This was a moment out of time, this whole damned trip. But reality is waiting back in Tulsa, and we've got a job to do here. Let's try to get it done and put this behind us."

She swallowed, tugging the sleeping bag closer around her. "You're right, of course," she managed shyly, embarrassed now that her heated skin had cooled. She couldn't meet his eyes. "I'm sorry about what...what I did. I...I can't think what came over me..."

He could feel her embarrassment. Odd, that, when she was twenty-seven and so beautiful. But she'd admitted herself that she'd been hurt, and it had been a long time for her. "Abstinence," he replied. "I know how it feels. You get to the point where you can't bear it any longer. I don't think less of you for wanting me, Jennifer," he added quietly. "I'm rather flattered," he confessed.

She relaxed a little. At least he wasn't ridiculing her. He couldn't know that her abstinence had been lifelong. And through it all, despite that shattering tenderness he'd shown her, he'd kept his head. He said she was beautiful, and he'd looked at her and kissed her. But he knew how badly she'd wanted him, so it might just have been pity. She didn't want to think about that, it hurt too much. She stared at him with soft, quiet eyes.

"How long has it been for you?" she asked gently. "Is it all right, if I ask you that?"

He drew in a slow breath, his broad chest lifting and falling, making his muscles ripple. "Two years," he said.

She searched his hard face. "Is it because I'm white that you won't take the risk?" she asked, her voice barely above a whisper. She had to know.

He stared at her for a long moment. Better to end it here, and temptation with it. "Yes," he said. "I want no possibility, ever, of a child coming from my desire for a woman with white skin."

Desire. Only desire, she thought miserably, and he'd just admitted it. She felt shamed, somehow. "Desire," she whispered.

He schooled his features not to give him away. He nodded his head, very slowly. "Isn't that what you felt for me?" He turned away. "I'll check the perimeter. Good night, Jennifer."

It would have hurt less if he'd hit her, but she didn't say a word. She lay down and closed her eyes. So now she knew. He felt nothing for her, nothing at all, except a desire that was so mild it couldn't even affect his control. And no way was he going to risk the possibility of creating a child. And she wanted nothing more, because she loved him. What a laugh!

Jenny shivered with mingled shame and bitter disappointment. It might have been better if he'd never touched her at all. She wouldn't be able to forget the expert touch of his hands, his mouth, the things he'd whispered to her. He was no novice, and now she was going to spend years remembering that. Tormenting herself with what might have been.

Jenny got up and managed to get another blouse from her suitcase and put it on. Her breasts were still sensitive from the rough contact with his chest. For such a torrid interlude, it had been remarkably innocent, she thought. He'd looked at her, he'd kissed her. But there had been no deep intimacy at all. Because he didn't want her enough, she supposed, and forced her eyes to close.

Outside, Hunter was lighting a cigarette. Smoking might calm his nerves. He looked at the hand holding the cigarette and watched it shake. Jennifer unclothed was a sight to do that to a stronger man than himself. He wondered how he'd ever managed to let her go. His body was burning and throbbing with need of her. She wanted him. He could go back into that tent right now and she'd open her arms for him.

But it would be a mistake. Despite her blatant desire for him, she was somehow less experienced than he'd expected. Shy and even a little afraid, but so hungry for him. He remembered her voice, whispering to him to teach her about deep kisses, the sight of her breasts in the light of the campfire...

He groaned out loud. Another beauty. Another white woman. She wanted him because he was someone out of her experience, and he'd better remember that. He'd already had a taste of being used for his uniqueness. Jennifer was beautiful enough to choose her own man. He couldn't believe that she'd keep him for long, once her desire was satisfied. Hilarious, really. It was usually the man who pressed the woman for physical satisfaction. Now he was the hunted, and Jennifer the predator. Other men might take what she offered. He couldn't. There was more to it than physical desire. He respected her, as a woman, as a scientist, as a person. He couldn't use her, even without the cultural barriers separating them. But it didn't make the night any easier for him. When he finally gave in to sleep, it was almost dawn.

Jennifer forced herself to work the next two days without thinking back. Hunter himself managed to keep his mind on his job, scouting the periphery, watching for signs of interest as they moved camp twice more. He hadn't been unkind, either. But his attitude toward her was suddenly impersonal. Employee to employee, with no personal comments of any kind. Only once, when she caught him staring at the stream where he'd seen her bathing, did any emotion show in his lean, hard face. She pretended not to see, because her own control was precarious. She wanted him still, now more than ever.

Because of that, she pushed herself, working at breakneck speed to do the samples of the outcrops and decide where seismic tests would have to be made by the geological technicians. Sound technology was the oilman's best friend, because it could save him millions by telling him where to drill. It was of the same benefit to the miner. Modern technology was invaluable when it came to determining underground mineral locations.

In no time, Jennifer had her fieldwork done and was ready to go back to Tulsa, back to sanity. It was almost a relief to have temptation out of the way, not to be alone with Hunter anymore, even if her heart was breaking at the thought of never having the experience again.

Hunter had registered her silence, her withdrawal. He'd thanked God for it during the past few days, because his desire for her had grown beyond bearing. Lying beside her in the tent at night had kept him sleepless. All he could think about was the way she'd looked in the firelight, the sweet vulnerability in her eyes when she'd offered herself to him, the ardent sweetness of her mouth under his. He wished he could forget. He had a feeling the memory was going to haunt him until he died. But if she even remembered what had happened, she gave no indication of it. She wouldn't look him in the eye anymore, as if her behavior had shamed her. He hated doing that to her, making her ashamed of such glorious abandon. But he couldn't give in. He'd fought his own need and won. But it was a hollow victory.

"Glad to be going home?" he asked when they were on the plane.

It was the first remark he'd made in two days that wasn't related to the job.

"Yes," she said without looking at him. "I'm glad."

"That makes two of us," he said with a rough sigh. "Thank God we can get back to normal now."

Normal, she thought, as if her life would ever be that again. Now that she knew his ardor, she knew the touch and feel and taste of him, she was going to starve to death without him. But he seemed completely unaffected by what had happened. And why not? He was experienced. Probably these interludes were part of his work background, and the encounter they'd had was a fairly innocent one. She shivered, thinking what might have happened if he'd wanted her back, if he'd been prepared. She'd never have gotten over him if they'd gone that far. She closed her eyes and tried to sleep. They'd be back in Tulsa soon, and they wouldn't be doing any more traveling together, thank God.

That peaceful thought lasted only until she was sitting in Eugene's office, giving her report. The land containing the potential moly strike was dead on government land, and Eugene cursed roundly.

"They're trading that tract. Look here," he muttered, showing her the area on the map. "They're trading it for a tract they like in Vermont. Damn! All right, there's only one thing to do. Pack an evening gown and some nice clothes. You and Cynthia and I are going to Washington to do some quick lobbying with one of our senators. I went to school with him and he's very Oklahoma-minded. Don't just sit there. Get going! I'll want to leave first thing in the morning."

"Yes, sir." She went home and packed. So much for her idea of staying at home for a while so that she could get over Hunter.

And there was one more unpleasant surprise waiting. When she got to the airport, to board Eugene's corporate jet, who should be waiting with Eugene and his blond wife, Cynthia, but Hunter, looking as irritated and put out as she felt.

6

Cynthia saw the flash of antagonism in Hunter's dark eyes as Jennifer approached, and she smiled to herself. "You look lovely, Jennifer," she told the younger woman, and linked her arm with Jennifer's. "Let's get buckled up while they finish the walkabout. How have you been?"

Hunter spared Jennifer one brief glance. His expression was as hard as stone. He'd spent days trying to forget her, and fate had thrown him a real curve today. He wanted to go off into the desert and spend some time alone. Maybe that was the answer, when Eugene could spare him. Maybe civilization was getting to him.

"You're brooding," Eugene muttered, glaring at him. "What's the matter?"

"I was just getting used to peace and quiet," Hunter murmured with a dry smile.

"God help us." Eugene shuddered. "Peace and quiet is for the grave, man. No good for healthy humans. Come on. I'll see if I can light a fire under the pilot."

"Better let him do his job," Hunter cautioned. "More than one plane has gone down because its owner was too impatient for the final check."

Eugene glared at him again, but that level stare intimidated even him. "Okay," he muttered. "Have it your own way."

Hunter smiled at the retreating figure, and all the while he was wondering how he was going to survive being close to Jenny without reaching for her.

The flight seemed to take forever. Hunter alternately read and glared at Jennifer, who pretended not to notice. Things had been so strained between them that she was uncomfortable with him. Her behavior in the desert and his reaction to it embarrassed and inhibited her. She sat with Cynthia, only half listening to the older woman's comments about clothes and Washington society while she wondered how she was going to cope with several days of the stoic Mr. Hunter.

They got off the plane at the airport in Washington at last, and Jennifer was momentarily left behind with Hunter while Eugene and Cynthia paused to check times for the return flight with the pilot.

She didn't know what to say to him. She averted her eyes and stared toward the other planes, with her purse and makeup case clutched tightly in her hand.

Hunter was smoking a cigarette. He glanced down at her impatiently and finally stopped and just stared at her until he made her nervous enough to look up. But when he saw her embarrassment, he was sorry he'd done it.

"Don't make it any harder than it already is," he said, his deep voice slow and terse. "What happened that night was just an interlude. I lost my head and so did you. Let it go."

She swallowed. "All right."

He scowled through a cloud of smoke as he searched her deep blue eyes. Involuntarily his gaze slid to her blouse and his eyes darkened with memories.

She turned away. That look was painful, and despite his assertion that it was over, it didn't seem as if he'd forgotten a single thing. Neither had she. The feel of his eyes on her, his mouth on her lips, haunted her night after lonely night. She didn't even like being near him because just his proximity made her shiver with need. It was a reaction unlike anything she'd ever experienced before in her life, a mad hunger that she could never satisfy.

Hunter was having problems of his own. God, she was lovely! Just looking at her hurt. He turned away to help get the luggage off the plane and carry it to the waiting limousine. He had to stop remembering.

The hotel they stayed at was four-star, very plush and service-oriented. Eugene had reserved two suites of rooms. Unfortunately, Jennifer was relegated to one with Hunter, which surprised and inhibited her.

Eugene noticed her uneasiness and averted his eyes before she could see the faint glimmer of amusement in them. "You'll survive it, Jenny," he said. "I want you where Hunter can watch you. You're the most important part of this enterprise. I can't have enemy agents trying to spirit you off under my nose, can I?"

"We have other security people…." she began hopefully.

"But Hunter's the best. No more arguments. I hope you brought an evening gown. There's an embassy ball tomorrow night."

"I did," she said reluctantly. It was a year old, but still functional, and it fit her like a second skin. She frowned bitterly, thinking of the exquisite white confection and regretting that she didn't still have the little red number she'd knocked Hunter's eyes out with a few months back. She'd thrown it away in a temper after that one bitter date with him.

Eugene had arranged appointments all over Washington, and he went alone, leaving Jennifer to go sightseeing with Cynthia and Hunter.

Cynthia was enchanted with everything she saw, from the Lincoln Memorial to the reflecting pool outside it, the spire of the Washington monument and the White House and the nation's Capital. But Jennifer was enchanted with Hunter and trying so hard not to let him see. She wore tan slacks with a colorful pink blouse and sandals for the sight-seeing tour, and Cynthia wore a similar ensemble. Hunter wore a suit.

He escorted them around the city with quiet impatience, and Jennifer knew without being told that he hated the noise and traffic, and that he would have preferred to be doing something else. But he didn't complain. He pointed out landmarks and hustled them in and out of cabs with singular forbearance. All the same, Jennifer noticed how relieved he looked when they were back at the hotel.

Eugene returned in time to go to supper, phoning Hunter to give him the time and place they were to eat. Hunter hung up, glancing at a nervous Jennifer poised in the doorway to her bedroom.

"You've got an hour to get dressed," he said. "Time for a shower, if you like. We're to meet him and Cynthia at the Coach and Whip for dinner."

"All right," she said. "I'll be ready."

He stared at her with quiet, steady dark eyes. "What are you going to wear?"

"Why?" she asked, startled.

He pursed his lips. "I hope it isn't something red," he murmured, turning away with an involuntary smile on his hard mouth.

"Oh!" she burst out.

But, he didn't look back or say a word. He just went into his own room and closed the door.

Except for that one unexpected incident, dinner went off without a hitch. But if she'd hoped for anything from Hunter, she was doomed for disappointment. He ate and excused himself, and she didn't see him again for the rest of the night or most of the next day. She and Cynthia amused themselves by going to a movie while Eugene had one last talk with someone on Capitol Hill. Then, almost before she knew it, Jennifer was getting ready to go to a real ball.

Jennifer felt like a girl on her first date as she put on the white satin gown to wear to the ball. She'd never been to anything really grand, although she'd come close once when she and Hunter were on assignment overseas. She put her long blond hair up in an elegant coiffure with tiny wisps of hair curling around her ears. She had a pair of satin-covered pumps that she wore with it, but the dress itself was the height of expensive luxury. She'd bought it on impulse, because at the time she'd had no place at all to wear it. It had a low-cut bodice and spaghetti straps that tied on each shoulder. The waist was fitted, but the skirt had yards and yards of material, and it flared gracefully when she walked. It covered all but the very tips of her pumps. She put on her makeup last, using just a little more than she usually did, but not too much. She looked in the mirror, fascinated because she looked totally different this way. Her whole face seemed radiant with the extra touch of rouge and the pale gray eye shadow with a tiny hint of light blue.

She looked at herself with faint satisfaction. She'd never been glad of her looks before, but tonight she was. She wanted Hunter to be proud of her, to want to be seen with her. She closed her eyes, imagining the music of a waltz. Would Hunter ask her to dance? She smiled. Surely he would. They'd waltz around the ballroom and all eyes would be on them... That jerked her back to reality. Attention would be the last thing Hunter would want, and probably the only dances he knew were done with war dances around a campfire.

She grimaced mentally. That would be just the thing to say to him, all right. It would put them quickly back on their old, familiar footing and he'd never speak to her again. Which might not be a bad idea, she told herself. At least if he hated her openly he wouldn't be making horrible remarks about the red dress she'd worn that one evening they'd gone out together.

On the other hand, why had he mentioned it at all? That was twice, she realized, that he'd made a remark about that particular dress. She smiled to herself. Well, well. He remembered it, did he? She'd go right out and find herself another red dress, one that was even more revealing, and she'd wear it until he screamed!

The sudden hard rap on the door made her jump. "Yes?" she called out.

"Time to go," Hunter replied quietly.

She grabbed her purse, almost upending the entire contents on the floor in the process, and rushed to their joint sitting room.

She stopped short at the sight of Hunter in a dinner jacket. It could have been made for him, she thought as she stared at him. The dark jacket with its white silk shirt and black tie might have been designed for his coloring. It made him look so elegant and handsome that she couldn't tear her eyes away.

He was doing some looking of his own. His dark eyes ran down the length of her body in the clinging white dress, growing narrower and glittering faintly as they lingered on her full breasts and worked their way back up to her soft mouth and then her dark blue eyes.

"Will I do?" she asked hesitantly.

"You'll do," he said, his voice terse with reluctant emotion. He met her eyes and held them, watching her cheeks go pink. "Oh, yes, you'll do, Jennifer. And you know it without having to be told."

She dragged her gaze down to his chest, to the quick rise and fall of it under the shirt. "You don't have to sound angry," she muttered.

"I am angry. You know it. And don't pretend you don't know why. I wouldn't buy that in a million years." He moved toward the door while she was still trying to puzzle out what he meant. "Let's go," he said, without looking at her again. "Eugene and Cynthia are waiting for us."

She started past him and paused without knowing why. Slowly she lifted her eyes to his and looked at him openly. Her heart ran wild at the fierce warmth she saw there, at the visible effort he made at control. "Is it all right if I tell you that you're devastating?" she asked softly.

He lifted his chin without replying, but something flashed in his dark eyes for an instant before he turned away with a faint smile. "Come on."

He was quiet when they joined the other couple, which was just as well, because Eugene monopolized the conversation—as usual. It was exciting to go to a ball in a big black limousine, and Jennifer wished her parents could see her now. She almost looked up at Hunter and said so, but he wouldn't find it interesting, she knew, so she kept her silence.

The big Washington mansion where the ball was being held was some embassy or other. Jennifer had been too excited about being with Hunter to care which one it was, or even where it was. She was trembling with contained excitement when Hunter helped her from the car and escorted her up the wide steps that led to the columned porch, which was ablaze with light. The faint sounds of music poured from the stately confines of the mansion.

"What a piece of real estate," Cynthia said mischievously, clasping Eugene's hand tightly in her own. "And I thought we had a nice house."

"We do have a nice house," he reminded her. "And we could have had one like this, but you seemed to think that it would be—what was the word you used?—pretentious."

"And it would have," she reassured him. "I was just admiring the pretentiousness of the embassy," she added, tongue-in-cheek.

Jennifer grinned. "Do you suppose the staff wear roller skates to get from room to room with the trays?"

"I wouldn't be a bit surprised," Eugene said, "but for God's sake don't make such a remark to our host. You can take it from me that he has absolutely no sense of humor."

"Can I ask why we're going to a ball at a foreign embassy to talk about land out West?" Jennifer asked.

"Sure!" Eugene assured her.

She glared at him.

He chuckled. "All right. There are two senators I have to see, and I was tipped off that they were both going to be at this shindig. You and Hunter go socialize until I need you—if I need you. I may be able to pull this one off alone."

"Then why are we here?" Jennifer persisted.

Eugene forcibly kept himself from glancing at Hunter. "Because I wanted to make sure you weren't abducted and held for ransom or some such thing while I was talking terms," he said. "Go and dance. Can you dance?" he taunted.

She drew herself up to her full height, an action that made her firm breasts thrust out proudly, and Hunter shifted a little jerkily and moved away. "Yes, I can dance," she told him. "In fact, I studied dancing for three years."

"So go and practice." His blue eyes narrowed on Hunter's averted face. "You might teach Hunter how."

Hunter cocked a thick eyebrow down at him. "My people could teach yours plenty about how to move to music." A wisp of a smile touched that hard face and his dark eyes twinkled. "We have dances for war, dances for peace, dances for rain, even dances for fertility," he added and had to grit his teeth to keep from glancing deliberately toward Jennifer.

"How about waltzes?" Eugene persisted.

"Ballroom dancing isn't included in the core curriculum for CIA operatives," he said, deadpan.

"Jennifer might be persuaded to teach you…" Eugene began.

But before he could even get the words out, Jennifer was suddenly swept away by a tall, balding man with a badge of office on the sash that arrowed across his thin chest. She was dancing before she knew it, and from that moment on, she didn't even get a peek at the hors d'oeuvres on the long, elegant table against the wall. She was dying of thirst, too, but one partner after another asked her to dance, and she was too entranced by the exquisite music of the live orchestra to refuse. Especially since Hunter didn't even bother to ask her for a dance, whether or not he knew how. When her first partner swept her off onto the dance floor, he'd walked away without even looking back and she hadn't seen him since.

She pleaded fatigue after a nonstop hour on the dance floor and found her way to the powder room upstairs. By the time she came down, Hunter had apparently come out of hiding because an older socialite had him cornered by a potted plant against one wall. He looked irritated and half angry, and Jennifer felt a surge of sympathy, although God alone knew why she should.

She started toward him, hesitated, and he looked up at that moment and his eyes kindled. He even smiled.

That had to mean he was desperate for rescue. He never smiled at her. Well, he was going to get his rescue, but she was going to enjoy it. She moved toward him with pure witchery in her movements, patting her hair back into place.

"Here I am, sweetheart!" she called in a rich exaggerated Southern drawl. "Did you think I'd gotten lost?" She draped herself over his side, feeling him stiffen. A mischievous sense of pleasure flooded through her. Well, he'd asked for it. She smiled thinly at the older woman, who was watching her with narrow, cold eyes. "Hello. I don't think we've met. I'm Jennifer Marist. Hunter and I work for an oil corporation in Oklahoma. It's so rarely that we get to enjoy a fabulous party like this, isn't it, darling?" she asked, blinking her long lashes up at him.

"Rarely," he agreed, but his eyes were promising retribution. He was already half out of humor from watching her pass from one pair of masculine arms to another. Then this social shark had attacked. He'd been desperate enough to encourage Jennifer to rescue him, but he hadn't exactly expected this type of rescue. Fortunately his expression gave nothing away.

"I was just telling Mr. Hunter that I'd love to have him join me for a late supper," the older woman said, blatantly ignoring

Jennifer's apparent possessiveness. She smiled at Hunter, diamonds dripping from her ears and her thin neck. "I want to hear all about his tribe. I've never met a real Indian before."

Hunter's jaw clenched, but Jennifer smiled.

"I know, isn't it fascinating?" Jennifer confided. "Did you know that he rubs himself all over with bear grease every night at bedtime? It's a ritual. And he keeps rattlesnakes," she whispered, "to use in fertility dances outside during full moons. You really must get him to show you the courting dance. It's done with deer heads and pouches full of dried buffalo chips...."

The older woman was looking a little frantic. "Excuse me," she said breathlessly, staring around as if she were looking for a life preserver. "I see someone I must speak to!"

She shot off without another word and Jennifer had to smother a giggle. "Oh, God, I'm sorry," she whispered. "It was the way she said it..."

He was laughing, too, if the glitter in his eyes and the faint uplift of his lips could be called that. "Bear grease," he muttered. "That wasn't the Apache, you idiot. And the dance a young girl does at her very special coming-of-age ceremony is done with a pouch of pollen, for fertility, not dried buffalo chips."

"Do you want me to call her back and tell her the truth?" she offered.

He shook his head. His dark eyes slid over her body in the clinging dress, and there was a definite appreciation in them. "If I have to suffer a woman for the rest of the evening, I'd prefer you," he said, startling her. "At least you won't ask embarrassing questions about my cultural background."

"Thanks a lot," she murmured. "And after that daring rescue, too."

"Rescue, yes. Daring?" He shook his head. "Hardly." He chuckled deeply. "You little terror. I ought to tie you to a chair and smear honey on you."

"You have to do that in the desert, where you can find ants," she reminded him. "You asked to be rescued, you know you did."

"This wasn't exactly what I had in mind," he muttered.

"Was she trying to put the make on you?" she asked, all eyes.

He glared at her. "No. She was trying to find out how many scalps I had in my teepee."

"Apaches didn't have teepees, they had wickiups," she said knowledgeably. "I hope you told her."

His eyebrows rose. "Who's the Indian here, you or me?"

"I think one of my great-grandfather's adoptive cousins was Lower Creek," she frowned thoughtfully.

"God help us!"

"I could have just kept on walking," she reminded him. "I didn't have to save you from that woman."

"No, you didn't. But before it happens again, I'm going to stand on the balcony and hope I get carried off by Russian helicopters. I hate these civilized hatchet parties."

"Mind if I join you?" she asked.

His eyes narrowed. "What for? You're the belle of the ball. You've danced every damned dance!"

"Only because you walked off and left me alone!" she threw back at him, her blue eyes flashing. "I thought we were together. But I suppose that's carrying the line of duty too far, isn't it? I mean, God forbid you should have to survive a whole evening in my company!"

"I said I was going outside," he replied with exaggerated patience. "If you want to come along, fine. I don't like being the only Indian around. Where were all these damned suicidal white women over a hundred years ago? I'll tell you, they were hiding behind curtains with loaded rifles! But now, all of a sudden, they can't wait to be thrown on a horse and carried off."

"You're shouting," she pointed out.

His dark eyes glittered down at her. "I am not," he said shortly.

"Besides, you don't have a horse."

"I have one at home," he replied. "Several, in fact. I like horses."

"So do I. But I haven't ridden much," she replied. "There was never much time for that sort of thing."

"People make time for the things they really want to do," he said, looking down at her.

She shrugged. "There are plenty of places to ride around Tulsa, but I think it's a mistake to get on a horse if you don't know how to control it."

"Well, well." He stood aside to let her precede him onto the balcony, past the colorful blur of dancing couples. The balcony was dark and fairly deserted, with huge potted plants and trees and a balustrade that overlooked the brilliant lights of the city.

7

Jennifer couldn't believe he'd actually allowed her to invade his solitude without a protest. It was sheer heaven being here beside him on the balcony, without another soul in sight.

She leaned forward on the balustrade. "Isn't it glorious?" she asked softly.

He studied her hungrily for a moment before he turned his gaze toward the horizon. "I prefer sunset on the desert." He lit a cigarette and smoked it silently for several seconds before his dark eyes cut sideways to study her. "Did you really want to dance with me?" he asked with a faint smile. Actually he danced quite well. But having Jenny close was a big risk. She went to his head even when they were several feet apart.

"Wasn't it obvious that I did?" she asked ruefully.

"Not to me." He blew out a cloud of smoke and stared at the distant horizon. "I won't dance, Jennifer. Not this kind of dancing, anyway." He was careful to say *won't* and not *can't*—lying was almost impossible for him. Apaches considered it bad manners to lie.

"Oh. I'm sorry. You do everything else so well, I just assumed that dancing would come naturally to you."

"It doesn't," he replied. "Where did you learn?"

"Dancing class," she said, grinning. Odd how comfortable she felt with him, despite the feverish excitement his closeness engendered in her slender body. She could catch the scent of his cologne, and it was spicy and sexy in her nostrils. He was the stuff dreams were made of. Her dreams, anyway.

"You studied ballroom dancing?" he persisted.

"Tap and ballet, actually. My mother thought I should be well-rounded instead of walking around with my nose stuck in a book or studying rocks most of the time."

"What are your parents like?" he asked, curious.

She smiled, picturing them. "My mother looks like me. My father's tall and very dark. They're both educators and I think they're nice people. Certainly they're intelligent."

"They'd have to be, with such a brainy daughter."

She laughed self-consciously. "I'm not brainy really. I had to study pretty hard to get where I am." She smiled wistfully.

"You know your job," he replied, glancing down at her. "I learned more about molybdenum than I wanted to know."

She blushed. "Yes, well, I tend to ramble sometimes."

"It wasn't a criticism," he said. "I enjoyed it." He looked out over the horizon. "God, I hate society."

"I guess it gets difficult for you when people start making insulting remarks about your heritage," she said. "It's hard for me when I get dragged on the dance floor by men I don't even know. I don't particularly like being handled."

He frowned. He hadn't thought of her beauty as being a handicap. Maybe it was. She'd had enough partners tonight. Enough, in fact, to make him jealous for the first time in memory.

"I don't like being an oddity," he agreed. "I've never thought of you that way."

She smiled. "Thank you. I could return the compliment."

He turned away from her, leaning against the balcony to look out at the city lights. "I suppose I'm less easily offended than I was before you joined the company. Maybe I'm learning to take that chip off my shoulder," he added, glancing at her with a rueful smile. "Isn't that what you once accused me of having?"

She joined him by the balcony, leaning her arms on it. "Yes. It was true. You got your back up every time I made a remark."

"You intimidated me," he said surprisingly. He lifted the cigarette to his firm lips, glancing down at her. "Beautiful, blond, intelligent…the kind of woman who could have any man she wanted. I didn't think a reservation Indian would appeal to you."

"I suppose you got the shock of your life that night by the creek," she remarked, a little shy at the admission.

"Indeed I did," he said huskily. His eyes darkened. "I never dreamed you wanted me like that."

"It wasn't enough, though," she said sadly, her eyes moving to the dark landscape. "Wanting on one side, I mean." She pushed back a loose strand of blond hair that had escaped her elegant upswept coiffure. "You didn't smoke while we were camping out."

"You didn't see me," he corrected. "It's my only vice, and just an occasional one. I have the infrequent can of beer, but I don't drink." His eyes narrowed. "Alcoholism is a big problem among my people. Some scientists have ventured the opinion that Indians lack the enzyme necessary to process alcohol."

"I didn't know. I don't drink, either. I like being in control of my senses."

"Do you?" He looked down at her quietly.

She wouldn't meet his eyes. "I always have been. Except with you."

He sighed angrily, lifting the cigarette to his mouth again before he ground it out under his heel. "So I noticed," he said gruffly. Her nearness was making him uncomfortable. He didn't like the temptation of being close to her, but he didn't want to spoil the evening for her by saying so.

She moved a little closer so that she could see his lean, dark face in the light from the ballroom. "Hunter, what's wrong?" she asked softly.

He hated the tenderness in her voice. It tempted him and made him angry. "Nothing."

She wanted to pursue the subject, but his expression was daunting. She smoothed down the soft material of the dress. With its sleeveless bodice that dipped almost to her waist, and the clingy chiffon outlining her narrow waist and full hips, she was a vision. She knew she looked pretty, but it would have made her evening to hear Hunter say so. Not that he would. She glanced back toward the dancers inside. "I guess this is familiar territory to you," she murmured absently. "High society, I mean."

He frowned. "I beg your pardon?"

"Well, you do a lot of work for Eugene, and this is his milieu," she explained, glancing up at him. "And I know you've had to look after politicians for him, so I suppose it entails a certain amount of socializing."

"Not that much." He folded his arms over his chest. "I don't care for this kind of civilized warfare. Too many people. Too much noise."

"I know how you feel." She sighed, staring toward the ballroom. "I'd much rather be outdoors, away from crowds."

He studied her with renewed interest. She wasn't lying. He remembered her delight in the desert those days they'd spent together, her laughter at the antics of the birds, her quiet contemplation of dusk and dawn. That pleasure hadn't been faked. But with her beauty and education, surely this was her scene.

"You look at home here, nevertheless," he said. He lit another cigarette and blew out a cloud of smoke. She was making him more nervous by the minute. Her dress was pure witchcraft.

"That's funny," she murmured, and smiled. "The closest to this kind of thing I ever got in my youth was the high school prom—or it would have been, if I'd been asked. I spent that night at home, baby-sitting the neighbor's little boy."

The cigarette froze en route to his mouth. "You weren't asked?"

"You sound surprised." She turned to look up at him. "All the boys assumed that I already had a date, because I was pretty. There was one special boy I liked, but he was just ordinary and not handsome at all. He didn't think he had a chance with me, so he never asked me out. I didn't find out until I was grown and he was married that he'd had a crush on me." She laughed, but it had a hollow sound. "Women hate me because they think I'm a threat to them. Men don't take me seriously at work if they don't know me because pretty blondes aren't supposed to be intelligent. And if I'm asked out on a date, it's automatically expected that I'll be dynamite in bed. You mentioned once that I don't date anybody. Now you know why."

"Are you?" he asked.

Her eyebrows lifted. "Am I what?"

"Dynamite in bed."

She glared up at him. There was something like amusement in his tone. "Don't you start, Hunter."

He tossed the cigarette down and ground it out under the heel of his dress shoe, but his eyes didn't leave hers. "Why not?" he asked, moving closer with a slow sensual step that made her heart beat faster. "I'm human."

"Are you, really?" she asked, remembering that night on the desert when he'd seen her bathing. She almost groaned. His restraint had overwhelmed her, then and since.

He caught her hands and slid them up around his neck. "Stop dithering and dance with me," he said quietly.

His voice was an octave lower. Deep, slow, sensuous, like the hands that, instead of holding her correctly, slid around her, against her bare back where the low cut of the dress left it vulnerable.

She gasped. "You said…you didn't dance," she whispered.

"You can teach me," he whispered back.

But it didn't feel as if he needed any instruction. He moved gracefully to the music, drawing her along with him. The feel of him this close, the brush of his warm, rough hands against her silky skin, made her tremble. When he felt the trembling, he drew her even closer. She shivered helplessly, feeling his hands slowly caressing her, his lips in her hair, against her forehead, as he made a lazy effort to move her to the rhythm of the slow bluesy tune the orchestra was playing. But it wasn't as much dancing as it was making love to music. She felt his chest dragging against her breasts with every step, his long, powerful legs brushing against hers at the thigh. She remembered his eyes on her bare breasts, his arms around her, the feel of his hard mouth. And she ached for him.

She tried to move back, before she gave herself away, but his hands were firm.

"What are you afraid of?" he asked at her forehead.

"You," she moaned. "What you make me feel." Her hands grasped the lapels of his jacket. Twenty-seven years of denial, of longing, of loneliness. Years of loving this man alone, of being deprived of even the most innocent physical contact. And now she was in his arms, he was holding her, touching her, and she couldn't hide her pleasure or her need.

"Jenny." He bent closer, his mouth tempting hers into lifting, his eyes dark and quiet and intent in the stillness. He stopped dancing, but his hands smoothed lazily up and down her back, and he watched the rapt, anguished need color her face, part her lips. She looked as if she'd die to have him make love to her. It was the same look he remembered from the night he'd seen her bathing, and it had the same overwhelming effect on him.

"Please," she whispered, and her voice broke. She was beyond hiding it, beyond pretence, totally vulnerable. "Would it kill you to kiss me again, just once? Oh, Hunter, please...!"

He lifted his head with a rough sigh, looking around them. He eased her into a small alcove, hidden to the rest of the balcony, and slowly moved her until she was against the wall. His hands rested on either side of her head against it, his body shielding hers, and then covering hers, trapping her between it and the wall in a slow, sensual movement.

"Lift your mouth to mine," he whispered.

She did, without a single protest, and had it taken in a succession of slow, brief, tormenting bites. She whimpered helplessly, shaking all over with the need to be close to him. He tasted of cigarette smoke and expensive brandy, and the kiss was almost like a narcotic, drugging her with slow, aching pleasure. She clung to him with something akin to desperation, so out of control that she couldn't begin to hide what she was feeling. Her body throbbed with it, trembled with it. Twenty-seven years of denial were going up in flames, in his arms.

"My God, you're starving for me," he said huskily, his voice rough with surprise as he looked down at her. "It's all right, little one," he breathed as his dark head bent again. "It's all right. I'll feed you..."

His mouth covered hers then, slowly building the pressure into something wild and deep and overwhelming. As if he understood her need for passion, he pushed down against her and his mouth became demanding, its very roughness filling the emptiness in her.

She slid her arms around his lean waist and pressed even closer, tears rolling down her flushed cheeks as she fed on his mouth, accepting the hard thrust of his tongue with awe, loving the feel of his aroused body bearing hers heavily against the wall. She wept against his hard lips and he lifted his head.

"Oh, don't...stop," she whispered brokenly. "Please, please... don't stop yet!"

He was losing it. His mouth ground into hers again, tasting the softness of her parted lips, inhaling the exquisite fragrance of her body into his nostrils. His body was rigid with desire, his hips already thrusting helplessly against hers with an involuntary rhythm. His mouth crushed hers roughly, his teeth nipping her full lower lip in a pagan surge of fierce need.

"I want you," she whispered into his mouth. All her control was gone, all her pride. She was beyond rational thought. "I want you. I want you so much!"

He dragged his head up. His hands gripped her upper arms hard while he fought for control. She'd already lost hers. Her eyes were dilated, wild with need, her body shaking helplessly with it. She was his. Here, now, standing up, she would have welcomed him and he knew it. It was all he could do to back away. But he had to remember who they were, and where they were.

"Jennifer," he said quietly. His voice sounded strained. He fought to steady it. "Jennifer!" He shook her. "Stop it!"

She felt the rough shake as if it was happening to somebody else. She stared up at him through a sensual veil, still shivering, her body throbbing with its urgent need of his. He shook her again, fiercely, and she caught her breath. The world spun around her and she suddenly realized where they were.

She swallowed hard with returning sanity. Her face went scarlet when she remembered begging him…

His hands tightened and released her arms. "Come on, now," he said, his voice gentle where it had been violent. "Come on, Jenny. Take a deep breath."

He knew she was vulnerable. He knew it all now. Tears ran down her cheeks, hot and salty, into the corners of her swollen mouth.

He drew her head to his jacket, his hands soothing at her nape. "It's all right, little one," he said quietly, his teeth clenched as he fought his own physical demons. He was hurting. "It's all right. Nothing happened."

"I want to die," she whispered brokenly. "I'm so…ashamed!"

"Of what?" he asked, frowning. He framed her face in his lean, warm hands and lifted it to his eyes. "Jenny, there's no shame in being a woman."

She could hardly see him through her tears. "Let me go…please," she pleaded, pushing at his chest.

He didn't like the way she looked. Desperate. Horrified. As if she'd committed some deadly sin. He couldn't let her leave in this condition.

"Calm down," he said firmly, taking her by the shoulders to

shake her again. "I'm not letting you out of my sight until you're rational."

She bit down on her swollen lower lip, hard, tasting him there. She closed her eyes. She couldn't bear to see his face.

"What in God's name is wrong with you?" he asked, leaning closer. "You wanted me, that's all. I've felt that kind of desire before, I know how helpless it can make you."

Yes, he'd felt it, but not with her. That was what hurt so much, that she felt it and he didn't. He'd kissed her because she'd begged him to, but she was sure there hadn't been anything else. Just pity and compassion. If only she knew more about men...

She lifted her cold hands and wiped at her tears. "I need to wash my face," she whispered. "I can't go back in there...like this."

He bent and brushed his lips tenderly against hers, but she jerked away from him, her blue eyes wide and terrified.

His head lifted and he studied her, realization kindling belatedly in his mind. So that was it. The hidden fear. She'd lost control. He'd made her helpless and she was going to fight tooth and nail to keep it from happening again. Was that why she didn't date anyone? Had she lost control before and was afraid of giving rein to her passionate nature? Or was it just years of denial catching up with her? Her violent desire for him had weakened his resolve painfully.

"Do you want me to do something about this?" he asked, his voice deep and quiet, posing a question he'd never meant to ask.

"What?" she asked numbly.

"A need that violent should be satisifed," he said matter-of-factly. "I know you want me. I've known that for a long time. But now I understand how desperate the need is."

She couldn't believe he was saying this. Her face was scarlet, she knew, but she stared up at him helplessly while he offered her the fulfillment of every dream she'd ever dreamed.

"Do you want me to take you back to the hotel and satisfy you, Jenny?" he asked quietly, his expression giving away nothing, although his body was still keeping him on the rack. He wanted her obsessively. He could taste her in his mouth. He wanted to taste all of her the way he'd savored her soft lips. He wanted to strip her and kiss every pink inch of her, from head to toe.

"I...might get pregnant," she whispered, too shaken to be rational, too hungry to refuse. "You said..."

He didn't like remembering what he'd said. "I'll take care of you," he said firmly. "In every way. There won't be consequences of any kind. Least of all the risk of a child torn between your culture and mine," he added bitterly.

She was twenty-seven, almost twenty-eight. She'd never known intimacy with anyone, but she wanted, so much, to know it with this man. She'd loved him forever, it sometimes seemed. He was offering her untold delights. She knew without asking that he was expert. The way he'd kissed her had told her that. He wouldn't hurt her. With luck, he'd never know that she was a virgin.

"I...want you," she whispered helplessly.

His chest expanded jerkily while he searched her eyes, curious about the faint fear and melancholy there. But one didn't question a gift like this. He caught her soft hand in his and led her back into the ballroom.

She remembered very little about the minutes that followed. They left. She said something polite to their host and hostess and to Eugene and Cynthia. There was a cab ride back to the hotel, she was at the door of his room. He put her inside without bothering to turn on the light.

Then she was in his arms. It was heaven. Pure, sweet heaven. He took her hair down and buried his face in it before his mouth slowly, inevitably, found her lips. She clung to him, tasting him, while he kissed her and kissed her until she couldn't stand. She felt his mouth and his hands on her bare skin as he removed her dress, her underthings, her hose. Then he lifted her and carried her to the bed.

"I want to look at you," he said huskily.

"Yes." She didn't flinch as the bedside light came on, although her cheeks reddened, even though he'd seen part of her like this before. He looked and she shivered at the bold hunger in his dark eyes as they went over her slowly, with fierce possessiveness.

"Pink satin," he whispered, his voice deep and slow in the stillness of the room. "I wanted to look at you like this that night you were bathing, at all of you. I wanted to touch you, but I didn't dare. I couldn't have stopped." He reached down and spread her hair on his pillow, his eyes darkening. "Exquisite," he whispered, his eyes sliding down her.

She shivered. She hadn't expected him to say things like that.

He sat down beside her, still fully clothed, not touching her. His eyes searched hers. "This is the first time," he said.

Her heart jumped. He knew!

"The first time," he continued, "that I've been with a white woman in years. This is something I never meant to happen."

She couldn't help the relief she felt that he hadn't guessed about her innocence. But what he was saying finally got through to her and she realized what it meant.

"You don't have to," she said uncertainly, because now that it was about to happen, she was nervous.

He reached out and traced one soft, firm breast, watching her body react helplessly and instantly to his touch. "I'm Apache," he said, studying her face. "There are places inside me that you can't see, can't touch. Different beliefs, different customs, different lifestyles. I live in your world, but I prefer the stark simplicity of mine." He traced around one dusky erect nipple, hearing her soft gasp. "I've spent years trying not to see you, Jennifer," he said, his voice barely above a whisper. "Years of dreams that kept my body in anguish…" He bent to her breasts, his mouth slow and ardent.

She couldn't believe he'd said that. She shivered and arched toward his lips, holding his face to her. "You mean…you want me, too?" she asked, fascinated.

He lifted his head and looked down into her eyes. "Yes," he said simply. "But only this once," he added, his voice stern. "Only tonight. Never again."

She swallowed. She wanted so much more than that, but it would have to do. She could live on this for the rest of her life. "All right," she whispered.

He stood with a long sigh and began to remove his own clothes. He did it with lazy grace, with a complete lack of inhibition that told her too well how familiar this was to him. She hated the other women in his life because they'd given him that expertise.

His keen eyes caught her expression and he lifted an eyebrow as he bent to remove the final barrier. "What was that hard look about?" he asked.

He turned back to her and the hard look was utterly forgotten as she stared blatantly at his nudity. He was all bronzed muscle and powerful etched lines and curves, so beautiful that she sat up and caught her breath at the perfection of his body.

"What is it?" he asked, frowning curiously.

"There was a statue in the Louvre," she stammered. "I saw photographs of it…Greek, I think. I remember being awed by the power and beauty of it and thinking that, well, that no mortal man could come close to that kind of perfection." She averted her eyes to the bed. "I didn't mean to stare. I guess you've been told ad nauseum how...beautifully masculine you are."

He felt the impact of that breathless adoration in her voice. He'd never heard himself described that way by anyone. His conquests had been sporadic, and even then more animal than sensual. He'd given in to his needs only when he couldn't bear them any longer, and in his later years, it hadn't been that often. With Jennifer, it was different. He was touched by her headlong, helpless need of him. He'd thought that it was purely physical, but her eyes were telling him otherwise. A woman didn't look at a man like this when her only concern was fulfillment, and her shy blushing face made him uneasy.

He slid onto the bed beside her, turning her so that she was lying against him. He felt her flinch at the first touch of his aroused body, and he tilted her face so that he could see it.

"It's frightening for a woman with every new man, isn't it?" he asked absently. "Not knowing if he'll be gentle or cruel, demanding or brutal?"

"Yes. Of course," she lied. She could feel the heat of him, the threatening masculinity in a way she'd never dreamed of feeling it. She had to be careful. If she gave herself away, he'd never touch her. She wanted this with him so badly, refusing to admit even to herself that pregnancy was a very big part of the wanting, that her need of him included that faint possibility.

"I'm not cruel," he said, moving her so that she was completely against him. He felt the soft little tremors in her body as she stiffened in reaction before she relaxed and let him hold her closer. "I'm not brutal." He slid one lean hand along her side, over the curve of breast and waist and hip down to her smooth, soft thigh. He eased his leg between both of hers and brought her into intimacy. "And for your sake, I'll try not to be too demanding."

She gasped at the sudden stark contact.

"Shhhh," he whispered, smoothing the hair at her nape. "Lie still. It's better like this, lying on our sides. It's more intimate. Lift your leg over mine."

She blushed scarlet, praying that she wouldn't blow her cover. She did as he told her, but her hands were gripping his shoulders for dear life, biting in, and her stiffness was making him curious.

"Haven't you ever done it like this?" he whispered at her ear as his hands began to touch her intimately.

"No," she choked. It was true. But she'd never done it any way at all, including like this.

"Look at me."

She had to force her shocked, frightened eyes to meet his, and then she saw the curiosity narrowing them. He touched her where she was most a woman and she clenched her teeth to keep from crying out.

His firm lips parted as he probed delicately, holding her eyes. He scowled, because something was different here. Very different.

"Are you...are you going to use something," she managed, trying to divert him.

But it didn't work. He was experienced enough to recognize what was different, because this particular difference was so blatant that he didn't have to be a doctor to know what it was.

"My God," he whispered explosively. His hand stilled, but it didn't withdraw.

"Hunter..." she began, passion growing cold at the look on his face.

He searched her eyes and his hand moved. She bit her lip and tears threatened.

"Does this hurt, little one?" he whispered softly, and did it again. She tried not to flinch, but the intimacy and faint discomfort defeated her. "Yes," he answered his own question. His face mirrored his shock. He looked at her as if he'd never seen her before, and still that maddening hand didn't move away. He couldn't believe it. A woman with her beauty, at her age. A virgin.

"I didn't think you'd know," she stammered. "The books say that even a doctor can't tell..."

"That's true," he replied gently. "But you're intact, little one. Do you understand? Almost completely intact."

She swallowed, lowering her embarrassed eyes to the jerky rise and fall of his bronzed chest. "The doctors said that it would be uncomfortable, but that I wouldn't have to have surgery when the time came," she said finally. "It's mine to give," she added, lifting her face back to his.

"And you want to give it to me?" he asked gently.

"Yes."

He eased her over onto her back, his eyes soft and quiet and very dark. "Then give it to me this way, for now," he whispered. His mouth touched hers so tenderly that her heart ached, and his hand began to move very slowly, expertly, on her.

She tensed at the sudden shock of pleasure and tried to get away, but he threw a long, powerful leg across both of hers.

"No," he whispered into her mouth. "I'm going to take you up to the stars. Don't fight me," he said softly.

She trembled as the pleasure bit into her body. It came again, and again. And all the while he kissed her, his lips tender on her face while he made magic in her body. He saw the fear and smiled reassuringly, his voice coaxing, softly praising. He felt the urgency, felt when it reached breaking point. He knew exactly what to do, and when. Her back arched and she gasped, weeping as the pleasure took her, convulsing her under his delighted, fascinated gaze. Heat washed over him, blinding fire exploding, racking him even as he heard her cry out. Then, ages later, she relaxed, her tears hot and salty in his mouth as he kissed them away. He relaxed, too, because in the midst of her own explosive fulfillment, her movements had triggered his. He kissed her closed eyelids, thinking that never in his life had he experienced anything quite so perfect. And from such relatively innocent love play.

He lifted his head, turning hers toward him to search her drowned, shamed eyes.

"Is sex a sin for you?" he said softly. "Is that why you're a virgin?"

"There was never anyone I wanted enough," she whispered, sobbing. "I wanted you so badly. So much that I would have died to have you…"

He brushed her mouth with his, feeling humble. "Virginity is a rare gift," he whispered. "Yours to give, certainly. But not outside marriage. I have my own kind of honor, Jennifer. Taking your innocence without a commitment would violate everything I believe in." He lifted his lips from hers and searched her eyes quietly. "I won't take you. And, yes, I want to. I always have."

She swallowed the tears, wiping them away with the back of her hand. "I'm sorry if I hurt you," she said, avoiding his bold gaze.

"Hurt me how?"

She flushed.

He laughed gently. "Oh. That. No. I had as much pleasure from it as you did." He rolled over onto his back lazily and stretched, feeling years younger and full of life. He sprawled, aware of her fascinated eyes on his body, drinking in that feminine appreciation. "God, that was good," he said huskily. "Good! Like the first sip of water after the desert."

She sat up, a little self-conscious of her nudity, but his eyes were warm and admiring and she forgot her shyness. "But we didn't do anything, really," she said.

He brought her hand to his chest and caressed it. "I felt exactly what you did. The same need, the same sweet release." His head turned toward her. "Sleep with me."

She colored. "You just said..."

"That I wouldn't have sex with you," he agreed. "That isn't what I asked. Stay the night. We'll lie in each other's arms and sleep."

Her breath caught. "Could we?"

He drew her to his side, pillowing her head on his broad shoulder. "Yes. We could." His hand reached for the light, and he turned it out, folding her closer. "For tonight," he whispered at her ear, "we're lovers. Even if not conventional ones."

She closed her eyes with ecstasy, wanting to tell him everything, how she felt, how deeply she loved him, needed him. But she didn't dare. He thought it was just desire, and she had to let him keep thinking it. If he knew how involved she was emotionally, his pride wouldn't let him near her again. He wouldn't want to hurt her.

She flattened her hand on his chest and sighed. "This is heaven," she whispered.

He didn't echo the words back, but he could have. He'd never spent an entire night in a woman's arms. The need to keep Jennifer here kept him awake long after she relaxed in sleep.

The next morning, he kissed her awake. He was already dressed, but his eyes were enjoying the sight of her with the covers pulled away in a purely masculine way.

"Nymph," he murmured, sweeping a possessive hand down her body. "How can you be a virgin?"

"Pure living," she said, and laughed delightedly.

He brought her to her feet and kissed her softly. "You'd better get dressed. Morning is a bad time for men, and all my noble scruples aren't going to protect you if I have to look at you this way much longer."

She sighed and leaned against him. "There won't be a man," she whispered. "Not now."

His teeth ground together. Why in God's name did she have to say things like that? "Get dressed," he said tersely.

She was shocked at the sudden change in attitude, at his fierce anger. She pulled back from him, wounded, and searched for her clothes.

He didn't turn his back. He couldn't. He watched her dress, his heart pounding, his body aching for hers. It had taken all his willpower to drag himself out of bed this morning, when he wanted her to the point of madness. It had taken a cold shower and a self-lecture to get himself back in control.

"I wanted you last night," he said huskily. "I want you even more this morning. I'm not trying to be cruel, but the risk is just too damned great, do you understand?"

She was back in her gown now, everything under it in place. She nodded without really understanding and without looking at him and went to get her purse off the dresser, where he must have put it this morning. She took out a small brush and made some sense of her disheveled hair. She shouldn't feel like a fallen woman, she told herself. But she did. She'd thrown herself at him, and he hadn't wanted her enough to take the risk of involvement. It had been just a pleasant interlude to him. But to her, it had been everything.

He stood behind her, in dress slacks and shirt and tie and sports jacket, very urbane and sophisticated. His lean hands held her shoulders and he looked at their joint reflection, his eyes narrowing at the contrast.

"Dark and light," he said curtly. "Indian and white. If I gave you a baby, it would belong to both worlds and neither world. We could never have a child together."

So that was why he was so afraid of not being prepared with her. Because he didn't want her to have his child. It was so final...

She broke down and cried. He whipped her around and held her, rocking her, his arms fiercely possessive, the tremor in her body echoing in his.

"I could love you," he said roughly. "You could become the most important thing in my life. But I won't let it happen. We can't become involved. You have your world, I have mine." He tilted her mouth up to his and his dark eyes were frightening as they searched hers intently. "Kiss me. This is goodbye."

Her mouth opened for his, inviting it, giving him everything he asked for, everything he didn't. He groaned, lifting her into an intimate, exquisite embrace, and she whimpered because the pleasure was overwhelming. She clung to his powerful shoulders, breathing him, while the kiss reached its climax and left them both shaking. He let her slide to the floor, letting her feel his stark, urgent arousal. She was the cause of it; he was proud that he was such a man with her.

She took a slow breath, her mouth red from the aching kiss, and stepped back from him. Something died in her soft blue eyes as she looked up at him, but she managed a smile.

"Do you have a first name?" she whispered.

He nodded. "Phillip. I don't think I've ever told it to anyone else."

She fought back the tears. "Thank you." She turned away from him, picking up her purse with hands that shook. "I'd better go back to my room." She glanced back at him. "It was the best night of my life. I'll live on it forever."

She opened the door and ran out, blind and deaf, almost stumbling in her haste to get across the parlor of the suite to her own room. Such a short distance, yet it was like moving from one life to another, she thought, blind to the tormented face of the man she'd left behind.

Hunter watched her door close, and he leaned heavily against his door facing. It was for the best, he kept telling himself. But the memory of Jennifer in his arms was going to take years to fade. Maybe more years than he even had left.

8

❦❦ ❦❦ ❦❦

Back in her own room, Jennifer changed from her evening dress into slacks and a short-sleeved red silk top, put her blond hair in a ponytail and tied it with a colorful red patterned scarf. But her heart wasn't in how she looked. Hunter had said goodbye, and what he meant was that they could work together for another ten years, but it would never again be more intimate than two colleagues.

She hoped that Eugene would be through with his politicking so that they could go home to Tulsa. She couldn't spend much more time around Hunter without going mad, especially after last night. He knew things about her now that no one else in the world did, and it was faintly unnerving.

His tenderness had surprised and delighted her, despite the circumstances. She wished she knew a little more about men. It occurred to her that a man who'd worked himself into a frenzy wanting a woman would have every right to be furious when he had to draw back. But Hunter hadn't been angry with her. He'd been kind. Did that mean that he hadn't wanted her very much in the first place, or did he care enough to put her feelings before his? She'd never been so confused, or so embarrassed. It was humiliating to have him know not only that she was on fire for him, but that she was a virgin to boot. If he wanted a weapon to use against her, he had a great one now. She dreaded facing him again. She had a feeling that last night wouldn't make any difference in his public treatment of her.

As it turned out, she was right. When she got downstairs to the restaurant for breakfast, Hunter stood, as did Eugene, for her to be seated, but his expression was stony and it gave away absolutely nothing.

"Good morning," Eugene said with a smile.

"You look very pretty," Cynthia added.

It wasn't a good morning, and Jennifer didn't feel pretty, she felt sick all over. She didn't quite meet Hunter's eyes as she sat down, mumbling something polite.

"Wasn't the ball wonderful?" Cynthia asked with a sigh. "I've never enjoyed anything quite as much."

"It was super," Jennifer said, staring blankly at her menu.

"I noticed that you were getting a lot of attention, Hunter," Eugene murmured dryly. "Especially from our host's sister."

"She wanted to see my scalps," he explained with a faint smile. He glanced toward Jennifer, his dark eyes giving nothing away. "Jennifer rescued me. We both had enough popularity to suit us by then, so we went back to the hotel."

"Sorry," Eugene said, sobering. "I hadn't realized I'd be putting you on the spot like that."

"I can handle social warfare," the younger man said imperturbably. "How did things work out?"

Eugene grinned. "Great. I got my deal. All we have to do is wait for the paperwork, and they're going to shoot that through. We should be able to send you two back down there to finalize the exact location within a month. I want to talk to two more people today. We'll fly home first thing in the morning."

At the mention of sending them back to the desert, Jennifer's face went paper white. Under the table, Hunter's lean hand caught hers where it lay on her lap. He enfolded it and his fingers contracted gently, sending a fiery thrill through Jennifer's body.

"I thought you knew where to look," Hunter replied.

Eugene nodded. "Oh, we do. What we're going to need you to do is camp out at a false location, to make sure our friends are led off the beaten track while we're running our seismic survey and doing flyovers."

"You don't think the agents will be able to hear dynamite blasts going off over the hill when our geologic technicians set up the seismic equipment to register the sound waves?" Jennifer asked with a smile. Hunter's strong fingers were warm and reassuring around her own, but they were making it hard to breathe normally.

"We'll work something out," Eugene said. He studied Jennifer's face with an intensity that made her nervous, especially when his calculating blue eyes went to Hunter. "Uh, you don't have any problem with spending a few more days out on the desert together?"

"Of course not," Hunter said easily.

"No," Jennifer agreed, and even smiled.

"You're both lying through your teeth." Eugene nodded slowly. "But I can't help it. You started this for me, you'll have to finish it. I'll try to work things so that we keep the field time to a minimum. Now. What shall we eat?"

Breakfast seemed to take forever. Jennifer still couldn't puzzle out Hunter's behavior. That lean hand wrapped around hers before breakfast had knocked half the breath out of her, even if his expression hadn't revealed anything.

While Eugene and Cynthia stood at the counter, Hunter caught Jennifer's arm and pulled her gently to one side.

"There's no need to look like that," he said softly, his dark eyes searching her shy ones. "It's all right."

"How do I look?" she asked.

"Embarrassed. Shamed." His hand dropped from her arm. "We did nothing last night that would have consequences. You understand?" he added, his dark eyes probing.

She turned red and swallowed hard. "Yes, I know," she said huskily. She couldn't meet his eyes.

"But it still embarrasses you to look at me?"

"Yes," she whispered.

His lean hand touched her long ponytail and he felt at a loss for words for the first time in recent memory. He didn't quite know what to say to her. She was nothing like the woman he'd thought her. He could hardly make himself believe that such a beautiful, desirable woman was totally innocent. And in so many ways. He looked at her mouth and felt again its soft, hungry response, felt the fierce need in her body that he'd wanted so desperately to satisfy. He still ached for her, but the shock of her chastity had spared him the shattering loss of honor he would have felt had he compromised her.

"You were a surprise, little one," he said half under his breath.

"And a big disappointment, I imagine, too," she replied.

"No." He gently tugged her ponytail until she looked up at him. "You don't have to worry about being alone with me on the desert. I'll take care of you. In every way."

She forced a smile. "I'll try not to be too much of a trial to you," she said quietly. "I'm...sorry...about what happened at the ball. I guess you know it all, now, don't you?"

"I know that you're vulnerable," he replied, his eyes soft and very dark. "I won't take advantage of it."

She searched his eyes with helpless attraction. "It's never been like that," she whispered worriedly. "Not ever..."

"We all have an Achilles' heel," he said. "Apparently I'm yours." He smiled gently. "It's all right. We'll muddle through."

"Do you have one?" she asked shyly.

"One what?"

"An Achilles' heel."

He chuckled softly. "Of course. Haven't you guessed yet what it is?"

"Your ancestry," she said with sudden insight.

"Smart lady." He noticed Eugene gesturing toward them and slid a careless arm around her shoulders. He couldn't help but feel the shiver that ran through her slender body, and he felt a little guilty at encouraging her physical infatuation for him. But it flattered his pride and touched his heart. If he didn't put some distance between them pretty soon, she could become a worse Achilles' heel even than his ancestry.

The day wore on, with Jennifer trying desperately not to look at Hunter with equal amounts of possession and wonder, and failing miserably. Eugene stayed in meetings until dinner, so Hunter escorted the women to all the places they hadn't seen before. Nothing had changed on the surface in Hunter's relationship with Jennifer. He didn't touch her except when it was necessary, and he didn't pay her any more attention than he paid Cynthia. Jennifer noticed that, and it made her feel even worse than she already did. The night before had been a revelation to her. But Hunter, even though he seemed a little less rigid with her, betrayed no sudden passion for her. By the time Eugene rejoined them and they had dinner at the restaurant that evening, Jennifer was more depressed than ever.

Hunter noticed her lack of spirit, and he was sorry. It had been equally difficult for him to pretend that nothing had happened. But for his sake as well as Jennifer's he had to keep things on a business basis from now on. He didn't dare risk a repeat of the night before. Having found Jennifer virginal had kept him awake all night. He wanted her more now than he ever had. It was agony to look at her and know that she'd give in to him with hardly any coaxing; to know that she'd give him what she'd never given another man.

He watched her all through dinner, hungry to get her alone, to kiss her until she was too weak to stand up. He didn't dare, of course. He was going to have to think of something to keep him occupied tonight and out of trouble.

Fate did it for him. He went with the women upstairs while Eugene had a drink with another contact. He'd suggested that they go by their suite first, to drop off Jennifer, trying not to notice the wounded look on her young face. But just as they rounded the corner off the elevator, they spotted a man coming out of Jennifer's room.

"Stay here," he said tersely, jerking out his .45 automatic. He was off in one single graceful movement.

Jennifer wanted to scream after him to be careful, her heart in her eyes, her pulses jerking wildly as he pursued the other man down the corridor and around another corner.

"Oh, Lord," Cynthia said huskily, putting a protective arm around Jenny.

"He was in my room," Jennifer said. "I hope he doesn't hurt

Hunter! It's got to be some of that same group who broke into my apartment before. They're after my maps!"

"But you didn't bring them, did you?" Cynthia asked worriedly.

"Hunter has them," Jennifer said huskily. "But he hides things well. I suppose my room was the natural one to search."

"Risky for them to come here," Cynthia commented.

Jenny's thoughts were occupied with the man chasing the prowlers. She didn't hear the other woman's words. "I wish Hunter would come back!" She stared down the corridor worriedly.

He did, a minute later, pushing his automatic back into its holster on the way. He looked and felt furiously angry. Just the thought that the agent could have broken into Jenny's room while she was in it, asleep, made him crazy.

"He got out on a fire escape. There was a car waiting, damn the luck," Hunter said angrily. "We'll have to arrange something for tonight."

"Jennifer can stay with me, and you can stay with Eugene," Cynthia volunteered.

"No." Hunter didn't look at Jennifer. "You're safer with Eugene. I'll be in the suite with Jennifer. Nobody will get in."

"You could sleep on the sofa," Jennifer volunteered with downcast eyes, thrilled that he was being so protective.

"We'll discuss it after we leave Cynthia at her door. I'll post an operative outside it tonight. You'll be safe until Eugene comes up," he promised Cynthia.

"You're very efficient," Cynthia said with a smile, and a teasing glance at Jennifer.

Jennifer didn't say a word. She went along to drop Cynthia off and then minutes later she was alone with Hunter in her room. He had some odd instrument and he went over the entire apartment with it, careful to check everywhere. He discovered two tiny metal devices, which he dealt with before he said a word.

"I've sent a man down to my room to play possum," he told her, shucking his jacket. The shoulder holster was firm around his broad chest, the dark butt of the handle stark against his white shirt.

She shivered at the sinister outline of the gun, at the memory of how Hunter earned his living. Sometimes she could forget it altogether, but not at times like this, and she feared for him.

He saw that nervous scrutiny and lifted an eyebrow. "I won't shoot you by mistake," he murmured dryly.

"It's not that." She wrapped her arms around his chest. "They never give up, do they?"

"From what you've told me about strategic metals, I'm not surprised." He moved closer, his lean hands smoothing over her shoulders. "Lie down and get some sleep, if you can. In the morning we'll go home. A couple of weeks in the desert while things are finalized, and we'll be home free. No more danger."

"Yes." And no more interludes like this. She thought it, but she didn't say it.

His dark eyes held hers. "Go on," he said gently. "I told you last night, there won't be any more close calls."

"I know. I'm a little nervous about the intruder, that's all," she lied.

"Of course." He knew she was lying. He watched her put away the clothes that had been disarranged, seeing the way she grimaced at the thought of strange hands on her things. But she packed them before she got out a nightgown. He was standing in the doorway, and his expression was grim.

"Are you...going to stay there while I change?" she asked huskily.

His jaw tautened. "If I did, you wouldn't spend the night alone."

He turned away and closed the door, trying not to picture Jennifer's soft, nude body in that room.

It was a long night, but there were no incidents. The next morning when Jennifer got up and dressed, Hunter was on his way out of the suite.

"Marlowe's outside the door," he said tersely. "We leave for the airport in thirty minutes."

"I'll be ready," she said quietly.

He nodded curtly and closed the door behind him.

They flew back to Tulsa that morning, but Jennifer barely had time to get settled back in her apartment before she and Hunter were on a plane heading to southern Arizona all over again.

"Same song, second verse," she murmured as they took the camping equipment back out to the desert, having gone through the process of renting a four-wheel-drive vehicle and buying camping equipment all over again.

He glanced at her, a smoking cigarette in his hand. "Well, it's not quite so bad. This time you don't have to do any real prospecting. We're only camping out."

"No television, no movies. Just the two of us and a handful of enemy agents, right?" she mused, trying not to give away how miserable she was.

"It won't be that bad," he said with a faint smile. "I'll teach you how to track and all about Apache customs. We'll get by."

She nodded. "With bullets whizzing around us and people trying to kill us for a mineral strike, right?"

"Stop that. Nobody's going to try to kill you. They want the land, not bodies."

She wished that was reassuring, but it wasn't.

They pitched the tent at the site they'd occupied the first night when they were here before. It was a good six miles from the actual site, but still close enough that seismic tests could be detected with the right monitors. But Eugene was an old fox, and her rock samples had been assayed by now. He used seismic tests extensively when he was searching for oil deposits, but moly was a different element and there were all sorts of detecting devices he could use to search out deposits.

"Nervous?" Hunter asked as they pitched camp.

She nodded. "A little."

He built a fire and proceeded to prepare food, a process Jennifer watched with fascination.

"Hunter, did you grow up around here?" he asked suddenly.

He nodded. "I used to wander all over this country as a boy. Within limits, of course. I kept to the reservation."

She studied him across the campfire. "And now?"

He looked up, studying her face in the flames. Even in jeans and a floppy T-shirt she was gorgeous, he thought. "Now I live in Tulsa."

"You said you kept horses."

"Yes. On the reservation. I own a small homestead. The house is my refuge. Actually I should say that the tribe owns the land, and ownership is overseen by the tribal council. We aren't allowed to sell any land without approval from the Bureau of Indian Affairs. The reasoning for that is a long story, and one I'd rather not go into right now," he added when she started to speak.

"All right," she said easily. He handed her a plate of stew and a cup of black coffee, adding a couple of slices of loaf bread to her plate. She ate hungrily. "Something about the night air gives me an appetite," she sighed when she finished. "Look at the stars. They're bigger here. And it's so quiet… Well, except for the coyotes and an occasional four-wheel-drive vehicle and the sound of rifle fire as people shoot road signs for amusement."

He glanced at her ruefully. "You're poetic."

"Oh, very." She wrapped her hands around her knees and stared at them.

He watched her for a minute, remembering another night alone, at another campsite, and her bare breasts in the moonlight. He got up suddenly.

"I'll have a look around. You might go ahead and turn in. It's been a long day."

"Yes, I think I will," she agreed easily. She went into the tent and got into her sleeping bag. Amazingly she was asleep when he finally came to bed.

The days went by all too slowly, and by the end of the week, Jennifer's nerves were raw and she was snapping at Hunter. He wasn't in any too good a humor himself. Jennifer lying beside him in the tent night after night was driving him out of his mind. The scent of her, the sound of her, the sight of her were so firmly imbedded in his brain that he felt part of her already.

The memories didn't help. He'd come so close to possessing her, and now his body knew the reality of hers and wanted it. The hunger kept gnawing at him, making him impatient and irritable.

"Must you keep turning those scanners on?" Jennifer asked when the police scanner began to get on her nerves the Friday night after they'd arrived.

"Yes, I must," he said tersely. "They're reporting an incident near here—presumably at the test site where Eugene's geologic technicians are working. I'm going to have a look. Stay close to the tent. Have you still got that .22 rifle I gave you?"

"Yes, and I can use it," she replied. "Was anybody hurt?" she asked.

"If I knew that, why would I be going to check it out?" he asked curtly. "What a damned stupid question!"

"Well, I'm not a trained agent, so you'll have to forgive my ignorance!" she shot back. "Go ahead and get shot! I won't cry over you!"

"I never expected that you would," he returned. He got into the four-wheel drive and took off without looking back.

Jennifer's nerve deserted her the minute the Jeep disappeared. She sat down beside the scanner and listened to it uneasily, glancing around with the rifle across her legs. She didn't know what had happened, and the fact that the agents were the most likely people to be bothering the technicians was unsettling news. What if they came here and tried to shake the information they wanted out of her while Hunter was gone?

That was ridiculous, of course. She laughed out loud. Of course they wouldn't come here...

The sound of a Jeep alerted her and she jumped up. Hunter, she thought with relief. She ran toward the rutted road with the rifle in time to be caught in the headlights of the vehicle that was approaching. There was an exclamation and a shot as the vehicle suddenly reversed and rushed off in the other direction.

Jennifer felt something hot against her arm, like a sudden sting. She touched it and her fingers came away wet.

She looked down at her arm. She could see a dark stain in the faint light from the campfire. She lifted her fingers closer and the unmistakable smell of blood was on her hand!

I've been shot, she thought in astonishment. My God, I've been shot!

She sat down heavily next to the campfire, with the rifle still in her shaking hands. If only Hunter would come back! She was alone and afraid and she didn't know what to do. Obviously the agents had come roaring into camp with the intention of seeking information. They hadn't expected her to come running toward them with a rifle. They'd shot at her in apparent self-defense and had raced away before she could get a shot off at them. It might be funny later. Right now, it was terrifying.

Her arm hurt. She grimaced. The sound of a vehicle approaching came again, but this time, she didn't run toward it. She raised the rifle, wincing as her arm protested, and leveled it at the dark shape spurting into camp.

"That's far enough!" she called out.

The engine and lights were cut off. The door opened. "Shoot and be damned," Hunter's deep voice replied.

9

Jenny thought that as long as she lived, she'd never forget the expression on Hunter's face when she collapsed in his arms and he discovered that she'd been shot.

She managed to explain what had happened while he laid her gently on her sleeping bag inside the tent and moved the Coleman lantern closer to check the wound.

"I must have passed them coming back. Damn it!" he burst out, adding something in a very gutteral language that seemed to raise and lower in pitch and stop suddenly between syllables.

"Is that...cursing?" she asked.

"Yes, and thank your stars you can't translate it," he added icily. He glanced down at her. "They raided the other camp, but they were a little too late. The technicians flew back to Tulsa this afternoon with the data. They left the tents and other gear, just as Eugene had instructed, to give them time to get away. They were supposed to contact us, but apparently they were being watched too closely."

"Eugene will kill them," she murmured, groaning when his fingers touched around the gash in her soft skin.

"If he doesn't, I will," he returned. "Which is nothing to what I intend doing to the man who shot you."

She stared up at him through waves of pain. His eyes were frightening, and at that moment he looked pagan, untamed.

"It isn't bad," she said, trying to ease the tension she could almost taste as his hard, deft fingers searched around the cut. They seemed just slightly unsteady. Imagine anything shaking the stoic Mr. Hunter, she thought with hysterical amusement.

"I can't see properly in this light. Come on." He helped her to the vehicle and helped her into the passenger side. He turned on the overhead light after he'd climbed quickly in beside her, and once more his eyes were on the cut. "You can manage without stitches, but it needs an antiseptic."

"There might be a drugstore..." she offered.

He turned off the light and started the engine. He never seemed to feel the need to answer questions, she sighed to herself. Amazing how he expected her to read his mind.

"But what about our things?" she asked.

He cursed again, turning around. "Wait here." He left the engine running, put out the campfire, got her case and his out of the tent along with the technical gear, and left the rest of it.

"But the tent, the sleeping bags..." she began. He glanced at her and she stopped when she saw his expression. She cleared her throat. "Never mind."

He set off into the desert and drove for what seemed forever until he came to a small house, set against the jagged peak of one of southern Arizona's endless mountain chains. He pulled into the dirt driveway, and Jenny wondered whose home it was. The house was livable, just, but it needed painting and patching and a new roof.

"Come on." He opened the door and helped her out.

"It's a beautiful setting," she murmured as she drank in the sweet, clear air and looked around the yard at the ocotillo and cholla and agave that surrounded the yard. "Like being alone in the world."

"I've always thought so," he said stiffly. He escorted her onto the porch and produced a key to unlock the door. He didn't look at her as he opened it and pulled the screen door back to let her enter the living room.

It was nothing like the exterior of the house, she noticed as he pulled a long chain and the bare light bulb in the ceiling came on. The living room was comfortable and neat, with padded arm-chairs and cane-bottomed chairs, Indian rugs on the floors and spread over the backs of the chairs. There was some kind of furry round shield with tiny fur tails hanging from it, and basketry every-where.

Hunter was watching her, waiting for disgust or contempt to show on her soft face. But she seemed fascinated; almost charmed by what she saw.

She turned back to him, her eyes shining despite the faint throb of the wound on her arm. "It's your house, isn't it?" she asked.

His dark eyebrows arched. "Yes."

"You're wondering how I knew," she murmured dryly. "It's simple. You're the only person I know who would enjoy living totally alone in the world with no nosy neighbors. And this," she gestured toward the living room, "is how I'd picture your living room."

He managed a faint smile. "Come on. I'll put a patch on the injury, then I'll find something to cook."

"All right."

"No comment about the cooking?" he added, leading her into a stark white bathroom with aging fixtures.

"I'd be surprised if you couldn't cook. You seem so self-sufficient."

"I've always had to be," he said simply. He stripped off his jacket, rolled up his sleeves and got out medicine and bandages from the cabinet over the sink. "My father died when I was small. I lived with my grandfather, on the reservation, until I was old enough to enlist. When I got out of the Green Berets, I kicked around for a few years doing other things. Eventually Ritter offered me a job and I've been there ever since."

"No wife, ever?" she asked hesitantly.

His dark, quiet eyes met hers. "Women don't fit in a place like this," he said. "It's stark and bare-bone comfort, and it's lonely. In case you haven't guessed, this is part of the reservation, too." He waited for her reaction, but there wasn't one. He shrugged and continued. "I'm away most of the time. I've never asked anyone to share it because I don't think a woman could. My job would be an immediate point of contention and my heritage would be another. I live on the reservation," he added with a mocking smile. "I can see how that would go over with most in-laws. And I believe in some of the old ways, especially in family life."

"A woman's place is three steps behind the man..." she began.

"A man should behave as one," he returned simply. "And a woman has her place—a very special place—in the order of things. She gives life, nurtures it. She gives warmth and light to her man, her children." He ran a basin of water, found a cloth and bathed the wound on Jenny's arm. "But, no, I don't think her place is three steps behind her man, or that she becomes property when she marries. Perhaps you don't know, but in the old days, many Apache women fought right alongside their men and were as re-spected as the warriors."

"No, I didn't know," she confessed. The touch of his fingers was painful delight. Her eyes glanced over the hard lines of his dark face with pure pleasure. "You're proud of your ancestry, aren't you?"

He looked down at her. "My people are like a separate state, under federal jurisdiction," he replied. "We have our own laws, our own reservation police, our own code of behavior. When we live in your world, we seem alien." He laughed coldly. "I wish I could tell you how many times in my life I've been called Tonto or Chief, and how many fights I've been into because of it."

She was beginning to understand him. He'd grown a shell, she supposed, because of the difficulties. And now he was trapped in it and couldn't find his way out.

"I know a little about prejudice," she said, surprising him. "I'm a female geologist and I work in the oil business." She smiled. "Equality is all the rage in accounting and law firms back east, and even in corporations. But out in the boondocks in the oil exploration game, there are Neanderthal men who think a woman goes to those lonely places for just one reason. I wish I had a nickel for every time I've had to threaten someone with a suit for sexual harassment."

"Looking the way you do, I can understand your problem," he mused, glancing at her with dancing dark eyes. "How does this feel?" he added when he'd put antiseptic on the wound and lightly bandaged it.

"It feels much better, thank you," she said. Her eyes searched his dark face while he put away the medicine. "What do you mean, the way I look?"

He closed the cabinet and gazed down at her. His face was expressionless except for the dark, disturbing glitter in his eyes as they slid down her body and up again. "Is it important to hear me say it?" he asked. "You know how lovely you are."

Her breath caught. "I've been told I was," she corrected. "It never meant anything. Before."

His jaw clenched. He stared at her until she flushed and still his eyes didn't waver or even blink. "Be careful," he said quietly. "I still want you very badly."

"I'm twenty-seven years old," she whispered. "If it isn't you, it won't be anybody. Ever. I said that once. I meant it."

His breath expelled roughly. He caught her around the waist and pulled her up from the edge of the bathtub where she'd been sitting. His arm was steely strong, and the feel and scent of him so close made her almost moan with pleasure.

"How much do you know about birth control?" he asked bluntly.

"I know that babies come if you don't use any," she replied, trying to sound sophisticated with a beet-red face.

His eyes were relentless. "And do you think I'm prepared for casual interludes with women all the time?"

"Most men are," she faltered.

"I'm not most men," he returned. "These days I think of sex as something that goes hand in hand with love, respect, honor. It used to be a casual amusement when I was a young man. I'm thirty-seven now, and it isn't casual or amusing anymore. It's serious business."

She could have reminded him that for a few minutes one night, he'd forgotten all those reasons, but she didn't. Her eyes fell to his firm chin. "It isn't casual with me, either," she whispered "But I'd give anything...!" She bit her lip. "I'm sorry."

His hand came up, framing her own chin, lifting her eyes to his. "You'd give anything...?" he prompted slowly.

She closed her eyes so that he wouldn't see the longing. So that she wouldn't throw herself at him again, as she had that night in Washington. "Nothing. I'm just tired. I wasn't thinking."

"I know you're infatuated with me," he said out of the blue.

Her eyes flew open, startled. "What?"

"It isn't something you hide well," he replied. His eyes narrowed. "I've had hell trying not to take advantage of it. I'm a new experience for you, something out of the ordinary, and I know already how you seek the unusual. But since you don't know, I'll tell you. Sex is the same with an Apache as it is with a white man, in case you—"

He broke off because she slapped him, with the full strength of her arm behind the blow. Tears welled in her eyes; her face had gone white with shock and grief.

He didn't flinch. He let her go, very gently, and moved away. "I'll see about something to eat," he said, with no inflection at all in his voice as he started toward the kitchen.

Jenny cried. She closed the bathroom door and cried until her throat hurt. If he'd tried for months to think up something hurtful, he couldn't have succeeded any better. She knew he was aware of her desire for him, but she hadn't known he was aware of her feelings, too. It made her too vulnerable.

Finally she dried her eyes and went out without looking in the small mirror. She could imagine what she looked like without having to see herself.

He glanced at her and his expression hardened as he proceeded to fry steak and eggs. "I'd expected to spend the weekend here, so I loaded up on supplies yesterday," he said. "You can set the table."

She took the dishes from the cabinet he gestured toward and set two places, including a mug for the coffee that was brewing in the modern coffeepot. She took her time meticulously folding two paper towels to go at each place.

"Utensils?" she asked in a totally defeated tone.

"Here." He opened the drawer beside him, but as she moved closer to reach inside it, he turned suddenly and pulled her to him. His mouth eased down over hers with a gentle, insistent pressure that caught her completely off guard. She felt his strong teeth nipping tenderly at her lower lip until her mouth opened for him. Then she felt his tongue inside, touching her own, his arm contracting, the sound that echoed out of his throat, deep and gruff and faintly threatening.

Her nails bit into his back where her arms had gone under his and around him, and she bit off a short, sharp little cry as the pleasure cut the ground from under her feet. The injury to her arm was still throbbing, but she held on for dear life, uncaring in the thrall of such aching pleasure. She didn't want him to stop, not ever!

All too soon, he lifted his head. His eyes were dark with emotion, his jaw clenched. "Finish setting the table," he said huskily, and abruptly let her go to concentrate on the Spanish omelet he was making.

She couldn't help the trembling of her hands as she complied with that request. It wasn't until they were halfway through the impromptu meal and the strong, fresh coffee that she was able to get some kind of control over herself.

"To continue what I started to say when we were in the bathroom, I'm not prepared for an intimate encounter," he said when she laid down her fork. He didn't look at her as he said it. His eyes were on the coffee cup in his hand. "And as I told you in Washington that night, half-breed children belong in no one's world."

Her eyes searched his face. A suspicion at the back of her mind began to take shape. He looked Apache. There was no doubt about that part of his heritage. But the way he felt about mixing the races, wasn't it violent if he'd never had experience of it?

"Which one of your parents was white, Phillip?" she asked softly.

His head jerked up. His eyes flashed at her. "What did you say?" he asked in a tone that should have backed her down. It didn't.

"I said, which one of your parents was white?"

"I'd forgotten that I told you my given name," he said softly. "You've never used it."

She began to realize, belatedly, that it was her use of his first name that had rattled him, not her reference to his parentage. She hesitated. "I didn't realize I had," she said after a minute.

He leaned back, troubled, the coffee cup still in his lean, dark hand. He watched her intently. "My mother was white, Jennifer," he said finally.

"Is she still alive?"

He shrugged. "I don't know. She couldn't take life on the reservation, and my father was too Apache to leave it. She left when I was five and I haven't seen her since. My father died a year later. He gave up. Life without her, he said, was no life. I always consider that I lost both my parents when I was five, so I don't qualify the statement. I don't know where my mother is." His face hardened. "I don't care. Her family put me through school and supported me while I was younger. I didn't find out until I was much older. My grandfather never would have told me, but I found a check stub. He was a proud man." He looked down at his hands. "Life on the reservation is hard. Unemployment, infant mortality, poverty... It's no one's idea of the American dream. He took the money for my sake, not for his. What he didn't spend on me, he sent back."

She stretched her hand toward his free one, lying on the table and abruptly stopped. He wouldn't want sympathy, she supposed.

But surprisingly, his own hand slid the remaining distance and enveloped hers, his thumb softly stroking her palm. "White and brown," he observed, staring at the differences in color. "I'm still Apache, Jenny, despite my white blood. But if I had a child with a white woman, he'd be a lost soul, like me. Caught between two worlds. My own people have a hard time accepting me, even though I look more Apache than white."

Her eyes adored him. "I can't imagine a more handsome man of either race," she said quietly.

His face went a ruddy color, and she wondered if it was possible to embarrass him.

She smiled wickedly. "My, my, are you *blushing?*"

He let go of her hand with an outright laugh. "Compliments are difficult for me," he said gruffly. "Eat your omelet."

She picked up her fork with a sigh, wincing a little as the movement made her arm uncomfortable. "Can I ask why we aren't having bacon or sausage with our eggs?" she murmured.

"Apaches don't eat pork," he said. "Or fish. Ever."

"Why?" she asked, astonished.

"Beats me. We just don't."

"I thought I knew something about your people. I suppose I don't know much at all."

He smiled to himself. "You know more than most whites."

"I guess that operative of yours who's Papago knows more," she murmured without looking at him. "She's the kind of woman you'll marry one day, isn't she?"

He frowned down at his omelet. "I don't know that I'll marry at all," he said. He lifted his eyes to her sad face and felt a wave of grief that almost knocked him flat. She was infatuated with him, but she could never endure life here. She was beautiful and sweet and he wanted her until she was all but an obsession. But his mind kept insisting that he couldn't risk having her turn out like his mother. His mother hadn't been able to take living in an Indian world.

She sighed wearily. "I've had the same feeling lately. I'm almost twenty-eight. Despite the fact that women are becoming mothers later and later in life, I don't really like the risk factors after thirty-five." She smiled at her omelet as she cut it. "Funny. I always thought I might make a pretty good mother."

"You've had the opportunity to marry," he said stiffly.

"Oh, of course. Soft, carefree city men who have affairs and look upon marriage as slow death. I had one proposal from a man who was twenty years older than me and wanted to live in Alaska." She glanced up. "I hate polar bears."

He smiled. "So do I."

"My other proposal was from a boy my age when I was eighteen, and he only wanted to marry me to get away from his parents. He was rich and I wasn't—it was a sort of rebellion." She put down her fork. "I've never been asked to marry anybody because I was loved. Wanted, yes. But that wasn't enough."

"You're not over the hill," he reminded her.

"It doesn't matter." She looked up at him, her eyes wide and soft and gentle. "I'm sorry you stopped that night in Washington," she said huskily. "I wouldn't have regretted it, ever."

His jaw tautened. He finished his steak and washed it down with coffee. "It would have hurt like hell."

She traced the rim of her plate, her heart beating madly at the memory of his arms around her, his body intimately over her own. "It wouldn't have hurt long," she whispered. "I wanted you too badly to care."

"God, yes, you did," he said through his teeth. The memories were driving him crazy. "Shaking in my arms, and I'd barely touched you. By the time I put my mouth on yours, you were trembling all over with the need. I never dreamed that women felt it like that."

"Maybe most women don't feel it like that," she said uneasily. "Maybe there's, well, something wrong with me...."

"There's nothing wrong with you that a night in my arms wouldn't cure," he said curtly. His dark eyes caught her blue ones and held them hotly. "But it would only be a night, and we'd have the rest of our lives to regret it."

Her lips parted as she searched his eyes. "No, we wouldn't," she whispered. "And you know it. You want me just as much as I want you."

He nodded slowly, his gaze dropping to her full breasts and back up again to her mouth and her eyes. "You can only give your chastity once."

"I know that, too," she replied. "I meant what I said. If it isn't you, it won't be anybody." Her breath sighed out raggedly. "I love you," she said achingly.

He let out a long, weary sigh. After a minute he got up and held out his hand. She took it, feeling his lean fingers enfold hers, wrap gently around them.

He led her into his bedroom without speaking and closed the door. "Do you want the light out?" he asked.

She bit her lower lip. She wanted to be sophisticated and worldly, but she was already blushing.

He smiled with bitter irony. "Never mind." He reached up and turned off the light, leaving the room in almost total darkness, except for the half moon that left its yellow shadow over the patchwork quilt on the bed.

"What do we do now?" she whispered, her voice husky with excitement and faint apprehension.

"What we did in my hotel room that night in Washington," he murmured as his hands reached for her. "Except that this time I won't pull back when I feel the barrier…"

"Phillip." She moaned his name into his mouth as it came down on hers, gasping when she felt him pull her hips roughly into the already aroused thrust of his.

"This is how badly I want you," he whispered, his breathing mingling with hers. "It happens the minute your body touches mine. Magic."

"Yes." She pulled his shirt out of his jeans and slid her hands up against his bare back, feeling the taut muscles, the rough silk of his skin. It was cool, and seconds later when her bare breasts melted into the hard wall of his chest, that was cool, too, against the heated warmth of her own skin.

When he had every scrap of material away from their bodies, he lifted her, with his mouth gently moving on her own, and laid her on the quilt. His hand went to the bedside table. He opened a drawer and removed something. Seconds later, he placed it in her hand and taught her how to put it in place. Even that was exciting and sensual in the hot darkness.

"This is so we won't make a baby," he whispered, his voice deep and slow as he moved over her. His teeth nibbled softly at her upper lip. His lean hands smoothed down her body, lingering on her soft thighs, making her tremble with the pleasure of his touch.

Her body was shivering. He kissed her tenderly, and then his mouth moved down to her breasts and caressed their hard tips until she was writhing under him.

"You like that, don't you?" he whispered. "I like it, too, little one.

You taste of satin here, and of desire here," he breathed against a taut nipple, his lips pulling at it with sensual tenderness.

She clung to his muscular arms, her breath coming in jerks while he kissed and touched and tasted, the darkness like a warm blanket over her fears.

When she was shuddering, he eased her trembling legs apart and levered himself down between them, his mouth poised just above her own, his eyes glittered into hers in the darkness. He probed tenderly and felt her tense.

"When I push down, try not to do that," he whispered. "If you tense up, it's going to hurt more."

She shivered with delicious anticipation, her body throbbing with a heat it had never felt before. Her legs moved to admit him even closer and her nails bit into his shoulders. "I'll try," she breathed.

His chest rose and fell deeply. His hips moved down, and she made a noise deep in her throat as she felt the burning pain. She tensed involuntarily. "I'm...sorry," she gasped.

"It can't be be helped," he said quietly. "I'm going to have to hurt you. Cry out if you want to. I'm sorry...!"

She did, because it was worse than she'd imagined it would be. But she didn't fight him or try to push him away even then. She bit her lip and moaned, trying to force her body to relax as it protested the invasion of his.

"Only a little longer," he whispered. His mouth came closer. "Kiss me. It will help."

She let him take her mouth, opened it to admit the slow, deep penetration of his tongue that imitated what his body was doing to hers. It was so erotic that it tricked her taut muscles into relaxing, and suddenly what had been almost impossible was easy and smooth.

He heard her intake of breath and lifted his head, smiling down at her through his own fierce excitement. The act of possession was almost enough to trigger his fulfillment. He had to stop and breathe himself to keep control.

"Phillip," she whispered achingly. Her eyes sought his, and she could barely believe it was happening, at last.

"How does it feel?" he whispered at her lips.

"Incredible," she managed, her voice shaking.

"And we haven't begun," he breathed as his mouth began to open on hers. His hips lifted and moved and she shivered, because the surge of pleasure she felt shocked her.

The sound of the car roaring up outside was an interruption that froze them both in incredulous shock.

"My God," he ground out. "No!"

But the car was stopping. Worse, there were lights flashing, so it had to be a police car.

He lifted himself away from her, shuddering as he fell onto his back and arched. He groaned and stiffened, while Jennifer tried to weather the frustration and anger she felt.

There were footsteps on the porch and a loud, heavy knock at the door.

"Just a minute!" Hunter shouted. He got up, pulling on his jeans with hands that shook. "God almighty, I'll kill someone for this!" he muttered. He leaned over Jennifer's shivering body and bent to kiss her with rough hunger. "Get dressed, quickly."

He left the room and she turned on the light, hurrying to get back into her clothes and make some kind of order in the room. She brushed her hair with his hairbrush and, satisfied that she looked as presentable as possible, she opened the bedroom door.

Hunter was talking to another man. They had to be speaking Apache, because Jennifer couldn't understand a word.

"This is Choya," Hunter introduced the shorter man. "He's chief of the reservation police. I've been telling him what happened. Since the incident occurred on Apache land, he'll be responsible for the investigation and any arrests."

"In other words, I get all the headaches," the newcomer grinned, perfect white teeth flashing. "My God, Hunter, I go home to a wife with buckteeth and you have her." He shook his head. "I need to change medicine men."

Hunter chuckled. "You know Maria's the prettiest woman around, so shut up. Is there anything else you need to know?"

"Not tonight," Choya said, and exchanged a knowing glance with Hunter. "Sorry about my timing. I'll get back on the road now. Good night."

"Good night," Jennifer said, blushing all over.

Hunter closed the door behind him and turned to Jennifer. He didn't move until the car drove away, his dark eyes sliding over her, his dark, bare chest lifting and falling slowly.

"Come here," he said curtly.

She went to him without hesitation. He lifted her, but instead of carrying her back into the bedroom, he carried her to the rocking chair and sat down with her across his lap.

"Thanks to Choya, we can't finish what we started," he said, smiling into her heated face. "I was prepared, but only for one time." He bent and drew his mouth slowly over hers. "Still burning?" he breathed.

His hand was on the buttons of her blouse, which she put on without her bra, and now he knew it. She arched, letting him look, letting him touch.

Her fingers tangled in his dark hair and pulled, tugging his face toward her bare breasts.

"All right," he whispered. "Is this what you want?"

It was. Oh, it was, she thought in sweet anguish, loving the touch of his mouth on her velvety skin. She lay in his arms and made no protest when he stripped off her jeans and underwear. His hand found her and moved, and his mouth reached up for hers. He rocked the chair and touched her rhythmically, and the combined force of the sensual movements very quickly brought an explosive culmination in her taut body.

She cried out and shivered and was still. He gathered her close beside him, her breasts brushing his bare chest, his cheek against her hair.

"It isn't enough," he whispered. "But it's safe. One day, so help me, I'll put you under me in bed and fill you until you scream."

She bit his shoulder in anguished need, and he shuddered and brought her even closer. "What about you?" she asked huskily.

"Don't worry about me," he said, ignoring his own need. He could handle it. He'd have to, he couldn't take the risk.

"You're no longer a virgin, technically," he said, lifting his head to search her eyes. "Despite the fact that we were barely together, I had your virginity tonight."

She smiled up at him with awe. "Yes."

He touched her mouth, tracing her lips with a finger that wasn't quite steady. "And you don't regret it?"

"No," she whispered.

His jaw clenched as his eyes fell to her bare breasts. "Neither do I," he said. "You belong to me."

"I know."

His eyes flashed as they met hers. "There won't be another man."

"I know that, too."

He stared into her eyes for a long moment, then he stood and carried her back into the bedroom. He stripped himself before he turned out the light and put her under the covers. He drew her body against his and pressed her cheek into his bare shoulder with a long, rough sigh.

"In the morning, get up as quickly as you can," he said at her ear. "A man awakens aroused and his wits are dulled by it. Don't be tempted to take chances. I won't forget and I won't forgive."

She sighed. "All right," she said reluctantly. She closed her eyes, pressing her hand flat on his chest and curling into his taut body. "Good night, Phillip."

His hand covered hers. "Good night, little one." He brushed a careless kiss against her forehead and then her eyes, lingering on the thick, long lashes.

"I'm sorry," she whispered.

"For what?"

"You had nothing."

His body was taut but he tried to ignore it. "I'll live," he murmured, trying to keep his voice light.

But she heard the stress in it. Hesitantly she slid her hand down his body and felt him tense. She waited for him to stop her, but he didn't. She heard his breathing change and felt his body arch in a slow, delicate rhythm. Her fingers moved down and he arched into them.

"Yes," he whispered, his eyes closed.

She stroked him, feeling him throb, feeling him tauten, hearing the anguished groan that broke from his lips as her hand explored him.

"Do it," he bit off.

He taught her, kicking the covers off, his eyes glittering in the darkness. She heard his breathing become tortured, watched his body react to her shy, loving touch. He watched her until it became impossible and then he arched up, crying out, and she learned things about men that all her reading hadn't prepared her for.

Eventually they slept. She supposed that she should regret what had happened. If she ever did marry, even if she hadn't been totally seduced, she was no longer completely chaste. But it was Hunter she'd given that privilege to, and she had no regrets. She loved him so deeply that she could live on tonight, forever if she had to.

She got up the next morning and went into the living room with shy reluctance. She never quite knew what to expect from Hunter, because he was so unpredictable.

He was putting food on the table. He glanced up. "I was about to call you," he said politely. "Sit down."

It was as if nothing had ever happened between them. She stared at him curiously as she sat in the chair.

He poured coffee with a straight face. "How's the arm?"

"It's sore, but I think it will be all right."

"We'll get you to a doctor before we leave for the airport. We're going home today."

"So soon?"

"It's past time," he returned tersely, and the eyes that met hers were angry. "Last night should never have happened. You have a very disturbing effect on my willpower, and I'm tired of it. I'm taking you back to Tulsa. If there's another assignment like this, I'll send one of my operatives with you instead. There aren't going to be any repeats."

She lowered her eyes to the table. "You can't bear to lose control in any way, can you?"

"No," he replied honestly. "You're becoming a liability, and I can't afford one. My job requires total concentration. What I feel when I'm around you could get us both killed. I made a mistake last night that could have been fatal. I left you alone. If we hadn't been at each other's throats out of simple physical frustration, I'd have had the presence of mind to take you with me. But I didn't."

"I'm all right," she said quietly.

"You could have died. Or I could have. I've had enough emotional stress to last me a lifetime, Jennifer," he said, his voice final. "From now on, I'll stick to women who can give out and get out. No more lovesick virgins."

She went scarlet. She couldn't even deny it. "I'll do my best to stay out of your way," she said.

"That would be appreciated," he replied. He couldn't look at her. It was hurting him to cut her up like this, but he had to make her angry enough to keep away from him. Wanting her was becoming an obsession that could cost him his job or his life under the right circumstances.

She dragged her eyes up for one brief instant. "Are you sorry we made love?" she asked huskily.

"Yes, I'm sorry," he said without a flicker of emotion. "I told you I'd been without a woman for a long time. You were handy, and you must know how beautiful you are." He forced a mocking smile. "It would have been a unique experience. I've never had a willing virgin before. But the newness would have worn off before morning, I'm afraid. I prefer an experienced woman in bed. Someone who knows how to play the game without expecting declarations of love and proposals of marriage."

Her face was very pale, but she smiled. "Well, no harm done," she said gamely. "Thanks for the instruction." She lowered her eyes to her coffee cup. "What time do you want to leave?"

He couldn't repress admiration for her bravery. No tears, no accusations, just acceptance despite her pain. That made it worse somehow. But he had to be strong.

He got up. "In half an hour," he said. "Leave the dishes. I'll be coming back here when I've put you on the plane."

"You aren't coming?" she exclaimed.

"No. I've got some leave due. I'm taking it now. I'll phone Eugene from the airport. Get your things together, please."

It was so hurried—the trip to the doctor's office, the antibiotic and tetanus shots, the rush to get to the airport in time to board a plane for Tulsa. She was en route before she realized how shocked and hurt she really was. It was a good thing that he hadn't let her say goodbye, so that she didn't break down. He'd given her the ticket, said something about having someone meet her at the airport, and then he'd left her at the right concourse gate without a goodbye or a backward glance.

She got off the plane in Tulsa and there was a car waiting. It whisked her back to her apartment. Once she got into it, she threw herself on her bed and cried until her eyes were red. But it didn't take away the sting of knowing that Hunter had only desired her. She'd given him everything she had to give, and he'd still walked away without a backward glance. She loved him more than her own life. How was she going to live without him?

10

꧁∾∾꧂ ꧁∾∾꧂ ꧁∾∾꧂

J ennifer couldn't decide what to do. She was so miserable that
she only went through the motions of doing a job that she'd
once loved. Her coworkers noticed the quiet pain in her
face, but they were too kind to mention it.

Eugene got his molybdenum mine. The deal went through with
flying colors, and the enemy agents went home in disgrace, having
pursued the wrong site and gotten themselves in eternal hot water
with their furious superiors.

Hunter stayed on vacation for a couple of weeks. When he came
back into the office, he pointedly ignored Jennifer, refusing to
even look her way when he passed her in the hall.

His attitude cut her to the bone. She lost weight and began to
give in to nerves. She jumped when people approached unexpectedly. She made mistakes on her charts——the kind that she never
would have made before. Eugene called her on the carpet for her
latest error, which had cost the company a good deal of money
drilling in what turned out to be a dry hole.

"Everybody hits a dry hole once or twice," he raged at her in the privacy of his office. "And under normal circumstances, it's excusable. But, damn it, this isn't! This was carelessness, Jennifer, plain and simple."

"Yes, it was. And I'm going to turn in my resignation," she said, amazed to hear the words coming from her lips.

Apparently Eugene was, too, because he stopped in midtirade to scowl at her. His blue eyes narrowed and he studied her. After a minute, he leaned back in his chair with a long sigh.

"It's Hunter, of course," he said out loud, nodding at her shocked expression. "He tried to quit a couple of weeks ago, too. I refused his resignation and I'm refusing yours. You don't have to see each other. I've already made arrangements to transfer him to our Phoenix office for a few months. He leaves at the end of the week."

She didn't know what to say. It wasn't going to do any good to deny it. But it puzzled her that Hunter had offered to resign. She knew how much he loved his job.

"Surprises you that he tried to quit, doesn't it?" he asked her. "He wouldn't give a reason, but he keeps trying to get assignments out of the country. You, on the other hand, keep refusing any assignment that would require him to look after you. Interesting, isn't it?" He leaned forward abruptly. "What happened out on the desert? Did he make a pass?"

She lowered her eyes to the floor so they wouldn't give her away. "We had some differences of opinion," she replied. "And we agreed that it would be better if we kept out of each other's way in the future."

"Is that why you're losing weight and making one mistake on top of another?" he asked pleasantly.

She lifted her face proudly and stared him down. "I cost you a lot of money, so I guess you're entitled to know. I'm in love with him."

"How does he feel?"

"Mr. Hunter doesn't tell anyone how he feels," she replied. "He said point-blank that he doesn't want to get mixed up with a white woman in any emotional or physical way, and he told me to get lost."

Eugene whistled through his teeth. "Well!"

"I'm trying to get lost, except that I keep bumping into him and he stares right through me." Her voice revealed the pain of the experience all too well. She averted her face. "If you'll send him to Phoenix, I think I can get over him."

"Do you? I wouldn't make any bets on it. And if his temper is any indication, he's having some problems of his own. He was livid about letting you get shot. I gather that he feels responsible."

"It was my fault as much as his," she replied. "I don't blame him. My arm is as good as new."

"Too bad we can't say the same of your brain," Eugene mused. "It's a very good brain, too. I'll send him off. We'll see how you both feel in a few months. If this blows over, he can come back."

"Fair enough." She got to her feet. "Thank you."

"Have you tried talking to him?" he asked as she started to leave.

"He won't," she replied. "Once he makes up his mind, nobody gets a chance to change it."

"Just a thought," Eugene said with a smile. "It would be one way of finding out if he shares your feelings."

Jennifer tormented herself with that thought for the rest of the day. But it would do no good to throw herself at him again, she mused bitterly. He'd already shown her that he wanted her physically. It was every other way that he was rejecting her.

Still, she couldn't resist one last try. So when he came down the hall the morning before he was to leave for Phoenix, she deliberately stepped into his path.

"Eugene says you're being transferred," she said, clutching a stack of topo maps to her breasts to still the trembling of her hands.

Hunter looked down at her. She was wearing gray slacks with a white pullover knit blouse, her blond hair long and soft around her shoulders. He drank in the sight of her without letting her see that it was killing him to leave her.

"I'm going home for a few months, yes," he replied, staring down at her with no particular emotion in his dark face. "It's been a long time since I've had the opportunity to see my grandfather and my cousins and visit old friends."

She wondered if any of the old friends were female, but she didn't dare ask. She looked up into his eyes with her heart in her own, with no idea of how powerfully she was affecting him.

"I'll miss you," she said softly.

He lifted an eyebrow and smiled mockingly. "Will you? Why?"

She bit her lower lip without answering.

He stuck his hands into his pockets and the smile left his face as he looked down at her. "Sex is a bad basis for a relationship," he said bluntly. "I wanted you. Any man would. But common ground is something we never had, and never could. I don't want a white lover, any more than I want a white wife. When I marry, if I marry, it will be to one of my own people. Is that clear enough?"

Her face went very pale, so that her blue eyes were the only color in it. "Yes," she said. "You told me that before."

"I want to make sure you get the message," he replied, forcing the words out. "It was a game. I play it with white women all the time. A little flirting, a little lovemaking, no harm done. But you're one of those throwbacks who equate sex with forever after. Sorry, honey, one night isn't worth my freedom, no matter how fascinating it was to have a virgin."

She dropped her wounded eyes to his sports jacket. "I see," she said, her voice haunted.

His fists clenched inside his pockets. It was killing him to do this! But he had to. He was so damned vulnerable that he wouldn't have the strength to resist her if she kept pursuing him. It had to end quickly. "Now go back to your office and stop trying to fan old flames. I've had all of you that I want...."

She whirled and ran before he finished, tears staining her cheeks. Nothing had ever hurt so much. She went into her office and slammed the door, grateful that her coworkers were still at lunch. She dried her tears after a while and forced herself to work. But she knew she'd never forget the horrible things Hunter had said to her. So much for finding out how he really felt. He'd told her.

Hunter was on his way to the airport, feeling like an animal. Tears on that sweet, loving face had hurt him. It had taken every ounce of willpower he had not to chase her into the office and dry them. But he'd accomplished what he set out to do, he'd driven her away. Now all he had to do was live with it, and he'd never have to worry about the threat of Jennifer again.

Simple words. But as the weeks turned into months, he grew morose. Not seeing Jennifer was far worse than having her around. He missed her. His grandfather noticed his preoccupation and mentioned it to him one evening as they watched the horses prance in the corral.

"It is the white woman, is it not?" Grandfather Sanchez Owl asked in Apache.

"Yes," Hunter replied, too sad to prevaricate.

"Go to her," he was advised.

Hunter's hands tightened on the corral. "I cannot. She could never live here."

"If she loved you, she could." He touched the younger man's shoulder. "Your mother never loved your father. She found him unique and she collected him, as a man collects fine horses. When his uniqueness began to pale, she left him. It is the way of things. There was no love to begin with."

"You never told me this."

Grandfather's broad shoulders rose and fell. "It was not necessary. Now it is. This woman...she loves you?"

Hunter stared out over the corral. "She did. But I have done my best to make her hate me."

"Love is a gift. One should not throw it away."

Hunter glanced at him. "I thought that I could not give up my freedom. I thought that she, like my mother, would betray me."

"A man should think with his heart, not his head, when he loves," the old man said quietly. "You do love, do you not?"

Hunter looked away, wounded inside, aching as he thought of Jennifer's soft eyes promising heaven, remembered the feel of her chaste body in his arms, loving him. He closed his eyes. "Yes," he said huskily, fiercely. "Yes, I love!"

"Then go back before it is too late."

"She is white!" Hunter ground out.

The old man smiled. "So are you, in your thinking. It is something you do not want to face, but you are as comfortable in the white man's world as you are here. Probably more so, because your achievements are there and not here. A man can live with a foot in two worlds. You have proven it."

"It wouldn't be fair to a child," he said slowly.

The old man chuckled. "A man should have a son," he said. "Many sons. Many daughters. If they are loved, they will find a place in life. This white woman...is she handsome?"

Hunter saw her face as clearly as if she were standing beside him. "She is sunset on the desert," he said quietly. "The first bloom on the cactus. She is the silence of night and the beauty of dawn."

The old man's eyes grew misty with memory. "If she is all those things," he replied, "then you are a fool."

Hunter looked over at him. "Yes, I am." He moved away from the fence. "I am, indeed!"

He caught a plane that very afternoon. All the way to Tulsa, he prayed silently that he wasn't going to be too late. There was every chance that Jennifer had taken him seriously and found someone else. If she had, he didn't know how he was going to cope. He should have listened to his heart in the first place. If he'd lost her, he'd never forgive himself.

To say that Eugene was shocked to see him was an understatement. The old man sat at his desk and gaped when Hunter came into the office.

"I sent you to Phoenix," he said.

"I came back," Hunter returned curtly. "Jennifer isn't here. Where is she?"

Eugene's eyebrows arched. "Don't tell me you care, one way or the other?"

The dark face hardened visibly. "Where is she?"

"At her apartment, taking a well-earned vacation."

"I see."

Eugene narrowed one eye. "Before you get any ideas, she's been seeing one of the other geologists."

Hunter felt his breath stop in his throat. His dark eyes cut into Eugene's. "Has she?"

"Don't hurt her any more than you already have," the old man said, suddenly stern and as icy as his security chief had ever been.

"She's just beginning to get over you. Leave her alone. Let her heal."

Something in Hunter wavered. He stared down at the carpeted floor, feeling uncertain for the first time in memory. "This geologist...is it serious?"

"I don't know. They've been dating for a couple of weeks. She's a little brighter than she has been, a little less brittle."

Hunter's hands clenched in his pockets. He looked up. "Is she well?" he asked huskily.

"She's better than she was just after you left," Eugene said noncommittally. He eyed the younger man quietly. "You've said often enough that you hated white woman. You finally convinced her. What do you want now—to torment her some more?"

Hunter averted his face and stared out the window. "My mother was white," he said after a minute, and felt rather than saw Eugene's surprise. "She walked out on my father when I was five. I thought she didn't love him enough to stay, but my grandfather said that she never loved him at all. It...made a difference in the way I looked at things. To ask a woman to marry a different culture, to accept a foreign way of life, is no small thing. But where love exists, perhaps hope does, too."

Eugene softened. "You love her."

Hunter turned back to him. "Yes," he said simply. "Life without her is no life at all. Whatever the risk, it can't be as bad as the past few months have been."

The older man smiled. He picked up a sheaf of papers and tossed them across the desk. "There's your excuse. Tell her I sent those for her to look over."

Hunter took them, staring at the old man. "Have I killed what she felt?" he asked quietly. "Does she speak of me at all?"

Eugene sighed. "To be honest, no, she doesn't. Whatever her feelings, she keeps them to herself. I'm afraid I can't tell you anything. You'll have to go and find out for yourself."

He nodded. After a minute, he went out and closed the door quietly behind him. He wondered if Jennifer would even speak to him. Whether she'd be furiously angry or cold and unapproachable, remembering the brutal things he'd said to her when they parted.

All the way to her apartment, he refused to allow himself to think about it. But when he pressed the doorbell, he found that he was holding his breath.

11

Jennifer left her dishes in the sink and went to answer the doorbell, a little irritated at the interruption. She'd spent the past few months in such misery that she was only beginning to get her head above water again. Missing Hunter had become a way of life, despite the fact that she'd started dating a very nice divorced geologist in her group. And if he did spend the whole of their evenings together talking about his ex-wife, what did that matter? Didn't she spend them talking about Hunter and things they'd done together?

She opened the door, and froze. So many lonely nights, dreaming of that hard, dark face, and here he stood. She felt her insides melting at just the sight of him, feeding on it like a starving woman.

She stared up at him with a helpless rapture in her eyes, the old warm vulnerability in her face. It had been so long since she'd seen him. The anguish of the time between lay helplessly in her face as she looked at him. He watched her with equal intensity. His dark eyes held hers for an endless, shattering moment before they slid down her thin body and back up again. She looked as if she was shattered to find him on her doorstep, but at least she wasn't actively hostile. He measured her against his memories for one long moment.

"You can't afford to lose this kind of weight," he said softly. "Are you all right?"

His concern was almost her undoing. She had to fight tears at the tenderness in his voice. She forced a smile. Act, girl, she told herself. You can do it. You did it before, when it was even harder. He's surely here on business, so don't throw yourself at his feet.

"I've been on a diet," she lied. "Come in and I'll brew some coffee. How are you?"

He stepped into the apartment, looking and feeling alien in it. His eyes were restless, wandering around. Her apartment reflected her personality and her life-style. There were souvenirs from her travels everywhere, along with the sunny colors that echoed her own personality, and the numerous whimsical objects she delighted in. Potted plants covered every inch of available space, and ferns and green plants trailed down from high shelves. There were Indian accents, too, including a war shield and some basketry. His eyes lingered on those. Apache. He smiled gently.

She saw where his gaze had fallen and tried to divert him. "My dad says it looks like a jungle in here, but I like green things," she said, leading him into the kitchen. She tugged nervously at her yellow tank top. "How have you been? Is this a business call? Did Eugene want me for something? I'm just off for this week, but I guess...!"

"Eugene wanted me to drop some papers off for you," he said, drawing them out of his inside jacket pocket. He dropped them onto the kitchen table. "Something about a new rock formation one of your colleagues wants to check out." He pulled out a chair and straddled it, his eyes narrowing as he watched her make coffee. "I thought you might go back into the field after I left. What happened?"

"I've decided I like desk work," she said. It was a bald-faced lie, but he couldn't be told that. "I'm getting too old for fieldwork. Twenty-eight next birthday," she added with a smile.

"I know." He leaned his chin on his dark hands, clasped on the high back of the chair. "Still alone?" he pursued.

"There's a nice man in my office. Divorced, two kids. We...go out together." She glanced at him. "You?"

The geologist made him angry. Jealous. His dark eyes glittered and he found a weapon of his own. "There's a widow who lives next door to my grandfather, on the reservation. No kids. She's a great cook. No alarming habits."

"And she's Apache," she said for him on a bitter, painful laugh.

"Yes," he bit off. "She's Apache. No complications. No social barriers. No adjustments."

"Good for you. Going to marry her?"

He pulled out a cigarette and lit it without answering. The snub made her nervous.

She got down coffee cups and filled them. "Are you going to take off your coat, or is it glued on?"

He chuckled in spite of himself, shedding the expensive raincoat. She took it from him and carried it into the bedroom, to drape it carefully over the foot of her bed. A few minutes, that was all she had to get through. Then he'd go away, and she could again begin to try to get over him.

She went back into the kitchen, all smiles and courtesy and they talked about everything in the world except themselves. No matter what tactics he used to draw her out about her feelings, she parried them neatly. He was beginning to believe Eugene, that she had no feelings left for him. And he had only himself to blame, he knew. He'd deliberately tried to hurt her, to chase her away. The fact that his motives had been good ones at the time counted for nothing. He felt empty and alone. He knew he was going to feel that way for the rest of his life. He'd almost certainly lost her. She talked about the fellow geologist as though he'd become her world.

He put out his second cigarette and glanced at his watch. "I've got to go," he said in a voice without expression.

"Another overseas assignment, no doubt," she tried to sound cheery.

"Internal," he replied. He glanced at her. "I've given up field-work, too. I lost the taste for it."

That was surprising. He didn't seem the type to thrive on a desk job. But then, she'd thought she wasn't the type, either. She managed. Probably the widow didn't want him in a dangerous job anymore, and he'd given it up for her sake. The thought made her sick.

"I'll get your coat," she said, smiling. Her face would be frozen in its assumed position by the time he left, she thought ruefully.

She picked up his coat from the bed. This would be the last time. He'd marry the widow and she'd never see him again. She'd lost him for good now. She drew his coat slowly to her breasts and cradled it against her, tears clogging her eyes, her throat. She brought it to her lips and kissed it with breathless tenderness, bending her head over it with a kind of pain she'd never felt before in her life. It held the faint scent of the cologne he wore, of the tobacco he smoked. It smelled of him, and the touch of it was precious. She was losing him forever. She didn't know how she was going to live.

She straightened, feeling old and alone, wondering how she was going to go back in there and pretend that it didn't matter about his widow. That the past few months had been happy and full. That her life was fine without him in it.

In the other room, the man who'd happened to glance toward her bedroom had seen something reflected in the mirror facing the door that froze him where he stood. Her lighthearted act had convinced him that she didn't care, that she never had. But that woman holding his coat loved him. The emotion he saw in her face would haunt him forever, humble him every time he remembered the anguish in those soft blue eyes. She wasn't happy without him. He knew now that she'd been pretending ever since he'd walked into the apartment. She'd only been putting on an act about not caring, to hide her real feelings. He grimaced, thinking how close a call it had been. If he'd taken her act for granted and left, his life would never have been the same.

He caught his breath and turned away. All his former arguments about the reasons they were better apart vanished in an agony of need. If he walked out that door, she was going to die. If not physically, surely emotionally. She loved him that much. He loved her that much, too. It was vaguely frightening, to love to that degree. But even with the obstacles, they were going to make it. He'd never been more certain of anything in his life.

He took the coat from her when she rejoined him, her mask firmly in place again. She couldn't know that he'd seen her through the mirror, so he didn't let on. He wanted to see how far she was willing to go with the charade, if she could keep it up until he walked out. Now that he knew how she felt, it was like anticipating a Christmas present that was desperately wanted.

"It was nice to see you again," she said as she went with him to the door.

"Same here." He opened the door and stood silhouetted in it,

with his long back to her, looking alien and somehow unapproachable. "You haven't said whether you were glad to see me,
Jennifer," he said quietly, without turning.

She lowered her eyes to the floor. "It's always good to see
old…friends, Phillip."

He drew in his breath sharply. The sound of his name in her soft
voice brought back unbearable memories. "Were we ever friends?"

"No. Not really. I'm…I'm glad…about your widow, I mean,"
she said, unable to conceal a faint note of bitter anguish in her tone.

He sighed, still with his back to her. "The widow just turned
eighty-two. She's my godmother."

Her heart jumped. She took a steadying breath. "The divorced
man only takes me out so he can talk about his ex-wife. He still
loves her."

He turned. He shook his head, the light in his eyes disturbing,
humbling. "Oh, God, what a close call we had! You little idiot, do
you really think I came here on business?" He held out his arms
and she went into them. And just that quickly, that easily, the obstacles were pushed aside, the loneliness of the past gone forever.

He bent to her mouth and hers answered it. She moaned, shuddering, her control gone forever.

He lifted his head, and had to fight her clinging arms. "I'm
going to close and lock the door, that's all," he whispered shakily,
reaching out to do it. "I don't want the neighbors to watch us make
love."

"Are we going to?" she asked helplessly.

He nodded. "Oh, yes," he said fervently. He bent, lifting her in
his arms. "I love you," he whispered at her lips, watching the soft,
incredulous wonder grow in her face as he said it. "And now I'm
going to prove it physically, in the intimacy of lovemaking. At least

I won't have to hurt you, will I, little one?" he asked, smiling gently at the memory of that night in his house.

She clung to him, shivering helplessly, her face buried in the heated skin of his throat. "You won't give me a child, ever, will you?" she whimpered.

His breath caught. He paused at the bedroom door, meeting her sad, hungry eyes. He started to speak, failed. He looked down at her mouth. "I won't...use anything, if you like," he whispered. His eyes went back up to hers, lost in their shocked delight. "It's all right," he said, his voice tender. "A child...will be all right."

She was crying. He undressed her gently, but she couldn't even see him through her tears. She loved him. He loved her. There would be children and years of being together, wherever they chose to live. On the reservation, off it, in the desert, anywhere at all.

She said so, seeing him come down on the bed beside her, a blur of mahogany skin and lean muscle.

"Say the words while I'm loving you," he whispered, his lips slow and tender on her yielded body.

"The...words?" she echoed, arching as his mouth pressed down on her flat belly.

"That you love me," he said lazily. "I said it, but you didn't."

"How could you not know?" she moaned achingly. "I offered myself every time you looked at me. I did everything but wear a button.... Oh!" She stiffened as his mouth touched her in an unexpected way.

He lifted his head, his eyes darkly smoldering. "Do you want that?" he whispered.

She almost didn't answer him. She had a feeling that the experienced women he'd known had expected it, and an equally strong feeling that it was something he'd do for her sake, but never for his own.

She sat up, touching his lean face lovingly. "If you want it," she whispered. "I…" Her eyes fell to his chest, and further. She caught her breath at the sight of him. "I'll do anything you want me to."

He tilted her eyes back up to his. "Is it something you want?"

She shook her head. "I'm sorry…"

"Sorry!" He laughed with soft delight and caught her close, his mouth rough on her bare shoulder. "I'm as old-fashioned as you are, in some ways. Not really modern enough for this day and age. But if you want that kind of intimacy, you can have it."

"Maybe someday," she whispered. "When I'm less inhibited." She flushed. "Right now, all of it is a little scary…"

He lifted his head and his dark eyes searched hers. "We'll sit up this time, and you can control when it happens."

She went scarlet. He brushed her mouth with his. "Don't be shy," he whispered into her lips. "It's as new to me as it is to you, to make love and be in love. I don't want to make it disappointing for you."

"It could never be that," she said gently. "Not with you."

"Try to remember that it's an art, like any other," he said, brushing back her hair. "It isn't perfection at first. It may be uncomfortable despite what we did in my bed that night, and there may not be much pleasure in it for you. I can make it up to you afterward." He drew in a slow breath. "I've been without a woman for a long time, and my body isn't always mine to control. I'll hold back as long as I can…."

His anguish made her feel protective. She lifted her lips to his face and kissed his eyes closed, loving the newness of being in love, of being loved in return, of being wanted. "Whatever you do to me will be all right," she whispered. "Love me, now, please. Teach me."

"God, what a thing to tempt a man with," he groaned. He eased her down on the bed, and his mouth found her with aching expertness. He kissed and touched and teased until the flames were blazing in her slender body, until she was crying and twisting up to his mouth and hurting with her need of him.

She was only dimly aware when he moved, sitting back against the headboard with her body over his. He lifted her, his hands faintly tremulous, and positioned her so that she felt him suddenly in stark, hot intimacy.

Her eyes dilated, looking straight into his. He took her hands and placed them on his hips.

"Now," he whispered.

She hesitated, but the strain in his face made her realize the torment he was enduring for her sake. She bit her lower lip and pushed. To her amazement, there was only a little discomfort, but not pain. She gasped.

He smiled gently, even through his excitement. "Yes," he whispered. "I thought it might be so. There's nothing to be afraid of now."

His hands settled, warm and hard on her hips. He whispered to her, something that made her body shiver, something so intimate that she gasped and her blood surged in her veins. And at that moment, his hands jerked mercilessly and she felt the white-hot fury of sudden pleasure biting into her.

He rolled over with her, still a part of her body, his voice whispering, coaxing. His mouth brushed against hers, his lips tender, his hands touching her. His mouth settled gently on hers and he began to move, very slowly.

She jerked helplessly. "Phillip!" she exclaimed as the sudden pleasure made her rigid.

"Hold on," he murmured against her mouth. "I'm going to make you want me so badly that you'll fly in my arms. Bite me. That's it, bite me!" he whispered fiercely.

She'd dreamed of a tender, slow initiation with moonbeams and pink clouds. Instead, it was like a vicious fever with pleasure so throbbing and fierce and merciless that she became wanton.

Her nails bit into him, like her teeth. He pushed her down into the mattress with the rough thrust of his body and she arched up to receive it, her legs tangling in his. She looked up at him, her eyes fastened to his, her breath gasping out as his face moved closer and then away, and the mattress rose and fell noisily.

"Look down," he said under his breath.

She did, too lost in him to be shy anymore. He looked, too, and when her eyes met his, passion was smoldering in them.

"Show me where, Jennifer," he whispered, moving her hands to his hips. "Teach me where you feel the most pleasure when I move."

She flushed, but she obeyed him, guided his body, and cried out when he followed her lead. And then it all seemed to explode at once. His movements were rough and quick, his powerful body strong enough for both of them, his hands controlling her wild thrashing, holding her down, making her submit. His mouth crushed into hers and she heard his tortured breathing, his harsh groans, as the pleasure arched him into her body.

Incredibly she went with him. Soaring. Up into the sun. Shivering with cold and heat so intricately mingled that she was only living as part of him. She was saying something, but she couldn't hear her own voice.

When she opened her eyes again, there was a new kind of lassitude in her limbs. They felt numb and boneless, like the rest of her body. She could breathe again. Her heartbeat was almost normal.

A dark, loving pair of eyes came into view above her. "That," he whispered, "is the sweetest expression of love I'll ever experience in my life. You're my woman."

"Yes." She said it with shy pride, because now it was over. The mystery was gone, but the magic remained. She touched his mouth, fascinated. "Will I get pregnant from it?" she whispered.

He smiled lazily. "I hope so," he whispered. "Creation should be like this, from seed so exquisitely planted in love. Now do you understand what I meant, about not making a casual entertainment out of something so profound? The ultimate glory of lovemaking is the act of creation." He bent and kissed her with rapt tenderness. "I want to plant my seed in you. If we can make a baby together, even if he is a product of two worlds, I want to."

She clung to him, her mouth ardent and loving. "So do I," she whispered huskily. "Oh, so do I! I love you."

"I love you just as much," he said with fierce possession. He was surprised at how quickly his body responded when he kissed her, at the kindling passion that bound them together almost at once.

"No, don't stop," she whispered when he hesitated.

"It's too soon…"

"No!" She pulled him down to her and put her mouth hungrily against his and felt him shudder. She opened her eyes as his body slid over hers and they melted together with delicious ease.

"You see?" she whispered shakily. "It's so easy now."

"So easy." He smiled tenderly and his mouth bent to hers. He bit at it, very gently, and his body echoed that tenderness, his arms enfolding hers. He rolled abruptly onto his side and smiled at her surprise. "That night in Washington, I wanted to do it like this, remember? Now we can. Put this leg over mine, here," he guided softly. "Now, like this…!"

She watched his face contort as his hand brought her hips

suddenly against his. It was fascinating to watch him, to see the passion kindle and ignite.

"Jennifer, you're staring," he whispered.

"I know. I want to watch you," she whispered back, her eyes wide and soft and curious. "Is it all right if I look?"

He shuddered. Her fascination with his pleasure brought it all too soon. His body buckled and began to shudder. He felt the familiar tension building to flashpoint, hamstringing him, racking him. He looked into her eyes and felt her hands shyly tugging at his hips and he cried out.

Convulsions of unbearable pleasure ripped through him. He was aware at some level of her stare, of her scarlet face as she saw him experience fulfillment. It made it all the more shattering. He was helpless and she was seeing him this way, but it didn't matter. Nothing mattered. He was burning. Burning. Burning!

He cried out, his body rippling beside hers. She pressed into his arms and helped him, loving the fury of his hands gripping her hips, loving the unbridled pleasure she saw in his face. He was truly hers, now. Completely hers. She shivered, amazed that his own satisfaction caused her body to fulfill itself in one long, hot wave of shuddering pleasure.

Long afterward, they slept. When she woke at last, it was to the smell of something delicious cooking in the kitchen. She got up and dressed, slowly, with the memory of what had happened like a candle in her mind.

Phillip was standing at the stove cooking steak. He was wearing only the trousers from his suit. His chest and feet were bare. He glanced up as she joined him, and his eyes were warm and tender.

"Are you hungry?" he asked, opening one arm to draw her to him and kiss her softly.

"A little," she whispered. Her eyes met his. "Do you really love me?"

"With all my heart," he whispered back, his eyes punctuating the words. "Life without you is no life, Jennifer. You'll have to get used to having an Apache husband."

"You want to marry me?" she asked, holding her breath.

He put down the fork he was using to turn the steak and brought her against him, bending to kiss her with fierce hunger. "Of course I want to marry you!" he said impatiently, when he lifted his head. "I always did. But the memory of how it was for my mother colored my whole life. Until my grandfather told me the truth—that my father was only a conversation piece for her; that she never loved him. He sent me to you," he added huskily. "He said that I was a fool."

She smiled gently. "No. Just a man afraid to trust. But I'll never hurt you, my darling," she said, sliding her arms around him, laying her blond head on his bare chest. "I'll give you children and live with you anywhere you say."

"Your job..." he began.

"Geology isn't something you forget. I'll have babies for a few years, then when they're in school, I'll work out of the Tucson or Phoenix offices. Eugene won't fire me completely."

His lean hands stilled on her back. "I can't let you make that kind of sacrifice for me."

She lifted her head. "You gave up fieldwork," she replied. "And I know how much you loved it. You did that because of me, didn't you?"

"Yes," he admitted finally. "I didn't want the risk. I was thinking about how it would be for you and the children while I was away."

She smiled with pure delight. "Me and the children," she

mused. "And yet you went away swearing that you wanted nothing to do with me."

"Lying through my teeth," he added with a dry chuckle. "I drove my grandfather crazy."

She reached up and touched his thick, dark eyebrows. "We're so different in coloring. I wonder if our children will look like you or me?"

"I hope they'll look like both of us," he replied. "My grandfather said that I was living proof that a man can have a foot in two worlds." He smiled at her. "He doesn't like whites, as a rule, but he'll like you."

"My parents will like you," she returned.

He frowned. "Are you sure?"

"Well, I did just happen to tell them about you a few thousand times over the past few years, and I had this picture that I begged out of the personnel files. My mother thought you were striking, and my father was sure you'd be able to keep me out of dangerous places if I ever married you."

"They don't mind the cultural differences?" he stressed.

"They raised me with a mind of my own and let me use it," she replied. "They're not rigid people, as you'll see when you meet them. They're very educated people with tolerant personalities. Besides all that, they want grandchildren."

"I see. That was the selling point, was it?" he murmured.

"Yes, it was. So we'd better set a date and get busy."

He bent and kissed her, ignoring the smell of burning steak. "How does next Friday suit you?" he asked.

"Just fine." She kissed him back, smiling. The steak went right on burning, and nobody noticed until it was the color of tar and the texture of old leather. Which was just as well, because they were in too much of a hurry to get to the courthouse for a marriage license to worry about food, anyway.

* * * * *

MAN IN CONTROL

PROLOGUE

꿈꿈꿈

Alexander Tyrell Cobb glared at his desk in the Houston Drug Enforcement Administration office with barely contained frustration. There was a photograph of a lovely woman in a ball gown in an expensive frame, the only visible sign of any emotional connections. Like the conservative clothes he wore to work, the photograph gave away little of the private man.

The photograph was misleading. The woman in it wasn't a close friend. She was a casual date, when he was between assignments. The frame had been given to him with the photo in it. He'd never put a woman's photo in a frame. Well, except for Jodie Clayburn. She and his sister, Margie, were best friends from years past. Most of the family photos he had included Jodie. She wasn't really family, of course. But there was no other Cobb family left, just as there was no other Clayburn family left. The three survivors of the two families were a forced mixture of different lifestyles.

Jodie was in love with Alexander. He knew it, and tried not to acknowledge it. She was totally wrong for him. He had no desire to marry and have a family. On the other hand, if he'd been seri-

ously interested in children and a home life, Jodie would have been
at the top of his list of potential mates. She had wonderful quali-
ties. He wasn't about to tell her so. She'd been hung up on him in
the past to a disturbing degree. He'd managed to keep her at arm's
length, and he had no plans to lessen the space between them. He
was married to his job.

Jodie, on the other hand, was an employee at a local oil corporation which was being used in an international drug smuggling
operation. Alexander was almost certain of it. But he couldn't
prove it. He was going to have to find some way to investigate one
of Jodie's acquaintances without letting anyone realize they were
being watched.

In the meantime, there was a party planned at the Cobb ranch in
Jacobsville, Texas, on Saturday. He dreaded it already. He hated
parties. Margie had already invited Jodie, probably because their
housekeeper, Jessie, refused to work that weekend. Jodie cooked
with a masterful hand, and she could make canapés. Kirry had been
invited, too, because Margie was a budding dress designer who
needed a friend in the business. Kirry was senior buyer for the department store where she worked. She was pretty and capable, but
Alexander found her good company and not much more. Their relationship had always been lukewarm and even now, it was slowly
fizzling out. She was demanding. He had enough demands on the job.

He put the picture facedown on his desk and pulled a file folder
closer, opening it to the photograph of a suspected drug smuggler
who was working out of Houston. He had his work cut out for him.
He wished he could avoid going home for the party, but Margie
would never forgive him. If he didn't show up, neither would Kirry,
and Alexander would never hear the end of it. He put the weekend
to the back of his mind and concentrated on the job at hand.

1

There was no way out of it. Margie Cobb had invited her to a party on the family ranch in Jacobsville, Texas. Jodie Clayburn had gone through her entire repertoire of excuses. Her favorite was that, given the right incentive, Margie's big brother, Alexander Tyrell Cobb, would feed her to his cattle. Not even that one had worked.

"He hates me, Margie," she groaned over the phone from her apartment in Houston, Texas. "You know he does. He'd be perfectly happy if I stayed away from him for the rest of my natural life and he never had to see me again."

"That's not true," Margie defended. "Lex really likes you, I know he does," she added with forced conviction, using the nickname that only a handful of people on earth were allowed to use. Jodie wasn't one of them.

"Right. He just hides his affection for me in bouts of bad temper laced with sarcasm," came the dry reply.

"Sure," Margie replied with failing humor.

Jodie lay back on her sofa with the freedom phone at her ear and pushed back her long blond hair. It was getting too long. She really needed to have it cut, but she liked the feel of it. Her gray eyes smiled as she remembered how much Brody Vance liked long hair. He worked at the Ritter Oil Corporation branch office in Houston with her, and was on the management fast track. As Jody was. She was administrative assistant to Brody, and if Brody had his way, she'd take his job as Human Resources generalist when he moved up to Human Resources manager. He liked her. She liked him, too. Of course he had a knockout girlfriend who was a Marketing Division manager in Houston, but she was always on the road somewhere. He was lonely. So he had lunch frequently with Jodie. She was trying very hard to develop a crush on him. He was beginning to notice her. Alexander had accused her of trying to sleep her way to the executive washroom...

"I was not!" she exclaimed, remembering his unexpected visit to her office with an executive of the company who was a personal friend. It had played havoc with her nerves and her heart. Seeing Alexander unexpectedly melted her from the neck down, despite her best efforts not to let him affect her.

"Excuse me?" Margie replied, aghast.

Jodie sat up quickly. "Nothing!" she said. "Sorry. I was just thinking. Did you know that Alexander has a friend who works for my company?"

There was a long pause. "He does?"

"Jasper Duncan, the Human Resources manager for our division."

"Oh. Yes. Jasper!" There was another pause. "How do you know about that?"

"Because Mr. Duncan brought him right to my desk while I was talking to a...well, to a good friend of mine, my boss."

"Right, the one he thinks you're sleeping with."

"Margie!" she exploded.

There was an embarrassed laugh. "Sorry. I know there's nothing going on. Alexander always thinks the worst of people. You know about Rachel."

"Everybody knows about Rachel," she muttered. "It was six years ago and he still throws her up to us."

"We did introduce him," Margie said defensively.

"Well, how were we to know she was a female gigolo who was only interested in marrying a rich man? She should have had better sense than to think Alexander would play that sort of game, anyway!"

"You do know him pretty well, don't you?" Margie murmured.

"We all grew up together in Jacobsville, Texas," Jodie reminded her. "Sort of," she added pensively. "Alexander was eight years ahead of us in school, and then he moved to Houston to work for the DEA when he got out of college."

"He's still eight years ahead of us," Margie chuckled. "Come on. You know you'll hate yourself if you miss this party. We're having a houseful of people. Derek will be there," she added sweetly, trying to inject a lure.

Derek was Margie's distant cousin, a dream of a man with some peculiar habits and a really weird sense of humor.

"You know what happened the last time Derek and I were together," Jodie said with a sense of foreboding.

"Oh, I'm sure Alexander has forgotten about *that* by now," she was assured.

"He has a long memory. And Derek can talk me into anything," Jodie added worriedly.

"I'll hang out with both of you and protect you from danger-ous impulses. Come on. Say yes. I've got an opportunity to show my designs. It depends on this party going smoothly. And I've made up this marvelous dress pattern I want to try out on you. For someone with the body of a clotheshorse, you have no sense of style at all!"

"You have enough for both of us. You're a budding fashion designer. I'm a lady executive. I have to dress the part."

"Baloney. When was the last time your boss wore a black dress to a party?"

Jodie was remembering a commercial she'd seen on television with men in black dresses. She howled, thinking of Alexander's hairy legs in a short skirt. Then she tried to imagine where he'd keep his sidearm in a short skirt, and she really howled.

She told Margie what she was thinking, and they both collapsed into laughter.

"Okay," she capitulated at last. "I'll come. But if I break a tree limb over your brother's thick skull, you can't say you weren't forewarned."

"I swear, I won't say a word."

"Then I'll see you Friday afternoon about four," Jodie said with resignation. "I'll rent a car and drive over."

"Uh, Jodie…"

She groaned. "All right, Margie, all right, I'll fly to the Jacobs-ville airport and you can pick me up there."

"Great!"

"Just because I had two little bitty fender benders," she muttered.

"You totaled two cars, Jodie, and Alexander had to bail you out of jail after the last one…"

"Well, that stupid thickheaded barbarian deserved to be hit! He called me a…well, never mind, but he asked for a punch in the mouth!" Jodie fumed.

Margie was trying not to laugh. Again.

"Anyway, it was only a small fine and the judge took my side when he heard the whole story," she said, ignoring Margie's quick reminder that Alexander had talked to the judge first. "Not that your brother ever let me forget it! Just because he works for the Justice Department is no reason for him to lecture me on law!"

"We just want you to arrive alive, darling," Margie drawled. "Now throw a few things into a suitcase, tell your boss you have a sick cousin you have to take care of before rush hour, and we'll... I'll...meet you at the airport Friday afternoon. You phone and tell me your flight number, okay?"

"Okay," Jodie replied, missing the slip.

"See you then! We're going to have a ball."

"Sure we are," Jodie told her. But when she hung up, she was calling herself all sorts of names for being such a weakling. Alexander was going to cut her up, she just knew it. He didn't like her. He never had. He'd gotten more antagonistic since she moved to Houston, where he worked, too. Further, it would probably mean a lot of work for Jodie, because she usually had to prepare meals if she showed up. The family cook, Jessie, hated being around Alexander when he was home, so she ran for the hills. Margie couldn't cook at all, so Jodie usually ended up with KP. Not that she minded. It was just that she felt used from time to time.

And despite Margie's assurances, she knew she was in for the fight of her life once she set foot on the Cobb ranch. At least Margie hadn't said anything about inviting Alexander's sometimes-girlfriend, Kirry Dane. A weekend with the elegant buyer for an exclusive Houston department store would be too much.

The thing was, she had to go when Margie asked her. She owed the Cobbs so much. When her parents, small Jacobsville ranchers, had been drowned in a riptide during a modest Florida vacation at the beach, it had been Alexander who flew down to take care of all the arrangements and comfort a devastated seventeen-year-old Jodie. When she entered business college, Alexander had gone with her to register and paid the fees himself. She spent every holiday with Margie. Since the death of the Cobbs' father, and their inheritance of the Jacobsville ranch property, she'd spent her vacation every summer there with Margie. Her life was so intertwined with that of the Cobbs that she couldn't even imagine life without them.

But Alexander had a very ambiguous relationship with Jodie. From time to time he was affectionate, in his gruff way. But he also seemed to resent her presence and he picked at her constantly. He had for the past year.

She got up and went to pack, putting the antagonism to the back of her mind. It did no good to dwell on her confrontations with Alexander. He was like a force of nature which had to be accepted, since it couldn't be controlled.

The Jacobsville Airport was crowded for a Friday afternoon. It was a tiny airport compared to those in larger cities, but a lot of people in south Texas used it for commuter flights to San Antonio and Houston. There was a restaurant and two concourses, and the halls were lined with beautiful paintings of traditional Texas scenery.

Jodie almost bowed under the weight of her oversized handbag and the unruly carry-on bag whose wheels didn't quite work. She looked around for Margie. The brunette wouldn't be hard to spot because she was tall for a woman, and always wore something striking—usually one of her own flamboyant designs.

But she didn't see any tall brunettes. What she did see, and what stopped her dead in her tracks, was a tall and striking dark-haired man in a gray vested business suit. A man with broad shoulders and narrow hips and big feet in hand-tooled leather boots. He turned, looking around, and spotted her. Even at the distance, those deep-set, cold green eyes were formidable. So was he. He looked absolutely furious.

She stood very still, like a woman confronted with a spitting cobra, and waited while he approached her with the long, quick stride she remembered from years of painful confrontations. Her chin lifted and her eyes narrowed. She drew in a quick breath, and geared up for combat.

Alexander Tyrell Cobb was thirty-three. He was a senior agent for the Drug Enforcement Administration. Usually, he worked out of Houston, but he was on vacation for a week. That meant he was at the family ranch in Jacobsville. He'd grown up there, with Margie, but their mother had taken them from their father after the divorce and had them live with her in Houston. It hadn't been until her death that they'd finally been allowed to return home to their father's ranch. The old man had loved them dearly. It had broken his heart when he'd lost them to their mother.

Alexander lived on the ranch sporadically even now, when he wasn't away on business. He also had an apartment in Houston. Margie lived at the ranch all the time, and kept things running smoothly while her big brother was out shutting down drug smugglers.

He looked like a man who could do that single-handed. He had big fists, like his big feet, and Jodie had seen him use them once on a man who slapped Margie. He rarely smiled. He had a temper like a scalded snake, and he was all business when he tucked that big .45 automatic into its hand-tooled leather holster and went out looking for trouble.

In the past two years, he'd been helping to shut down an international drug lord, Manuel Lopez, who'd died mysteriously in an explosion in the Bahamas. Now he was after the dead drug lord's latest successor, a Central American national who was reputed to have business connections in the port city of Houston.

She'd developed a feverish crush on him when she was in her teens. She'd written him a love poem. Alexander, with typical efficiency, had circled the grammatical and spelling errors and bought her a supplemental English book to help her correct the mistakes. Her self-esteem had taken a serious nosedive, and after that, she kept her deepest feelings carefully hidden.

She'd seen him only a few times since her move to Houston when she began attending business college. When she visited Margie these days, Alexander never seemed to be around except at Christmas. It was as if he'd been avoiding her. Then, just a couple of weeks ago, he'd dropped by her office to see Jasper. It had been a shock to see him unexpectedly, and her hands had trembled on her file folders, despite her best efforts to play it cool. She wanted to think she'd outgrown her flaming crush on him. Sadly, it had only gotten worse. It was easier on her nerves when she didn't have to see him. Fortunately it was a big city and they didn't travel in the same circles. But she didn't know where Alexander's office or apartment were, and she didn't ask.

In fact, her nerves were already on edge right now, just from the level, intent stare of those green eyes across a crowded concourse. She clutched the handle of her wheeled suitcase with a taut grip. Alexander made her knees weak.

He strode toward her. He never looked right or left. His gaze was right on her the whole way. She wondered if he was like that on the job, so intent on what he was doing that he seemed relentless.

He was a sexy beast, too. There was a tightly controlled sensuality in every movement of those long, powerful legs, in the way he carried himself. He was elegant, arrogant. Jodie couldn't remember a time in her life when she hadn't been fascinated by him. She hoped it didn't show. She worked hard at pretending to be his enemy.

He stopped in front of her and looked down his nose into her wide eyes. His were green, clear as water, with dark rims that made them seem even more piercing. He had thick black eyelashes and black eyebrows that were as black as his neatly cut, thick, straight hair.

"You're late," he said in his deep, gravelly voice, throwing down the gauntlet at once. He looked annoyed, half out of humor and wanting someone to bite.

"I can't fly the plane," she replied sarcastically. "I had to depend on *men* for that."

He gave her a speaking glance and turned. "The car's in the parking lot. Let's go."

"Margie was supposed to meet me," she muttered, dragging her case behind her.

"Margie knew I had to be here anyway, so she had me wait for you," he said enigmatically. "I never knew a woman who could keep an appointment, anyway."

The carry-on bag fell over for the tenth time. She muttered and finally just picked the heavy thing up. "You might offer to help me," she said, glowering at her companion.

His eyebrows arched. "Help a woman carry a heavy load? My God, I'd be stripped, lashed to a rail and carried through Houston by torchlight!"

She gave him a seething glance. "Manners don't go out of style!"

"Pity I never had any to begin with." He watched her struggle with the luggage, green eyes dancing with pure venom.

She was sweating already. "I hate you," she said through her teeth as she followed along with him.

"That's a change," he said with a shrug, pushing back his jacket as he dug into his slacks pocket for his car keys.

A security guard spotted the pistol on his belt and came forward menacingly. With meticulous patience, and very carefully, Alexander reached into the inside pocket of his suit coat and produced his badge and ID. He had it out before the guard reached them.

The man took it. "Wait a minute," he said, and moved aside to check it out over the radio.

"Maybe you're on a wanted list somewhere," Jodie said enthusiastically. "Maybe they'll put you in jail while they check out your ID!"

"If they do," he replied nonchalantly, "rent-a-cop over there will be looking for another job by morning."

He didn't smile as he said it, and Jodie knew he meant what he was saying. Alexander had a vindictive streak a mile wide. There was a saying among law enforcement people that Cobb would follow you all the way to hell to get you if you crossed him. From their years of uneasy acquaintance, she knew it was more than myth.

The security guard came back and handed Alexander his ID. "Sorry, sir, but it's my job to check out suspicious people."

Alexander glared at him. "Then why haven't you checked out the gentleman in the silk suit over there with the bulge in his hatband? He's terrified that you're going to notice him."

The security guard frowned and glanced toward the elegant man, who tugged at his collar. "Thanks for the tip," he murmured, and started toward the man.

"You might have offered to lend him your gun," she told Alexander.

"He's got one. Of a sort," he added with disgust at the pearl-handled sidearm the security guard was carrying.

"Men have to have their weapons, don't they?" she chided.

He gave her a quick glance. "With a mouth like yours, you don't need a weapon. Careful you don't cut your chin with that tongue."

She aimed a kick at his shin and missed, almost losing her balance.

"Assault on a law enforcement officer is a felony," he pointed out without even breaking stride.

She recovered her balance and went out the door after him without another word. If they ever suspended the rules for one day, she knew who she was going after!

Once they reached his car, an elegant white Jaguar S-type, he did put her bags in the trunk—but he left her to open her own door and get in. It wasn't surprising to find him driving such a car, on a federal agent's salary, because he and Margie were independently wealthy. Their late mother had left them both well-off, but unlike Margie, who loved the social life, Alexander refused to live on an inheritance. He enjoyed working for his living. It was one of many things Jodie admired about him.

The admiration didn't last long. He threw down the gauntlet again without hesitation. "How's your boyfriend?" he asked as he pulled out into traffic.

"I don't have a boyfriend!" she snapped, still wiping away sweat. It was hot for August, even in south Texas.

"No? You'd like to have one, though, wouldn't you?" He adjusted the rearview mirror as he stopped at a traffic light.

"He's my boss. That's all."

"Pity. You could hardly take your eyes off him, that day I stopped by your office."

"*He's* handsome," she said with deliberate emphasis.

His eyebrow jerked. "Looks don't get you promoted in the Drug Enforcement Administration," he told her.

"You'd know. You've worked for it half your life."

"Not quite half. I'm only thirty-three."

"One foot in the grave..."

He glanced at her. "You're twenty-five, I believe? And never been engaged?"

He knew that would hurt. She averted her gaze to the window. Until a few months ago, she'd been about fifty pounds overweight and not very careful about her clothing or makeup. She was still clueless about how to dress. She dressed like an overweight woman, with loose clothing that showed nothing of her pretty figure. She folded her arms over her breasts defensively.

"I can't go through with this," she said through her teeth. "Three days of you will put me in therapy!"

He actually smiled. "That would be worth putting up with three days of you to see."

She crossed her legs under her full skirt and concentrated on the road. Her eyes caressed the silky brown bird's-eye maple that graced the car's dash and steering wheel.

"Margie promised she'd meet me," she muttered, repeating herself.

"She told me you'd be thrilled if I did," he replied with a searing glance. "You're still hung up on me, aren't you?" he asked with faint sarcasm.

Her jaw fell. "She lied! I did not say I'd be thrilled for you to meet me!" she raged. "I only came because she promised that she'd be here when I landed. I wanted to rent a car and drive!"

His green eyes narrowed on her flushed face. "That would have been suicide," he murmured. "Or homicide, depending on your point of view."

"I can drive!"

"You and the demolition derby guys," he agreed. He accelerated around a slow-moving car and the powerful Jaguar growled like the big cat it was named for. She glanced at him and saw the pure joy of the car's performance in his face as he slid effortlessly back into the lane ahead of the slow car. He enjoyed fast cars and, gossip said, faster women. But that side of his life had always been concealed from Jodie. It was as if he'd placed her permanently off-limits and planned to keep her there.

"At least I don't humiliate other drivers by streaking past them at jet fighter speed!" she raged. She was all but babbling, and after only ten minutes of his company. Seething inwardly, she turned toward the window so that she wouldn't have to look at him.

"I wasn't streaking. I'm doing the speed limit," he said. He glanced at the speedometer, smiled faintly and eased up on the accelerator. His eyes slid over Jodie curiously. "You've lost so much weight, I hardly recognized you when I stopped by to talk to Jasper."

"Right. I looked different when I was fat."

"You were never fat," he shot back angrily. "You were voluptuous. There's a difference."

She glanced at him. "I was terribly overweight."

"And you think men like to run their hands over bones, do you?"

She shifted in her seat. "I wouldn't know."

"You had a low self-image. You still have it. There's nothing wrong with you. Except for that sharp tongue," he added.

"Look who's complaining!"

"If I don't yell, nobody listens."

"You never yell," she corrected. "You can look at people and make them run for cover."

He smiled without malice. "I practice in my bathroom mirror."

She couldn't believe she'd heard that.

"You need to start thinking about a Halloween costume," he murmured as he made a turn.

"For what? Are you going to hire me out for parties?" she muttered.

"For our annual Halloween party next month," he said with muted disgust. "Margie's invited half of Jacobsville to come over in silly clothes and masks to eat candy apples."

"What are you coming as?"

He gave her a careless glance. "A Drug Enforcement Agency field agent."

She rolled her eyes toward the ceiling of the car.

"I make a convincing DEA field agent," he persisted.

"I wouldn't argue with that," she had to agree. "I hear that Manuel Lopez mysteriously blew up in the Bahamas the year before last, and nobody's replaced him yet," she added. "Did you have anything to do with his sudden demise?"

"DEA agents don't blow up drug lords. Not even one as bad as Lopez."

"Somebody did."

He glanced at her with a faint smile. "In a manner of speaking."

"One of the former mercs from Jacobsville, I heard."

"Micah Steele was somewhere around when it happened. He's never been actually connected with Lopez's death."

"He moved back here and married Callie Kirby, didn't he? They have a little girl now."

He nodded. "He's practicing medicine at Jacobsville General as a resident, hoping to go into private practice when he finishes his last semester of study."

"Lucky Callie," she murmured absently, staring out the window. "She always wanted to get married and have kids, and she was crazy about Micah most of her life."

He watched her curiously. "Didn't you want to get married, too?"

She didn't answer. "So now that Lopez is out of the way, and nobody's replaced him, you don't have a lot to do, do you?"

He laughed shortly. "Lopez has a new successor, a Peruvian national living in Mexico on an open-ended visa. He's got colleagues in Houston helping him smuggle his product into the United States."

"Do you know who they are?" she asked excitedly.

He gave her a cold glare. "Oh, sure, I'm going to tell you their names right now."

"You don't have to be sarcastic, Cobb," she said icily.

One thick eyebrow jerked. "You're the only person I know, outside work, who uses my last name as if it were my first name."

"You don't use my real name, either."

"Don't I?" He seemed surprised. He glanced at her. "You don't look like a Jordana."

"I never thought I looked like a Jordana, either," she said with a sigh. "My mother loved odd names. She even gave them to the cats."

Remembering her mother made her sad. She'd lost both parents in a freak accident during a modest vacation in Florida after her high school graduation. Her parents had gone swimming in the ocean, having no idea that the pretty red flags on the beach warned of treacherous riptides that could drown even experienced swimmers. Which her mother and father were not. She could still remember the horror of it. Alexander had come to take care of the details, and to get her back home. Odd how many tragedies and crises he'd seen her through over the years.

"Your mother was a sweet woman," he recalled. "I'm sorry you lost her. And your father."

"He was a sweet man, too," she recalled. It had been eight years ago, and she could remember happy times now, but it still made her sad to think of them.

"Strange, isn't it, that you don't take after either of them?" he asked caustically. "No man in his right mind could call you 'sweet.'"

"Stop right there, Cobb," she threatened, using his last name again. It was much more comfortable than getting personal with the nickname Margie used for him. "I could say things about you, too."

"What? That I'm dashing and intelligent and the answer to a maiden's prayer?" He pursed his lips and glanced her way as he pulled into the road that led to the ranch. "Which brings up another question. Are you sleeping with that airheaded boss of yours at work yet?"

"He is not airheaded!" she exclaimed, offended.

"He eats tofu and quiche, he drives a red convertible of uncertain age, he plays tennis and he doesn't know how to program a computer without crashing the system."

That was far too knowledgeable to have come from a dossier. Her eyes narrowed. "You've had him checked out!" she accused with certainty.

He only smiled. It wasn't a nice smile.

2

❧❧❧❧❧❧

"You can't go around snooping into people's private lives like that," Jodie exclaimed heatedly. "It's not right!"

"I'm looking for a high-level divisional manager who works for the new drug lord in his Houston territory," he replied calmly. "I check out everybody who might have an inkling of what's going on." He turned his head slightly. "I even checked you out."

"Me?" she exclaimed.

He gave her a speaking look. "I should have known better. If I had a social life like yours, I'd join a convent."

"I can see you now, in long skirts…"

"It was a figure of speech," he said curtly. He pulled into the road that led up to the ranch house. "You haven't been on a date in two years. Amazing, considering how many eligible bachelors there are in your building alone, much less the whole of Houston." He gave her a penetrating stare. "Are you sure you aren't still stuck on me?"

She drew in a short breath. "Oh, sure, I am," she muttered. "I only come down here so that I can sit and moon over you and think of ways to poison all your girlfriends."

He chuckled in spite of himself. "Okay. I get the idea."

"Who in my building do you suspect, exactly?" she persisted.

He hesitated. His dark brows drew together in a frown as the ranch house came into view down the long, dusty road. "I can't tell you that," he said. "Right now it's only a suspicion."

"I could help you trap him," she volunteered. "If I get a gun, that is. I won't help you if I have to be unarmed."

He chuckled again. "You shoot like you drive, Jodie."

She made an angry sound in her throat. "I could shoot just fine if I got enough practice. Is it my fault that my landlord doesn't like us busting targets in my apartment building?"

"Have Margie invite you down just to shoot. She can teach you as well as I can."

It was an unpleasant reminder that he wasn't keen on being with her.

"I don't remember asking you to teach me anything," she returned.

He pulled up in front of the house. "Well, not lately, at least," he had to agree.

Margie heard the car drive up and came barreling out onto the porch. She was tall, like Alexander, and she had green eyes, too, but her dark hair had faint undertones of auburn. She was pretty, unlike poor Jodie, and she wore anything with flair. She designed and made her own clothes, and they were beautiful.

She ran to Jodie and hugged her, laughing. "I'm so glad you came!"

"I thought you were going to pick me up at the airport, Margie," came the droll reply.

Margie looked blank for an instant. "Oh, gosh, I was, wasn't I?

I got busy with a design and just lost all track of time. Besides, Lex had already gone to the airport to pick up Kirry, but she couldn't get his cell phone, so she phoned me and said she was delayed until tomorrow afternoon. He was right there already, so I just phoned him and had him bring you home."

Kirry was Alexander's current girlfriend. The fashion buyer had just returned home recently from a buying trip to Paris. It didn't occur to Margie that it would have been pure torture to have to ride to the ranch with Alexander and his girlfriend. But, then, Margie didn't think things through. And to give her credit, she didn't realize that Jodie was still crazy about Alexander Cobb.

"She's coming down tomorrow to look at some of my new designs," Margie continued, unabashed, "and, of course, for the party in her honor that we're giving here. She leads a very busy life."

Jodie felt her heart crashing at her feet, and she didn't dare show it. A weekend with Kirry Dane drooling over Alexander, and vice versa. Why hadn't she argued harder and stayed home?

Alexander checked his watch. "I've got to make a few phone calls, then I'm going to drive into town and see about that fencing I ordered."

"That's what we have a foreman for," Margie informed him.

"Chayce went home to Georgia for the weekend. His father's in the hospital."

"You didn't tell me that!"

"Did you need to know?" he shot right back.

Margie shook her head, exasperated, as he just walked away without a backward glance. "I do live here, too," she muttered, but it was too late. He'd already gone into the house.

"I'm going to be in the way if the party's for Kirry," Jodie said worriedly. "Honestly, Margie, you shouldn't have invited me. No wonder Alexander's so angry!"

"It's my house, too, and I can invite who I like," Margie replied curtly, intimating that she and Alexander had argued about Jodie's inclusion at the party. That hurt even more. "You're my best friend, Jodie, and I need an ego boost," Margie continued unabashed. "Kirry is so worldly and sophisticated. She hates it here and she makes me feel insecure. But I need her help to get my designs shown at the store where she works. So, you're my security blanket." She linked her arm with Jodie's. "Besides, Kirry and Lex together get on my nerves."

What about my nerves? Jodie was wondering. And my heart, having to see Alexander with Kirry all weekend? But she only smiled and pretended that it didn't matter. She was Margie's friend, and she owed her a lot. Even if it was going to mean eating her heart out watching the man she loved hang on to that beautiful woman, Kirry Dane.

Margie stopped just before they went into the house. She looked worried. "You have gotten over that crush you had on my brother...?" she asked quickly.

"You and your brother!" Jodie gasped. "Honestly, I'm too old for schoolgirl crushes," she lied through her teeth, "and besides, there's this wonderful guy at the office that I like a lot. It's just that he's going with someone."

Margie grimaced. "You poor kid. It's always like that with you, isn't it?"

"Go right ahead and step on my ego, don't mind me," Jodie retorted.

Margie flushed. "I'm a pig," she said. "Sorry, Jodie. I don't know what's the matter with me. Yes, I do," she added at once. "Cousin Derek arrived unexpectedly this morning. Jessie's already threatened to cook him up with a pan of eggs, and one of the cowboys ran a tractor through a fence trying to get away from him. In fact, Jessie remembered that she could have a weekend off whenever she wanted, so she's gone to Dallas for the weekend to see her brother. And here I am with no cook and a party tomorrow night!"

"Except me?" Jodie ventured, and her heart sank again when she saw Margie's face. No wonder she'd been insistent. There wouldn't be any food without someone to cook it, and Margie couldn't cook.

"You don't mind, do you, dear?" Margie asked quickly. "After all, you do make the most scrumptious little canapés, and you're a great cook. Even Jessie asks you for recipes."

"No," Jodie lied. "I don't mind."

"And you can help me keep Derek out of Alexander's way."

"Derek." Jodie's eyes lit up. She loved the Cobbs' renegade cousin from Oklahoma. He was a rodeo cowboy who won belts at every competition, six foot two of pure lithe muscle, with a handsome face and a modest demeanor—when he wasn't up to some horrible devilment. He drove housekeepers and cowboys crazy with his antics, and Alexander barely tolerated him. He was Margie's favorite of their few cousins. Not that he was really a cousin. He was only related by marriage. Of course, Margie didn't know that. Derek had told Jodie once, but asked her not to tell. She wondered why.

"Don't even think about helping him do anything crazy while you're here," Margie cautioned. "Lex doesn't know he's here yet. I, uh, haven't told him."

"Margie!" came a thunderous roar from the general direction of Alexander's office.

Margie groaned. "Oh, dear, Lex does seem to know about Derek."

"My suitcase," Jodie said, halting, hoping to get out of the line of fire in time.

"Lex will bring it in, dear, come along." She almost dragged her best friend into the house.

Derek was leaning against the staircase banister, handsome as a devil, with dancing brown eyes and a lean, good-looking face under jet-black hair. In front of him, Alexander was holding up a rubber chicken by the neck.

"I thought you liked chicken," Derek drawled.

"Cooked," Alexander replied tersely. "Not in my desk chair pretending to be a cushion!"

"You could cook that, but the fumes would clear out the kitchen for sure," Derek chuckled.

Cobb threw it at the man, turned, went back into his office and slammed the door. Muttered curses came right through two inches of solid mahogany.

"Derek, how could you?" Margie wailed.

He tossed her the chicken and came forward to lift her up and kiss her saucily on the nose. "Now, now, you can't expect me to be dignified. It isn't in my nature. Hi, sprout!" he added, putting Margie down only to pick up Jodie and swing her around in a bear hug. "How's my best girl?"

"I'm just fine, Derek," she replied, kissing his cheek. "You look great."

"So do you." He let her dangle from his hands and his keen dark eyes scanned her flushed face. "Has Cobb been picking on you all the way home?" he asked lazily.

"Why can't you two call him Lex, like I do?" Margie wanted to know.

"He doesn't look like a Lex," Derek replied.

"He always picks on me," Jodie said heavily as Derek let her slide back onto her feet. "If he had a list of people he doesn't like, I'd lead it."

"We'd tie for that spot, I reckon," Derek replied. He gave Margie a slow, steady appraisal. "New duds? I like that skirt."

Margie grinned up at him. "I made it."

"Good for you. When are you going to have a show of all those pretty things you make?"

"That's what I'm working on. Lex's girlfriend Kirry is trying to get her store to let me do a parade of my designs."

"Kirry." Derek wrinkled his straight nose. "Talk about slow poison. And he thought Rachel was bad!"

"Don't mention Rachel!" Margie cautioned quickly.

"Kirry makes her look like a church mouse," Derek said flatly. "She's a social climber with dollar signs for eyes. Mark my words, it isn't his body she's after."

"He likes her," Margie replied.

"He likes liver and onions, too," Derek said, and made a horrible face.

Jodie laughed at the byplay.

Derek glanced at her. "Why doesn't he ever look at you, sprout? You'd be perfect for him."

"Don't be silly," Jodie said with a forced smile. "I'm not his type at all."

"You're not mercenary. You're a sucker for anyone in trouble. You like cats and dogs and children, and you don't like night life. You're perfect."

"He likes opera and theater," she returned.

"And you don't?" Derek asked.

Margie grabbed him by the arm. "Come on and let's have coffee while you tell us about your latest rodeo triumph."

"How do you know it was?" he teased.

"When have you ever lost a belt?" she replied with a grin.

Jodie followed along behind them, already uneasy about the weekend. She had a feeling that it wasn't going to be the best one of her life.

Later, Jodie escaped from the banter between Margie and her cousin and went out to the corral near the barn to look at the new calves. One of the older ranch hands, Johnny, came out to join her. He was missing a tooth in front from a bull's hooves and a finger from a too-tight rope that slipped. His chaps and hat and boots were worn and dirty from hard work. But he had a heart of pure gold, and Jodie loved him. He reminded her of her late father.

"Hey, Johnny!" she greeted, standing on the top rung of the wooden fence in old jeans, boots, and a long-sleeved blue checked shirt. Her hair was up in a ponytail. She looked about twelve.

He grinned back. "Hey, Jodie! Come to see my babies?"

"Sure have!"

"Ain't they purty?" he drawled, joining her at the fence, where she was feeding her eyes on the pretty little white-faced, red-coated calves.

"Yes, they are," she agreed with a sigh. "I miss this up in Houston. The closest I get to cattle is the rodeo when it comes to town."

He winced. "You poor kid," he said. "You lost everything at once, all them years ago."

That was true. She'd lost her parents and her home, all at once. If Alexander hadn't gotten her into business college, where she could live on campus, she'd have been homeless.

She smiled down at him. "Time heals even the worst wounds, Johnny. Besides, I still get to come down here and visit once in a while."

He looked irritated. "Wish you came more than that Dane

woman," he said under his breath. "Can't stand cattle and dust, don't like cowboys, looks at us like we'd get her dirty just by speaking to her."

She reached over and patted him gently on the shoulder. "We all have our burdens to bear."

He sighed. "I reckon so. Why don't you move back down here?" he added. "Plenty of jobs going in Jacobsville right now. I hear tell the police chief needs a new secretary."

She chuckled. "I'm not going to work for Cash Grier," she assured him. "They said his last secretary emptied the trash can over his head, and it was full of half-empty coffee cups and coffee grounds."

"Well, some folks don't take to police work," he said, but he chuckled.

"Nothing to do, Johnny?" came a deep, terse voice from behind Jodie.

Johnny straightened immediately. "Just started mucking out the stable, boss. I only came over to say howdy to Miss Jodie."

"Good to see you again, Johnny," she said.

"Same here, miss."

He tipped his hat and went slowly back into the barn.

"Don't divert the hired help," Alexander said curtly.

She got down from the fence. It was a long way up to his eyes in her flat shoes. "He was a friend of my father's," she reminded him. "I was being polite."

She turned and started back into the house.

"Running away?"

She stopped and faced him. "I'm not going to be your whipping boy," she said.

His eyebrows arched. "Wrong gender."

"You know what I mean. You're furious that Derek's here, and Kirry's not, and you want somebody to take it out on."

He moved restlessly at the accusation. His scowl was suddenly darker. "Don't do that."

She knew what he meant. She could always see through his bad temper to the reason for it, something his own sister had never been able to do.

"Derek will leave in the morning and Kirry will be here by afternoon," she said. "Derek can't do that much damage in a night. Besides, you know how close he and Margie are."

"He's too flighty for her, distant relation or not," he muttered.

She sighed, looking up at him with quiet, soft eyes full of memories. "Like me," she said under her breath.

He frowned. "What?"

"That's always been your main argument against me—that I'm too flighty. That's why you didn't like it when Derek was trying to get me to go out with him three years ago," she reminded him.

He stared at her for a few seconds, still scowling. "Did I say that?"

She nodded then turned away. "I've got to go help Margie organize the food and drinks," she added. "Left to her own devices, we'll be eating turkey and bacon roll-ups and drinking spring water."

"What did you have in mind?" he asked amusedly.

"A nice baked chicken with garlic-and-chives mashed potatoes, fruit salad, homemade rolls and biscuits, gravy, fresh asparagus and a chocolate pound cake for dessert," she said absently.

"You can cook?" he asked, astonished.

She glared at him over one shoulder. "You didn't notice? Margie hasn't cooked a meal any time I've been down here for the weekend, except for one barbecue that the cowboys roasted a side of beef for."

He didn't say another word, but he looked unusually thoughtful.

* * *

The meal came out beautifully. By the time she had it on the table, Jodie was flushed from the heat of the kitchen and her hair was disheveled, but she'd produced a perfect meal.

Margie enthused over the results with every dish she tasted, and so did Derek. Alexander was unusually quiet. He finished his chocolate pound cake and a second cup of coffee before he gave his sister a dark look.

"You told me you'd been doing all the cooking when Jessie wasn't here and Jodie was," he said flatly.

Margie actually flushed. She dropped her fork and couldn't meet Jodie's surprised glance.

"You always made such a fuss of extra company when Jessie was gone," she protested without realizing she was only making things worse.

Alexander's teeth ground together when he saw the look on Jodie's face. He threw down his napkin and got noisily to his feet. "You're as insensitive as a cactus plant, Margie," he said angrily.

"You're better?" she retorted, with her eyebrows reaching for her hairline. "You're the one who always complains when I invite Jodie, even though she hasn't got any family except us…oh, dear."

Jodie had already gotten to her own feet and was collecting dirty dishes. She didn't respond to the bickering. She felt it, though. It hurt to know that Alexander barely tolerated her; almost as much as it hurt to know Margie had taken credit for her cooking all these years.

"I'll help you clear, darlin'," Derek offered with a meaningful look at the Cobbs. "Both of you could use some sensitivity training. You just step all over Jodie's feelings without the least notice. Some 'second family' you turned out to be!"

He propelled Jodie ahead of him into the kitchen and closed the door. For once, he looked angry.

She smiled at him. "Don't take it so personally, Derek," she said. "Insults just bounce off me. I'm so used to Alexander by now that I hardly listen."

He tilted her chin up and read the pain in her soft eyes. "He walks on your heart every time he speaks to you," he said bluntly. "He doesn't even know how you feel, when a blind man could see it."

She patted his cheek. "You're a nice man, Derek."

He shrugged. "I've always been a nice man, for all the good it does me. Women flock to hang all over Cobb while he glowers and insults them."

"Someday a nice, sweet woman will come along and take you in hand, and thank God every day for you," she told him.

He chuckled. "Want to take me on?"

She wrinkled her nose at him. "You're very sweet, but I've got my eye on a rather nice man at my office. He's sweet, too, and his girlfriend treats him like dirt. He deserves someone better."

"He'd be lucky to get you," Derek said.

She smiled.

They were frozen in that affectionate tableau when the door opened and Alexander exploded into the room. He stopped short, obviously unsettled by what he thought he was seeing. Especially when Jodie jerked her hand down from Derek's cheek, and he let go of her chin.

"Something you forgot to say about Jodie's unwanted presence in your life?" Derek drawled, and for an instant, the smiling, gentle man Jodie knew became a threatening presence.

Alexander scowled. "Margie didn't mean that the way it sounded," he returned.

"Margie never means things the way they sound," Derek said coldly, "but she never stops to think how much words can hurt, either. She walks around in a perpetual Margie-haze of self-absorption. Even now, Jodie's only here because she can make canapés for the party tomorrow night—or didn't you know?" he added with absolute venom.

Margie came into the room behind her brother, downcast and quiet. She winced as she met Derek's accusing eyes.

"I'm a pig," she confessed. "I really don't mean to hurt people. I love Jodie. She knows it, even if you don't."

"You have a great way of showing it, honey," Derek replied, a little less antagonistic to her than to her brother. "Inviting Jodie down just to cook for a party is pretty thoughtless."

Margie's eyes fell. "You can go home if you want to, Jodie, and I'm really sorry," she offered.

"Oh, for heaven's sake, I don't mind cooking!" Jodie went to Margie and hugged her hard. "I could always say no if I didn't want to do it! Derek's just being kind, that's all."

Margie glared at her cousin. "Kind."

Derek glared back. "Sure I am. It runs in the family. Glad you could come, Jodie, want to wash and wax my car when you finish doing the dishes?" he added sarcastically.

"You stop that!" Margie raged at him.

"Then get in here and help her do the dishes," Derek drawled. "Or do your hands melt in hot water?"

"We do have a dishwasher," Alexander said tersely.

"Gosh! You've actually seen it, then?" Derek exclaimed.

Alexander said a nasty word and stormed out of the kitchen.

"One down," Derek said with twinkling eyes and looking at Margie. "One to go."

"Quit that, or she'll toss you out and I'll be stuck here with them and Kirry all weekend," Jodie said softly.

"Kirry?" He gaped at Margie. "You invited Kirry?"

Margie ground her teeth together and clenched her small hands. "She's the guest of honor!"

"Lord, give me a bus ticket!" He moved toward the door. "Sorry, honey, I'm not into masochism, and a night of unadulterated Kirry would put me in a mental ward. I'm leaving."

"But you just got here!" Margie wailed.

He turned at the door. "You should have told me who was coming to the party. I'd still be in San Antonio. Want to come with me, Jodie?" he offered. "I'll take you to a fiesta!"

Margie looked murderous. "She's my friend."

"She's not, or you wouldn't have forced her down here to suffer Kirry all weekend," he added.

"Give me a minute to get out of the line of fire, will you?" Jodie held up her hands and went back to the dining room to scoop up dirty dishes, forcibly smiling.

Derek glanced at the closed door, and moved closer to Margie. "Don't try to convince me that you don't know how Jodie feels about your brother."

"She got over that old crush years ago, she said so!" Margie returned.

"She lied," he said shortly. "She's as much in love with him as she ever was, not that either of you ever notice! It's killing her just to be around him, and you stick her with Kirry. How do you think she's going to feel, watching Kirry slither all over Cobb for a whole night?"

Margie bit her lower lip and looked hunted. "She said..."

"Oh, sure, she's going to tell you that she's in love with Cobb." He nodded. "Great instincts, Marge."

"Don't call me Marge!"

He bent and brushed an insolent kiss across her parted lips, making her gasp. His dark eyes narrowed as he assayed the unwilling response. "Never thought of me like that, either, huh?" he drawled.

"You're…my…cousin," she choked.

"I'm no close relation to you at all, despite Cobb's antagonism. One day I'm going to walk out the door with you over my shoulder, and Cobb can do his worst." He winked at her. "See you, sweetheart."

He turned and ambled out the door. Margie was still staring after him helplessly and holding her hand to her lips when Jodie came in with another stack of dishes.

"What's wrong with you?" Jodie asked.

"Derek kissed me," she said in a husky tone.

"He's always kissing you."

Margie swallowed hard. "Not like this."

Jodie's eyebrows went up and she grinned. "I thought it was about time."

"What?"

"Nothing," Jodie said at once. "Here, can you open the dishwasher for me? My hands are full."

Margie broke out of her trance and went to help, shell-shocked and quiet.

"Don't let Derek upset you," Jodie said gently. "He thinks he's doing me a favor, but he's not. I don't mind helping out, in any way I can. I owe you and Cobb so much…"

"You don't owe us a thing," Margie said at once. "Oh, Jodie, you shouldn't let me make use of you like this. You should speak up for yourself. You don't do that enough."

"I know. It's why I haven't advanced in the company," she had to admit. "I just don't like confrontations."

"You had enough of them as a kid, didn't you?" Margie asked.

Jodie flushed. "I loved my parents. I really did."

"But they fought, too. Just like ours. Our mother hated our father, even after he was dead. She drank and drank, trying to forget him, just the same. She soured my brother on women, you know. She picked on him from the time he was six, and every year it got worse. He had a roaring inferiority complex when he was in high school."

"Yes? Well, he's obviously got over it now," Jodie said waspishly.

Margie shook her head. "Not really. If he had, he'd know he could do better than Kirry."

"I thought you liked her!"

Margie looked shamefaced. "I do, sort of. Well, she's got an important job and she could really help me get my foot in the door at Weston's, the exclusive department store where she works."

"Oh, Margie," Jodie said wearily, shaking her head.

"I use people," Margie admitted. "But," she added brightly, "I try to do it in a nice way, and I always send flowers or presents or something afterward, don't I?"

Jodie laughed helplessly. "Yes, you do," she admitted. "Here, help me load up the dishes, and then you can tell me what sort of canapés you want me to make for tomorrow."

She didn't add that she knew she'd spend the whole day tomorrow making them, because the party was for almost forty people, and lunch had to be provided, as well. It was a logistical nightmare. But she could cope. She'd done it before. And Margie was her best friend.

3

⚜⚜⚜

J odie was up at dawn making biscuits and dough for the canapés. She'd only just taken up breakfast when Alexander came into the kitchen, wearing jeans and boots and a long-sleeved chambray shirt. He looked freshly showered and clean-shaven, his dark hair still damp.

"I've got breakfast," Jodie offered without looking too closely at him. He was overpowering in tight jeans and a shirt unbuttoned to his collarbone, where thick curling black hair peeked out. She had to fight not to throw herself at him.

"Coffee?" he murmured.

"In the pot."

He poured himself a cup, watching the deft motions of her hands as she buttered biscuits and scooped eggs onto a platter already brimming over with bacon and sausages.

"Aren't you eating?" he asked as he seated himself at the table.

"Haven't time," she said, arranging a layer of canapés on a baking sheet. "Most of your guests are coming in time for lunch, so these have to be done now, before I get too busy."

His sensuous lips made a thin line. "I can't stand him, but Derek is right about one thing. You do let Margie use you."

"You and Margie were there when I had nobody else," she said without seeing the flinch of his eyelids. "I consider that she's entitled to anything I can ever do for her."

"You sell yourself short."

"I appreciate it when people do things for me without being asked," she replied. She put the canapés in the oven and set the timer, pushing back sweaty hair that had escaped from her bun.

His eyes went over her figure in baggy pants and an oversize T-shirt. "You dress like a bag lady," he muttered.

She glanced at him, surprised. "I dress very nicely at work."

"Like a dowager bag lady," he corrected. "You wear the same sort of clothes you favored when you were overweight. You're not anymore. Why don't you wear things that fit?"

It was surprising that he noticed her enough to even know what she was wearing. "Margie's the fashion model, not me," she reminded him. "Besides, I'm not the type for trendy stuff. I'm just ordinary."

He frowned. She had a real ego problem. He and Margie hadn't done much for it, either. She accepted anything that was thrown at her, as if she deserved it. He was surprised how much it bothered him, to see her so undervalued even by herself. Not that he was interested in her, he added silently. She wasn't his type at all.

"Kirry's coming this morning," he added. "I have to pick her up at the airport at noon."

Jodie only smiled. "Margie's hoping she'll help her with a market for her designs."

"I think she'll try," he said conservatively. "Eat breakfast," he said. "You can't go all day without food."

"I don't have time," she repeated, starting on another batch of canapés. "Unless you want to sacrifice yourself in a bowl of dough?" she offered, extending the bowl with a mischievous smile.

His green eyes twinkled affectionately in spite of himself. "No, thanks."

"I didn't think so."

He watched her work while he ate, nebulous thoughts racing through his mind. Jodie was so much a part of his life that he never felt discomfort when they were together. He had a hard time with strangers. He appeared to be stoic and aloof, but in fact he was an introvert who didn't quite know how to mix with people who weren't in law enforcement. Like Jodie herself, he considered. She was almost painfully shy around people she didn't know——and tonight, she was going to be thrown in headfirst with a crowd she probably wouldn't even like.

Kirry's friends were social climbers, high society. Alexander himself wasn't comfortable with them, and Jodie certainly wouldn't be. They were into expensive cars, European vacations, diamonds, investments, and they traveled in circles that included some of the most famous people alive, from movie stars to Formula 1 race car drivers, to financial geniuses, playwrights and authors. They classified their friends by wealth and status, not by character. In their world, right and wrong didn't even exist.

"You're not going to like this crowd," he said aloud.

She glanced at him. "I'll be in the kitchen most of the time," she said easily, "or helping serve."

He looked outraged. "You're a guest, not the kitchen help!"

"Don't be absurd," she murmured absently, "I haven't even got the right clothes to wear to Kirry's sort of party. I'd be an embarrassment."

He set his coffee cup down with muted force. "Then why the hell did you come in the first place?" he asked.

"Margie asked me to," she said simply.

He got up and went out without another word. Jodie was going to regret this visit. He was sorry Margie had insisted that she come.

The party was in full swing. Alexander had picked up Kirry at the airport and lugged her suitcases up to the second guest room, down the hall from Jodie's. Kirry, blond and svelte and from a wealthy background was like the Cobbs, old money and family ties. She looked at Jodie without seeing her, and talked only to Margie and Alexander during lunch. Fortunately there were plenty of other people there who didn't mind talking to Jodie, especially an elderly couple apparently rolling in wealth to judge by the diamonds the matron was decked out in.

After lunch, Kirry had Alexander drive her into town and Jodie silently excused herself and escaped to the kitchen.

She had a nice little black dress, off the rack at a local department store, and high heels to match, which she wore to the party. But it was hidden under the big apron she wore most of the evening, heating and arranging canapés and washing dishes and crystal glasses in between uses.

It was almost ten o'clock before she was able to join Margie and her friends. But by then, Margie was hanging on to Kirry like a bat, with Alexander nearby, and Jodie couldn't get near her.

She stood in a corner by herself, wishing that Derek hadn't run from this weekend, so that she'd at least have someone to talk to. But that wasn't happening. She started talking to the elderly matron she'd sat beside at lunch, but another couple joined them and mentioned their week in Paris, and a mutual friend, and Jodie was out of her depth. She moved to another circle, but they were discussing annuities and investments, and she knew nothing to contribute to that discussion, either.

Alexander noticed, seething, that she was alone most of the evening. He started to get up, but Kirry moved closer and clung to his sleeve while Margie talked about her latest collection and offered to show it to Kirry in the morning. Kirry was very possessive. They weren't involved, as he'd been with other women. Perhaps that was why she was reluctant to let him move away. She hated the very thought of any other woman looking at him. That possessiveness was wearing thin. She was beautiful and she carried herself well, but she had an attitude he didn't like, and she was positively rude to any of his colleagues that spoke to him when they were together. Not that she had any idea what Alexander actually did for a living. He was independently wealthy and people in his and Margie's circle of friends assumed that the ranch was his full-time occupation. He'd taught Jodie and Margie never to mention that he worked in Drug Enforcement. They could say that he dabbled in security work, if they liked, but nothing more. When he'd started out with the DEA, he'd done a lot of undercover work. It wasn't politic to let people know that.

Jodie, meanwhile, had discovered champagne. She'd never let herself drink at any of the Cobb parties in the past, but she was feeling particularly isolated tonight, and it was painful. She liked the bubbles, the fragrance of flowers that clung to the exquisite beverage and the delicious taste. So she had three glasses, one after the other, and pretty soon she didn't mind at all that Margie and Alexander's guests were treating her like a barmaid who'd tried to insert herself into their exalted circles.

She noticed that she'd had too much to drink when she walked toward a doorway and ran headfirst into the door facing. She began to giggle softly. Her hair was coming down from its high coiffure, but she didn't care. She took out the circular comb that had held it in place and shook her head, letting the thick, waving wealth of hair fall to her shoulders.

The action caught the eye of a man nearby, a bored race car driver who'd been dragged to this hick party by his wife. He sized up Jodie, and despite the dress that did absolutely nothing for her, he was intrigued.

He moved close, leaning against the door facing she'd hit so unexpectedly.

"Hurt yourself?" he asked in a pleasant deep drawl, faintly accented.

Jodie looked up at the newcomer curiously and managed a lopsided grin. He was a dish, with curly black hair and dancing black eyes, an olive complexion and the body of an athlete.

"Only my hard head," she replied with a chuckle. "Who are you?"

"Francisco," he replied lazily. He lifted his glass to her in a toast. "You're the first person tonight who even asked." He leaned down so that he was eye to eye with her. "I'm a foreigner, you see."

"Are you, really?"

He was enchanted. He laughed, and it wasn't a polite social laugh at all. "I'm from Madrid," he said. "Didn't you notice my accent?"

"I don't speak any foreign languages," she confessed sadly, sipping what was left of her champagne. "I don't understand high finance or read popular novels or know any movie stars, and I've never been on a holiday abroad. So I thought I'd go sit in the kitchen."

He laughed again. "May I join you, then?" he asked.

She looked pointedly at his left hand. There was no ring.

He took a ring out of his slacks pocket and dangled it in front of her. "We don't advertise our commitment at parties. My wife likes it that way. That's my wife," he added with pure disdain, nodding toward a blond woman in a skintight red dress that looked sprayed on. She was leaning against a very handsome blond man.

"She's beautiful," she remarked.

"She's anybody's," he returned coldly. "The man she's stalking is a rising motion picture star. He's poor. She's rich. She's financing his career in return for the occasional loan of his body."

Her eyes almost popped out of her eyelids.

He shook his head. "You're not worldly, are you?" he mused. "I have an open marriage. She does what she pleases. So do I."

"Don't you love her?" she asked curiously.

"One marries for love, you think." He sighed. "What a child you are. I married her because her father owned the company. As his son-in-law, I get to drive the car in competition."

"You're the race car driver!" she exclaimed softly. "Kirry mentioned you were coming."

"Kirry." His lips curled distastefully and he glanced across the room into a pair of cold, angry green eyes above the head of Kirry Dane. "She was last year's diversion," he murmured. "She wanted to be seen at Monaco."

Jodie was surprised by his lack of inhibition. She wondered if Alexander knew about this relationship, or if he cared. She'd never thought whether he bothered asking about his date's previous entanglements.

"Her boyfriend doesn't like me," he murmured absently, and smiled icily, lifting his glass.

Jodie looked behind her. Kirry had turned away, but Alexander was suddenly making a beeline across the room toward them.

Francisco made a face. "There's one man you don't want to make an enemy of," he confided. "Are you a relation of his, by any chance?"

Jodie laughed a little too loudly. "Good Lord, no." She chuckled. "I'm the cook!"

"I beg your pardon?" he asked.

By that time, Alexander was facing her. He took the crystal champagne flute from her hands and put it gingerly on a nearby table.

"I wasn't going to break it, Alexander," she muttered. "I do know it's Waterford crystal!"

"How many glasses have you had?" he demanded.

"I don't like your tone," she retorted, moving clumsily, so that Francisco had to grab her arm to keep her upright. "I had three glasses. It's not that strong, and I'm not drunk!"

"And ducks don't have feathers," Alexander replied tersely. He caught her other arm and pulled her none too gently from Francisco's grasp. "I'll take care of Jodie. Hadn't you better reacquire your wife?" he added pointedly to the younger man.

Francisco sighed, with a long, wistful appraisal of Jodie. "It seems so," he replied. "Nice to have met you—Jodie, is it?"

Jodie grinned woozily. "It's Jordana, actually, but most people call me Jodie. And I was glad to meet you, too, Francisco! I never met a real race car driver before!"

He started to speak, but it was too late, because Alexander was already marching her out of the room and down the hall.

"Will you stop dragging me around?!" she demanded, stumbling on her high heels.

He pulled her into the dark-paneled library and closed the door with a muted thud. He let go of her arm and glared down at her. "Will you stop trying to seduce married men?" he shot back.

"Gomez and his wife are on the cover of half the tabloids in Texas right now," he added bluntly.

"Why?"

"Her father just died and she inherited the car company. She's trying to sell it and her husband is fighting her in court, tooth and nail."

"And they're still married?"

"Apparently, in name, at least. She's pregnant, I hear, with another man's child."

She looked up at him coldly. "Some circles you and Margie travel in," she said with contempt.

"Circles you'd never fit into," he agreed.

"Not hardly," she drawled ungrammatically. "And I wouldn't want to. In my world, people get married and have kids and build a home together." She nodded her head toward the closed door. "Those people in there wouldn't know what a home was if you drew it for them!"

His green eyes narrowed on her face. "You're smashed. Why don't you go to bed?"

She lifted her chin and smiled mistily. "Why don't you come with me?" she purred.

The look on his face would have amused her, if she'd been sober. He just stared, shocked.

She arched her shoulders and made a husky little sound in her throat. She parted her lips and ran her tongue slowly around them, the way she'd read in a magazine article that said men were turned on by it.

Apparently they were. Alexander was staring at her mouth with an odd expression. His chest was rising and falling very quickly. She could see the motion of it through his white shirt and dinner jacket.

She moved closer, draping herself against him as she'd seen that slinky blond woman in the red dress do it. She moved her leg against his and felt his whole body stiffen abruptly.

Her hands went to the front of his shirt under the jacket. She drew her fingers down it, feeling the ripple of muscle. His big hands caught her shoulders, but he wasn't pushing.

"You look at me, but you never see me," she murmured. Her lips brushed against his throat. He smelled of expensive cologne and soap. "I'm not pretty. I'm not sexy. But I would die for you…!"

His hard mouth cut off the words. He curled her into his body with a rigid arm at her back, and his mouth opened against her moist, full, parted lips with the fury of a summer storm.

It wasn't premeditated. The feel of her against him had triggered a raging arousal in his muscular body. He went in headfirst, without thinking of the consequences.

If he was helpless, so was she. As he enveloped her against him, her arms slid around his warm body under the jacket and her mouth answered the hunger of his. She made a husky little moan that apparently made matters worse. His mouth became suddenly insistent, as if he heard the need in her soft cry and was doing his best to satisfy the hunger it betrayed.

Her hands lifted to the back of his head and her fingers dug into his scalp as she arched her body upward in a hopeless plea.

He whispered something that she couldn't understand before he bent and lifted her, with her mouth still trapped under his demanding lips, and carried her to the sofa.

He spread her body onto the cold leather and slid over it, one powerful leg inserting itself between both of hers in a frantic, furious exchange of passion. He'd never known such raging need, not only in himself, but in Jodie. She was liquid in his embrace, yielding to everything he asked without a word being spoken.

He moved slightly, just enough to get his hand in between them. It smoothed over her collarbone and down into the soft dip of her dress, over the lacy bra she was wearing underneath. He felt the hard little nipple in his palm as he increased the insistent pressure of the caress and heard her cry of delight go into his open mouth.

Her hands were on the buttons of his shirt. It was dangerous. It was reckless. She'd incited him to madness, and he couldn't stop. When he felt the buttons give, and her hands speared into the thick hair over his chest, he groaned harshly. His body shivered with desire.

His mouth ground into hers as his leg moved between hers. One lean hand went under her hips and gathered her up against the fierce arousal of his body, moving her against him in a blatant physical statement of intent.

Jodie's head was spinning. All her dreams of love were coming true. Alexander wanted her! She could feel the insistent pressure of his body over hers. He was kissing her as if he'd die to have her, and she gloried in the fury of his hunger. She relaxed with a husky little laugh and kissed him back languidly, feeling her body melt under him, melt into him. She was on fire, burning with unfamiliar needs, drowning in unfamiliar sensations that made her whole body tingle with pleasure. She lifted her hips against his and gasped at the blatant contact.

Alexander lifted his head and looked at her. His face was a rigid mask. Only his green eyes were alive in it, glittering down at her in a rasping, unsteady silence of merged breathing.

"Don't stop," she whispered, moving her hips again.

He was tempted. It showed. But that iron control wouldn't let him slip into carelessness. She'd been drinking. In fact, she was smashed. He had his own suspicions about her innocence, and they wouldn't shut up. His body was begging him to forget her lack of experience and give it relief. But his will was too strong. He was the man in control. It was his responsibility to protect her, even from himself.

"You're drunk, Jodie," he said. His voice was faintly unsteady, but it was terse and firm.

"Does it matter?" she asked lazily.

"Don't be ridiculous."

He moved away, getting to his feet. He looked down at her sprawled body in its disheveled dress and he ached all the way to his toes. But he couldn't do this. Not when she was so vulnerable.

She sighed and closed her eyes. It had been so sweet, lying in his arms. She smiled dreamily. Was she dreaming?

"Get up, for God's sake!" he snapped.

When her eyes opened, he was standing her firmly on her feet. "You're going to bed, right now, before you make an utter fool of yourself!"

She blinked, staring up at him. "I can't go to bed. Who'll do the dishes?"

"Jodie!"

She giggled, trying to lean against him. He thrust her away and took her arm, moving her toward the door. "I told Francisco I was the cook. That's me," she drawled cheerfully. "Cook, bottle-washer, best friend and household slave." She laughed louder.

He propelled her out the door, back down the hall toward the staircase, and urged her up it. She was still giggling a little too loudly for comfort, but the noise of the music from the living room covered it nicely.

He got her to the guest room she was occupying and put her inside. "Go to bed," he said through his teeth.

She leaned against the door facing, totally at sea. "You could come inside," she murmured wickedly. "There's a bed."

"You need one," he agreed tersely. "Go get in it."

"Always bossing me around," she sighed. "Don't you like kissing me, Alexander?"

"You're going to hate yourself in the morning," he assured her.

She yawned, her mind going around in circles, like the room. "I think I'll go to bed now."

"Great idea."

He started to walk out.

"Could you send Francisco up, please?" she taunted. "I'd like to lie down and discuss race cars with him."

"In your dreams!" he said coldly.

He actually slammed the door, totally out of patience, self-control and tact. He waited a minute, to make sure she didn't try to come back out. But there was only the sound of slow progress toward the bed and a sudden loud whoosh. When he opened the door again and peeked in, she was lying facedown in her dress on the covers, sound asleep. He closed the door again, determined not to get close to her a second time. He went back to the party, feeling as if he'd had his stomach punched. He couldn't imagine what had possessed him to let Jodie tempt him into indiscretion. His lack of control worried him so much that he was twice as attentive to Kirry as he usually was.

When he saw her up to her room, after the party was over, he kissed her with intent. She was perfectly willing, but his body let him down. He couldn't manage any interest at all.

"You're just tired," she assured him with a worldly smile. "We have all the time in the world. Sleep tight."

"Sure. You, too."

He left her and went back downstairs. He was restless, angry at his attack of impotence with the one woman who was capable of curing it. Or, at least, he imagined she was. He and Kirry had never been lovers, although they'd come close at one time. Now, she was a pleasant companion from time to time, a bauble to show off, to take around town. It infuriated him that he could be whole with Jodie, who was almost certainly a virgin, and he couldn't even function with a sophisticated woman like Kirry. Maybe it was his age.

The rattle of plates caught his attention. He moved toward the sound and found a distressed Margie in the kitchen trying to put dishes in the dishwasher.

"That doesn't look right," he commented with a frown when he noticed the lack of conformity in the way she was tossing plates and bowls and cups and crystal all together. "You'll break the crystal."

She glared at him. "Well, what do I know about washing dishes?" she exclaimed. "That's why we have Jessie!"

He cocked his head. "You're out of sorts."

She pushed back her red-tinged dark hair angrily. "Yes, I'm out of sorts! Kirry said she doesn't think I'm ready to show my collection yet. She said her store had shows booked for the rest of the year, and she couldn't help me!"

"All that buttering up and dragging Jodie down here to work, for nothing," he said sarcastically.

"Where is Jodie?" she demanded. "I haven't seen her for two hours, and here's all this work that isn't getting done except by me!"

He leaned back against the half open door and stared at his sister. "She's passed out on her bed, dead drunk," he said distastefully. "After trying to seduce the world's number one race car driver, and then me."

Margie stood up and stared back. "You?"

"I wish I could impress on you how tired I am of finding Jodie underfoot every time I walk into my own house," he said coldly. "We can't have a party without her, we can't have a holiday without her. My own birthday means an invitation! Why can't you just hire a cook when you need one instead of landing me with your erstwhile best friend?"

"I thought you liked Jodie, a little," Margie stammered.

"She's blue collar, Margie," he persisted, still smarting under his loss of control and furious that Jodie was responsible for it. "She'll never fit in our circles, no matter how much you try to force her into them. She was telling people tonight that she was the cook, and it's not far wrong. She's a social disaster with legs. She knows nothing about our sort of lifestyle, she can't carry on a decent conversation and she dresses like a homeless person. It's an embarrassment to have her here!"

Margie sighed miserably. "I hope you haven't said things like that to her, Lex," she worried. "She may not be an upper class sort of person, but she's sweet and kind, and she doesn't gossip. She's the only real friend I've ever had. Not that I've behaved much like one," she added sadly.

"You should have friends in your own class," he said coldly. "I don't want Jodie invited down here again," he added firmly, holding up a hand when Margie tried to speak. "I mean it. You find some excuse, but you keep her away from here. I'm not going to be stalked by your bag lady of a friend. I don't want her underfoot at any more holidays, and God forbid, at my birthday party! If you want to see her, drive to Houston, fly to Houston, stay in Houston! But don't bring her here anymore."

"Did she really try to seduce you?" Margie wondered aloud.

"I don't want to talk about it," he said flatly. "It was embarrassing."

"She'll probably be horrified when she wakes up and remembers what happened. Whatever did," Margie added, fishing.

"I'll be horrified for months myself. Kirry is my steady girl," he added deliberately. "I'm not hitting on some other woman behind her back, and Jodie should have known it. Not that it seemed to matter to her, about me or the married racer."

"She's never had a drink, as far as I know," Margie ventured gently. "She's not like our mother, Lex."

His face closed up. Jodie's behavior had aroused painful memories of his mother, who drank often, and to excess. She was a constant embarrassment anytime people came to the house, and she delighted in embarrassing her son any way possible. Jodie's unmanageable silliness brought back nightmares.

"There's nothing in the world more disgusting than a drunk woman," he said aloud. "Nothing that makes me sicker to my stomach."

Margie closed the dishwasher and started it. There was a terrible cracking sound. The crystal! She winced. "I don't care what's broken. I'm not a cook. I can't wash dishes. I'm a dress designer!"

"Hire help for Jessie," he said.

"Okay," she said, giving in. "I won't invite Jodie back again. But how do I tell her, Lex? She's never going to understand. And it will hurt her."

He knew that. He couldn't bear to know it. His face hardened. "Just keep her away from me. I don't care how."

"I'll think of something," Margie said weakly.

Outside in the hall, a white-faced Jodie was stealthily making

her way back to the staircase. She'd come down belatedly to do
the dishes, still tingling hours after Alexander's feverish lovemaking. She'd been floating, delirious with hope that he might have
started to see her in a different light. And then she'd heard what
he said. She'd heard every single word. She disgusted him. She was
such a social disaster, in fact, that he never wanted her to come to
the house again. She'd embarrassed him and made a fool of herself.

He was right. She'd behaved stupidly, and now she was going
to pay for it by being an outcast. The only family she had no longer
wanted her.

She went back to her room, closed the door quietly, and picked
up the telephone. She changed her airplane ticket for an early-
morning flight.

The next morning, she went to Margie's room at daybreak. She
hadn't slept a wink. She'd packed and changed her clothes, and
now she was ready to go.

"Will you drive me to the airport?" she asked her sleepy friend.
"Or do you want me to ask Johnny?"

Margie sat up, blinking. Then she remembered Lex's odd
comments and her own shame at how she'd treated her best friend.
She flushed.

"I'll drive you," Margie said at once. "But don't you want to wait
until after breakfast?" She flushed again, remembering that Jodie
would have had to cook it.

"I'm not hungry. There's leftover sausage and bacon in the
fridge, along with some biscuits. You can just heat them up. Alexander can cook eggs to go with them," she added, almost choking
on his name.

Margie felt guilty. "You're upset," she ventured.

Keeping quiet was the hardest thing Jodie had ever done. "I got drunk last night and did some...really stupid things," she summarized. "I'd just like to go home, Margie. Okay?"

Margie tried not to let her relief show. Jodie was leaving without a fuss. Lex would be pleased, and she'd be off the hook. She smiled. "Okay. I'll just get dressed, and then we'll go!"

4

⋙∽∿∾ ∾∿∽∿ ⋙∽∿∾

If running away seemed the right thing to do, actually doing it became complicated the minute Jodie went down the staircase with her suitcase.

The last thing she'd expected was to find the cause of her flight standing in the hall watching her. She ground her teeth together to keep from speaking.

Alexander was leaning against the banister, and he looked both uncomfortable and concerned when he saw Jodie's pale complexion and swollen eyelids.

He stood upright, scowling. "I'm driving Kirry back to Houston this afternoon," he said at once, noting Jodie's suitcase. "You can ride with us."

Jodie forced a quiet smile. Her eyes didn't quite meet his. "Thanks for the offer, Alexander, but I have an airplane ticket."

"Then I'll drive you to the airport," he added quietly.

Her face tightened. She swallowed down her hurt. "Thanks, but Margie's already dressed and ready to go. And we have some things to talk about on the way," she added before he could offer again.

He watched her uneasily. Jodie was acting like a fugitive evading the police. She wouldn't meet his eyes, or let him near her. He'd had all night to regret his behavior, and he was still blaming her for it. He'd overreacted. He knew she'd had a crush on him at one time. He'd hurt her with his cold rejection. She'd been drinking. It hadn't been her fault, but he'd blamed her for the whole fiasco. He felt guilty because of the way she looked.

Before he could say anything else, Margie came bouncing down the steps. "Okay, I'm ready! Let's go," she told Jodie.

"I'm right behind you. So long, Alexander," she told him without looking up past his top shirt button.

He didn't reply. He stood watching until the front door closed behind her. He still didn't understand his own conflicting emotions. He'd hoped to have some time alone with Jodie while he explored this suddenly changed relationship between them. But she was clearly embarrassed about her behavior the night before, and she was running scared. Probably letting her go was the best way to handle it. After a few days, he'd go to see her at the office and smooth things over. He couldn't bear having her look that way and knowing he was responsible for it. Regardless of his burst of bad temper, he cared about Jodie. He didn't want her to be hurt.

"You look very pale, Jodie," Margie commented when she walked her best friend to the security checkpoint. "Are you sure you're all right?"

"I'm embarrassed about how I acted last night, that's all," she assured her best friend. "How did you luck out with Kirry, by the way?"

"Not too well," she replied with a sigh. "And I think I broke all the crystal by putting it in the dishwasher."

"I'm sorry I wasn't able to do that for you," Jodie apologized.

"It's not your fault. Nothing is your fault." Margie looked tormented. "I was going to ask you down to Lex's birthday party next month…"

"Margie, I can't really face Alexander right now, okay?" she interrupted gently, and saw the relief plain on the taller woman's face. "So I'm going to make myself scarce for a little while."

"That might be best," Margie had to admit.

Jodie smiled. "Thanks for asking me to the party," she managed. "I had a good time."

That was a lie, and they both knew it.

"I'll make all this up to you one day, I promise I will," Margie said unexpectedly, and hugged Jodie, hard. "I'm not much of a friend, Jodie, but I'm going to change. I am. You'll see."

"I wouldn't be much of a friend if I wanted to remake you," Jodie replied, smiling. "I'll see you around, Margie," she added enigmatically, and left before Margie could ask what she meant.

It was a short trip back to Houston. Jodie fought tears all the way. She couldn't remember anything hurting so much in all her life. Alexander couldn't bear the sight of her. He didn't want her around. She made him sick. She…disgusted him.

Most of her memories of love swirled around Alexander Cobb. She'd daydreamed about him even before she realized her feelings had deepened into love. She treasured unexpected meetings with him, she tingled just from having him smile at her. But all that had been a lie. She was a responsibility he took seriously, like his job. She meant nothing more than that to him. It was a painful realization, and it was going to take time for the hurt to lessen.

But for the moment it was too painful to bear. She drew the air carrier's magazine out of its pocket in the back of the seat ahead of her and settled back to read it. By the time she finished, the plane was landing. She walked through the Houston concourse with a new resolution. She was going to forget Alexander. It was time to put away the past and start fresh.

Alexander was alone in the library when his sister came back from the airport.

He went out into the hall to meet her. "Did she say anything to you?" he asked at once.

Surprised by the question, and his faint anxiety, she hesitated. "About what?"

He glowered down at her. "About why she was leaving abruptly. I know her ticket was for late this afternoon. She must have changed it."

"She said she was too embarrassed to face you," Margie replied.

"Anything else?" he persisted.

"Not really." She felt uneasy herself. "You know Jodie. She's painfully shy, Lex. She doesn't drink, ever. I guess whatever happened made her ashamed of herself and uncomfortable around you. She'll get over it in time."

"Do you think so?" he wondered aloud.

"What are you both doing down here?" Kirry asked petulantly with a yawn. She came down the staircase in a red silk gown and black silk robe and slippers, her long blond hair sweeping around her shoulders. "I feel as if I haven't even slept. Is breakfast ready?"

Margie started. "Well, Jessie isn't here," she began.

"Where's that little cook who was at the party last night?" she asked carelessly. "Why can't she make breakfast?"

"Jodie's not a cook," Alexander said tersely. "She's Margie's best friend."

Kirry's eyebrows arched. "She looked like a lush to me," Kirry said unkindly. "People like that should never drink. Is she too hung over to cook, then?"

"She's gone home," Margie said, resenting Kirry's remarks.

"Then who's going to make toast and coffee for me?" Kirry demanded. "I have to have breakfast."

"I can make toast," Margie said, turning. She wanted Kirry's help with her collection, but she disliked the woman intensely.

"Then I'll get dressed. Want to come up and do my zip, Lex?" Kirry drawled.

"No," he said flatly. "I'll make coffee." He went into the kitchen behind Margie.

Kirry stared after him blankly. He'd never spoken to her in such a way before, and Margie had been positively rude. They shouldn't drink, either, she was thinking as she went back upstairs to dress. Obviously it was hangovers and bad tempers all around this morning.

Two weeks later, Jodie sat in on a meeting between Brody and an employee of their information systems section who had been rude and insulting to a fellow worker. It was Brody's job as Human Resources Generalist to oversee personnel matters, and he was a diplomat. It gave Jodie the chance to see what sort of duties she would be expected to perform if she moved up from Human Resources Generalist to manager.

"Mr. Koswalski, this is Ms. Clayburn, my administrative assistant. She's here to take notes," he added.

Jodie was surprised, because she thought she was there to learn the job. But she smiled and pulled out her small pad and pen, perching it on her knee.

"You've had a complaint about me, haven't you?" Koswalski asked with a sigh.

Brody's eyebrows arched. "Well, yes..."

"One of our executives hired a systems specialist with no practical experience in oil exploration," Koswalski told him. "I was preparing an article for inclusion in our quarterly magazine and the system went down. She was sent to repair it. She saw my article and made some comments about the terms I used, and how unprofessional they sounded. Obviously she didn't understand the difference between a rigger and a roughneck. When I tried to explain, she accused me of talking down to her and walked out." He threw up his hands. "Sir, I wasn't rude, and I wasn't uncooperative. I was trying to teach her the language of the industry."

Brody looked as if he meant to say something, but he glanced at Jodie and cleared his throat instead. "You didn't call her names, Mr. Koswalski?"

"No, sir, I did not," the young man replied courteously. "But she did call me several. Besides that, quite frankly, she had a glazed look in her eyes and a red nose." His face tautened. "Mr. Vance, I've seen too many people who use drugs to mistake signs of drug use. She didn't repair the system, she made matters worse. I had to call in another specialist to undo her damage. I have his name, and his assignment," he added, producing a slip of paper, which he handed to Brody. "I'm sorry to make a countercharge of incompetence against another employee, but my integrity is at stake."

Brody took the slip of paper and read the name. He looked at the younger man again. "I know this technician. He's the best we have. He'll confirm what you just told me?"

"He will, Mr. Vance."

Brody nodded. "I'll check with him and make some investigation of your charges. You'll be notified when we have a resolution. Thank you, Mr. Koswalski."

"Thank you, Mr. Vance," the young man replied, standing. "I enjoy my job very much. If I lose it, it should be on merit, not lies."

"I quite agree," Brody replied. "Good day."

"Good day." Koswalski left, very dignified.

Brody turned to Jodie. "How would you characterize our Mr. Koswalski?"

"He seems sincere, honest, and hardworking."

He nodded. "He's here on time every morning, never takes longer than he has for lunch, does any task he's given willingly and without protest, even if it means working late hours."

He picked up a file folder. "On the other hand, the systems specialist, a Ms. Burgen, has been late four out of five mornings she's worked here. She misses work on Mondays every other week. She complains if she's asked to do overtime, and her work is unsatisfactory." He looked up. "Your course of action, in my place?"

"I would fire her," she said.

He smiled slowly. "She has an invalid mother and a two-year-old son," he said surprisingly. "She was fired from her last job. If she loses this one, she faces an uncertain future."

She bit her lower lip. It was one thing to condone firing an incompetent employee, but given the woman's home life the decision was uncomfortable.

"If you take my place, you'll be required to make such recommendations. In fact, you'll be required to make them to me," he added. "You can't wear your heart on your sleeve. You work for a business that depends on its income. Incompetent employees will cost us time, money, and possibly even clients. No business can exist that way for long."

She looked up at him with sad eyes. "It's not a nice job, Brody."

He nodded. "It's like gardening. You have to separate the weeds from the vegetables. Too many weeds, no more vegetables."

"I understand." She looked at her pad. "So what will you recommend?" she added.

"That our security section make a thorough investigation of her job performance," he said. "If she has a drug problem that relates to it, she'll be given the choice of counseling and treatment or separation. Unless she's caught using drugs on the job, of course," he added coolly. "In that case, she'll be arrested."

She knew she was growing cold inside. What had sounded like a wonderful position was weighing on her like a rock.

"Jodie, is this really what you want to do?" he asked gently, smiling. "Forgive me, but you're not a hardhearted person, and you're forever making excuses for people. It isn't the mark of a manager."

"I'm beginning to realize that," she said quietly. She searched his eyes. "Doesn't it bother you, recommending that people lose their jobs?"

"No," he said simply. "I'm sorry for them, but not sorry enough to risk my paycheck and yours keeping them on a job they're not qualified to perform. That's business, Jodie."

"I suppose so." She toyed with her pad. "I was a whiz with computers in business college," she mused. "I didn't want to be a systems specialist because I'm not mechanically-minded, but I could do anything with software." She glanced at him. "Maybe I'm in the wrong job to begin with. Maybe I should have been a software specialist."

He grinned. "If you decide, eventually, that you'd like to do that, write a job description, give it to your Human Resources manager, and apply for the job," he counseled.

"You're kidding!"

"I'm not. It's how I got my job," he confided.

"Well!"

"You don't have to fire software," he reminded her. "And if it doesn't work, it won't worry your conscience to toss it out. But all this is premature. You don't have to decide right now what you want to do. Besides," he added with a sigh, "I may not even get that promotion I'm hoping for."

"You'll get it," she assured him. "You're terrific at what you do, Brody."

"Do you really think so?" he asked, and seemed to care about her reply.

"I certainly do."

He smiled. "Thanks. Cara doesn't think much of my abilities, I'm afraid. I suppose it's because she's so good at marketing. She gets promotions all the time. And the travel...! She's out of town more than she's in, but she loves it. She was in Mexico last week and in Peru the week before that. Imagine! I'd love to go to Mexico and see Chichen Itza." He sighed.

"So would I. You like archaeology?" she fished.

He grinned. "Love it. You?"

"Oh, yes!"

"There's a museum exhibit of Mayan pottery at the art museum," he said enthusiastically. "Cara hates that sort of thing. I don't suppose you'd like to go with me to see it next Saturday?"

Next Saturday. Alexander's birthday. She'd mourned for the past two weeks since she'd come back from the Cobbs' party, miserable and hurting. But she wouldn't be invited to his birthday party, and she wouldn't go even if she was.

"I'd love to," she said with a beaming smile. "But... won't your girlfriend mind?"

He frowned. "I don't know." He looked down at her. "We, uh, don't have to advertise it, do we?"

She understood. It was a little uncomfortable going out with a committed man, but it wasn't as if he were married or anything. Besides, his girlfriend treated him like dirt. She wouldn't.

"No, we don't," she agreed. "I'll look forward to it."

"Great!" He beamed, too. "I'll phone you Friday night and we'll decide where and when to meet, okay?"

"Okay!"

She was on a new track, a new life, and she felt like a new person. She'd started going to a retro coffeehouse in the evenings, where they served good coffee and people read poetry on stage or played folk music with guitars. Jodie fit right in with the artsy crowd. She'd even gotten up for the first time and read one of her poems, a sad one about rejected love that Alexander had inspired. Everyone applauded, even the owner, a man named Johnny. The boost of confidence she felt made her less inhibited, and the next time she read her poetry, she wasn't afraid of the crowd. She was reborn. She was the new, improved Jodie, who could conquer the world. And now Brody wanted to date her. She was delighted.

That feeling lasted precisely two hours. She came back in after lunch to find Alexander Cobb perched on her desk, in her small cubicle, waiting for her.

She hadn't had enough time to get over her disastrous last

meeting with him. She wanted to turn and run, but that wasn't going to work. He'd already spotted her.

She walked calmly to her desk—although her heart was doing cartwheels—and put her purse in her lower desk drawer.

"Hello, Alexander," she said somberly. "What can I do for you?"

Her attitude sent him reeling. Jodie had always been unsettled and full of joy when she came upon him unexpectedly. He didn't realize how much he'd enjoyed the headlong reaction until it wasn't there anymore.

He stared at her across the desk, puzzled and disturbed. "What happened wasn't anybody's fault," he said stiffly. "Don't wear yourself out regretting it."

She relaxed a little, but only a little. "I drank too much. I won't do it a second time," she assured him. "How's Margie?"

"Quiet," he said. The one word was alarming. Margie was never quiet.

"Why?" she asked.

Shrugging, he picked up a paper clip from her desk and studied it. "She can't get anywhere with her designs. She expected immediate success, and she can't even get a foot in the door."

"I'm sorry. She's really good."

He nodded and his green eyes met hers narrowly. "I need to talk to you," he said. "Can you meet me downstairs at the coffee bar when you get off from work?"

She didn't want to, and it was obvious. "Couldn't you just phone me at home?" she countered.

He scowled. "No. I can't discuss this over the phone." She was still hesitating. "Do you have other plans?" he asked.

She shook her head. "No. I don't want to miss my bus."

"I can drive you…"

"No! I mean——" she lowered her voice "——no, I won't put you to any trouble. There are two buses. The second runs an hour after the first one."

"It won't take an hour," he assured her. But he felt as if something was missing from their conversation. She didn't tease him, taunt him, antagonize him. In fact, she looked very much as if she wanted to avoid him altogether.

"All right, then," she said, sitting down at her desk. "I'll see you there about five after five."

He nodded, pausing at the opening of the cubicle to look back at her. It was a bad time to remember the taste of her full, soft mouth under his. But he couldn't help it. She was wearing a very businesslike dark suit with a pale pink blouse, her long hair up in a bun. She should have looked like a businesswoman, but she was much too vulnerable, too insecure, to give that image. She didn't have the self-confidence to rate a higher job, but he couldn't tell her that. Jodie had a massive inferiority complex. The least thing hurt her. As he'd hurt her.

The muscles in his jaw tautened. "This doesn't suit you," he said abruptly, nodding around the sterile little glass and wood cage they kept her in. "Won't they even let you have a potted plant?"

She was aghast at the comment. He never made personal remarks. She shifted restlessly in her chair. "It isn't dignified," she stammered.

He moved a step closer. "Jodie, a job shouldn't mimic jail. If you don't like what you do, where you do it, you're wasting the major part of your life."

She knew that. She tasted panic when she swallowed. But jobs were thin on the ground and she had the chance for advancement in this one. She put to the back of her mind Brody's comments on her shortcomings as a manager.

"I like my job very much," she lied.

His eyes slid over her with something like possession. "No, you don't. Pity. You have a gift for computer programming. I'll bet you haven't written a single routine since you've been here."

Her face clenched. "Don't you have something to do? Because I'm busy."

"Suit yourself. As soon after five as you can make it, please," he said, adding deliberately, "I have a dinner date."

With Kirry. Always with Kirry. She knew it. She hated Kirry. She hated him, too. But she smiled. "No problem. See you." She turned on her computer and pulled up her memo file to see what tasks were upcoming. She ignored Alexander, who gave her another long, curious appraisal before he left her alone.

She felt the sting of his presence all the way to her poor heart. He was so much a part of her life that it was like being amputated when she thought of a lifetime without his complicated presence.

For the first time, she thought about moving to another city. Ritter Oil Corporation had a headquarters office in Tulsa, Oklahoma. Perhaps she could get a transfer there...and do what, she asked herself? She was barely qualified for the predominantly clerical job she was doing now, and painfully unqualified for firing people, even if they deserved it. She'd let her pride force her into taking this job, because Alexander kept asking when she was going to start working after her graduation from business college. He probably hadn't meant that he thought she was taking advantage of his financial help—but she took it that way. So she went to work for the first company that offered her a job, just to shut him up.

In retrospect, she should have looked a little harder. She'd been under consideration for a job with the local police department, as a computer specialist. She had the skills to write programs, to restructure software. She was a whiz at opening protected files, finding lost documents, tracking down suspicious e-mails and finding ways to circumvent write-protected software. Her professor had recommended her for a career in law enforcement as a cyber crime specialist, but she'd jumped at the first post-college job that came her way.

Now here she was, stuck in a dead-end job that she didn't even like, kept in a cubicle like a box of printer paper and only taken out when some higher-up needed her to take a letter or organize a schedule, or compile his notes…

She had a vision of herself as a cardboard box full of supplies and started giggling.

Another administrative assistant stuck her head in the cubicle. "Better keep it down," she advised softly. "They've had a complaint about the noise levels in here."

"I'm only laughing to myself," Jodie protested, shocked.

"They want us quiet while we're working. No personal phone calls, no talking to ourselves—and there's a new memo about the length of time people are taking in the bathroom…"

"Oh, good God!" Jodie burst out furiously.

The other woman put a feverish hand to her lips and looked around nervously. "Shhh!" she cautioned.

Jodie stood up and gave the woman her best military salute.

Sadly the vice president in charge of personnel was walking by her cubicle at the time. He stopped, eyeing both women suspiciously.

Already in trouble, and not giving a damn anymore, Jodie saluted him, too.

Surprisingly he had to suppress a smile. He wiped it off quickly. "Back to work, girls," he cautioned and kept walking.

The other woman moved closer. "Now see what you've done!" she hissed. "We'll both be on report!"

"If he tries to put me on report, I'll put him on report, as well," Jodie replied coolly. "Nobody calls me a 'girl' in a working office!"

The other woman threw up her hands and walked out.

Jodie turned her attention back to her chores and put the incident out of her mind. But it was very disturbing to realize how much authority the company had over her working life, and she didn't like it. She wondered if old man Ritter, the head of the corporation, encouraged such office politics. From what she'd heard about him, he was something of a renegade. He didn't seem to like rules and regulations very much, but, then, he couldn't be everywhere. Maybe he didn't even know the suppressive tactics his executives used to keep employees under control here.

Being cautioned never to speak was bad enough, and personalization of cubicles was strictly forbidden by company policy. But to have executives complain about the time employees spent in the bathroom made Jodie furious. She had a girlfriend who was a diabetic, and made frequent trips to the rest room in school. Some teachers had made it very difficult for her until her parents had requested a teacher conference to explain their daughter's health problem. She had a feeling no sort of conference would help at this job.

She went back to work, but the day had been disturbing in more ways than one.

At exactly five minutes past quitting time, she walked into the little coffee shop downstairs. Alexander had a table, and he was waiting for her. He'd already ordered the French Vanilla cappuccino she liked so much, along with chocolate biscotti.

She was surprised by his memory of her preferences. She draped her old coat over the empty chair at the corner table and sat down. Fortunately the shop wasn't crowded, as it was early in the evening, and there were no customers anywhere near them.

"Right on time," Alexander noted, checking his expensive wristwatch.

"I usually am," she said absently, sipping her cappuccino. "This is wonderful," she added with a tiny smile.

He seemed puzzled. "Don't you come here often?"

"Actually, it's not something I can fit into my budget," she confessed.

Now it was shock that claimed his features. "You make a good salary," he commented.

"If you want to rent someplace with good security, it costs more," she told him. "I have to dress nicely for work, and that costs, too. By the time I add in utilities and food and bus fare, there isn't a lot left. We aren't all in your income tax bracket, Alexander," she added without rancor.

He let his attention wander to his own cappuccino. He sipped it quietly.

"I never think of you as being in a different economic class," he said.

"Don't you?" She knew better, and her thoughts were bitter. She couldn't forget what she'd overheard him say to his sister, that she was only blue collar and she didn't fit in with them.

He sat up straight. "Something's worrying you," he said flatly. "You're not the same. You haven't been since the party."

Her face felt numb. She couldn't lower her pride enough to tell him what she'd overheard. It was just too much, on top of everything else that had gone haywire lately.

"Why can't you talk to me?" he persisted.

She looked up at him with buried resentments, hurt pride, and outraged sentiment plain in her cold eyes. "It would be like talking to the floor," she said. "If you're here, it's because you want something. So, what is it?"

His expression was eloquent. He sipped cappuccino carefully and then put the delicate cup in its saucer with precision.

"Why do you think I want something?"

She felt ancient. "Margie invites me to parties so that I can cook and clean up the kitchen, if Jessie isn't available," she said in a tone without inflection. "Or if she's sick and needs nursing. You come to see me if you need something typed, or a computer program tweaked, or some clue traced back to an ISP online. Neither of you ever come near me unless I'm useful."

His breath caught. "Jodie, it's not like that!"

She looked at him steadily. "Yes, it is. It always has been. I'm not complaining," she added at once. "I don't know what I would have done if it hadn't been for you and Margie. I owe you more than I can ever repay in my lifetime. It's just that since you're here, there's something you need done, and I know it. No problem. Tell me what you want me to do."

His eyes closed and opened again, on a pained expression. It was true. He and Margie had used her shamelessly, but without realizing they were so obvious. He hated the thought.

"It's a little late to develop a conscience," she added with a faint smile. "It's out of character, anyway. Come on. What is it?"

He toyed with his biscotti. "I told you that we're tracking a link to the drug cartel."

She nodded.

"In your company," he added.

"You said I couldn't help," she reminded him.

"Well, I was wrong. In fact, you're the only one who can help me with this."

A few weeks ago, she'd have joked about getting a badge or a gun. Now she just waited for answers. The days of friendly teasing were long gone.

He met her searching gaze. "I want you to pretend that we're developing a relationship," he said, "so that I have a reason to hang around your division."

She didn't react. She was proud of herself. It would have been painfully easy to dump the thick, creamy cappuccino all over his immaculate trousers and anoint him with the cream.

His eyebrow jerked. "Yes, you're right, I'm using you. It's the only way I can find to do surveillance. I can't hang around Jasper or people will think I'm keen on him!"

That thought provoked a faint smile. "His wife wouldn't like it."

He shrugged. "Will you do it?"

She hesitated.

He anticipated that. He took out a photograph and slid it across the table to her.

She picked it up. It was of two young boys, about five or six, both smiling broadly. They had thick, straight black hair and black eyes and dark complexions. They looked Latin. She looked back up at Alexander with a question in her eyes.

"Their mother was tired of having drug users in her neighborhood. They met in an abandoned house next door to her. There were frequent disputes, usually followed by running gun battles. The dealer who made the house his headquarters got ambitious. He decided to double-cross the new drug leadership that came in after Manuel Lopez's old territory was finally divided," he said carelessly. "Mama Garcia kept a close eye on what was going on, and kept the police informed. She made the fatal error of telling her infrequent neighbor that his days in her neighborhood were numbered. He told his supplier.

"All this got back to the new dealer network. So when they came to take out the double-crossing dealer, they were quite particular about where they placed the shots. They knew where Mama Garcia lived, and they targeted her along with their rival. Miguel and Juan were hit almost twenty times with automatic weapon fire. They died in the firefight, along with the rebellious dealer. Their mother was wounded and will probably never walk again."

She winced as she looked at the photograph of the two little boys, so happy and smiling. Both dead, over drugs.

He saw her discomfort and nodded. "The local distributor I'm after ordered the hit. He works in this building, in this corporation, in this division." He leaned forward, and she'd never seen him look so menacing. "I'm going to take him out. So, I'll ask you one more time, Jodie. Will you help me?"

5

~∽~ ~∽~ ~∽~

J odie groaned inwardly. She knew as she looked one last time at the photograph that she couldn't let a child-killer walk the streets, no matter what the sacrifice to herself.

She handed him back the photograph. "Yes, I'll do it," she said in a subdued tone. "When do I start?"

"Tomorrow at lunch. We'll go out to eat. You can give me the grand tour on the way."

"Okay."

"You still look reluctant," he said with narrowed eyes.

"Brody just asked me out, for the first time," she confessed, trying to sound more despondent than she actually was. It wouldn't hurt to let Alexander know that she wasn't pining over him.

His expression was not easily read. "I thought he was engaged."

She grimaced. "Well, things are cooling off," she defended herself. "His girlfriend travels all over the world. She just came back from trips to Mexico and Peru, and she doesn't pay Brody much attention even when she's here!" she muttered.

"Peru?" He seemed thoughtful. He studied her quietly for a long moment before he spoke. "They're still engaged, Jodie."

And he thought less of her because she was ignoring another woman's rights. Of course he did. She didn't like the idea, either, and she knew she wasn't going to go out with Brody a week from Saturday. Not now. Alexander made her feel too guilty.

She traced the rim of her china coffee cup. "You're right," she had to admit. "It's just that she treats him so badly," she added with a wistful smile. "He's a sweet man. He's always encouraging me in my job, telling me I can do things, believing in me."

"Which is no damned reason to have an affair with a man," he said furiously. It made him angry to think that another man was trying to uplift Jodie's ego when he'd done nothing but damage to it.

She lowered her voice. "I am not having an affair with him!"

"But you would, if he asked," he said, his eyes as cold as green glass.

She started to argue, then stopped. It would do no good to argue. Besides, it was her life, and he had no business telling her how to live it.

"How do you want me to act while we're pretending to get involved?" she countered sourly. "Do you want me to throw myself at you and start kissing you when you walk into my cubicle?"

His eyes dilated. "I beg your pardon?"

"Never mind," she said, ruffled. "I'll play it by ear."

He really did seem different, she thought, watching him hesitate uncharacteristically. He drew a diskette in a plastic holder out of his inside jacket pocket and handed it to her.

"Another chore," he added, glancing around to make sure they weren't being observed. "I want you to check out these Web sites, and the e-mail addresses, without leaving footprints. I want to know if they're legitimate and who owns them. They're password protected and in code."

"No problem," she said easily. "I can get behind any firewall they put up."

"Don't leave an address they can trace back to you," he emphasized. "These people won't hesitate to kill children. They wouldn't mind wasting you."

"I get the point. I'm not sloppy." She slipped the diskette into her purse and finished her coffee. "Anything else?"

"Yes. Margie said to tell you that she's sorry."

Her eyebrows arched. "For what?"

"For everything." He searched her eyes. "And for the record, you don't owe us endless favors, debt or no debt."

She got to her feet. "I know that. I'll have this information for you tomorrow by the time you get here."

He got up, too, catching the bill before she had time to grab it. "My conference, my treat," he said. He stared down at her with an intensity that was disturbing. "You're still keeping something back," he said in a deep, low tone.

"Nothing of any importance," she replied. It was disconcerting that he could read her expressions that well.

His eyes narrowed. "Do you really like working here, Jodie?"

"You're the one who said I needed to stop loafing and get a job," she accused with more bitterness than she realized. "So I got one."

He actually winced. "I said you needed to get your priorities straight," he countered. "Not that you needed to jump into a job you hate."

"I like Brody."

"Brody isn't the damned job," he replied tersely. "You're not cut out for monotony. It will kill your soul."

She knew that; she didn't want to admit it. "Don't you have a hot date?" she asked sarcastically, out of patience with his meddling.

He sighed heavily. "Yes. Why don't you?"

"Men aren't worth the trouble they cause," she lied, turning.

"Oh, you'd know?" he drawled sarcastically. "With your hectic social life?"

She turned, furious. "When Brody's free, look out," she said.

He didn't reply. But he watched her all the way down the hall.

She fumed all the way home. Alexander had such a nerve, she thought angrily. He could taunt her with his conquests, use her to do his decryption work, force her into becoming his accomplice in an investigation...!

Wait a minute, she thought suddenly, her hand resting on her purse over the diskette he'd entrusted her with. He had some of the best cyber crime experts in the country on his payroll. Why was he farming out work to an amateur who didn't even work for him?

The answer came in slowly, as she recalled bits and pieces of information she'd heard during the Lopez investigation. She knew people in Jacobsville who kept in touch with her after her move to Houston. Someone had mentioned that there were suspicions of a mole in the law enforcement community, a shadowy figure who'd funneled information to Lopez so that he could escape capture.

Then Alexander's unusual request made sense. He suspected somebody in his organization of working with the drug dealers, and he wanted someone he could trust to do this investigation for him.

She felt oddly touched by his confidence, not only in her ability, but also in her character. He'd refused to let her help him before, but now he was trusting her with explosive information. He was letting her into his life, even on a limited basis. He had to care about her, a little.

Sure he did, she told herself glumly. She was a computer whiz, and he knew it. Hadn't he paid for the college education that had honed those skills? He trusted her ability to manipulate software and track criminal activity through cyberspace. That didn't amount to a declaration of love. She had to stop living in dreams. There was no hope of a future with Alexander. She wasn't even his type. He liked highly intelligent, confident women. He liked professionals. Jodie was more like a mouse. She kept in her little corner, avoiding confrontation, hiding her abilities, speaking only when spoken to, never demanding anything.

She traced the outline of the diskette box through the soft leather of her purse, bought almost new at a yard sale. She pursed her lips. Well, maybe it was time she stopped being everybody's lackey and started standing up for herself. She was smart. She was capable. She could do any job she really wanted to do.

She thought about firing a woman with a dependent elderly mother and child and ground her teeth together. It was becoming obvious that she was never going to enjoy that sort of job.

On the other hand, tracking down criminals was exciting. It made her face flush as she considered how valuable she could be to Alexander in this investigation. She thought of the two little Garcia boys and their poor mother, and her eyes narrowed angrily. She was going to help Alexander catch the animal who'd ordered that depraved execution. And she was just the woman with the skills to do it.

Jodie spent most of the evening and the wee hours of the morning tracking down the information Alexander had asked her to find for him. She despaired a time or two, because she ran into one dead end after another. The drug dealers must have cyber experts of their own, and of a high caliber, if they could do this sort of thing.

She finally found a Web site that listed information which was, on the surface, nothing more than advisories about the best sites to find UFO information. But one of the addresses coincided with the material she'd printed out from Alexander's diskette, as a possible link to the drug network. She opened site after site, but she found nothing more than double-talk about possible landing sites and dates. Most covered pages and pages of data, but the last one had only one page of information. It was oddly concise, and the sites were all in a defined area—Texas and Mexico and Peru. Strange, she thought. But, then, Peru was right next door to Colombia. And while drugs and Colombia went together like apples and pie, few people outside law enforcement would connect Peru with drug smuggling.

It was two in the morning, and she was so sleepy that she began to laugh at her own inadequacy. But as she looked at the last site she made sudden sense of the numbers and landing sites. Quickly she printed out the single page of UFO landing sites.

There was a pattern in the listings. It was so obvious that it hit her in the face. She grabbed a pencil and pad and began writing down the numbers. From there, it was a quick move to transpose them with letters. They spelled an e-mail address.

She plugged back into her ISP and changed identities to avoid leaving digital footprints. Then she used a hacker's device to find the source of the e-mail. It originated from a foreign server, and linked directly to a city in Peru. Moreover, a city in Peru near the border with Colombia. She copied down the information without risking leaving it in her hard drive and got out fast.

She folded the sheets of paper covered with her information—because she hadn't wanted to leave anything on her computer that could be accessed if she were online—and placed them in her purse. She smiled sleepily as she climbed into bed with a huge yawn. Alexander, she thought, was going to be impressed.

In fact, he was speechless. He went over the figures in his car in the parking lot on the way to lunch. His eyes met Jodie's and he shook his head.

"This is ingenious," he murmured.

"They did do a good job of hiding information…" she agreed.

"No! Your work," he corrected instantly. "This is quality work, Jodie. Quality work. I can't think of anyone who could have done it better."

"Thanks," she said.

"And you're taking notes for Brody Vance," he said with veiled contempt. "He should be working for you."

She chuckled at the thought of Brody with a pad and pen sitting with his legs crossed under a skirt, in front of her desk. "He wouldn't suit."

"You don't suit the job you're doing," he replied. "When this case is solved, I want you to consider switching vocations. Any law enforcement agency with a cyber crime unit would be proud to have you."

Except his, she was thinking, but she didn't say it. A compliment from Alexander was worth something. "I might do that," she said noncommittally.

"I'll put this to good use," he said, sliding the folded sheets into his inside suit pocket. "Where do you want to eat?" he added.

"I usually eat downstairs in the cafeteria. They have a blue plate special…"

"Where does your boss have lunch?"

"Brody?" She blinked. "When his girlfriend's in town, he usually goes to a Mexican restaurant, La Rancheria. It's three blocks over near the north expressway," she added.

"I know where it is. What's his girlfriend like?"

She shrugged. "Very dark, very beautiful, very chic. She's District Marketing manager for the whole southwest. She oversees our sales force for the gas and propane distribution network. We sell all over the world, of course, not just in Texas."

"But she travels to Mexico and Peru," he murmured as he turned the Jaguar into traffic.

"She has family in both places," she said disinterestedly. "Her mother was moving from a town in Peru near the Colombian border down to Mexico City, and Cara had to help organize it. That's what she told Brody." She frowned. "Odd, I thought Brody said her mother was dead. But, then, I didn't really pay attention. I've only seen her a couple of times. She leads Brody around by the nose. He's not very forceful."

"Do you like Mexican food?"

"The real thing, yes," she said with a sigh. "I usually get my chili fix from cans or TV dinners. It's not the same."

"No, it's not."

"You used to love eggs ranchero for breakfast," she commented, and then could have bitten her tongue out for admitting that she remembered his food preferences.

"Yes. You made them for me at four in the morning, the day my father died. Jessie was in tears, so was Margie. Nobody was awake. I'd come from overseas and didn't even have supper. You heard me rattling around in the kitchen trying to make a sandwich," he recalled with a strangely tender smile. "You got up and started cooking. Never said a word, either," he added. "You put the plate in front of me, poured coffee, and went away." He shrugged. "I couldn't have talked to save my life. I was too broken up at losing Dad. You knew that. I never understood how."

"Neither did I," she confessed. She looked out the window. It was a cold day, misting rain. The city looked smoggy. That wasn't surprising. It usually did.

"What is it about Vance that attracts you?" he asked abruptly.

"Brody? Well, he's kind and encouraging, he always makes people feel good about themselves. I like being with him. He's...I don't know...comfortable."

"Comfortable." He made the word sound insulting. He turned into the parking lot of the Mexican restaurant.

"You asked," she pointed out.

He cut off the engine and glanced at her. "God forbid that a woman should ever find me comfortable!"

"That would take a miracle," she said sweetly, and unfastened her seat belt.

He only laughed.

They had a quiet lunch. Brody wasn't there, but Alexander kept looking around as if he expected the man to materialize right beside the table.

"Are you looking for someone?" she asked finally.

He glanced at her over his dessert, a caramel flan. "I'm always looking for someone," he returned. "It's my job."

She didn't think about what he did for a living most of the time. Of course, the bulge under his jacket where he carried his gun was a dead giveaway, and sometimes he mentioned a case he was working on. Today, their combined efforts on the computer tracking brought it up. But she could go whole days without realizing that he put himself at risk to do the job. In his position, it was inevitable that he would make enemies. Some of them must have been dangerous, but he'd never been wounded.

"Thinking deep thoughts?" he asked her as he registered her expression.

"Not really. This flan is delicious."

"No wonder your boss frequents the place. The food is good, too."

"I really like the way they make coffee…"

"Kennedy!" Alexander called to a man just entering the restaurant, interrupting Jodie's comment.

An older man glanced his way, hesitated, and then smiled broadly as he joined them. "Cobb!" he greeted. "Good to see you!"

"I thought you were in New Orleans," Alexander commented.

"I was. Got through quicker than I thought I would. Who's this?" he added with a curious glance at Jodie.

"Jodie's my girl," Alexander said carelessly. "Jodie, this is Bert Kennedy, one of my senior agents."

They shook hands.

"Glad to meet you, Mr. Kennedy."

"Same here, Miss…?"

Alexander ignored the question. Jodie just smiled at him.

"Uh, any luck on the shipyard tip?" Kennedy asked.

Alexander shook his head. "Didn't pan out." He didn't meet the older man's eyes. "We may put a man at Thorn Oil next week," he said in a quiet tone, glancing around to make sure they weren't subject to eavesdroppers. "I'll tell you about it later."

Kennedy had been nervous, but now he relaxed and began to grin. "Great! I'd love to be in on the surveillance," he added. "Unless you have something bigger?"

"We'll talk about it later. See you."

Kennedy nodded, and walked on to a table by the window.

"Is he one of your best men?" she asked Alexander.

"Kennedy is a renegade," he murmured coolly, watching the man from a distance. "He's the bird who brought mercenaries into my drug bust in Jacobsville the year before last, without warning me first. One of their undercover guys almost got killed because we didn't know who he was."

"Eb Scott's men," she ventured.

He nodded. "I was already upset because Manuel Lopez had killed my undercover officer, Walt Monroe. He was my newest agent. I sent him to infiltrate Lopez's organization." His eyes were bleak. "I wanted Lopez. I wanted him badly. The night of the raid, I had no idea that Scott and his gang were even on the place. They were running a Mexican national undercover. If Kennedy knew, he didn't tell me. We could have killed him, or Scott, or any of his men. They weren't supposed to be there."

"I expect Mr. Kennedy lived to regret that decision."

He gave her a cool look. "Oh, he regretted it, all right."

She wasn't surprised that Mr. Kennedy was intimidated by Alexander. Most people were, herself included.

She finished her coffee. "Thanks for lunch," she said. "I really enjoyed it."

He studied her with real interest. "You have exquisite manners," he commented. "Your mother did, too."

She felt her cheeks go hot. "She was a stickler for courtesy," she replied.

"So was your father. They were good people."

"Like your own father."

"I loved him. My mother never forgave him for leaving her for a younger woman," he commented in a rare lapse. "She drank like a fish. Margie and I were stuck with her, because she put on such a good front in court that nobody believed she was a raging alcoholic. She got custody and made us pay for my father's infidelities until she finally died. By then, we were almost grown. We still loved him, though."

She hadn't known the Cobbs' mother very well. Margie had been reluctant to invite her to their home while the older woman was still alive, although Margie spent a lot of time at Jodie's home. Margie and Alexander were very fond of Mr. and Mrs. Clayburn, and they brought wonderful Christmas presents to them every year. Jodie had often wondered just how much damage his mother had done to Alexander in his younger, formative years. It might explain a lot about his behavior from time to time.

"Did you love your mother?" she asked.

He glared at her. "I hated her."

She swallowed. She thought back to the party, to her uninhibited behavior when she'd had those glasses of champagne. She'd brought back terrible memories for Alexander, of his mother, his childhood. Only now did she understand why he'd reacted so violently. No wonder she'd made him sick. He identified her behavior with his mother's. But he'd said other things, as well, things she couldn't forget. Things that hurt.

She dropped her eyes and looked at her watch. "I really have to get back," she began.

His hand went across the table to cover hers. "Don't," he said roughly. "Don't look like that! You don't drink normally, not ever. That's why the champagne hit you so hard. I overreacted. Don't let it ruin things between us, Jodie."

She took a slow breath to calm herself. She couldn't meet his eyes. She looked at his mouth instead, and that was worse. It was a chiseled, sensuous mouth and she couldn't stop remembering how it felt to be kissed by it. He was expert. He was overwhelming. She wanted him to drag her into his arms and kiss her blind, and that would never do.

She withdrew her hand with a slow smile. "I'm not holding grudges, Alexander," she reassured him. "Listen, I really have to get back. I've got a diskette full of letters to get out by quitting time."

"All right," he said. "Let's go."

Kennedy raised his hand and waved as they went out. Alexander returned the salute, sliding his hand around Jodie's waist as they left the building. But she noticed that he dropped it the minute they entered the parking lot. He was putting on an act, and she'd better remember it. She'd already been hurt once. There was no sense in inviting more pain from the same source.

He left her at the front door of her building with a curious, narrow-eyed gaze that stayed with her the rest of the day.

The phone on her desk rang early the following morning and she answered it absently while she typed.

"Do you still like symphony concerts?" came a deep voice in reply.

Alexander! Her fingers flew across the keys, making errors. "Uh, yes."

"There's a special performance of Debussy tomorrow night."

"I read about it in the entertainment section of the newspaper," she said. "They're doing 'Afternoon of a Faun' and 'La Mer,' my two favorites."

He chuckled. "I know."

"I'd love to see it," she admitted.

"I've got tickets. I'll pick you up at seven. Will you have time to eat supper by then?" he added, implying that he was asking her to the concert only, not to dinner.

"Of course," she replied.

"I have to work late, or I'd include dinner," he said softly.

"No problem. I have leftovers that have to be eaten," she said.

"Then I'll see you at seven."

"At seven." She hung up. Her hands were ice cold and shaking. She felt her insides shake. Alexander was taking her to a concert. Mentally her thoughts flew to her closet. She only had one good dress, a black one. She could pair it with her winter coat and a small strand of pearls that Margie and Alexander had given her when she graduated from college. She could put her hair up. She wouldn't look too bad.

She felt like a teenager on her first date until she realized why they were going out together. Alexander hadn't just discovered love eternal. He was putting on an act. But why put it on at a concert?

The answer came in an unexpected way. Brody stopped by her office a few minutes after Alexander's call. He came into the cubicle, looking nervous.

"Is something wrong?" she asked.

He drew in a long breath. "About next Saturday..." he began.

"I can't go," she blurted out.

His relief was patent. "I'm so glad you said that," he replied, relief making him limp. "Cara's going to be home and she wants to spend the day with me."

"Alexander's having a birthday party that day," she replied, painfully aware that she wouldn't be invited, although Alexander would surely want her coworkers to think that she was.

"I, uh, couldn't help but notice that he took you out to lunch yesterday," he said. "You've known him for a long time."

"A very long time," she confessed. "He just phoned, in fact, to invite me to a concert of Debussy…"

"Debussy?" he exclaimed.

"Well, yes…?"

"I'll see you there," he said. "Cara and I are going, too. Isn't *that* a coincidence?"

She laughed, as he did. "I can't believe it! I didn't even know you liked Debussy!"

He grimaced. "Actually, I don't," he had to confess. "Cara does."

She smiled wickedly. "I don't think Alexander's very keen on him, either, but he'll pretend to be."

He smiled back. "Forgive me, but he doesn't seem quite your type," he began slowly, flushing a little. "He's a rather tough sort of man, isn't he? And I think he was wearing a gun yesterday, too…Jodie?" he added when she burst out laughing.

"He's sort of in security work, part-time," she told him, without adding where he worked or what he did. Alexander had always made a point of keeping his exact job secret, even among his friends, for reasons Jodie was only beginning to understand.

"Oh. Oh!" He laughed with sheer relief. "And here I thought maybe you were getting involved with a mobster!"

She'd have to remember to tell Alexander that. Not that it would impress him.

"No, he's not quite that bad," she assured him. "About next Saturday, Brody, I would have canceled anyway. It didn't feel right."

"No, it didn't," he seconded. "You and I are too conventional, Jodie. Neither of us is comfortable stepping out of bounds. I'll bet you never had a speeding ticket."

"Never," she agreed. "Not that I drive very much anymore. It's so convenient to take buses," she added, without mentioning that she'd had to sell her car months ago. The repair bills, because it was an older model, were eating her alive.

"I suppose so. Uh, I did notice that your friend drives a new Jaguar."

She smiled sedately. "He and his sister are independently wealthy," she told him. "They own a ranch and breed some of the finest cattle in south Texas. That's how he can afford to run a Jaguar."

"I see." He stuck his hands in his pockets and watched her. "Debussy. Somehow I never thought of you as a classical concert-goer."

"But I am. I love ballet and theater, too. Not that I get the opportunity to see much of them these days."

"Does your friend like them, too?"

"He's the one who taught me about them," she confided. "He was forever taking me and his sister to performances when we were in our teens. He said that we needed to learn culture, because it was important. We weren't keen at the time, but we learned to love it as he did. Except for Debussy," she added on a chuckle. "And I sometimes think I like that composer just to spite him."

"It's a beautiful piece, if you like modern. I'm a Beethoven man myself."

"And I don't like Beethoven, except for the Ninth Symphony."

"That figures. Well, thanks for understanding. I, uh, I guess we'll see you at the concert tonight, then!"

"I guess so."

They exchanged smiles and then he left. She turned her attention back to her computer, curious about the coincidence.

Had Alexander known that Brody and his girlfriend Cara were going to the same performance? Or had it really been one of those inexplicable things?

Then another thought popped into her mind. What if Alexander was staking out her company because he suspected Brody of being in the drug lord's organization?

6

~∞∾ ∾∾ ∽∞∾

The suspicion that Alexander was after Brody kept Jodie brooding for the rest of the day. Brody was a gentle, sweet man. Surely he couldn't be involved in anything as unsavory as drug smuggling!

If someone at the corporation was under investigation, she couldn't blow Alexander's cover by mentioning anything to her boss. But, wait, hadn't Alexander told his agent, Kennedy, that they were investigating a case at Thorn Oil Corporation? Then she remembered why Alexander wanted to pretend to be interested in Jodie. Something was crazy here. Why would he lie to Kennedy?

She shook her head and put the questions away. She wasn't going to find any answers on her own.

She'd been dressed and ready for an hour when she buzzed Alexander into her apartment building. By the time he got to her room and knocked at the door, she was a nervous wreck.

She opened the door, and he gave her a not very flattering scrutiny. She thought she looked nice in her sedate black dress and high heels, with her hair in a bun. Obviously he didn't. He was dashing, though, in a dinner jacket and slacks and highly polished black shoes. His black tie was perfectly straight against the expensive white cotton of his shirt.

"You never wear your hair down," Alexander said curtly. "And you've worn that same dress to two out of three parties at our house."

She flushed. "It's the only good dress I have, Alexander," she said tightly.

He sighed angrily. "Margie would love to make you something, if you'd let her."

She turned to lock her door. Her hands were cold and numb. He couldn't let her enjoy one single evening without criticizing something about her. She felt near tears...

She gasped as he suddenly whipped her around and bent to kiss her with grinding, passionate fervor. She didn't have time to respond. It was over as soon as it had begun, despite her rubbery legs and wispy breathing. She stood looking up at him with wide, misty, shocked eyes in a pale face.

His own green eyes glittered into hers as he studied her reaction. "Stop letting me put you down," he said unexpectedly. "I know I don't do much for your ego, but you have to stand up for yourself. You're not a carpet, Jodie, stop letting people walk on you."

She was still trying to breathe and think at the same time.

"And now you look like an accident victim," he murmured. He pulled out a handkerchief, his eyes on her mouth. "I suppose I'm covered with pink lipstick," he added, pressing the handkerchief into her hand. "Clean me up."

"It...doesn't come off," she stammered.

He cocked an eyebrow and waited for an explanation.

"It's that new kind they advertise. You put it on and it lasts all day. It won't come off on coffee cups or even linen." She handed him back the handkerchief.

He put it up, but he didn't move. His hands went to the pert bun on the top of her head and before she could stop him, he loosed her hair from the circular comb that held the wealth of hair in place. It fell softly, in waves, to her shoulders.

Alexander caught his breath. "Beautiful," he whispered, the comb held absently in one hand while he ran the other through the soft strands of hair.

"It took forever…to get it put up," she protested weakly.

"I love long hair," he said gruffly. He bent, tilting her chin up, to kiss her with exquisite tenderness. "Leave it like that."

He put the comb in her hand and waited while she stuck it into her purse. Her hands shook. He saw that, too, and he smiled.

When she finished, he linked her fingers into his and they started off down the hall.

The concert hall was full. Apparently quite a few people in Houston liked Debussy, Jodie thought mischievously as they walked down the aisle to their seats. She knew that Alexander didn't like it at all, but it was nice of him to suffer through it, considering her own affection for the pieces the orchestra was playing.

Of course, he might only be here because he was spying on Brody, she thought, and then worried about that. She couldn't believe Brody would ever deal in anything dishonest. He was too much like Jodie herself. But why would Alexander be spending so much time at her place of work if he didn't suspect Brody?

It was all very puzzling. She sat down in the reserved seat next to Alexander and waited for the curtain to go up. They'd gotten into a traffic jam on the way and had arrived just in the nick of time. The lights went out almost the minute they sat down.

In the darkness, lit comfortably by the lights from the stage where the orchestra was placed, she felt Alexander's big, warm hand curl into hers. She sighed helplessly, loving the exciting, electric contact of his touch.

He heard the soft sound, and his fingers tightened. He didn't let go until intermission.

"Want to stretch your legs?" he invited, standing.

"Yes, I think so," she agreed. She got up, still excited by his proximity, and walked out with him. He didn't hold her hand this time, she noticed, and wondered why.

When they were in the lobby, Brody spotted them and moved quickly toward them, his girlfriend in tow.

She was pretty, Jodie noted, very elegant and dark-haired and long-legged. She wished she was half as pretty. Brody's girlfriend looked Hispanic. She was certainly striking.

"Well, hello!" Brody said with genuine warmth. "Sweetheart, this is my secretary, Jodie Clayburn...excuse me," he added quickly, with an embarrassed smile at Jodie's tight-lipped glance, "I mean, my administrative assistant. And this is Jodie's date, Mr., uh, Mr...."

"Cobb," Alexander prompted.

"Mr. Cobb," Brody parroted. "This is my girlfriend, Cara Dominguez," he introduced.

"Pleased to meet you," Cara said in a bored tone.

"Same here," Jodie replied.

"Cara's in marketing," Brody said, trying to force the conversation to ignite. "She works for Bradford Marketing Associates, down the street. They're a subsidiary of Ritter Oil Corporation. They sell drilling equipment and machine parts for oil equipment all over the United States. Cara is over the southwestern division."

"And what do you do, Mr. Cobb?" Cara asked Alexander, who was simply watching her, without commenting.

"Oh, he's in security work," Brody volunteered.

Cara's eyebrows arched. "Really!" she asked, but without much real interest.

"I work for the Drug Enforcement Administration," Alexander said with a faint smile, his eyes acknowledging Jodie's shock. "I'm undercover and out of the country a lot of the time," he added with the straightest face Jodie had ever seen. "I don't have to work at all, of course," he added with a cool smile, "but I like the cachet of law enforcement duties."

Jodie was trying not to look at him or react. It was difficult.

"How nice," Cara said after a minute, and she seemed disconcerted by his honesty. "You are working on a case now?" she fished.

One of the first things Jodie and Margie had learned from Alexander when he went with the DEA was not to mention what he did for a living, past the fact that he did "security work." She'd always assumed it had something to do with his infrequent undercover assignments. And here he was spilling all the beans!

"Sort of," Alexander said lazily. "We're investigating a company with Houston connections," he added deliberately.

Cara was all ears. "That would not be Thorn Oil Corporation?"

Alexander gave her a very nice shocked look.

She laughed. "One hears things," she mused. "Don't worry, I never tell what I know."

"Right," Brody chuckled, making a joke of it. He hadn't known what Alexander did for a living until now.

Alexander laughed, too. "I have to have the occasional diversion," he confessed. "My father was wealthy. My sister and I were his only beneficiaries."

Cara was eyeing him with increased interest. "You live in Houston, Mr. Cobb?"

He nodded.

"Are you enjoying the concert?" Brody broke in, uncomfortable at the way his girlfriend was looking at Alexander.

"It's wonderful," Jodie said.

"I understand the Houston ballet is doing *The Nutcracker* starting in November," Cara purred, smiling at Alexander. "If you like ballet, perhaps we will meet again."

"Perhaps we will," Alexander replied. "Do you live in Houston, also, Miss Dominguez?"

"Yes, but I travel a great deal," she said with careless detachment. "My contacts are far reaching."

"She's only just come back from Mexico," Brody said with a nervous laugh.

"Yes, I've been helping my mother move," Cara said tightly. "After my father...died, she lost her home and had nowhere to go."

"I'm very sorry," Jodie told her. "I lost my parents some years ago. I know how it feels."

Cara turned back to Brody. "We need to get back to our seats. Nice to have met you both," she added with a social smile as she took Brody's hand and drew him along with her. He barely had time to say goodbye.

Alexander glanced down at Jodie. "Your boss looked shocked when I told him what I did."

She shook her head. "You told me never to do that, but you told them everything!"

"I told them nothing Cara didn't know already," he said enigmatically. He slid his hand into hers and smiled secretively. "Let's go back."

"It's a very nice concert," she commented.

"Is it? I hate Debussy," he murmured unsurprisingly.

The comment kept her quiet until they were out of the theater and on their way back to her apartment in his car.

"Why did you ask me out if you don't like concerts?" she asked.

He glanced at her. "I had my reasons. What do you think of your boss's girlfriend?"

"She's nice enough. She leads Brody around like a child, though."

"Most women would," he said lazily. "He's not assertive."

"He certainly is," she defended him. "He has to fire people."

"He's not for you, Jodie, girlfriend or not," he said surprisingly. "You'd stagnate in a relationship with him."

"It's my life," she pointed out.

"So it is."

They went the rest of the way in silence. He walked her to her apartment door and stood staring down at her for a long moment. "Buy a new dress."

"Why?" she asked, surprised.

"I'll take you to see *The Nutcracker* next month. As I recall, it was one of your favorite ballets."

"Yes," she stammered.

"So I'll take you," he said. He checked his watch. "I've got a late call to make, and meetings the first of the week. But I'll take you to lunch next Wednesday."

"Okay," she replied.

He reached out suddenly and drew her against him, hard. He held her there, probing her eyes with his until her lips parted. Then he bent and kissed her hungrily, twisting his mouth against hers until she yielded and gave him what he wanted. A long, breathless moment later, he lifted his head.

"Not bad," he murmured softly. "But you could use a little practice. Sleep well."

He let her go and walked away while she tried to find her voice. He never looked back once. Jodie stood at her door watching until he stepped into the elevator and the doors closed.

She usually left at eleven-thirty to go to lunch, and Alexander knew it. But he was late the following Wednesday. She'd chewed off three of her long fingernails by the time he showed up. She was in the lobby where clients were met, along with several of her colleagues who were just leaving for lunch. Alexander came in, looking windblown and half out of humor.

"I can't make it for lunch," he said at once. "I'm sorry. Something came up."

"That's all right," she said, trying not to let her disappointment show. "Another time."

"I'll be out of town for the next couple of days," he continued, not lowering his voice, "but don't you forget my birthday party on Saturday. Call me from the airport and I'll pick you up. If I'm not back by then, Margie will. All right?"

Amazing how much he sounded as if he really wanted her to come. But she knew he was only putting on an act for the employees who were listening to him.

"All right," she agreed. "Have a safe trip. I'll see you Saturday."

He reached out and touched her cheek tenderly. "So long," he said, smiling. He walked away slowly, as if he hated to leave her, and she watched him go with equal reluctance. There were smiling faces all around. It was working. People believed they were involved, which was just what he wanted.

Later, while Brody was signing the letters he'd dictated earlier, she wondered where Alexander was going that would keep him out of town for so long.

"You look pensive," Brody said curiously. "Something worrying you?"

"Nothing, really," she lied. "I was just thinking about Alexander's birthday party on Saturday."

He sighed as he signed the last letter. "It must be nice to have a party," he murmured. "I stopped having them years ago."

"Cara could throw one for you," she suggested.

He grimaced. "She's not the least bit sentimental. She's all business, most of the time, and she never seems to stop working. She's on a trip to Arizona this week to try to land a new client."

"You'll miss her, I'm sure," Jodie said.

He shrugged. "I'll try to." He flushed. "Sorry, that just popped out."

She smiled. "We all have our problems, Brody."

"Yes, I noticed that your friend, Cobb, hardly touches you, except when he thinks someone is watching. He must be one cold fish," he added with disgust.

Jodie flushed then, remembering Alexander's ardor.

He cleared his throat and changed the subject, and not a minute too soon.

Jodie was doing housework in her apartment when the phone rang Saturday morning.

"Jodie?" Margie asked gently.

"Yes. How are you, Margie?" she asked, but not with her usual cheerful friendliness.

"You're still angry at me, aren't you?" She sighed. "I'm so sorry for making you do all the cooking..."

"I'm not angry," Jodie replied.

There was a long sigh. "I thought Kirry would help me arrange a showing of my designs at her department store," she confessed miserably. "But that's never going to happen. She only pretended to be my friend so that she could get to Alexander. I guess you know she's furious because he's been seen with you?"

"She has nothing to be jealous about," Jodie said coldly. "You can tell her so, for me. Was that all you wanted?"

"Jodie, that's not why I called!" Margie exclaimed. She hesitated. "Alexander wanted me to phone you and make sure you were coming to his birthday party."

"There's no chance of that," Jodie replied firmly.

"But...but he's expecting you," Margie stammered. "He said you promised to come, but that I had to call you and make sure you showed up."

"Kirry's invited, of course?" Jodie asked.

"Well...well, yes, I assumed he'd want her to come so I invited her, too."

"I'm invited to make her jealous, I suppose."

There was a static pause. "Jodie, what's going on? You won't return my calls, you won't meet me for lunch, you don't answer notes. If you're not mad at me, what's wrong?"

Jodie looked down at the floor. It needed mopping, she thought absently. "Alexander told you that he was sick of tripping over me every time he came back to the ranch, and that you were especially not to ask me to his birthday party."

There was a terrible stillness on the end of the line for several seconds. "Oh, my God," Margie groaned. "You heard what he said that night!"

"I heard every single word, Margie," Jodie said tightly. "He thinks I'm still crazy about him, and it...disgusts him. He said I'm not in your social set and you should make friends among your own social circle." She took a deep, steadying breath. "Maybe he's right, Margie. The two of you took care of me when I had nobody else, but I've been taking advantage of it all these years, making believe that you were my family. In a way I'm grateful that Alexander opened my eyes. I've been an idiot."

"Jodie, he didn't mean it, I know he didn't! Sometimes he just says things without thinking them through. I know he wouldn't hurt you deliberately."

"He didn't know I could hear him," she said. "I drank too much and behaved like an idiot. We both know how Alexander feels about women who get drunk. But I've come to my senses now. I'm not going to impose on your hospitality..."

"But Alexander wants you to come!" Margie argued. "He said so!"

"No, he doesn't, Margie," Jodie said wistfully. "You don't understand what's going on, but I'm helping Alexander with a case. He's using me as a blind while he's surveilling a suspect, and don't you dare let on that you know it. It's not personal between us. It couldn't be. I'm not his sort of woman and we both know it."

Margie's intake of breath was audible. "What am I going to tell him when you don't show up?"

"You won't need to tell him anything," Jodie said easily. "He isn't expecting me. It was just for show. He'll tell you all about it one day. Now I have to go, Margie. I'm working in the kitchen, and things are going to burn," she added, lying through her teeth.

"We could have lunch next week," the other woman offered.

"No. You need to find friends in your class, Margie. I'm not part of your family, and you don't owe me anything. Now, goodbye!"

She hung up and unplugged the phone in case Margie tried to call back. She felt sick. But severing ties with Margie was the right thing to do. Once Alexander was through with her, once he'd caught his criminal, he'd leave her strictly alone. She was going to get out of his life, and Margie's, right now. It was the only sensible way to get over her feelings for Alexander.

The house was full of people when Alexander went inside, carrying his bag on a shoulder strap.

Margie met him at the door. "I'll bet you're tired, but at least you got here." She chuckled, trying not to show her worry. "Leave your bag by the door and come on in. Everybody's in the dining room with the cake."

He walked beside her toward the spacious dining room, where about twenty people were waiting near a table set with china and crystal, punch and coffee and cake. He searched the crowd and began to scowl.

"I don't see Jodie," he said at once. "Where is she? Didn't you phone her?"

"Yes," she groaned, "but she wouldn't come. Please, Lex, can't we talk about it later? Look, Kirry's here!"

"Damn Kirry," he said through his teeth, glaring down at his sister. "Why didn't she come?"

She drew in a miserable breath. "Because she heard us talking the last time she was here," she replied slowly. "She said you were right about her not being in our social class, and that she heard you say that the last thing you wanted was to trip over her at your birthday party." She winced, because the look on his face was so full of pain.

"She heard me," he said, almost choking on the words. "Good God, no wonder she looked at me the way she did. No wonder she's been acting so strangely!"

"She won't go out to lunch with me, she won't come here, she doesn't even want me to call her anymore," Margie said sadly. "I feel as if I've lost my own sister."

His own loss was much worse. He felt sick to his soul. He'd never meant for Jodie to hear those harsh, terrible words. He'd been reacting to his own helpless loss of control with her, not her hesitant ardor. It was himself he'd been angry at. Now he understood why Jodie was so reluctant to be around him lately. It was ironic that he found himself thinking about her around the clock, and she was as standoffish as a woman who found him bad company when they were alone. If only he could turn the clock back, make everything right. Jodie, so sweet and tender and loving, Jodie who had loved him once, hearing him tell Margie that Jodie disgusted him...!

"I should be shot," he ground out. "Shot!"

"Don't. It's your birthday," Margie reminded him. "Please. All these people came just to wish you well."

He didn't say another word. He simply walked into the room and let the congratulations flow over him. But he didn't feel happy. He felt as if his heart had withered and died in his chest.

That night, he slipped into his office while Kirry was talking to Margie, and he phoned Jodie. He'd had two straight malt whiskeys with no water, and he wasn't quite sober. It had taken that much to dull the sharp edge of pain.

"You didn't come," he said when she answered.

She hadn't expected him to notice. She swallowed, hard. "The invitation was all for show," she said, her voice husky. "You didn't expect me."

There was a pause. "Did you go out with Brody after all?" he drawled sarcastically. "Is that why you didn't show up?"

"No, I didn't," she muttered. "I'm not spending another minute of my life trying to fit into your exalted social class," she added hotly. "Cheating wives, consciousless husbands, social climbing friends…that's not my idea of a party!"

He sat back in his chair. "You might not believe it, but it's not mine, either," he said flatly. "I'd rather get a fast food hamburger and talk shop with the guys."

That was surprising. But she didn't quite trust him. "That isn't Kirry's style," she pointed out.

He laughed coldly. "It would become her style in minutes if she thought it would make me propose. I'm rich. Haven't you noticed?"

"It's hard to miss," she replied.

"Kirry likes life in the fast lane. She wants to be decked out in diamonds and taken to all the most expensive places four nights a week. Five on holidays."

"I'm sure she wants you, too."

"Are you?"

"I'm folding clothes, Alexander. Was there anything else?" she added formally, trying to get him to hang up. The conversation was getting painful.

"I never knew that you heard me the night of our last party, Jodie," he said in a deep, husky, pained sort of voice. "I'm more sorry than I can say. You don't know what it was like when my mother had parties. She drank like a fish…"

So Margie had told him. It wasn't really a surprise. "I had some champagne," she interrupted. "I don't drink, so it overwhelmed me. I'm very sorry for the way I behaved."

There was another pause. "I loved it," he said gruffly.

Now she couldn't even manage a reply. She just stared at the receiver, waiting for him to say something else.

"Talk to me!" he growled.

"What do you want me to say?" she asked unsteadily. "You were right. I don't belong in your class. I never will. You said I was a nuisance, and you were ri—"

"Jodie!" Her name sounded as if it were torn from his throat. "Jodie, don't! I didn't mean what I said. You've never been a nuisance!"

"It's too late," she said heavily. "I won't come back to the ranch again, ever, Alexander, not for you or even for Margie. I'm going to live my own life, make my own way in the world."

"By pushing us out of it?" he queried.

She sighed. "I suppose so."

"But not until I solve this case," he added after a minute. "Right?"

She wanted to argue, but she kept seeing the little boys' faces in that photograph he'd shown her. "Not until then," she said.

There was a rough sound, as if he'd been holding his breath and suddenly let it out. "All right."

"Alexander, where are you?!" That was Kirry's voice, very loud.

"In a minute, Kirry! I'm on the phone!"

"We're going to open the presents. Come on!"

Jodie heard the sound Alexander made, and she laughed softly in spite of herself. "I thought it was your birthday?" she mused.

"It started to be, but my best present is back in Houston folding clothes," he said vehemently.

Her heart jumped. She had to fight not to react. "I'm nobody's present, Alexander," she informed him. "And now I really do have to go. Happy birthday."

"I'm thirty-four," he said. "Margie is the only family I have. Two of my colleagues just had babies," he remarked, his voice just slightly slurred. "Their desks are full of photographs of the kids and their wives. Know what I've got in a frame on my desk, Jodie? Kirry, in a ball gown."

"I guess the married guys would switch places with you..."

"That's not what I mean! I didn't put it there, she did. Instead of a wife and kids, I've got a would-be debutante who wants to own Paris."

"That was your choice," she pointed out.

"That's what you think. She gave me the framed picture." There was a pause. "Why don't you give me a photo?"

"Sure. Why not? Who would you like a photo of, and I'll see if I can find one for you."

"You, idiot!"

"I don't have any photos of myself."

"Why not?"

"Who'd take them?" she asked. "I don't even own a camera."

"We'll have to do something about that," he murmured. "Do you like parks? We could go jogging early Monday in that one near where you live. The one with the goofy sculpture."

"It's modern art. It isn't goofy."

"You're entitled to your opinion. Do you jog?"

"Not really."

"Do you have sweats and sneakers?"

She sighed irritably. "Well, yes, but..."

"No buts. I'll see you bright and early Monday." There was a pause. "I'll even apologize."

"That would be a media event."

"I'm serious," he added quietly. "I've never regretted anything in my life more than knowing you heard what I said to Margie that night."

For an apology, it was fairly headlong. Alexander never made apologies. It was a red letter event.

"Okay," she said after a few seconds.

He sighed, hard. "We can start over," he said firmly.

"Alexander, are you coming out of there?" came Kirry's petulant voice in the background.

"Better tell Kirry first," she chided.

"I'll tell her…get the hell out of my study!" he raged abruptly, and there was the sound of something heavy hitting the wall. Then there was the sound of a door closing with a quick snap.

"What did you do?" Jodie exclaimed.

"I threw a book in her general direction. Don't worry. It wasn't a book I liked. It was something on Colombian politics."

"You could have hit her!"

"In pistol competition, I hit one hundred targets out of a hundred shots. The book hit ten feet from where she was standing."

"You shouldn't throw things at people."

"But I'm uncivilized," he reminded her. "I need someone to mellow me out."

"Kirry's already there."

"Not for long, if she opens that damned door again. I'll see you Monday. Okay?"

There was a long hesitation. But finally she said, "Okay."

She put down the receiver and stared at it blankly. Her life had just shifted ten degrees and she had no idea why. At least, not right then.

7

Jodie had just changed into her sweats and was making breakfast in her sock feet when Alexander knocked on the door.

He was wearing gray sweats, like hers, with gray running shoes. He gave her a long, thorough appraisal. "I don't like your hair in a bun," he commented.

"I can't run with it down," she told him. "It tangles."

He sniffed the air. "Breakfast?" he asked hopefully.

"Just bacon and eggs and biscuits."

"Just! I had a granola bar," he said with absolute disdain.

She laughed nervously. It was new to have him in her apartment, to have him wanting to be with her. She didn't understand his change of attitude, and she didn't really trust it. But she was too enchanted to question it too closely.

"If you'll feed me," he began, "I'll let you keep up with me while we jog."

"That sounds suspiciously like a bribe," she teased, moving toward the table. "What *would* your bosses say?"

"You're not a client," he pointed out, seating himself at the table. "Or a perpetrator. So it doesn't count."

She poured him a mug of coffee and put it next to his plate, frowning as she noted the lack of matching dishes and even silverware. The table—a prize from a yard sale—had noticeable scratches and she didn't even have a tablecloth.

"What a comedown this must be," she muttered to herself as she fetched the blackberry jam and put it on the table, along with another teaspoon that didn't match the forks.

He gave her an odd look. "I'm not making comparisons, Jodie," he said softly, and his eyes were as soft as his deep voice. "You live within your means, and you do extremely well at it. You'd be surprised how many people are mortgaged right down to the fillings in their teeth trying to put on a show for their acquaintances. Which is, incidentally, why a lot of them end up in prison, trying to make a quick buck by selling drugs."

She made a face. "I'd rather starve than live like that."

"So would I," he confessed. He bit into a biscuit and moaned softly. "If only Jessie could make these the way you do," he said.

She smiled, pleased at the compliment, because Jessie was a wonderful cook. "They're the only thing I do well."

"No, they aren't." He tasted the jam and frowned. "I didn't know they made blackberry jam," he noted.

"You can buy it, but I like to make my own and put it up," she said. "That came from blackberries I picked last summer, on the ranch. They're actually your own blackberries," she added sheepishly.

"You can have as many as you like, if you'll keep me supplied with this jam," he said, helping himself to more biscuits.

"I'm glad you like it."

They ate in a companionable silence. When she poured their second cups of strong coffee, there weren't any biscuits left.

"Now I need to jog," he teased, "to work off the weight I've just put on. Coffee's good, too, Jodie. Everything was good."

"You were just hungry."

He sat back holding his coffee and stared at her. "You've never learned how to take a compliment," he said gently. "You do a lot of things better than other people, but you're modest to the point of self-abasement."

She moved a shoulder. "I like cooking."

He sipped coffee, still watching her. She was pretty early in the morning, he mused, with her face blooming like a rose, her skin clean and free of makeup. Her lips had a natural blush, and they had a shape that was arousing. He remembered how it felt to kiss her, and he ached to do it again. But this was new territory for her. He had to take his time. If he rushed her, he was going to lose her. That thought, once indifferent, took on supreme importance now. He was only beginning to see how much a part of him Jodie already was. He could have kicked himself for what he'd said to her at the ill-fated party.

"The party was a bust," he said abruptly.

Her eyes widened. "Pardon?"

"Kirry opened the presents and commented on their value and usefulness until the guests turned to strong drink," he said with a twinkle in his green eyes. "Then she took offense when a former friend of hers turned up with her ex-boyfriend and made a scene. She left in a trail of flames by cab before we even got to the live band."

She was trying not to smile. It was hard not to be amused at Kirry's situation. The woman was trying, even to people like Margie, who wanted to be friends with her.

"I guess there went Margie's shot at fashion fame," she said sadly.

"Kirry would never have helped her," he said carelessly, and finished his coffee. "She never had any intention of risking her job on a new designer's reputation. She was stringing Margie along so that she could hang out with us. She was wearing thin even before Saturday night."

"Sorry," she said, not knowing what else to say.

"We weren't lovers," he offered blatantly.

She blushed and then caught her breath. "Alexander...!"

"I wanted you to know that, in case anything is ever said about my relationship with her," he added, very seriously. "It was never more than a surface attraction. I can't abide a woman who wears makeup to bed."

She wouldn't ask, she wouldn't ask, she wouldn't...! "How do you know she does?" she blurted out.

He grinned at her. "Margie told me. She asked Kirry why, and Kirry said you never knew when a gentleman might knock on your door after midnight." He leaned forward. "I never did."

"I wasn't going to ask!"

"Sure you were." His eyes slid over her pretty breasts, nicely but not blatantly outlined under the gray jersey top she was wearing. "You're possessive about me. You don't want to be, but you are."

She was losing ground. She got to her feet and made a big thing of checking to see that her shoelaces were tied. "Shouldn't we go?"

He got up, stretched lazily, and started to clear the table. She was shocked to watch him.

"You've never done that," she remarked.

He glanced at her. "If I get married, and I might, I think marriage should be a fifty-fifty proposition. There's nothing romantic about a man lying around the apartment in a dirty T-shirt watching football while his wife slaves in the kitchen." He frowned thoughtfully. "Come to think of it, I don't like football."

"You don't wear dirty T-shirts, either," she replied, feeling sad because he'd mentioned marrying. Maybe there was another woman in his life, besides Kirry.

He chuckled. "Not unless I'm working in the garage." He came around the table after he'd put the dishes in the sink and took her gently by the shoulders, his expression somber. "We've never discussed personal issues. I know less about you than a stranger does. Do you like children? Do you want to have them? Or is a career primary in your life right now?"

The questions were vaguely terrifying. He was going from total indifference to intent scrutiny, and it was too soon. Her face took on a hunted look.

"Never mind," he said quickly, when he saw that. "Don't worry about the question. It isn't important."

She relaxed, but only a little. "I...love children," she faltered. "I like working, or I would if I had a challenging job. But that doesn't mean I'd want to put off having a family if I got married. My mother worked while I was growing up, but she was always there when I needed her, and she never put her job before her family. Neither would I." She searched his eyes, thinking how beautiful a shade of green they were, and about little children with them. Her expression went dreamy. "Fame and fortune may sound enticing, but they wouldn't make up for having people love you." She shrugged. "I guess that sounds corny."

"Actually, it sounds very mature." He bent and drew his mouth gently over her lips, a whisper of contact that didn't demand anything. "I feel the same way."

"You do?" She was unconsciously reaching up to him, trying to prolong the contact. It was unsettling that his lightest touch could send her reeling like this. She wanted more. She wanted him to crush her in his arms and kiss her blind.

He nibbled her upper lip slowly. "It isn't enough, is it?"

"Well...no..."

His arms drew her up, against the steely length of his body, and his mouth opened her lips to a kiss that was consuming with its heat. She moaned helplessly, clinging to him.

He lifted his mouth a breath away. His voice was strained when he spoke. "Do you have any idea what those little noises do to me?" he groaned.

"Noises?" she asked, oblivious, as she stared at his mouth.

"Never mind." He kissed her again, devouring her soft lips. The sounds she made drugged him. He was measuring the distance from the kitchen to her bedroom when he realized how fast things were progressing.

He drew back, and held her away from him, his jaw taut with an attempt at control.

"Alexander," she whispered, her voice pleading as she looked up at him with misty soft eyes.

"I almost never get women pregnant on Monday, but this could be an exception," he said in a choked tone.

Her eyes widened like saucers as she realized what he was saying.

He burst out laughing at her expression. He moved back even more. "I only carry identification and twenty dollars on me when I jog," he confessed. "The other things I keep in my wallet are still in it, at my apartment," he added, his tone blatantly expressive.

She divined what he was intimating and she flushed. She pushed back straggly hair from her face as she searched for her composure.

"Of course, a lot of modern women keep their own supply," he drawled. "I expect you have a box full in your medicine cabinet."

She flushed even more, and now she was glaring at him.

He chuckled, amused. "Your parents were very strict," he recalled. "And deeply religious. You still have those old attitudes about premarital sex, don't you?"

She nodded, grimacing.

"Don't apologize," he said wistfully. "In ten minutes or so, the ache will ease and I can actually stand up straight... God, Jodie!" he burst out laughing at her horrified expression. "I'm kidding!"

"You're a terrible man," she moaned.

"No, I'm just normal," he replied. "I'd love nothing better than a few hours in bed with you, but I'm not enough of a scoundrel to seduce you. Besides all that—" he sighed "—your conscience would kill both of us."

"Rub it in."

He shrugged. "You'd be surprised how many women at my office abstain, and make no bones about it to eligible bachelors who want to take them out," he said, and he smiled tenderly at her. "We tend to think of them as rugged individualists with the good sense not to take chances." He leaned forward. "And there are actually a couple of the younger male agents who feel the same way!"

"You're kidding!"

He shook his head, smiling. "Maybe it's a trend. You know, back in the early twentieth century, most women and men went to their weddings chaste. A man with a bad reputation was as untouchable as a woman with one."

"I'll bet you never told a woman in your life that you were going to abstain," she murmured wickedly.

He didn't smile back. He studied her for a long moment. "I'm telling you that I am. For the foreseeable future."

She didn't know how to take that, and it showed.

"I'm not in your class as a novice," he confessed, "but I'm no rake, either. I don't find other women desirable lately. Just you." He shrugged. "Careful, it may be contagious."

She laughed. Her whole face lit up. She was beautiful.

He drew her against him and kissed her, very briefly, before he moved away again. "We should go," he said. "I have a meeting at the office at ten. Then we could have lunch."

"Okay," she said. She felt lighthearted. Overwhelmed. She started toward the door and then stopped. "Can I ask you a question?"

"Shoot."

"Are you staking out my company because you're investigating Brody for drug smuggling?"

He gave her an old, wise look. "You're sharp, Jodie. I'll have to watch what I say around you."

"That means you're not going to tell me. Right?"

He chuckled. "Right." He led the way into the hall and then waited for her to lock her door behind them.

She slipped the key into her pocket.

"No ID?" he mused as they went downstairs and started jogging down the sparsely occupied sidewalk.

"Just the key and five dollars, in case I need money for a bottle of water or something," she confessed.

He sighed, not even showing the strain as they moved quickly along. "One of our forensic reconstruction artists is always lecturing us on carrying identification. She says that it's easier to have something on you that will identify you, so that she doesn't have to take your skull and model clay to do a reconstruction of your face. She helps solve a lot of murder victims' identities, but she has plenty that she can't identify. The faces haunt her, she says."

"I watched a program about forensic reconstruction on educational television two weeks ago."

"I know the one you mean. I saw it, too. That was our artist," he said with traces of pride in his deep voice. "She's a wonder."

"I guess it wouldn't hurt to carry my driver's license around with me," she murmured.

He didn't say another word, but he grinned to himself.

The meeting was a drug task force formed of a special agent from the Houston FBI office, a Houston police detective who specialized in local gangs, a Texas Ranger from Company A, an agent from the U.S. Customs Service and a sheriff's deputy from Harris County who headed her department's drug unit.

They sat down in a conference room in the nearest Houston police station to discuss intelligence.

"We've got a good lead on the new division chief of the Culebra cartel in Mexico," Alexander announced when it was his turn to speak. "We know that he has somebody on his payroll from Ritter Oil Corporation, and that he's funneling drugs through a warehouse where oil regulators and drilling equipment are kept before they're shipped out all over the southwest. Since the parking lot of that warehouse is locked by a key code, the division chief has to have someone on the inside."

"Do we know how it's being moved and when?" the FBI agent asked.

Alexander had suspicions, but no concrete evidence. "Waiting for final word on when. But we do have an informant, a young man who got cold feet and came to U.S. Customs with information about the drug smuggling. I interviewed the young man, with help from Customs," he added, nodding with a smile at the petite brunette customs official at the table with them.

"That would be me," she said with a grin.

"The informant says that a shipment of processed cocaine is on the way here, one of the biggest in several years. It was shipped from the Guajira Peninsula in Colombia to Central America and transshipped by plane to an isolated landing site in rural Mexico. From there it was carried to a warehouse in Mexico City owned by a subsidiary of an oil company here in Houston. It was reboxed with legitimate oil processing equipment manufactured in Europe, in boxes with false bottoms. It was shipped legally to the oil company's district office in Galveston where it was inspected briefly and passed through customs."

"The oil company is one that's never been involved in any illegal activity," the customs representative said wistfully, "so the agent didn't look for hidden contraband."

"To continue," Alexander said, "it's going to be shipped into the Houston warehouse via the Houston Ship Canal as domestic inventory from Galveston."

"Which means, no more customs inspections," the Texas Ranger said.

"Exactly," Alexander agreed.

The brunette customs agent shook her head. "A few shipments get by our inspectors, but not many. We have contacts everywhere, too, and one of those tipped us off about the young man who was willing to inform on the perpetrators of an incoming cocaine shipment," she told the others. "So we saved our bacon."

"You had the contacts I gave you, don't forget," the blond lieutenant of detectives from Houston reminded her with a smile, as she adjusted her collar.

"Do we even have a suspect?" the customs agent asked.

Alexander nodded. "I've got someone on the inside at Ritter

Oil, and I'm watching a potential suspect. I don't have enough evidence yet to make an accusation, but I hope to get it, and soon. I'm doing this undercover, so this information is to be kept in this room. I've put it out that we have another company, Thorn Oil, under surveillance, as a cover story. Under no circumstances are any of you to discuss any of this meeting, even with another DEA agent—*especially* with another DEA agent—until further notice. That's essential."

The police lieutenant gave him a pointed look. "Can I ask why?"

"Because the oil corporation isn't the only entity that's harboring an inside informant," Alexander replied flatly. "And that's all I feel comfortable saying."

"You can count on us," the Texas Ranger assured him. "We won't blow your cover. The person you're watching, can you tell us why you're watching him?"

"In order to use that warehouse for storage purposes, the drug lord has to have access to it," Alexander explained. "I'm betting he has some sort of access to the locked gate and that he's paying the night watchman to look the other way."

"That would make sense," the customs agent agreed grimly. "These people know how little law enforcement personnel make. They can easily afford to offer a poorly paid night watchman a six figure 'donation' to just turn his head at the appropriate time."

"That much money would tempt even a law-abiding citizen," Alexander agreed. "But more than that, very often there's a need that compromises integrity. A sheriff in another state had a wife dying of cancer and no insurance. He got fifty thousand dollars for not noticing a shipment of drugs coming into his county."

"They catch him?" the policewoman asked.

"Yes. He wasn't very good at being a crook. He confessed, before he was even suspected of being involved."

"How many people in your agency know about this?" the deputy sheriff asked Alexander.

"Nobody, at the moment," he replied. "It has to stay that way, until we make the bust. I'll depend on all of you to back me up. The mules working for the new drug lord carry automatic weapons and they've killed so many people down in Mexico that they won't hesitate to waste anyone who gets in their way."

"Good thing the president of Mexico isn't intimidated by them," the customs agent said with a grin. "He's done more to attack drug trafficking than any president before him."

"He's a good egg," Alexander agreed. "Let's hope we can shut down this operation before any more kids go down."

"Amen to that," the FBI agent said solemnly.

Alexander showed up at Jodie's office feeling more optimistic than he had for weeks. He was close to an arrest, but the next few days would be critical. After their meeting, the task force had gleaned information from the informant that the drug shipment was coming into Houston the following week. He had to be alert, and he had to spend a lot of time at Jodie's office so that he didn't miss anything.

He took her out to lunch, but he was preoccupied.

"You're onto something," she guessed.

He nodded, smiling. "Something big. How would you like to be part of a surveillance?"

"Me? Wow. Can I have a gun?"

He glared at her. "No."

She shrugged. "Okay. But don't expect me to save your life without one."

"Not giving you one might save my life," he said pointedly.

She ignored the jibe. "Surveillance?" she prodded. "Of what?"

"You'll find out when we go, and not a word to anybody."

"Okay," she agreed. "How do you do surveillance?"

"We sit in a parked car and drink coffee and wish we were watching television," he said honestly. "It gets incredibly boring. Not so much if we have a companion. That's where you come in," he added with a grin. "We can sit in the car and neck and nobody will guess we're spying on them."

"In a Jaguar," she murmured. "Sure, nobody will notice us in one of those!"

He gave her a long look. "We'll be in a law enforcement vehicle, undercover."

"Right. In a car with government license plates, four antennae and those little round hubcaps..."

"Will you stop?" he groaned.

"Sorry!" She grinned at him over her coffee. "But I like the necking part."

He pursed his lips and gave her a wicked grin. "So do I."

She laughed a little self-consciously and finished her lunch.

They were on the way back to his Jaguar when his DEA agent, Kennedy, drove up. He got out of his car and approached them with a big smile.

"Hi, Cobb! How's it going?" he asked.

"Couldn't be better," Alexander told him complacently. "What's new?"

"Oh, nothing, I'm still working on that smuggling ring." He glanced at Alexander curiously. "Heard anything about a new drug task force?"

"Just rumors," Alexander assured him, and noticed a faint reaction from the other man. "Nothing definite. I'll let you know if I hear anything."

"Thanks." Kennedy shrugged. "There are always rumors."

"Do you have anybody at Thorn Oil, just in case?" Alexander asked him pointedly.

Kennedy cleared his throat and laughed. "Nobody at all. Why?"

"No reason. No reason at all. Enjoy your lunch."

"Sure. I never see you at staff meetings lately," he added. "You got something undercover going on?"

Alexander deliberately tugged Jodie close against his side and gave her a look that could have warmed coffee. "Something," he said, with a smile in Kennedy's direction. "See you."

"Yeah. See you!"

Kennedy walked on toward the restaurant, a little distracted.

Jodie waited until they were closed up in Alexander's car before she spoke. "You didn't tell him anything truthful," she remarked.

"Kennedy's got a loose tongue," he told her as he cranked the car. "You don't tell him anything you don't want repeated. Honest to God, he's worse than Margie!"

"So that's it," she said, laughing. "I just wondered. Isn't it odd that he seems to show up at places where we eat a lot?"

"Plenty of the guys eat where we do," he replied lazily. "We know where the good food is."

"You really do," she had to admit. "That steak was wonderful!"

"Glad you liked it."

"I could cook for you, sometime," she offered, and then flushed at her own boldness.

"After I wind up this case, I'll let you," he said, with a warm smile. "Meanwhile, I've got a lot of work to do."

She wondered about that statement after he left her at the office. She was still puzzling over it when she walked right into Brody when she got off the elevator at her floor.

"Oh, sorry!" she exclaimed, only then noticing that Cara was with him. "Hello," she greeted the woman as she stopped to punch her time card before entering the cubicle area.

Cara wasn't inclined to be polite. She gave Jodie a cold look and turned back to Brody. "I don't understand why you can't do me this one little favor," she muttered. "It isn't as if I ask you often for anything."

"Yes, but dear, it's an odd place to leave your car. There are garages..."

"My car is very expensive," she pointed out, her faint accent growing in intensity, like the anger in her black eyes. "All I require is for you to let me in, only that."

Jodie's ears perked up. She pretended to have trouble getting her card into the time clock, and hummed deliberately to herself, although not so loudly that she couldn't hear what the other two people were saying.

"Company rules..." he began.

"Rules, rules! You are to be an executive, are you not? Do you have to ask permission for such a small thing? Or are you not man enough to make such decisions for yourself?" she added cannily.

"Nice to see you both," Jodie said, and moved away—but not quickly. She fumbled in her purse and walked very slowly as she did. She was curious to know what Cara wanted.

"I suppose I could, just this once," Brody capitulated. "But you know, dear, a warehouse isn't as safe as a parking garage, strictly speaking."

Jodie's heart leaped.

"Yours certainly is, you have an armed guard, do you not?

Besides, I work for a subsidiary of Ritter Oil. It is not as if I had no right to leave my car there when I go out of town for the company."

"All right, all right," Brody said. "Tomorrow night then. What time?"

"At six-thirty," she told him. "It will be dark, so you must flash your lights twice to let me know it is you."

They spoke at length, but Jodie was already out of earshot. She'd heard enough of the suspicious conversation to wonder about it. But she was much too cautious to phone Alexander from her work station.

She would have to wait until the end of the day, even if it drove her crazy. Meanwhile she pretended that she'd noticed nothing.

Brody came by her cubicle later that afternoon, just before quitting time, while she was finishing a letter he'd dictated.

"Can I help you?" she asked automatically, and smiled.

He smiled back and looked uncomfortable. "No, not really. I just wondered what you thought about what Cara asked me?"

She gave him a blank look. "What she asked you?" she said. "I'm sorry, I'd just come from having lunch with Alexander." She smiled and sighed and lowered her eyes demurely. "To tell you the truth, I wasn't paying attention to anything except the time clock. What did she ask you?" She opened her eyes very wide and looked blank.

"Never mind. She phoned and made a comment about your being there. It's nothing. Nothing at all."

She smiled up at him. "Did you enjoy the concert that night?"

"Yes, actually I did, despite the fact that Cara went out to the powder room and didn't show up again for an hour." He shook his head. "Honestly, that woman is so mysterious! I never know what she's thinking."

"She's very crisp, isn't she?" she mused. "I mean, she's assertive and aggressive. I guess she's a good marketer."

"She is," he sighed. "At least, I guess she is. I haven't heard much from the big boss about her work. In fact, there was some talk about letting her go a month or two ago, because she lost a contract. Funny, it was one she was supposedly out of town negotiating at the time, but the client said he'd never seen her. Mr. Ritter talked him into staying, but he had words with Cara about the affair."

"Could that have been when her mother was ill?" she asked.

"Her mother hasn't ever been ill, as far as I know," he murmured. "She did move from Peru to Mexico, but you know about that." He put his hands in his pockets. "She wants me to do something that isn't quite acceptable, and I'm nervous about it. I'm due for a promotion. I don't want to get mixed up in anything the least bit suspicious."

"Why, Brody, what does she want you to do?" she asked innocently.

He glanced at her, started to speak, and then smiled sheepishly. "Well, it's nothing, really. Just a favor." He shrugged. "I'm sure I'm making a big deal out of nothing. You never told me that your boyfriend works for the Drug Enforcement Administration."

"He doesn't advertise it," she stammered. "He does a lot of undercover work at night," she added.

Brody sighed. "I see. Well, I'll let you finish. You and Cobb seem to get along very well," he added.

"I've known him a long time."

"So you have. You've known me a long time, too, though," he added with a slow smile.

"Not really. Only three years."

"Is it? I thought it was longer." He toyed with his tie. "You and Cobb seem to spend a lot of time together."

"Not as much as we'd like," she said, seeing a chance to help Alexander and throw Cara off the track. "And I have a cousin staying with me for a few days, so we spend a lot of time in parked cars necking," she added.

Brody actually flushed. "Oh." He glanced at his watch and grimaced. "I've got a meeting with our vice president in charge of human resources at four, I'd better get going. See you later."

"See you, Brody."

She was very glad that she'd learned to keep what she knew to herself. What Brody's girlfriend had let slip was potentially explosive information, even if it was only circumstantial. She'd have a lot to tell Alexander when she saw him. Furthermore, she'd already given Alexander some cover by telling Brody about the company car, and the fact that they spent time at night necking in one. He was going to be proud of her, she just knew it!

8
❧❧❧ ❧❧❧ ❧❧❧

The minute she got to her apartment, Jodie grabbed the phone and called Alexander.

"Can you come by right away?" Jodie asked him quickly.

He hesitated. "To your apartment? Why?"

She didn't know if her phone might be bugged. She couldn't risk it. She sighed theatrically. "Because I'm wearing a see-through gown with a row of prophylactics pinned to the hem…!"

"Jodie!" He sounded shocked.

"Listen, I have something to tell you," she said firmly.

He hesitated again and then he groaned. "I can't right now…"

"Who's on the phone, Alex?" came a sultry voice from somewhere in the background.

Jodie didn't need to ask who the voice belonged to. Her heart began to race with impotent fury. "Sorry I interrupted," she said flatly. "I'm sure you and Kirry have lots to talk about."

She hung up and then unplugged the phone. So much for any feeling Alexander had for her. He was already seeing Kirry again, alone and at his apartment. No doubt he was only seeing Jodie to avert suspicion at Ritter Oil. The sweet talk was to allay any suspicion that he was using her. Why hadn't she realized that? The Cobbs were always using her, for one reason or another. She was being a fool again. Despite what he'd said, it was obvious now that Alexander had no interest in her except as a pawn.

She fought down tears and went to her computer. She might as well use some of her expertise to check out Miss Cara Dominguez and see if the woman had a rap sheet. With a silent apology to the local law enforcement departments, she hacked into criminal files and checked her out.

What she found was interesting enough to take her mind off Alexander. It seemed that Cara didn't have a lily-white past at all. In fact, she'd once been arrested for possession with intent to distribute cocaine and had managed to get the charges dropped. Besides that, she had some very odd connections internationally. It was hinted in the records of an international law enforcement agency—whose files gave way to her expertise also—that her uncle was one of the Colombian drug lords. She wondered if Alexander knew that.

Would he care? He was with Kirry. Damn Kirry! She threw a plastic coffee cup at the wall in impotent rage.

Just as it hit, there was a buzz at the intercom. She glowered at it, but the caller was insistent. She pushed the button.

"Yes?" she asked angrily.

"Let me in," Alexander said tersely.

"Are you alone?" she asked with barely contained sarcasm.

"In more ways than you might realize," he replied, his voice deep and subdued. "Let me in, Jodie."

She buzzed him in with helpless reluctance and waited at her opened door for him to come out of the elevator.

He was still in his suit. He looked elegant, expensive, and very irritated. He walked into the apartment ahead of her and went straight to the kitchen.

"I was going to take you out to eat when Kirry showed up, in tears, and begged to talk to me," he said heavily, examining pots until he found one that contained a nice beef stew. He got a bowl out of the cupboard and proceeded to fill it. "Any corn bread?" he asked wistfully, having sniffed it when he entered the apartment.

"It's only just getting done," she said, reaching around him for a pot holder. She opened the oven and produced a pone of corn bread.

"I'm hungry," he said.

"You're always hungry," she accused, but she was feeling better.

He caught her by the shoulders and pulled her against him, tilting her chin up so that he could see into her mutinous eyes. "I don't want Kirry. I said that, and I meant it."

"Even if you didn't, you couldn't say so," she muttered. "You need me to help you smoke out your drug smuggler."

He scowled. "Do you really think I'm that sort of man?" he asked, and sounded wounded. "I'll admit that Margie and I don't have a good track record with you, but I'd draw the line at pretending an emotion I didn't feel, just to catch crooks."

She shifted restlessly and didn't speak.

He shook his head. "No ego," he mused, watching her. "None at all. You can't see what's right under your nose."

"My chin, and no, I can't see it…"

He chuckled, bending to kiss her briefly, fiercely. "Feed me. Then we might watch television together for a while. I'll be working most evenings during the week, but Friday night we could go see a movie or something."

Her heart skipped. "A movie?"

"Or we could go bowling. I used to like it."

Her mind was spinning. He actually wanted to be with her! But cold reality worked its way between them again. "You haven't asked why I wanted you to come over," she began as he started for the table with his bowl of stew.

"No, I haven't. Why?" he asked, pouring himself a cup of freshly brewed coffee and accepting a dish of corn bread from her.

She put coffee and corn bread at her place at the table and put butter next to it before she sat down and gave Alexander a mischievous smile. "Cara talked Brody into letting her into the warehouse parking lot after hours tomorrow—about six-thirty in the evening. She said she wanted to park her car there, but it sounded thin to me."

He caught his breath. "Jodie, you're a wonder."

"That's not all," she added, sipping coffee and adding more cream to it. "She was arrested at the age of seventeen for possession with intent to distribute cocaine, and she got off because the charges were dropped. There's an unconfirmed suspicion that her uncle is one of the top Colombian drug lords."

"Where did you get that?"

She flushed. "I can't tell you. Sorry."

"You've hacked into some poor soul's protected files, haven't you?" he asked sternly, but with twinkling eyes.

"I can't tell you," she repeated.

"Okay, I give up." He ate stew and corn bread with obvious enthusiasm. "Then I guess you and I will go on stakeout tomorrow night."

She smiled smugly. "Yes, in your boss's borrowed security car, because my cousin is visiting and we can't neck in the apartment. I told Brody that, and he'll tell Cara that, so if we're seen near my office, they won't think a thing of it."

"Sheer genius," he mused, studying her. "Like I said, you're a natural for law enforcement work. You've got to get your expert computer certification and change professions, Jodie. You're wasted in personnel work."

"Human resources work," she reminded him.

"New label, same job."

She wrinkled her nose. "Maybe so."

They finished their supper in pleasant silence, and she produced a small loaf of pound cake for dessert, with peaches and whipped cream.

"If I ate here often, I'd get fat," he murmured.

She laughed. "Not likely. The cake was made with margarine and reduced-fat milk. I make rolls the same way, except with light olive oil in place of margarine. I don't want clogged arteries before I'm thirty," she added. "And I especially don't want to look like I used to."

He smiled at her warmly. "I like the way you used to look," he said surprisingly. "I like you any way at all, Jodie," he continued softly. "That hasn't changed."

She didn't know whether or not to trust him, and it showed in her face.

He sighed. "It's going to be a long siege," he said enigmatically.

Later, they curled up together on the couch to watch the evening news. There was a brief allusion to a drug smuggling catch by U.S. Customs in the Gulf of Mexico, showing the helicopters they used to catch the fast little boats used in smuggling.

"Those boats go like the wind," Jodie remarked.

He yawned. "They do, indeed. The Colombian National Police busted an operation that was building a submarine for drug smuggling a couple of years ago."

"That's incredible!"

"Some of the smuggling methods are, too, like the tunnel under the Mexican border that was discovered, and having little children swallow balloons filled with cocaine to get them through customs."

"That's barbaric," she said.

He nodded. "It's a profitable business. Greed makes animals of men sometimes, and of women, too."

She cuddled close to him. "It isn't Brody you were after, is it? It's his girlfriend."

He chuckled and wrapped her up in his arms. "You're too sharp for me."

"I learned from an expert," she said, lifting her eyes to his handsome face.

He looked down at her intently for a few seconds before he bent to her mouth and began to kiss her hungrily. Her arms slid up around his neck and she held on for dear life as the kiss devoured her.

Finally he lifted his head and put her away from him, with visible effort. "No more of that tonight," he said huskily.

"Spoilsport," she muttered.

"You're the one with the conscience, honey," he drawled meaningfully. "I'm willing, but you'd never live it down."

"I probably wouldn't," she confessed, but her eyes were misty and wistful.

He pushed back her hair. "Don't look like that," he chided. "It isn't the end of the world. I like you the way you are, Jodie, hangups and all. Okay?"

She smiled. "Okay."

"And I'm not sleeping with Kirry!"

The smile grew larger.

He kissed the tip of her nose and got up. "I've got some preparations to make. I'll pick you up tomorrow at 6:20 sharp and we'll park at the warehouse in the undercover car." He hesitated. "It might be better if I had a female agent in the car with me..."

"No, you don't," she said firmly, getting to her feet. "This is my stakeout. You wouldn't even know where to go, or when, if it wasn't for me."

"True. But it could be very dangerous," he added grimly.

"I'm not afraid."

"All right," he said finally. "But you'll stay in the car and out of the line of fire."

"Whatever you say," she agreed at once.

The warehouse parking lot was deserted. The night watchman was visible in the doorway of the warehouse as he opened the door to look out. He did that twice.

"He's in on it," Alexander said coldly, folding Jodie closer in his arms. "He knows they're coming, and he's watching for them."

"No doubt. Ouch." She reached under her rib cage and touched a small hard object in his coat pocket. "What is that, another gun?"

"Another cell phone," he said. "I have two. I'm leaving one with you, in case you see something I don't while I'm inside," he added, indicating a cell phone he'd placed on the dash.

"You do have backup?" she worried.

"Yes. My whole team. They're well concealed, but they're in place."

"Thank goodness!"

He shifted her in his arms so that he could look to his left at the warehouse while he was apparently kissing her.

"Your heart is going very fast," she murmured under his cool lips.

"Adrenaline," he murmured. "I live on rushes of it. I could never settle for a nine-to-five desk job."

She smiled against his mouth. "I don't like it much, either."

He nuzzled her cheek with his just as a car drove past them toward the warehouse. It hesitated for a few seconds and then sped on.

"That's Brody's car," she murmured.

"And that one, following it?" he asked, indicating a small red hardtop convertible of some expensive foreign make.

"Cara."

"Amazing that she can afford a Ferrari on thirty-five thousand a year," he mused, "and considering that her mother is poor."

"I was thinking the same thing," she murmured. "Kiss me again."

"No time, honey." He pulled out a two-way radio and spoke into it. "All units, stand by. Target in motion. Repeat, target in motion. Stand by."

Several voices took turns asserting their readiness. Alexander watched as Brody's car suddenly reappeared and he drove away. The gates of the warehouse closed behind his car. He paused near Alexander's car again, and then drove off down the road.

As soon as he was out of sight, a van came into sight. Cara appeared at the parking lot entrance, inserted a card key into the lock, opened the gate and motioned the van forward. The gate didn't close again, but remained open.

Alexander gave it time to get to a loading dock and its occupants to exit the cab and begin opening the rear doors before he took out the walkie-talkie again.

"All units, move in. I repeat, all units, move in. We are good to go!"

He took the cell phone from the dash and put it into Jodie's hands. "You sit right here, with the doors locked, and don't move until I call you on that phone and tell you it's safe. Under no circumstances are you to come into the parking lot. Okay?"

She nodded. "Okay. Don't get shot," she added.

He kissed her. "I don't plan to. See you later."

He got out of the car and went toward a building next door to the warehouse. He was joined by another figure in black. They went down an alley together, out of sight.

Jodie slid down into her seat, so that only her eyes and the top of her head were visible in the concealing darkness, barely lit by a nearby street light. She waited with her heart pounding in her chest for several minutes, until she heard a single gunshot. There was pandemonium in the parking lot. Dark figures ran to and fro. More shots were fired. Her heart jumped into her throat. She gritted her teeth, praying that Alexander wasn't in the line of fire.

Then, suddenly, she spotted him, with another dark figure. They had two people in custody, a man and a woman. They were standing near another loading dock, apparently conversing with the men, when Jodie spotted a solitary figure outside the gates, on the sidewalk, moving toward the open gate. The figure was slight, and it held what looked like an automatic weapon. She'd seen Alexander with one of those, a rare time when he'd been arming himself for a drug bust.

She had a single button to push to make Alexander's cell phone ring, but when she pressed in the number, nothing happened. The phone went dead in her hand.

The man with the machine gun was moving closer to where Alexander and the other man stood with their prisoners, their backs to the gate.

The key was in the car. She only saw one way to save Alexander. She got behind the wheel, cranked the car, put it in gear and aimed it right for the armed man, who was now framed in the gate.

She ran the car at him. He whirled at the sudden noise of an approaching vehicle and started spraying it with machine gun fire.

Jodie ducked down behind the wheel, praying that the weapon didn't have bullets that would penetrate the engine block as easily as they shattered the windshield of the car she was driving. There was a loud thud.

She had to stop the car, because she couldn't see where she was going, but the windshield didn't catch any more bullets. Now she heard gunshots that didn't sound like that of the small automatic her assailant was carrying.

The door of the car was suddenly jerked open, and she looked up, wide-eyed and panicky, into Alexander's white face.

"Jodie!" he ground out. "Put the car out of gear!"

She put it into Park with trembling hands and cut off the ignition.

Alexander dragged her out of it and began going over her with his hands, feeling for blood. She was covered with little shards of glass. Her face was bleeding. So were her hands. She'd put them over her face the instant the man started firing.

Slowly she became aware that Alexander's hands had a faint tremor as they searched her body.

"I'm okay," she said in a thin voice. "Are you?"

"Yes."

But he was rattled, and it showed.

"He was going to shoot you in the back," she began.

"I told you to use the cell phone!" he raged.

"It wouldn't work!"

He reached beside her and picked it up. His eyes closed. The battery was dead.

"And you stop yelling at me," she raged back at him. "I couldn't let him kill you!"

He caught her up in his arms, bruisingly close, and kissed her furiously. Then he just held her, rocked her, riveted her to his hard body with fierce hunger. "You crazy woman," he bit off at her ear. "You brave, crazy, wonderful woman!"

She held him, too, content now, safe now. Her eyes closed. It was over, and he was alive. Thank God.

He let her go reluctantly as two other men came up, giving them curious looks.

"She's all right," he told them, moving back a little. "Just a few cuts from the broken windshield."

"That was one of the bravest things I've ever seen a woman do," one of the men, an older man with jet black hair and eyes, murmured. "She drove right into the bullets."

"We'd be dead if she hadn't," the other man, equally dark-haired and dark-eyed, said with a grin. "Thanks!"

"You're welcome," she said with a sheepish smile as she moved closer to Alexander.

"The car's a total write-off," the older man mused.

"Like you've never totaled a car in a gun battle, Hunter," Alexander said with a chuckle.

The other man shrugged. "Maybe one or two. What the hell. The government has all that money we confiscate from drug smugglers to replace cars. You might ask your boss for that cute little Ferrari, Cobb."

"I already drive a Jaguar," he said, laughing. "With all due respect to Ferrari, I wouldn't trade it for anything else."

"I helped make the bust," Jodie complained. "They should give it to me!"

"I wouldn't be too optimistic about that," came a droll remark from the second of the two men. "I think Cobb's boss is partial to Italian sports cars, and he can't afford a Ferrari on his salary."

"Darn," Jodie said on a sigh. "Just my luck."

"You should take her to the hospital and have her checked," Hunter told Alexander. "She's bleeding."

"She could be dead, pulling a stunt like that," Alexander said with renewed anger as he looked at her.

"That's no way to thank a person for saving your life," Jodie pointed out, still riding an adrenaline high.

"You're probably right, but you took a chance you shouldn't have," Alexander said grimly. "Come on. We'll hitch a ride with one of my men."

"Your car might still be drivable," she said, looking at it. The windshield was shattered but still clinging to the frame. She winced. "Or maybe not."

"Maybe not," Alexander agreed. "See you, Hunter. Lane. Thanks for the help."

"Any time," Hunter replied, and they walked back toward the warehouse with Alexander and Jodie. "Colby Lane was in town overnight and bored to death, so I brought him along for the fun."

"Fun!" Jodie exclaimed.

The older man chuckled. "He leads a mundane nine-to-five life. I've talked him into giving it up for international intrigue at Ritter Oil."

"I was just convinced," the man named Colby Lane said with a chuckle.

"Good. Tomorrow you can tell Ritter you'll take the job. See you, Cobb."

"Sure thing."

"Who were those two guys you were talking to?" Jodie asked when the hospital had treated her cuts and Alexander had commandeered another car to take her home in.

"Phillip Hunter and Colby Lane. You've surely heard of Hunter."

"He's a local legend," she replied with a smile, "but I didn't recognize him in that black garb. He's our security chief."

"Lane's doing the same job for the Hutton corporation, but they're moving overseas and he isn't keen on going. So Hunter's trying to get him to come down here as his second-in-command at Ritter Oil."

"Why was Mr. Lane here tonight?"

"Probably just as Phillip said—Lane just got into town, and Hunter volunteered him to help out. He and Hunter are old friends."

"He looked very dark," she commented.

"They're both Apache," he said easily. "Hunter's married to a knockout blond geologist who works for Ritter. They have a young daughter. Lane's not married."

"They seem to know each other very well."

Alexander chuckled. "They have similar backgrounds in black ops. Highest level covert operations," he clarified. "They used to work for the 'company.'"

"Not Ritter's company," she guessed.

He chuckled. "No. Not Ritter's."

"Did you arrest Cara?"

"Our Houston policewoman made the actual arrest, so that Cara wouldn't know I headed the operation. Cara was arrested along with two men she swears she doesn't know," he replied. "We had probable cause to do a search anyway, but I had a search warrant in my pocket, and I had to use it. We found enough cocaine in there to get a city high, and the two men in the truck had some on them."

"How about Cara?"

He sighed. "She was clean. Now we have to connect her." He glanced at her apologetically. "That will mean getting your boss involved. However innocently, he did let her into a locked parking lot."

"But wasn't the night watchman working for them? Couldn't he have let them in?"

"He could have. But I have a feeling Cara wanted Brody involved, so that he'd be willing to do what she asked so that she didn't give him away for breaking a strict company rule," he replied. He saw her expression and he smiled. "Don't worry. I won't let him be prosecuted."

"Thanks, Alexander."

He moved closer and studied the cuts on her face and arms. He winced. "You poor baby," he said gently. "I wouldn't have had you hurt for the world."

"You'd have been dead if I hadn't done something," she said matter-of-factly. "The phone went dead and you were too far away to hear me if I yelled. Besides," she added with a chuckle, "I hate going to funerals."

"Me, too." He swept her close and kissed the breath out of her. "I have to go back to work, tie up loose ends. You'll need to come with me to the nearest police precinct and give a statement, as well. You're a material witness." He hesitated, frowning.

"What's wrong?" she asked.

"Cara knows who you are, and she can find out where you live," he said. "She's a vengeful witch. Chances are very good that she's going to make bond. I'm going to arrange some security for you."

"Do you think that's necessary?"

He nodded grimly. "I'm afraid it is. Would you like to know the estimated street value of the cocaine we've just confiscated?"

"Yes."

"From thirty to thirty-five million dollars."

She whistled softly. "Now I understand why they're willing to kill people. And that's just one shipment, right?"

"Just one, although it's unusually large. There's another drug smuggling investigation going on right now involving Colombian rebels, but I can't tell you about that one. It's top secret." He smoothed back her hair and looked at her as if she were a treasure trove. "Thank you for what you did," he said after a minute. "Even if it was crazy, it saved my life, not to mention Lane's and Hunter's."

She reached up a soft hand to smooth over his cheek, where it was slightly rough from a day's growth of beard. "You're welcome. But you would have done the same thing, if it had been me, or Margie."

"Yes, I'm afraid I would have."

He still looked worried. She tugged his head down and kissed him warmly, her body exploding inside when he half-lifted her against him and kissed her until her lips were sore.

"I could have lost you tonight," he said curtly.

"Oh, I'm a weed," she murmured into his throat. "We're very hard to uproot."

His arms tightened. "Just the same, you watch your back. If Brody asks what you know, and he will, you tell him nothing," he added. "You were with me when things started happening, you didn't even know what was going on until bullets started flying. Right?"

"Right."

He sighed heavily and kissed her one last time before he put her back onto her own feet. "I've got to go help the guys with the paperwork," he said reluctantly. "I'd much rather be with you. For tonight, lock your doors and keep your freedom phone handy. If you need me, I'm a phone call away. Tomorrow, you'll have security."

"I've got a nice, big, heavy flashlight like the one you keep in your car," she told him pertly. "If anybody tries to get in, they'll get a headache."

Unless they had guns, he added silently, but he didn't say that. "Don't be overconfident," he cautioned. "Never underestimate the enemy."

She saluted him.

He tugged her face up and kissed her, hard. "Incorrigible," he pronounced her. "But I can't imagine life without you, so be cautious!"

"I will. I promise. You have to promise, too," she added.

He gave her a warm smile. "Oh, I have my eye on the future, too," he assured her. "I don't plan to cash in my chips right now. I'll phone you tomorrow."

"Okay. Good night."

"Good night. Lock this," he added when he went out the door.

She did, loudly, and heard him chuckle as he went down the hall. Once he was gone, she sank down into her single easy chair and shivered as she recalled the feverish events of the evening. She was alive. He was alive. But she could still hear the bullets, feel the shattering of the windshield followed by dozens of tiny, painful cuts on her skin even through the sweater she'd been wearing. It was amazing that she'd come out of a firefight with so few wounds.

She went to bed, but she didn't sleep well. Alexander phoned very early the next morning to check on her and tell her that he'd see her at lunch.

She put on her coat and went to work, prepared for some comments from her coworkers, despite the fact that she was wearing a long-sleeved, high-necked blouse. Nothing was going to hide the tiny cuts that lined her cheeks and chin. She knew better than to mention where she got them, so she made up a nasty fall down the steps at her apartment building.

It worked with everyone except Brody. He came in as soon as she'd turned on her computer, looking worried and sad.

"Are you all right?" he asked abruptly. "I was worried sick all night."

Her wide-eyed look wasn't feigned. "How did you know?" she faltered.

"I had to go and bail Cara out of jail early this morning," he said coolly. "She's been accused of drug smuggling, can you imagine it? She was only parking her car when those lunatics opened fire!"

9

⸜⸝⸜⸝⸜⸝

Remembering what Alexander had cautioned her about, Jodie managed not to laugh out loud at Brody. How could a man be so naive?

"Drug smuggling?" she exclaimed, playing her part. "Cara?"

"That's what they said," he replied. "Apparently some of Ritter's security people had the warehouse staked out. When the shooting started, they returned fire, and I guess they called in the police. In fact, your friend Cobb was there when they arrested Cara."

"Yes, I know. He heard the shooting and walked right into it," she said, choosing her words carefully. "We were parked across the street..."

"I saw you when I let Cara into the parking lot," Brody said, embarrassed. "One of the gang came in with a machine gun and they say you aimed Cobb's car right at him and drove into a hail of bullets to save his life. I guess you really do care about him."

"Yes," she confessed. "I do."

"It was a courageous thing to do. Cara said you must be crazy about the guy to do that."

"Poor Cara," she replied, sidestepping the question. "I'm so sorry for the trouble she's in. Why in the world do they think she was involved? She was just in the wrong place at the wrong time."

Brody seemed to relax. "That's what Cara said. Uh, Cobb wasn't in on that bust deliberately, was he?"

"We were in a parked car outside the gate. We didn't know about any bust," she replied.

"So that's why he was there," he murmured absently, nodding. "I thought it must be something of the sort. Cara didn't know any of the others, but one was a female detective and another was a female deputy sheriff. The policewoman arrested her."

"Don't mess with Texas women," Jodie said, adding on a word to the well-known Texas motto.

He laughed. "So it seems. Uh, there was supposed to be a DEA agent there, as well. Cara has a friend who works out of the Houston office, but he's been out of town a lot lately and she hasn't been able to contact him. She says it's funny, but he seems to actually be avoiding her." He gave her an odd look. "I gather that it wasn't Cobb. But do you know anything about who the agent was?"

"No," she said straight-faced. "And Alexander didn't mention it, either. He tells me everything, so I'd know if it was him."

"I see."

She wondered if Cara's friend at the DEA was named Kennedy, but she pretended to know nothing. "What's Cara going to do?" she asked, sounding concerned.

"Get a good lawyer, I suppose," he said heavily.

"I wish her well. I'm so sorry, Brody."

He sighed heavily. "I seem to have a knack for getting myself into tight corners, but I think Cara's easily superior to me in that respect. Well, I'd better phone the attorney whose name she gave me. You're sure you're all right?"

"I'm fine, Brody, honestly." She smiled at him.

He smiled back. "See you."

She watched him go with relief. She'd been improvising widely to make sure he didn't connect Alexander with the surveillance of the warehouse.

When Alexander phoned her, she arranged to meet him briefly at the café downstairs for coffee. He was pushed for time, having been in meetings with his drug unit most of the day planning strategy.

"You've become a local legend," he told her with a mischievous smile when they were drinking cappuccino.

"Me?" she exclaimed.

He grinned at her. "The oil clerk who drove through a hail of bullets to save her lover."

She flushed and glared at him. "Point one, I am not a clerk, I'm an administrative assistant. And point two, I am not your—!"

"I didn't say I started the rumor." He chuckled. His eyes became solemn as he studied her across the table. "But the part about being a heroine, I endorse enthusiastically. That being said, would you like to add to your legend?"

She paid attention. "Are you kidding? What do you want me to do?"

"Cara made bond this afternoon," he told her. "We've got a tail on her, but she's sure to suspect that. She'll make contact with one of her subordinates, in some public place where she thinks we won't be able to tape her. When she does, I'm going to want you to accidentally happen upon her and plant a microphone under her table."

"Wow! 'Jane Bond' stuff!"

"Jane?" he wondered.

She shrugged. "A woman named James would be a novelty."

"Point taken. Are you game?"

"Of course. But why wouldn't you let one of your own people do it?"

His face was revealing. "The last hearty professional we sent to do that little task stumbled over his own feet and pitched head-first into the table our target was occupying. In the process he overturned a carafe of scalding coffee, also on the target, who had to be taken to the hospital for treatment."

"What if I do the same thing?" she worried.

He smiled gently. "You don't have a clumsy bone in your body, Jodie. But even if you did, Cara knows you. She might suspect me, but she won't suspect you."

"When do I start?"

"I'll let you know," he promised. "In the meantime, keep your eyes and ears open, and don't..."

Just as he spoke, there was a commotion outside the coffee shop. A young woman with long blond hair was trailing away a dark-haired little girl with a shocked face. Behind them, one of the men Jodie recognized from the drug bust—one of Alexander's friends—was waving his arms and talking loudly in a language Jodie had never heard before, his expression furious.

The trio passed out of sight, but not before Jodie finally recognized the man Alexander had called Colby Lane.

"What in the world...?" she wondered.

"It's a long story," Alexander told her. "And I'm not at liberty to repeat it. Let's just say that Colby has been rather suddenly introduced to a previously unknown member of his family."

"Was he cursing—and in what language?" she persisted.

"You can't curse in Apache," he assured her. "It's like Japanese—if you really want to tick somebody off in Japan, you say something about their mother's belly button. But giving them the finger doesn't have any meaning."

"Really?" She was fascinated.

He chuckled. "Anyway, Native Americans—whose origins are also suspected to be Asian—don't use curse words in their own language."

"Mr. Lane looked very upset. And I thought I recognized that blond woman. She was transferred here from their Arizona office just a few weeks ago. She has a little girl, about the same age as Mr. Hunter's daughter."

"Let it lie," Alexander advised. "We have problems of our own. I meant to mention that we've located one of Cara's known associates serving as a waiter in a little coffeehouse off Alameda called The Beat…"

"I go there!" she exclaimed. "I go there a lot! You can get all sorts of fancy coffees and it's like a retro 'beatnik' joint. They play bongos and wear all black and customers get up and read their poetry." She flushed. "I actually did that myself, just last week."

He was impressed. "You, getting up in front of people to read poetry? I didn't know you still wrote poetry, Jodie."

"It's very personal stuff," she said, uneasy.

He began to look arrogant. "About me?"

She glared at him. "At the time I wrote it, you were my least favorite person on the planet," she informed him.

"Ouch!" He was thinking again. "But if they already know you there, it's even less of a stretch if you show up when Cara does—assuming she even uses the café for her purposes. We'll have to wait and see. I don't expect her to arrange a rendezvous with a colleague just to suit me."

"Nice of you," she teased.

He chuckled. He reached across the table and linked her fingers with his. His green eyes probed hers for a long moment. "Those cuts are noticeable on your face," he said quietly. "Do they hurt?"

"Not nearly as much as having you gunned down in front of me would have," she replied.

His eyes began to glitter with feeling. His fingers contracted around hers. "Which is just how I felt when I saw those bullets slamming into the windshield of my car, with you at the wheel."

Her breath caught. He'd never admitted so much in the past.

He laughed self-consciously and released her hand. "We're getting morose. A miss is as good as a mile, and I still have paperwork to finish that I haven't even started on." He glanced at his watch. "I can't promise anything, but we might see a movie this weekend."

"That would be nice," she said. "You'll let me know...?"

He frowned. "I don't like putting you in the line of fire a second time."

"I go to the coffee shop all the time," she reminded him. "I'm not risking anything." Except my heart, again, she thought.

He sighed. "I suppose so. Just the same, don't let down your guard. I hope you can tell if someone's tailing you?"

"I get goose bumps on the back of my neck," she assured him. "I'll be careful. You do the same," she added firmly.

He smiled gently. "I'll do my best."

Having settled down with a good book the following day after a sandwich and soup supper, it was a surprise to have Alexander phone her and ask her to go down to the coffee shop on the double.

"I'll meet you in the parking lot with the equipment," he said. "Get a cab and have it drop you off. I'll reimburse you. Hurry, Jodie."

"Okay. I'm on my way," she promised, lounging in pajamas and a robe.

She dashed into the bedroom, threw on a long black velvet skirt, a black sweater, loafers, and ran a quick brush through her loosed hair before perching her little black beret on top of her head. She grabbed her coat and rushed out the door, barely pausing except to lock it. She was at the elevator before she remembered her purse, lying on the couch. She dashed back to get it, cursing her own lack of preparedness in an emergency.

Minutes later, she got out of the cab at the side door of The Beat coffeehouse.

Alexander waited by his company car while Jodie paid the cab. She joined him, careful to notice that she was unobserved.

He straightened at her approach. In the well-lit parking lot, she could see his eyes. They were troubled.

"I'm here," she said, just for something to say. "What do you want me to do?"

"I'm not sure I want you to do anything," he said honestly. "This is dangerous. Right now, she has no reason to suspect you. But if you bug her table for me, and she finds out that you did, your life could be in danger."

"Hey, listen, you were the one who told me about the little boys being shot by her henchmen," she reminded him. "I know the risk, Alexander. I'm willing to take it."

"Your knees are knocking," he murmured.

She laughed, a little unsteadily. "I guess they are. And my heart's pounding. But I'm still willing to do it. Now what exactly do I do?"

He opened the passenger door for her. "Get in. I'll brief you."

"Is she here?" she asked when they were inside.

"Yes. She's at the table nearest the kitchen door, at the left side of the stage. Here." He handed her a fountain pen.

"No, thanks," she said, waving it away. "I've got two in my purse..."

He opened her hand and placed the capped pen in it. She looked at it, surprised by its heaviness. "It's a miniature receiver," he told her. He produced a small black box with an antenna, and what looked like an earplug with a tiny wire sticking out the fat end. "The box is a receiver, linked to a tape recorder. The earplug is also a receiver, which we use when we're in close quarters and don't want to attract attention. Since the box has a range of several hundred feet, I'll be able to hear what comes into the pen from my car."

"Do you want me to accidentally leave the pen on her table?"

"I want you to accidentally drop it under her table," he said. "If she sees it, the game's up. We're not the only people who deal in counterespionage."

She sucked in her breath. She was getting the picture. Cara was no dummy. "Okay. I'll lean over her table to say hello and make sure I put it where she won't feel it with her foot. How will that do?"

"Yes. But you have to make sure she doesn't see you do it."

"I'll be very careful."

He was having second thoughts. She was brave, but courage wasn't the only requirement for such an assignment. He remembered her driving through gunfire to save him. She could have died then. He'd thought about little else, and he hadn't slept well. Jodie was like a silver thread that ran through his life. In recent weeks, he'd been considering, seriously, how hard it would be to go on without her. He wasn't certain that he could.

"Why are you watching me like that?" she wanted to know, smiling curiously. "I'm not a dummy. I won't let you down, honest."

"It wasn't that." He closed her fingers around the pen. "Are you sure you want to go through with this?"

"Very sure."

"Okay." He hesitated. "What are you going to give as an excuse for being there?"

She gave him a bright smile. "I phoned Johnny—the owner—earlier, just after you phoned me and told him I had a new poem, but I was a little nervous about getting up in front of a big crowd. He said there was only a small crowd and I'd do fine."

"You improvise very well."

"I've been observing you for years," she teased. "But it's true. I do have a poem to read, which should throw Cara off the track."

He tugged her chin up and kissed her, hard. "You're going to be fine."

She smiled at him. "Which one of us are you supposed to be reassuring?"

"Both of us," he said tenderly. He kissed her again. "Go to work."

"What do I do when she leaves?"

"Get a cab back to your apartment. I'll meet you there. If anything goes wrong," he added firmly, "or if she acts suspicious, you stay in the coffeehouse and phone my cell number. Got that?" He handed her a card with his mobile phone number on it.

"I've got it."

She opened the car door and stepped out into the cool night air. With a subdued wave, she turned, pulled her coat closer around her and walked purposefully toward the coffeehouse. What she didn't tell Alexander was that her new poem was about him.

She didn't look around noticeably as she made her way through the sparse crowd to the table where she usually sat on her evenings here. She held the pen carefully in her hand, behind a long fold of her coat. As she pulled out a chair at the table, her eyes swept the room and she spotted Cara at a table with another woman. She smiled and Cara frowned.

Uh-oh, she thought, but she pinned the smile firmly to her face and moved to Cara's table.

"I thought it was you," she said cheerily. "I didn't know you ever came here! Brody never mentioned it to me."

Cara gave her a very suspicious look. "This is not your normal evening entertainment, surely?"

"But I come here all the time," Jodie replied honestly. "Johnny's one of my fans."

"Fans." Cara turned the word over on her tongue as if she'd never heard it.

"Aficionados," Jodie persisted. "I write poetry."

"You?"

The other woman made it sound like an insult. The woman beside her, an even older woman with a face like plate steel, only looked.

Jodie felt a chill of fear and worked to hide it. Her palm sweated against the weight of the pen hidden in her hand. As she hesitated, Johnny came walking over in his apron.

"Hey, Jodie!" he greeted. "Now don't worry, there's only these two unfamiliar ladies in here, you know everybody else. You just get up there and give it your best. It'll be great!"

"Johnny, you make me feel so much better," she told the man.

"These ladies friends of yours?" he asked, noticing them—especially Cara—with interested dark eyes.

"Cara's boyfriend is my boss at work," Jodie said.

"Lucky boyfriend," Johnny murmured, his voice dropping an octave.

Cara relaxed and smiled. "I am Cara Dominguez," she introduced herself. "This is my *amiga,* Chiva."

Johnny leaned over the table to shake hands and Jodie pretended to be overbalanced by him. In the process of righting herself and accepting his apology, she managed to let the pen drop under the table where it lay unnoticed several inches from either woman's foot.

"Sorry, Jodie, meeting two such lovely ladies made me clumsy." He chuckled.

She grinned at him. "No harm done. I'm not hurt."

"Okay, then, you go get on that stage. Want your usual French Vanilla cappuccino?"

"You bet. Make it a large one, with a croissant, please."

"It'll be on the house," he informed her. "That's incentive for you."

"Gee, thanks!" she exclaimed.

"My treat. Nice to meet you ladies."

"It is for us the same," Cara purred. She glanced at Jodie, much less suspicious now. "So you write poetry. I will enjoy listening to it."

Jodie chuckled. "I'm not great, but people here are generally kind. Good to see you."

Cara shrugged. The other woman said nothing.

Jodie pulled off her coat and went up onto the stage, trying to ignore her shaking knees. Meanwhile she prayed that Alexander could hear what the two women were saying. Because the minute she pulled the microphone closer, introduced herself, and pulled out the folded sheet of paper that contained her poem, Cara leaned toward the other woman and started speaking urgently.

Probably exchanging fashion tips, or some such thing, Jodie

thought dismally, but she smiled at the crowd, unfolded the paper, and began to read.

Apparently her efforts weren't too bad, because the small crowd paid attention to every line of the poem. And when she finished reading it, there was enthusiastic applause.

Cara and her friend, however, were much too intent on conversation to pay Jodie any attention. She went back to her seat, ate her croissant and drank her cappuccino with her back to the table where Cara and the other woman were sitting, just to make sure they knew she wasn't watching them.

A few minutes later, Johnny came by her table and patted her on the back. "That was some good work, girl!" he exclaimed. "I'm sorry your friend didn't seem to care enough to listen to it."

"She's not into poetry," she confided.

"I guess not. She and that odd-looking friend of hers didn't even finish their coffee."

"They're gone?" she asked without turning.

He nodded. "About five minutes ago, I guess. No great loss, if you ask me."

"Thanks for the treat, Johnny, and for the encouragement," she added.

"Um, I sure would like to have a copy of that poem."

Her eyes widened. "You would? Honestly?"

He shrugged. "It was really good. I know this guy. He works for a small press. They publish poetry. I'd like to show it to him. If you don't mind."

"Mind!" She handed him the folded paper. "I don't mind! Thanks, Johnny!"

"No problem. I'll be in touch." He turned, and then paused, digging into his apron pocket. "Say, is this yours? I'm afraid I may have stepped on it. It was under that table where your friend was sitting."

"Yes, it's mine," she said, taking it from him. "Thanks a lot."

He winced. "If I broke it, I'll buy you a new one, okay?"

"It's just a pen," she said with determined carelessness. "No problem."

"You wait, I'll call you a cab."

"That would be great!"

She settled back to wait, her head full of hopeful success, and not only for Alexander.

"Is it broken?" she asked Alexander when she was back at her apartment, and he was examining his listening device.

"I'll have the lab guys check it out," he told her.

"Could you hear anything?"

He grinned hugely. "Not only did I hear plenty, I taped it. We've got a lead we'd never have had without you. There's just one bad thing."

"Oh?"

"Cara thinks your poetry stinks," he said with a twinkle in his eyes.

"She can think what she likes, but Johnny's showing it to a publisher friend of his. He thought it was wonderful."

He searched her face. "So did I, Jodie."

She felt a little nervous, but certainly he couldn't have known that he was the subject of it, so she just thanked him offhandedly.

"Now I'm sure I'm cut out for espionage," she murmured.

"You may be, but I don't know if my nerves could take it."

"You thought I'd mess up," she guessed.

He shook his head, holding her hand firmly in his. "It wasn't that.

I don't like having you at risk, Jodie. I don't want you on the firing line ever again, even if you did save my skin last night."

She searched his green eyes hungrily. "I wouldn't want to live in a world that didn't contain you, too," she said. Then, backtracking out of embarrassment, she laughed and added, "I really couldn't live without the aggravation."

He laughed, as he was meant to. "Same here." He checked his watch. "I don't want to go," he said unexpectedly, "but I've got to get back to my office and go through this tape. Tomorrow, I'll be in conference with my drug unit. You pretend that nothing at all was amiss, except you saw Cara at your favorite evening haunt. Right?"

"Right," she assured him.

"I'll call you."

"That's what they all say," she said dryly.

He paused at the door and looked at her. "Who?"

"Excuse me?"

"Who else is promising to call you?" he persisted.

"The president, for my advice on his foreign policy, of course," she informed him.

He laughed warmly. "Incorrigible," he said to himself, winked at her, and let himself out. "Lock it!" he called through it.

She snicked the lock audibly and heard him chuckle again. She leaned back against the door with a relieved sigh. It was over. She'd done what he asked her, and she hadn't fouled it up. Most of all, he was pleased with her.

She was amazed at the smiles she got from him in recent weeks. He'd always been reserved, taciturn, with most other people. But he enjoyed her company and it showed.

The next day, Brody seemed very preoccupied. She took dictation, which he gave haltingly, and almost absently.

"Are you okay?" she wanted to know.

He moved restively around his office. He turned to stare at her curiously. "Are you involved in some sort of top secret operation or something?"

Her eyes popped. "Pardon?"

He cleared his throat. "I know you were at a coffeehouse where Cara went last night with a friend. I wondered if you were spying on her…?"

"I go to The Beat all the time, Brody," she told him, surprised. "Alexander's idea of an evening out is a concert or the theater, but my tastes run to bad poetry and bongos. I've been going there for weeks. It's no secret. The owner knows me very well."

He relaxed suddenly and smiled. "Thank goodness! That's what Cara told me, of course, but it seemed odd that you'd be there when she was. I mean, like you and your boyfriend showed up at the restaurant where we had lunch that day, and then you were at the concert, too. And your friend does work for the DEA…"

"Coincidences," she said lazily. "That's all. Unless you think I've been following you," she added with deliberate emphasis, demurely lowering her eyes.

There was a long, shocked pause. "Why, I never thought… considered…really?"

She crossed her legs. "I think you're very nice, Brody, and Cara treats you like a pet dog," she said with appropriate indignation. She peered at him covertly. "You're too good for her."

He was obviously embarrassed, flattered, and uncertain. "My gosh…I'm sorry, but I knew about Cobb working for the DEA, and then the drug bust came so unexpectedly. Well, it seemed logical that he might be spying on Cara with your help…"

"I never dreamed that I looked like a secret agent!" she exclaimed, and then she chuckled. "As if Alexander would ever trust me with something so dangerous," she added, lowering her eyes so that he couldn't see them.

He sighed. "Forgive me. I've had these crazy theories. Cara thought I was nuts, especially after she told me the owner of that coffeehouse knew you very well and encouraged you to read...well...very bad poetry. She thought maybe he had a case on you."

"It was not bad poetry! And he had a case on Cara, not me," she replied with just the right amount of pique.

"Did he!"

"I told him she was your girlfriend, don't worry," she said, and managed to sound regretful.

"Jodie, I'm very flattered," he faltered.

She held up a hand. "Let's not talk about it, Brody, okay? You just dictate, and I'll write."

He sighed, studying her closely. After a minute, he shrugged, and began dictating. This time, he was concise and relaxed. Jodie felt like collapsing with relief, herself. It had been a close call, and not even because Cara was suspicious. It was Brody who seemed to sense problems.

10

It was a relief that Cara didn't suspect Jodie of spying, but it was worrying that Brody did. He was an intelligent man, and it wouldn't be easy to fool him. She'd have to mention that to Alexander when she saw him.

He came by the apartment that evening, soon after Jodie got home from work, taciturn and worried.

"Something happened," she guessed uneasily.

He nodded. "Got any coffee?"

"Sure. Come on into the kitchen."

He sat down and she poured him a cup from the pot full she'd just made. He sipped it and studied her across the table. "Kennedy came back to town today. He's Cara's contact."

"Oh, dear," she murmured, sensing that something was very wrong.

He nodded. "I called him into my office and told him I was firing him, and why. I have sworn statements from two witnesses who are willing to testify against him in return for reduced sentences." He sighed. "He said that he knew you were involved, that you'd helped me finger Cara, and that he'd tell her if I didn't back down."

"Don't feel bad about it," she said, mentally panicking while trying not to show it. "You couldn't let him stay, after what he did."

He looked at her blankly. "You're a constant surprise to me, Jodie. How did you know I wouldn't back down?"

She smiled gently. "You wouldn't be Alexander if you let people bluff you."

"Yes, baby, but he's not bluffing."

The endearment caught her off guard, made her feel warm inside, warm all over. "So what do we do now?" she asked, a little disconcerted.

He noted her warm color and smiled tenderly. "You go live with Margie for a few days, until I wrap up this case. Our cover's blown now for sure."

"Margie can shoot a gun, but she's not all that great at it, Alexander," she pointed out.

"Our foreman, Chayce, is, and so is cousin Derek," he replied. "He was involved in national security work when he was just out of college. He's a dead shot, and he'll be bringing his two brothers with him." He chuckled. "Funny. All I had to say was that Margie might be in danger along with you, and he volunteered at once."

"You don't like him," she recalled.

He shrugged. "I don't like the idea of Margie getting involved with a cousin. But Derek seemed to know that, too, and he told me something I didn't know before when I phoned him. He wasn't my uncle's son. His mother had an affair with an old beau and he was the result. It was a family secret until last night. Which means," he added, "that he's only related to us by marriage, not by blood."

"He told you himself?" she asked.

"He told me. Apparently, he told you, too. But he didn't tell Margie."

"Have you?" she wondered.

"That's for him to do," he replied. "I've interfered enough." He checked his watch. "I've got to go. I have a man watching the apartment," he added. "The one I told you about. But tomorrow, you tell Brody you're taking a few days off to look after a sick relative and you go to Margie. Got that?"

"But my job...!"

"It's your life!" he shot back, eyes blazing. "This is no game. These people will kill you as surely as they killed those children. I am not going to watch you die, Jodie. Least of all for something I got you into!"

She caught her breath. This was far more serious than she'd realized.

"I told you," he emphasized, "Cara knows you were involved. The secret's out. You leave town. Period."

She stared at him and knew she was trapped. Her job was going to be an afterthought. They'd fire her. She was even afraid to take a day off when she was sick, because the company policy in her department was so strict.

"If you lose that job, it will be a blessing," Alexander told her flatly. "You're too good to waste your life taking somebody else's dictation. When this is over, I'll help you find something better. I'll take you to classes so that you can get your expert computer certification, then I'll get an employment agency busy to find you a better job."

That was a little disappointing. Obviously he didn't have a future with her in mind, or he wouldn't be interested in getting her a job.

He leaned back in his chair, sipping coffee. "Although," he added suddenly, his gaze intent, "there might be an alternative."

"An alternative?"

"We'll talk about that later," he said. He finished his coffee. "I have to go."

She got up and walked him to the door. "You be careful, too," she chided.

He opened his jacket and indicated the .45 automatic in its hand-tooled leather holster.

"It won't shoot itself," she reminded him pertly.

He chuckled, drew her into his arms, and kissed her until her young body ached with deep, secret longings.

He lifted his head finally, and he wasn't breathing normally. She felt the intensity of his gaze all the way to her toes as he looked at her. "All these years," he murmured, "and I wasted them sniping at you."

"You seemed to enjoy it at the time," she remarked absently, watching his mouth hover over hers.

"I didn't want a marriage like my parents had. I played the field, to keep women from getting serious about me," he confessed. He traced her upper lip with his mouth, with breathless tenderness. "Especially you," he added roughly. "No one else posed the threat you did, with your old-fashioned ideals and your sterling character. But I couldn't let you see how attracted to you I was. I did a pretty good job. And then you had too much champagne at a party and did what I'd been afraid you'd do since you graduated from high school."

"You were afraid...?"

He nibbled her upper lip. "I knew that if you ever got close, I'd never be able to let you go," he whispered sensuously. "What I spouted to Margie was a lot of hot air. I ached from head to toe after what we did together. I wanted you so badly, honey. I didn't sleep all night thinking about how easy it would have been."

"I didn't sleep thinking that you hated me," she confessed.

He sighed regretfully. "I didn't know you'd overheard me, but I said enough when I left you at your bedroom. I felt guilty when I went downstairs and saw your face. You were shamed and humiliated, and it was my fault. I only wanted a chance to make amends, but you started backing away and you wouldn't stop. That was when I knew what a mistake I'd made."

She toyed with his shirt button. "And then you needed help to catch a drug smuggler," she mused.

There was a pause long enough to make her look up. "You're good, Jodie, and I did need somebody out of the agency to dig out that information for me. But..."

"But?"

He smiled sheepishly. "Houston P.D. owes me a favor. They'd have been glad to get the information for me. So would the Texas Rangers, or the county sheriff."

"Then why did you ask me to do it?" she exclaimed.

His hands went to frame her face. They felt warm and strong against her soft skin. "I was losing you," he whispered as he bent again to rub his lips tenderly over her mouth. "You wouldn't let me near you any other way."

His mouth was making pudding of her brain. She slid her arms up around his neck and her hands tangled in the thick hair above his nape. "But there was Kirry..."

"Window dressing. I didn't even like her, especially by the time my birthday rolled around. I gave Margie hell for inviting her to my birthday party, did she tell you?"

She shook her head, dazed.

He caught her upper lip in his mouth and toyed with it. His breathing grew unsteady. His hands on her face became insistent. "I got drunk when Margie told me you'd overheard us," he whispered. "It took two neat whiskeys for me to even phone you. Too much was riding on my ability to make an apology. And frankly, baby, I don't make a habit of giving them."

She melted into his body, hungry for closer contact. "I was so ashamed of what I'd done..."

His mouth crushed down onto hers with passionate intent. "I loved what you did," he ground out. "I wasn't kidding when I told you that. I could taste you long after I went to bed. I dreamed about it all night."

"So did I," she whispered.

His lips parted hers ardently. "I thought you were hung up on damned Brody," he murmured, "until you aimed that car at the gunman. I prayed for all I was worth until I got to you and knew that you were all right. I could have lost you forever. It haunts me!"

"I'm tougher than old cowboy boots," she whispered, elated beyond belief at what he was saying to her.

"And softer than silk, in all the right places. Come here." He moved her against the wall. His body pressed hers gently against it while he kissed her with all the pent-up longing he'd been suppressing for weeks. When she moaned, he felt his body tremble with aching need.

"You're killing me," he ground out.

"Wh...what?"

He lifted his head and looked down into soft, curious brown eyes. "You haven't got a clue," he muttered. "Can't you tell when a man's dying of lust?"

Her eyebrows arched as he rested his weight on his hands next to her ears on the wall and suddenly pressed his hips into hers, emphatically demonstrating the question.

She swallowed hard. "Alexander, I was really only kidding about having a dress with prophylactics pinned to the hem...."

He burst out laughing and forced his aching body away from hers. "I've never laughed as much in my life as I do with you," he said on a long sigh. "But I really would give half an arm to lay you down on the carpet right now, Jodie."

She flushed with more delight than fear. "One of us could run to the drugstore, I guess," she murmured dryly.

"Not now," he whispered wickedly. "But hold that thought until I wind up this case."

She laughed. "Okay."

He nibbled her upper lip. "I'll pick you up at work about nine in the morning," he murmured as he lifted his head. "And I'll drive you down to Jacobsville."

"You're really worried," she realized, when she saw the somber expression.

"Yes, Jodie. I'm really worried. Keep your doors locked and don't answer the phone."

"What if it's you?" she worried.

"Do you still have the cell phone I loaned you?"

"Yes."

She produced it. He opened it, turned it on, and checked the battery. "It's fully charged. Leave it on. If I need to call you, I'll use this number. You can call me if you're afraid. Okay?"

"Okay."

He kissed her one last time, gave her a soulful, enigmatic look, and went out the door. She bolted it behind him and stood there for several long seconds, her head whirling with the changes that were suddenly upsetting her life and career. Alexander was trying to tell her something, but she couldn't quite decide what. Did he want an affair? He certainly couldn't be thinking about marriage, he hated the whole thought of it. But, what did he want? She worried the question until morning, and still had no answers.

"You're going to leave for three days, just like that?" Brody exploded at work the next morning, his face harder than Jodie had ever seen it. "How the hell am I going to manage without a secretary?" he blustered. "I can't type my own letters!"

The real man, under the facade, Jodie thought, fascinated with her first glimpse of Brody's dark side. She'd never seen him really angry.

"I'm not just a secretary," she reminded him.

"Oh, hell, you do mail and requisition forms," he said coldly. "Call it what you like, it's donkey work." His eyes narrowed. "It's because of what you did to Cara, isn't it? You're scared, so you're running away!"

Her face flamed with temper. She stood up from her desk and gave him a look that would have melted steel. "Would you be keen to hang around if they were gunning for you? You listen to me, Brody, these drug lords don't care who dies as long as they get their money. There are two dead little children who didn't do a thing wrong, except stand between a drug dealer and their mother, who was trying to shut down drug dealing in her neighborhood. Cara is part of that sick trade, and if you defend her, so are you!"

He gaped at her. In the years they'd worked together, Jodie had never talked back to him.

She grabbed up her purse and got the few personal belongings out of her desk. "Never mind holding my job open for me. I quit!" she told him flatly. "There must be more to life than pandering to the ego of a man who thinks I'm a donkey. One more thing, Brody," she added, facing him with her arms full of her belongings. "You and your drug-dealing girlfriend can both go to hell, with my blessing!"

She turned and stalked out of her cubicle. She imagined a trail of fire behind her. Brody's incredulous gasp had been music to her ears. Alexander was right. She was wasted here. She'd find something better, she knew it.

On her way out the door, she almost collided with Phillip Hunter. He righted her, his black eyebrows arching.

"You're leaving, Miss Clayburn?" he asked.

"I'm leaving, Mr. Hunter," she said, still bristling from her encounter with Brody.

"Great. Come with me."

He motioned with his chin. She followed him, puzzled, because he'd never spoken to her before except in a cordial, impersonal way.

He led her into the boardroom and closed the door. Inside was the other dark man she'd met briefly during the drug bust at the warehouse, Colby Lane, and the owner of the corporation himself, Eugene Ritter.

"Sit down, Ms. Clayburn," Ritter said with a warm smile, his blue eyes twinkling under a lock of silver hair.

She dropped into a chair, with her sack full of possessions clutched close to her chest.

"Mr. Ritter," she began, wondering what in the world she was going to do now. "I can explain..."

"You don't have to," he said gently. "I already know everything. When this drug case is wrapped up—and Cobb assures me it will be soon—how would you like to come back and work for me in an area where your skills won't be wasted?"

She was speechless. She just stared at him over her bulging carry-all.

"Phillip wants to go home to Arizona to work in our branch office there, and Colby Lane here—" he indicated the other dark man "—is going to replace him. He knows about your computer skills and Cobb's already told him that you're a whiz with investigations. How would you like to work for Lane as a computer security consultant? It will pay well and you'll have autonomy within the corporation. The downside," he added slowly, "is that you may have to do some traveling eventually, to our various branch offices, to work with Hunter and our other troubleshooters. Is that a problem?"

She shook her head, still grasping for a hold on the situation.

"Good!" He rubbed his hands together. "Then we'll draw up a contract for you, and you can have your attorney read and approve it when you come back." He was suddenly solemn. "There are going to be a lot of changes here in the near future. I've been coasting along in our headquarters office in Oklahoma and letting the outlying divisions take care of themselves, with near-disastrous results. If Hunter hadn't been tipped off by Cobb about the warehouse being used as a drug drop, we could have been facing federal charges, with no intentional involvement whatsoever on our part, on international drug smuggling. Tell Cobb we owe him one for that."

She grinned. "I will. And, Mr. Ritter, thank you very much for the opportunity. I won't let you down."

"I know that, Ms. Clayburn," he told her, smiling back. "Hunter will walk you outside. Just in case. Not that I think you need too much protection," he added, tongue-in-cheek. "There aren't a lot of people who'll drive into gunfire to save another person."

She laughed. "If I'd had time to think about it, I probably wouldn't have done it. Just the same, I won't mind having an escort to the front entrance," she confessed, standing. "I'm getting a cab to my apartment."

"We'll talk again," Ritter assured her, standing. He was tall and very elegant in a gray business suit. "All right, come on, Lane. We'll inspect the warehouse one last time."

"Yes, sir," Lane agreed.

"I'm just stunned," Jodie murmured when they reached the street, where the cab she'd called was waiting. She'd also phoned Cobb to meet her at her apartment.

"Ritter sees more than people think he does," Hunter told her, chuckling. "He's sharp, and he doesn't miss much. Tell Cobb I owe him one, too. My wife and I have been a little preoccupied lately— we just found out that we're expecting again. My mind hasn't been as much on the job as it should have been."

"Congratulations!"

He shrugged. "I wouldn't mind another girl, but Jennifer wants a son this time, a matched set, she calls it. She wants to be near her cousin Danetta, who's also expecting a second child. She and Cabe Ritter, the old man's son, have a son but they want a daughter." He chuckled. "We'll see what we both get. Meanwhile, you go straight to your apartment with no stops," he directed, becoming solemn. He looked over the top of the cab, saw something, and nodded approvingly. "Cobb's having you tailed. No, don't look back. If anyone makes a try for you, dive for cover and let your escort handle it, okay?"

"Okay. But I'm not really nervous about it now."

"So I saw the other night," he replied. "You've got guts, Ms. Clayburn. You'll be a welcome addition to security here."

She beamed. "I'll do my best. Thanks again."

"No problem. Be safe."

He closed the door and watched the taxi pull away. Her escort, in a dark unmarked car, pulled right out behind the cab. She found herself wishing that Cara and her group would make a try for her. It wouldn't bother her one bit to have the woman land in jail for a long time.

Alexander was waiting for her at her apartment. He picked up the suitcase she'd packed and then he drove her down to the Jacobsville ranch. She didn't have time to tell him about the changes in her life. She was saving that for a surprise. She was feeling good about her own abilities, and her confidence in herself had a surprising effect on her friend Margie, who met her at the door with faint shock.

Margie hugged her, but her eyes were wary. "There's something different about you," she murmured sedately.

"I've been exercising," she assured the other woman amusedly.

"Sure she has." Alexander chuckled. "By aiming cars at men armed with automatic weapons."

"What!" Margie exclaimed, gasping.

"Well, they were shooting at Alexander," Jodie told her. "What else could I do?"

Margie and her brother exchanged a long, serious look. He nodded slowly, and then he smiled. Margie beamed.

"What's that all about?" Jodie wondered aloud.

"We're passing along mental messages," Margie told her with wicked eyes. "Never mind. You're just in time to try on the flamenco dress I made you for our Halloween party."

"Halloween party." Jodie nodded blankly.

"It's this Saturday," Margie said, exasperated. "We always have it the weekend before Halloween, remember?"

"I didn't realize it was that far along in the month," Jodie said. "I guess I've been busier than I realized."

"She writes poetry about me," Alexander said as he went up the staircase with Jodie's bag.

"I do not write poetry about you!" Jodie called after him.

He only laughed. "And she reads it on stage in a retro beatnik coffeehouse."

"For real?" Margie asked. "Jodie, I have to come stay with you in Houston so you can take me there. I love coffeehouses and poetry!" She shook her head. "I can't imagine you reading poetry on a stage. Or driving a car into bullets, for that matter." She looked shocked. "Jodie, you've changed."

Jodie nodded. "I guess I have."

Margie hugged her impulsively. "Are we still friends?" she wondered. "I haven't been a good one, but I'm going to try. I can actually make canapés!" she added. "I took lessons. So now you can come to parties when Jessie's not here, and I won't even ask you to do any of the work!"

Jodie burst out laughing. "This I have to see."

"You can, Friday. I expect it will take all day, what with the decorating, and I'm doing all that myself, too. Derek thinks I'm improving madly," she added, and a faint flush came to her cheeks.

"Cousin Derek's here already?" she asked.

"He's not actually my cousin at all, except by marriage, although I only just found out," Margie said, drawing Jodie along with her into the living room. "He's got two brothers and they're on the way here. One of them is a cattle rancher and the other is a divorced grizzly bear."

"A what?"

Margie looked worried. "He's a Bureau of Land Management

enforcement agent," she said. "He tracks down poachers and people who deal in illegal hunting and such. He's the one whose wife left him for a car salesman. He's very bitter."

"Is Derek close to them?"

"To the rancher one," Margie said. "He doesn't see the grizzly bear too often, thank goodness."

"Thank goodness?" Jodie probed delicately.

Margie flushed. "I think Cousin Derek wants to be much more than my cousin."

"It's about time," Jodie said with a wicked smile. "He's just your type."

Margie made a face. "Come on into the kitchen and we'll see what there is to eat. I don't know about you, but I'm hungry." She stopped suddenly. "Don't take this the wrong way, but why are Derek and his brothers moving in and why are you and Alexander here in the middle of the week?"

"Oh, somebody's just going to try to kill me, that's all," Jodie said matter-of-factly. "But Alexander's more than able to handle them, with Cousin Derek's help and some hard work by the DEA and Alexander's drug unit."

"Trying to kill you." Margie nodded. "Right."

"That's no joke," Alexander said from the doorway. He came into the room and pulled Jodie to his side, bending to kiss her gently. "I have to go. Derek's on the job, and his brothers will be here within an hour or two. Nothing to worry about."

"Except you getting shot," Jodie replied worriedly.

He opened his jacket and showed her his gun.

"I know. You're indestructible. But come back in one piece, okay?" she asked softly.

He searched her eyes and smiled tenderly. "That's a deal. See you later." He winked at Margie and took one last look at Jodie before he left.

"How people change," Margie murmured dryly.

But Jodie wasn't really listening. Her eyes were still on Alexander's broad back as he went out the door.

Alexander and his group met somberly that evening to compare notes and plan strategy. They knew by now where Cara Dominguez was, who her cohorts were and just how much Brody Vance knew about her operation. The security guard on the job at the Ritter warehouse was linked to the organization, as well, but thought he was home free. What he didn't know was that Alexander had a court order to wiretap his office, and the agent overseeing that job had some interesting information to impart about a drug shipment that was still concealed in Ritter's warehouse. It was one that no one knew about until the wiretap. And it was a much bigger load than the one the drug unit had just busted.

The trick was going to be catching the thieves with the merchandise. It wasn't enough to know they were connected with it. They had to have hard evidence, facts that would stand up in court. They had to have a chain of evidence that would definitively link Cara to the drug shipment.

Just when Alexander thought he was ready to spring the trap, Cara Dominguez disappeared off the face of the earth. The security guard was immediately arrested, before he could flee, but he had nothing to say under advice of counsel.

When they went to the Ritter warehouse, with Colby Lane and Phillip Hunter, to appropriate the drug shipment, they found cartons of drilling equipment parts. Even with drug-sniffing dogs, they found no trace of the missing shipment. And everybody connected with Cara Dominguez suddenly developed amnesia and couldn't remember anything about her.

The only good thing about it was that the operation had obviously changed locations, and there was no further reason for anyone to target Jodie. Where it had moved was a job for the DEA to follow up on. Alexander was sure that Kennedy had something to do with the sudden disappearance of Cara, and the shipment, but he couldn't prove a thing. The only move he had left was to prosecute Kennedy for giving secret information to a known drug dealer, and that he could prove. He had Kennedy arraigned on charges of conspiracy to distribute controlled substances, which effectively removed the man from any chance of a future job in law enforcement—even if he managed to weasel out of a long jail term for what he'd already done.

Alexander returned to the Jacobsville ranch on Friday, to find Margie and Jodie in the kitchen making canapés while Cousin Derek and two other men sat at the kitchen table. Derek was sampling the sausage rolls while a taller dark-eyed man with jet-black hair oiled his handgun and a second dark-haired man with eyes as green as Alexander's sat glaring at his two companions.

"She's gone," Alexander said heavily. "Took a powder. We can't find a trace of her, so far, and the drug shipment vanished into thin air. Needless to say, I'm relieved on your behalf," he told a radiant Jodie. "But it's not what I wanted to happen."

"Your inside man slipped up," the green-eyed stranger said in a deep bass voice.

"I didn't have an inside man, Zeke," Alexander said, dropping into a chair with the other men. "More's the pity."

"Don't mind him," the other stranger said easily. "He's perfect. He never loses a case or misses a shot. And he can cook."

Zeke glared at him. "You could do with a few lessons in marksmanship, Josiah," he returned curtly. "You can't even hit a target."

"That's a fact," Derek agreed at once, dark eyes dancing. "He tried to shoot a snake once and took the mailbox down with a shotgun."

"I can hit what I aim at when I want to," Josiah said huffily. "I hated that damned mailbox. I shot it on purpose."

His brothers almost rolled on the floor laughing. Josiah sighed and poured himself another cup of coffee. "Then I guess I'm on a plane back to Oklahoma."

"And I'm on one to Wyoming." Zeke nodded.

Derek glared at them. "And I'm booked for a rodeo in Arizona. Listen, why don't we sell up and move down here? Texas has lots of ranches. In fact, I expect we could find one near here without a lot of trouble."

"You might at that," Alexander told them as he poured his own cup of coffee, taking the opportunity to ruffle Jodie's blond hair and smile tenderly down at her. "I hear the old Jacobs place is up for sale again. That eastern dude who took it over lost his shirt in the stock market. It's just as well. He didn't know much about horses anyway."

"It's a horse farm?" Josiah asked, interested.

Alexander nodded. "A seed herd of Arabians and a couple of foals they bred from racing stock. He had pipe dreams about entering a horse in the Kentucky Derby one day."

"Why'd he give it up?"

"Well, for one thing, he didn't know anything about horses. He wouldn't ask for advice from anybody who did, but he'd read this book. He figured he could do it himself. That was before he got kicked out of the barn the first time," he added in a droll tone.

Zeke made a rough sound. "I'm not keen on horses. And I work in Wyoming."

"You're a little too late, anyway," Margie interrupted, but she was watching Derek with new intensity. "We heard that one of Cash Grier's brothers came down here to look at it. Apparently, they're interested."

"Grier has brothers?" Jodie exclaimed. "What a horrifying thought! How many?"

"Three. They've been on the outs for a long time, but they're making overtures. It seems the ranch would get them close enough to Cash to try and heal the breach."

"That's one mean hombre," Derek ventured.

"He keeps the peace," Alexander defended him. "And he makes life interesting in town. Especially just lately."

"What's going on lately?" Derek wanted to know.

Alexander, Jodie and Margie exchanged secretive smiles. "Never mind," Alexander said. "There are other properties, if you're really interested. You might stop by one of the real estate agencies and stock up on brochures."

"He'll never leave Oklahoma," Derek said, nodding toward Josiah. "And Wyoming's the only place left that's sparsely popu-lated enough to appeal to our family grizzly." He glanced at Margie and grinned. "However, I only need a temporary base of opera-tions since I'm on the road so much. I might buy me a little cabin nearby and come serenade Margie on weekends when I'm in town."

Margie laughed, but she was flushed with excitement. "Might you, now?"

"Of course, you're set on a designing career," he mused.

"And you're hooked on breaking bones and spraining muscles in the rodeo circuit."

"We might find some common ground one day," Derek replied.

Margie only smiled. "Are you all staying for my Halloween party?" she asked the brothers.

Zeke finished his coffee and got up. "I don't do parties. Excuse me. I have to call the airline."

"I'm right behind you," Josiah said, following his brother with an apologetic smile.

"Well, I guess it's just me," Derek said. "What do you think, Marge, how about if I borrow one of Alex's suits and come as a college professor?"

She burst out laughing.

Alexander caught Jodie by the hand and pulled her out of the kitchen with him.

"Where are we going?" she asked.

"For a walk, now that nobody's shooting at us," he said, linking her fingers into his.

He led her out the front door and around to the side of the house, by the long fences that kept the cattle in.

"When do you have to go back to work?" he asked Jodie reluctantly.

"That wasn't exactly discussed," she confessed, with a secret smile, because he didn't know which job she was returning to take. "But I suppose next week will do nicely."

"I still think Brody Vance is involved in this somehow," he said flatly, turning to her. "I can't prove it yet, but I'm certain he's not as innocent as he's pretending to be."

"That's exactly what I think," she agreed, surprising him. "By the way," she added, "I quit my job before we came down here."

"You quit...good for you!" he exclaimed, hugging her close. "I'm proud of you, Jodie!"

She laughed, holding on tight. "Don't be too proud. I'm still working for Mr. Ritter. But it's going to be in a totally different capacity."

"Doing what?" he asked flatly.

"I'm going to be working with Colby Lane as a computer security consultant," she told him.

"What about Hunter?" he asked.

"He's going back to Arizona with his wife. They're expecting a second child, and I think they want a little less excitement in their life right now," she confided with a grin. "So Colby Lane is taking over security. Mr. Ritter said I might have to do some traveling later on as a troubleshooter, but it wouldn't be often."

He was studying her with soft, quiet eyes. "As long as it's sporadic and not for too long, that's fine. You'll do well in security," he said. "Old man Ritter isn't as dense as I thought he was. I'm glad he's still keeping an eye on the company. Colby Lane will keep his security people on their toes just as well as Hunter did."

"I think Mr. Hunter is irritated that Cara managed to get into that warehouse parking lot," she ventured.

"He is. But it could have happened to anyone. Brody Vance is our wild card. He's going to need watching. And no, you can't offer to do it," he added firmly. "Let Lane set up his own surveillance. You stick to the job you're given and stop sticking your neck out."

"I like that!" she exclaimed. "And who was it who encouraged me to stick my neck out in the first place planting bugs near people in coffeehouses?"

He searched her eyes quietly. "You did a great job. I was proud of you. I always thought we might work well together."

"We did, didn't we?" she mused.

He pushed back wispy strands of loose hair from her cheek and studied her hungrily. "I have in mind another opportunity for mutual cooperation," he said, bending to her mouth.

11

～∞～ ～∞～ ～∞～

"What sort of mutual cooperation?" she whispered against his searching lips. "Does it involve guns and bugs?"

He smiled against her soft mouth. "I was thinking more of prophylactics…"

While Jodie was trying to let the extraordinary statement filter into her brain, and trying to decide whether to slug him or kiss him back, a loud voice penetrated their oblivion.

"Jodie!" Margie yelled. "Where are you?"

Alexander lifted his head. He seemed as dazed as she felt.

"Jodie!" Margie yelled more insistently.

"On my way!" Jodie yelled back.

"Sisters are a pain," he murmured on a long sigh.

She smiled at him. "I'm sure it's a minor disaster that only I can cope with," she assured him.

He chuckled. "Go ahead. But tonight," he added in a deep, husky tone, "you're mine."

She flushed at the way he said it. She started to argue, but Margie was yelling again, so she ran toward the house instead.

Alexander stared hungrily at Jodie when she came down the stairs just before the first party guest arrived the next evening. They'd spent the day together, riding around the ranch and talking. There hadn't been any more physical encounters, but there was a new closeness between them that everyone noticed.

Jodie's blond hair was long and wavy. She was wearing a red dress with a long, ruffled hem, an elasticized neckline that was pushed off the shoulders, leaving her creamy skin visible. She was wearing high heels and more makeup than she usually put on. And she was breathtaking. He just shook his head, his eyes eating her as she came down the staircase, holding on to the banister.

"You could be dessert," he murmured when she reached him.

"So could you," she replied, adoring him with her eyes. "But you aren't even wearing a costume."

"I am so," he argued with a wry smile. "I'm disguised as a government agent."

"Alexander!" she wailed.

He chuckled and caught her fingers in his. "I look better than Derek does. He's coming as a rodeo cowboy, complete with banged-up chaps, worn-out boots, and a championship belt buckle the size of my foot."

"He'll look authentic," she replied.

He smiled. "So do I. Don't I?"

She sighed, loving the way he looked. "I suppose you do, at that. There's going to be a big crowd, Margie says."

He tilted her chin up to his eyes. "There won't be anyone here except the two of us, Jodie," he said quietly.

The way he was looking at her, she could almost believe it.

"I think Margie feels that way with Derek," she murmured absently. "Too bad his brothers wouldn't stay."

"They aren't the partying type," he said. "Neither are we, really."

She nodded. Her eyes searched his and she felt giddy all over at the shift in their relationship. It was as if all the arguments of years past were blown away like sand. She felt new, young, on top of the world. And if his expression was anything to go by, he felt the same way.

He traced her face with his eyes. "How do you feel about short engagements?" he asked out of the blue.

She was sure that it was a rhetorical question. "I suppose it depends on the people involved. If they knew each other well..."

"I've known you longer than any other woman in my life except my sister," he interrupted. His face tightened as he stared down at her with narrow, hungry eyes. "I want to marry you, Jodie."

She opened her mouth to speak and couldn't even manage words. The shock robbed her of speech.

He grimaced. "I thought it might come as a shock. You don't have to answer me this minute," he said easily, taking her hand. "You think about it for a while. Let's go mingle with the guests as they come in and spend the night dancing. Then I'll ask you again."

She went along with him unprotesting, but she was certain she was hearing things. Alexander wasn't a marrying man. He must be temporarily out of his mind with worry over his unsolved case. But he didn't look like the product of a deranged mind, and the way he held Jodie's hand tight in his, and the way he watched her, were convincing.

Not only that, but he had eyes for her alone. Kirry didn't come, but there were plenty of other attractive women at the party. None of them attracted so much as a glance from Alexander. He danced only with Jodie, and held her so closely that people who knew both of them started to speculate openly on their changed relationship.

"People are watching us," Jodie murmured as they finished one dance only to start right into another one.

"Let them watch," he said huskily. His eyes fell to her soft mouth. "I'm glad you work in Houston, Jodie. I won't have to find excuses to commute to Jacobsville to see you."

"You never liked me before," she murmured out loud.

"I never got this close to you before," he countered. "I've lived my whole life trying to forget the way my mother was, Jodie," he confessed. "She gave me emotional scars that I still carry. I kept women at a safe distance. I actually thought I had you at a safe distance, too," he added on a chuckle. "And then I started taking you around for business reasons and got caught in my own web."

"Did you, really?" she murmured with wonder.

"Careful," he whispered. "I'm dead serious." He bent and brushed his mouth beside hers, nuzzling her cheek with his nose. "It's too late to go back, Jodie. I can't let go."

His arm contracted. She gasped softly at the increased intimacy of the contact. She could feel the hunger in him. Her own body began to vibrate faintly as she realized how susceptible she was.

"You be careful," she countered breathlessly. "I'm on fire! You could find yourself on the floor in a closet, being ravished, if you keep this up."

"If that's a promise, lead me to a closet," he said, only half joking.

She laughed. He didn't.

In fact, his arm contracted even more and he groaned softly at her ear. "Jodie," he said in a choked tone, "how do you feel about runaway marriages?"

"Excuse me?"

He lifted his head and looked down into her eyes with dark intensity. "Runaway marriage. You get in a car, run away to Mexico in the middle of somebody's Halloween party and get married." His arm brought her closer. "They're binding even in this country. We could get to the airport in about six minutes, and onto a plane in less than an hour."

"To where?" she burst out, aghast.

"Anywhere in Mexico," he groaned, his eyes biting into hers as he lifted his head. "We can be married again in Jacobsville whenever you like."

"Then why go to Mexico tonight?" she asked, flustered.

His hand slid low on her spine and pulled her hips into his with a look that made her blush.

"That is not a good reason to go to Mexico on the spur of the moment," she said, while her body told her brain to shut up.

"That's what you think." His expression was eloquent.

"But what if I said yes?" she burst out. "You could end up tied to me for life, when all you want is immediate relief! And speaking of relief, there's a bedroom right up the stairs...!"

He stopped dancing. His face was solemn. "Tell me you wouldn't mind a quick fling in my bed, Jodie," he challenged. "Tell me your conscience wouldn't bother you at all."

She sighed. "I'd like to," she began.

"But your parents didn't raise you that way," he concluded for her. "In fact, my father was like that," he added quietly. "He was old-fashioned and I'm like him. There haven't even been that many women, if you'd like to know, Jodie," he confessed. "And right now, I wish there hadn't been even one."

"That is the sweetest thing to say," she whispered, and pulled his face down so that she could kiss him.

"As it happens, I mean it." He kissed her back, very lightly. "Run away with me," he challenged. "Right now!"

It was crazy. He had to be out of his mind. But the temptation to get him to a minister before he changed his mind was all-consuming. She was suddenly caught up in the same excitement she saw in his face. "But you're so conventional!"

"I'll be very conventional again first thing tomorrow," he promised. "Tonight, I'm going for broke. Grab a coat. Don't tell anybody where we're going. I'll think up something to say to Margie."

She glanced toward the back of the room, where Margie was watching them excitedly and whispering something to Derek that made him laugh.

"All right. We're both crazy, but I'm not arguing with you. Tell her whatever you like. Make it good," she told him, and dashed up the staircase.

He was waiting for her at the front door. He looked irritated.

"What's wrong?" Jodie asked when she reached him. Her heart plummeted. "Changed your mind?"

"Not on your life!" He caught her arm and pulled her out the door, closing it quickly behind them. "Margie's too smart for her own good. Or Derek is."

"You can't put anything past Margie," she said, laughing with relief as they ran down the steps and toward the garage, where he kept his Jaguar.

"Or Derek," he murmured, chuckling.

He unlocked the door with his keyless entry and popped out the laser key with his thumb on the button. He looked down at her hesitantly. "I'm game if you are," he told her. "But you can still back out if you want to."

She shook her head, her eyes full of dreams. "You might never be in the mood again."

"That's a laugh." He put her inside and minutes later, they were en route to the airport.

Holding hands all the way during the flight, making plans, they arrived in El Paso with bated breath. Alexander rented a car at the airport and they drove across the border, stopping at customs and looking so radiant that the guard guessed their purpose immediately.

"You're going over to get married, I'd bet," the man said with a huge grin. *"Buena suerte,"* he added, handing back their identification. "And drive carefully!"

"You bet!" Alexander told him as he drove off.

They found a small chapel and a minister willing to perform the ceremony after a short conversation with a police officer near a traffic light.

Jodie borrowed a peso from the minister's wife for luck and was handed a small bouquet of silk flowers to hold while the words were spoken, in Spanish, that would make them man and wife.

Alexander translated for her, his eyes soft and warm and possessive as the minister pronounced them man and wife at last. He drew a ring out of his pocket, a beautiful embossed gold band, which he slid onto her finger. It was a perfect fit. She recognized it as one she'd sighed over years ago in a jewelry shop she'd gone to with Margie when they were dreaming about marriage in the distant future.

She'd been back to the shop over the years to make sure it was still there. Apparently Margie had told Alexander about it.

They signed the necessary documents, Alexander paid the minister, and they got back into the car with a marriage license.

Jodie stared at her ring and her new husband with wide-eyed wonder. "We must be crazy," she commented.

He laughed. "We're not crazy. We're very sensible. First we have an elopement, then we have a honeymoon, then we have a normal wedding with Margie and our friends." He glanced at her with twinkling eyes. "You said you didn't have to be back at work until next week. We'll have our honeymoon before you go back."

"Where, exactly, did you have in mind for a honeymoon?" she asked.

Three hours later, tangled with Alexander in a big king-size bed with waves pounding the shore outside the window, she lay in the shadows of the moonlit Gulf of Mexico. The hotel was first class, the food was supposed to be the best in Galveston, the beach was like sugar sand. But all she saw was Alexander's face above hers as her body throbbed in the molasses slow rhythm of his kisses on her breasts on cool, crisp sheets.

"You taste like candy," he whispered against her belly.

"You never said I was sweet before," she teased breathlessly.

"You always were. I didn't know how to say it. You gave me the shakes every time I got near you." His mouth opened on her diaphragm and pressed down, hard.

She gasped at the warm pleasure of it. Her hands tangled in his thick, dark hair. "That was mutual, too." She drew his face to her breasts and coaxed his mouth onto them. "This is very nice," she murmured unsteadily.

"It gets better." His hands found her in a new and invasive way. She started to protest, only to find his mouth crushing down over her parted lips about the same time that his movements lifted her completely off the bed in a throbbing wave of unexpected pleasure.

"Oh, you like that, do you?" he murmured against her mouth. "How about this...?"

She cried out. His lips stifled the sound and his leg moved between both of hers. He kissed her passionately while his lean hips shifted and she felt him in an intimacy they hadn't yet shared.

He felt her body jerk as she tried to reject the shock of invasion, but his mouth gentled hers, his hands soothed her, teased her, coaxed her into allowing the slow merging of their bodies.

She gasped, her hands biting into his back in mingled fear and excitement.

"It won't hurt long," he whispered reassuringly, and his tongue probed her lips as he began a slow, steady rhythm that rippled down her nerves like pure joy on a roller coaster of pleasure.

"That's it," he murmured against her eager lips. "Come up against me and find the pressure and the rhythm that you need. That's it. That's...it!"

She was amazed that he didn't mind letting her experiment, that he was willing to help her experience him. She'd heard some horror stories about wedding nights from former friends. This wasn't one. She'd found a man who wanted eager participation, not passive acceptance. She moved and shifted and he laughed roughly, his deep voice throbbing with pleasure, as her seeking body kindled waves of delight in his own.

She was on fire with power. She moved under him, invited him, challenged him, provoked him. And he went with her, every step of the way up the ladder to a mutual climax that groaned out at her ear in ripples of satiation. She clung to him, shivering in the explosive aftermath of an experience that exceeded her wildest hopes.

"And now you know," he whispered, kissing her eyelids closed.

"Now I know." She nose-dived into his damp throat and clung while they slowly settled back to earth again.

"I love you, baby," he whispered tenderly.

Joy flooded through her. "I love you, too!" she whispered breathlessly.

He curled her into his body with a long yawn and with the ocean purring like a wet kitten outside the windows, they drifted off into a warm, soft sleep.

"Hey."

She heard his voice at her ear. Then there was an aroma, a delicious smell of fresh coffee, rich and dark and delicious.

Her eyes didn't even open, but her head followed the retreat of the coffee.

"I thought that would do it. Breakfast," Alexander coaxed. "We've got your favorite, pecan waffles with bacon."

Her eyes opened. "You remembered!"

He grinned at her. "I know what you like." His lips pursed. "Especially after last night."

She laughed, dragging herself out of bed in the slip she'd worn to bed, because it was still too soon to sleep in nothing at all. She was shy with him.

He was completely dressed, right down to his shoes. He gave her an appreciative sweep of his green eyes that took in her bare feet and her disheveled hair.

"You look wonderful like that," he said. "I always knew you would."

"When was that, exactly?" she chided, taking a seat at the table facing the window. "Before or after you accused me of being a layabout?"

"Ouch!" he groaned.

"It's okay. I forgive you," she said with a wicked glance. "I could never hold a grudge against a man who was that good in bed."

"And just think, I was very subdued last night, in deference to your first time."

She gasped. "Well!"

His eyebrows arched. "Think of the possibilities. If you aren't too delicate after last night, we could explore some of them later."

"Later?"

"I had in mind taking you around town and showing you off," he said, flipping open a napkin. "They have all sorts of interesting things to see here."

She sipped coffee, trying to ignore her body, which was making emphatic statements about what *it* wanted to do with the day.

He was watching her with covert, wise eyes. "On the other hand," he murmured as he nibbled a pancake, "if you were feeling lazy, we could just lie around in the bed and listen to the ocean, while we…"

Her hand poised over the waffle. "While we…?"

He began to smile. She laughed. The intimacy was new and secret, and exciting. She rushed through the waffle and part of the bacon, and then pushed herself away from the table and literally threw herself into his arms across the chair. He prided himself on his control, because they actually almost made it to the bed….

Two days later, worn-out, and not because of any sightseeing trip, they dragged themselves into the ranch house with a bag full of peace offerings for Margie which included seashells, baskets, a pretty ruffled sundress and some taffy.

Margie gave them a long, amused look. "There is going to have to be a wedding here," she informed them. "It won't do to run off to Mexico and get married, you have to do it in Jacobsville before anybody will believe you're really man and wife."

"I don't mind," Alexander said complacently, "but I'm not making the arrangements."

"Jodie and I can do that."

"But I have to go back to work," she told Margie, and went forward to hand her the bag and hug her. "And I haven't even told you about my new job!"

"What about your new husband?" Alexander groaned. "Are you going to desert me?"

She gave him a wicked glance. "Don't you have to talk to somebody about ranch business? Margie doesn't even know that I'm changing jobs!"

He sighed. "That's all husbands are good for," he murmured to himself. "You marry a woman, and she runs off and leaves you to gossip with a girlfriend."

"My sister-in-law, if you please," Jodie corrected him with a grin. "I'll cook you a nice apple pie for later, Alexander," she promised.

"Okay, I do take bribes," he had to confess. He grinned at her. "But now that we're married, couldn't you find something else to call me? Something a little less formal?"

She thought about it for a minute. "Darling," she said.

He looked at her with an odd expression, smiled as if he couldn't help himself, and made a noise like a tiger. He went out the back door while they were still laughing.

* * *

Jodie moved into her new job with a little apprehension, because of what she'd said to Brody Vance, but he was as genial as if no cross words had ever been spoken between them. Cara Dominguez still hadn't been heard from or seen, neither had her accomplice. There was still a shipment of drugs missing, that had to be in the warehouse somewhere, but guards and stepped up surveillance assured that the drug dealers couldn't get near the warehouse to search for it.

One of Cara's rivals in the business was arrested in a guns-for-drugs deal in Houston that made national and international headlines. Alexander told Jodie about it just before the wire services broke the story, and assured her that Cara's organization was going to be next on the list of objectives for his department.

Meanwhile, Jodie learned the ropes of computer security and went back to school to finish her certification, with Alexander's blessing. Margie came up to see her while she was arranging a showing of her new designs with a local modeling agency and a department store that Kirry didn't work for.

Alexander kept shorter hours and did more delegating of chores, so that he could be at home when Jodie was. They bought a small house on the outskirts of Houston. Margie arranged to help Jodie with the decorating scheme. She was still amazed at the change in her best friend, who was now independent, strong-willed, hardworking and nobody's doormat.

There was still the retro coffeehouse, of course, and one night Jodie had a phone call from the owner, Johnny. She listened, exploded with delight, and ran to tell Alexander the news.

"The publisher wants to buy my poems!" she exclaimed. "He wants to include them in an anthology of Texas poetry! Isn't it exciting?"

"It's exciting," he agreed, bending to kiss her warmly. "Now tell the truth. They're about me, aren't they?"

She sighed. "Yes, they're about you. But I'm afraid this will be the only volume of poetry I ever create."

"Really? Why?"

She nibbled his chin. "Because misery is what makes good poetry. And just between us two," she added as her fingers went to his shirt buttons, "I'm far too happy to write good poetry ever again."

He guided her fingers down his shirt, smiling secretively. "I have plans to keep you that way, too," he murmured deeply.

And he did.

* * * * *

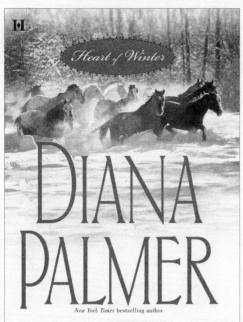

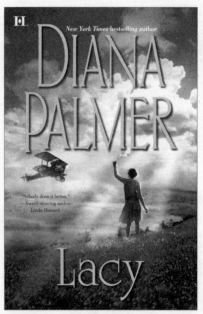